Dalwan and the Sword Fallonrod

by J. Christopher Frazer

CHAPTER 1

A radiant mist began to form in the blackness that was now so familiar to his nightlong journeys of terror. Five-year-old Dalwan watched it swirl and billow as if driven by unseen winds. Two eyes suddenly appeared out of the darkness... the mist vanished as if blown away by a powerful breath. The eyes, bright with their own light, now squinted with pitiless concentration... peering through the darkness... searching... seeking something with fierce determination. Fear squeezed the air from Dalwan's chest; he knew they sought him... looked only for him. He wanted to hide... his throat spasmed closed, he couldn't cry out! This time, he would be found! "Daddy... help me!" moved his lips without the slightest whisper of sound. The eyes strained and turned, sensing, relentlessly searching, then narrowing to a heart-stopping slit looking into Dalwan's own terrified eyes, "There he is!" The eyes widened with the treacherous delight of discovery. Dalwan's heart began to pound wildly. Wicked sharp claws on a black hand streaked toward him out of the darkness. Dalwan's mind screamed, but in his frantic sleep, only a muffled groan escaped his lips. The hand missed him by only a breath. It retracted then flashed past him again, controlled by an arm of powerfully knotted muscles. There was a loud curse, and the hand began to thrash in mindless anger, grasping at the air as if trying to catch an elusive gnat. Finally, the hand doubled into a tight fist and pounded down with incredible violence on an invisible surface. A sound like thunder exploded in Dalwan's ears, bringing tears to his eyes and a renewed attempt to cry out... still nothing escaped his lips but a whimper.

The house was dark in those predawn hours when a bright flash of light filled the bedroom. Reela woke her husband Kindron with a gasp as she suddenly sat up, startled in their bed.

"What is it, Reela?" Kindron asked, annoyed at being woken again by his overreactive wife. "What now!?"

"There's something wrong with Dalwan!" she whispered in a panicked voice.

"You're dreaming again. Just..."

He was cut short by a brilliant flash from the doorway leading into Dalwan's room.

"What the..." Kindron was on his feet, grabbing a short sword, and he bounded toward his boy's bedroom, with Reela only a step behind him.

The smell of burning cloth greeted him as he entered the room, which was illuminated by small flames burning at the edge of Dalwan's blankets in several places.

Before he could get to the bed, Dalwan stirred fitfully and mumbled unintelligible words in a fearful voice as a ball of fire formed in his exposed hand. It exploded in another brilliant flash, sending out a shower of sparks.

"Dalwan! Stop it!!!" yelled Kindron as he grabbed Dalwan by the shoulders and jerked him out of his smoldering bed.

"Kin! easy, he's only five..."

"Reela, I know what I'm doing... Dalwan are you awake? Look at me..."

"Kindron, you're scaring him..." shouted Reela as she tried to take Dalwan out of his powerful hands.

Dalwan burst into terrorized sobbing.

"Let go of him...KINDRON, GIVE HIM TO ME!"

Kindron loosened his grip on Dalwan and let him slip into her arms. He then busied himself putting out the smoldering spots and a few small flames which were now burning in various places throughout the dark little room. He opened the shutter to air out the room. Reela held Dalwan with his face into her shoulder, rocking his quivering frame in her lap as she settled down on his bed.

Finally, his deep sobbing subsided, and he looked up into Reela's wet eyes, "Mama... I'm... scared." He said in quivering gasps.

"Were you having bad dreams?"

"The eyes, they were looking for me again." He buried his face in her night coat.

"Reela, we can't just let him go on this way. Now he's got fire... I don't know anything about fire magic... it scares me... Reela, I can't help him through this."

"He's just a boy..."

"...who's throwing fire all over his room ten years before other children even get a hint of what their gifts are!"

"I'm sorry daddy...I'm sorry...I didn't mean to..." Dalwan sobbed out the words and began to cry uncontrollably again.

Kindron sat down next to them and put his arms around them both. "I know...I know. We aren't mad at you son...we're scared." He reached down and gently turned Dalwan's face towards his own. "Do you understand that we are afraid that you might..."

Reela cut him off by putting her hand gently to his lips. "Dalwan, we just want to make sure that you're safe...that the 'eyes' don't hurt you."

"How did fire get in my room?"

Reela and Kindron looked at each other hoping to find answers in each other's eyes.

Kindron took Dalwan and pulled him to his lap. "Dalwan, you made the fire. You already have magic, magic that only one in a hundred thousand people get. You're very special."

"Is it going to hurt me?"

"No son. But you'll have to learn to control it... to use it safely."

"Will you teach me?"

"Neither your mother nor I know anything about fire arts. But your great uncle Shaylan is one of the best of all the fire makers in the whole land. He may be willing to teach you."

"I'm scared... can he make the eyes and the hand go away... Can Uncle Shaylan help me?"

"Maybe he can, Dalwan. We'll ask him real soon, O.K?"

"If he can help me, I want to go see him. Can we go tomorrow?"

Reela rose quietly, silent tears streaming down her face, and left the room as Kindron finished, "Maybe we can go see him tomorrow. Now, lie back down and try to get some sleep."

That night, through many more tears, they decided to take Dalwan to live with Shaylan in his mountain home near Burkeston. He was indeed the greatest and most gifted firewielder in Pretoria and would be their only hope of training Dalwan to use and control his gifts while protecting him and keeping his identity secret from those who would try to take him and use his powers toward their own ends.

CHAPTER 2

A little over one hundred and twenty-five years prior, Maylor, the possessor of the mighty power-sword Fallonrod, died of old age in Castle Crest. Even in his elder years, he had been revered throughout the many lands. Armed with Fallonrod, he remained a deterrent to any who would make trouble for his homeland, Pretoria. In his death, he left behind a sword that everyone wanted but no one could control. During the three years that followed his death, talented men of numerous arts tried to engage the sword. Each perished in their attempts, some in spectacular fashion. During the final attempt, which occurred in the private library of the Lord of Castle Crest, the user was incinerated as he held the sword. The power of the sword's blast created such extreme heat that when the sword fell from the charcoal hand, its blade melted straight into the stone floor, sinking almost to its hilt. Only a double handbreadth of the blade was left visible.

The Lord of Castle Crest decided to seal up the room containing the sword by completely encasing it in stone. The Swordroom, as it was to be called, was an interior room near the lord's living quarters. There were no exterior walls or windows. To seal the room, the Lord of Castle Crest had a search conducted throughout all Pretoria to find the greatest stone molder (a shaper and joiner of stone by magical art). Once located, he was charged with sealing up the entire room in thick, magically molded stone. After it was completed, the room remained sealed for well over one hundred years, entombing Fallonrod and its incredible, unmanageable power.

Now the earth-power was rising, and the sword had again become the topic of tales and speculation. The three Lords of Pretoria had a mutual protection agreement that they guarded jealously and that provided security in their part of the world. A powermaster who could wield the sword would be a powerful ally or a very dangerous enemy. With the rise in earth-power, men's ability to wield the power of their individual magical art would increase manyfold. Each kingdom would jockey for political position and align with one another in covenants of war and protection. Wielders of magic would become the commodity of kings, each of whom hoped to own or control the greatest magicians. Then would come the inevitable conflicts as each kingdom sought to expand its borders and realm of influence. Power would be the ultimate determinant, and Fallonrod, if the tales were true, could be the ultimate key to success.

****

Creydek was a tall, stout man with a dark, overly bushy beard and eyebrows, and large boned arms fitted with massive hands. His bulk made him look like a giant. His current task was to manage a group of five talented stone molders who were charged with creating a tunnel. The armies of Malmoria were waiting on the completion of this secret attack tunnel, which would open a corridor from the maze of natural caverns under the Magnon Mountains to the high vertical cliffs at the back side of the Castle Crest fortress. Creydek's mastery of the magic art of stonemolding had finally paid off. His power with stone was greater than any two or three of those who now served him. Under his direction, the group had made quick work in cutting a series of shafts between the caverns in the mountain, which would open a corridor for the troops to move quickly through when the time came for the attack. Scouts had discovered a cave opening high over Castle Crest on the mountain wall 20 days earlier, which he had used to calculate the positioning of this last tunnel to exit the mountain at ground level. Two days earlier, Creydek himself had broken a small hole through to the outside and discovered that the tunnel was indeed right on target; he was coming out directly next to the castle wall on the virtually unguarded back side of Castle Crest.

He shaped the floor of the tunnel in a downward slope, the few steps necessary to facilitate a quick, orderly exit from the caverns. On their knees, the molder's hands moved over the sloping stone without ever touching it, and the stone began to flow upward into small heaps large enough for a strong man to lift as they cut broad stairs down into the floor. The molders severed each heap into a blob of stone so it could be carried off. The men who moved the stone had to wear thick gloves because the stone was very hot after being molded in this fashion.

In this way, they shaped the stairway down the sloped floor to match the ground level outside. After consultation with the military leaders, they widened the corridor near the intended exit, leaving only a thin wall of rock as a facade to hide the attack tunnel from the few sentries posted on the castle wall outside. When completed, it would be large enough to provide a quick exit for the army gathered in the caverns behind them.

Astenor, the famed shadowmaster, paced atop the newly created stairway only feet from Creydek, impatiently awaiting their completion of the breech in the mountain wall.

"I'm ready now," said Creydek triumphantly to Astenor.

"Good," answered Astenor in a voice that evidenced much less respect for Creydek than Creydek held for him. "Make a hole in the wall just large enough for me to crawl through. Make it about waist high...and not too big," he said in a scolding, demeaning tone.

Creydek felt his face heat to scalding hot; his eyes narrowed to a slit. There wasn't another stonemolder in the entire land that could have done what he had done in such a short time. He stood staring, burning with rage at Astenor's arrogant underestimation of him.

"Any time now will be fine, Creydek," Astenor said, raising his voice as if lecturing a child.

Creydek was almost a head taller than Astenor and could have knocked him unconscious, no! killed him, with a single blow if he chose. He took a step toward Astenor with doubled fists the size of small ale kegs, which both rose to an intimidating fighting position, his face still blushing bright red.

Creydek's advance caused the vale of arrogance to drop from Astenor's eyes, alerting him to his imminent peril.

He began to backstep, calling aloud, "Captain, Captain!! We have a situation here."

Captain Vance, the officer in charge of the attack from the tunnel, turned his attention to the petty ego warfare between the two men and jogged the dozen steps needed to position himself between them, yelling as he came, "You fools, save your fight and your presumptive vanity until after we've won the battle. It's not like you two are winning the war for us by yourselves. You're just getting the army to the battlefield!" With a passing glance of disgust in Astenor's direction, he grabbed Creydek by the arm and pulled him around with some serious effort. "Get the wall open, NOW!" As he turned to rejoin his officers for their last-minute briefing, he added over his shoulder, "If you really want to be a hero, do so in the castle by getting us into the vault where the sword is."

Creydek moved back to the remaining shell of rock that separated them from the outside world. He glanced at Astenor, "The little man isn't worth getting upset over," he thought as he loathed Astenor's self-important posturing. He made quick work of cutting a seam around a chunk of wall large enough for Astenor to crawl out through. He fashioned it in such a way that it could be removed quickly as a single piece.

"Captain Vance," he shouted, "It's ready to open at your command."

"Excellent!" he answered with a look that restored Creydek's dignity. "Are you ready, Astenor?"

Astenor nodded.

"Very well then. Remember, Lord Falock has a few well-trained sensors in the castle. If they're alert, it won't take them any time at all to pick up your magic once you're outside the caverns. You've gotta work fast. And Astenor, be sure to hold the illusion of the mountain until Creydek has opened the castle wall." Turning to Creydek, "Which shouldn't take long at all from what we've seen here today."

Creydek straightened up and nodded gratefully with a smiled, "Let's hope you can do as well with your craft, shortly," he said with a vengeful glance toward Astenor. Two soldiers helped him pull the stone out of the wall, leaving a smooth, almost perfectly round hole.

Astenor quickly slipped out. In a virtual instant, he shouted back inside, "The illusion is complete, you can take the rest of the wall down." His words oozed with arrogant confidence.

As soon as he made the announcement, another man crawled through and sprinted toward the north end of the castle fortress, running as close to the wall as possible, to avoid detection. Once at the front, he would signal the attacking forces, hidden up the valley, to begin their assault.

Turning back to Creydek, Captain Vance slapped him on the back and said in a friendly but challenging tone, "Just how quickly can you and your boys get this wall open?"

A broad smile crept across Creydek's face, "Get some men ready to move rock...lots of rock!" he said in a raspy whisper.

"Stand clear of the wall," said Creydek. They quickly moved into position, and two of his men held their hands against the stone and began to work their way across the bottom edge of the rock facade. The other two worked feverishly from the scaffolds on both sides of the passage. Credek worked across the middle from a bridge between the two scaffolds. He returned to the floor after only a short time of working and announced with showman-like confidence, "If Balore would like to do the honors, the wall will fall at his command."

A call went back down the corridor for Balore. Balore was the true hope of Malmoria, their very own powermaster, the one they knew would soon own Fallonrod and its magnificent power. He came down through the corridor crowded with soldiers. He was wearing a royal blue cape with a gold chain securing it around his neck. A cheer went up in a wave as he passed by.

With his approach, Captain Vance called all those present to attention.

Creydek stepped forward. "If you will do the honor of throwing a strong green flame at the center of the wall, it will open for you," he said, speaking with pride and respect.

Creydek was standing next to the hole in the wall. He looked out and warned Astenor about the coming noise and the attention it might bring, then turned back to Balore and said, "It's all yours, sir."

A tense hush fell over the crowd of soldiers that now totally filled the corridor back far past where the light would let anyone see. Hundreds of curious eyes reflected the flickering light from the rows of torches spaced along the walls.

With the soldiers behind him and himself a respectable distance from the wall, Balore held up his hands shoulder-width apart over his head. A green light began to form between them, quickly becoming a monstrous, blinding fury of spinning flame which he hurled like a blazing curtain against the wall. It impacted the wall with such force that its concussion painfully pounded the ears of everyone within eyeshot of the wall. Most of the wall toppled outward with an equally deafening roar, sending much of the debris rumbling away from the opening through the image Astenor was holding.

The guard on the wall nearest the scene jumped to life and scrambled to look over the rampart for the cause of this disturbance. Several other soldiers came running to the edge of the wall and peered over it, combing the terrain for any sign of trouble. "It's just a rockslide," said one of the soldiers to those joining him, "See where that dust is? Look, there, some of the rocks are still moving." The hitherto bored soldiers stared at the debris for a few moments, a harrowing eternity for those in the tunnel. This had less to do with any suspicion on their part and more to do with the fact that this was the most action any of them had seen in months. One by one, the wall sentries shuffled off and returned to their posts. Astenor breathed a sigh of relief.

After the initial shock to their ears, the men in the corridor had great difficulty controlling their urge to cheer when the wall fell, but settled for a few good slaps on the back and butting forearms together in their traditional victory gesture. Their long wait was almost over. Only one more wall to go! They began to clear the rubble from the floor as the final breach was being made, this time, in the castle wall.

At the northwest end of the castle, the runner stopped. He faced the rocky valley that traverses northwest toward Brenton Pass, connecting Pretoria with Malmoria through the Magnon Mountains. Using a set of magics in a predetermined sequence, he signaled a sensor awaiting his signal to the commanders of the army. They were hiding in some of the many caves along the crags and in the heavily forested canyon walls near the entrance to the pass. Within a short time, the army was on the move. They were more than ready for action after ten days of restless seclusion. They moved into the center of the valley and fanned out so as to make a formidable impression on the fortress dwellers. They worked their way toward the castle at a forced-march pace.

Back at the castle, Creydek avoided detection by the soldier on the wall and began to tunnel through the exterior wall at a place he surmised was near a street, judging the soldier's long stares in that direction. He hoped the use of his magical art and that of Astenor, who kept the image of the canyon wall vivid, would be missed or overlooked as the advancing army became visible. One at a time, he caused the edges of the individual stones in the wall to flow like thick syrup and loosen themselves from their carefully worked positions. Stone after stone was then segmented and removed effortlessly by gloved soldiers who carried them to places along the base of the wall so they wouldn't attract attention from those above them. The other stone molders used their magic to secure the sides and top of the tunnel until he had shaped a passageway through the entire sixteen feet of the wall's thickness. This went much quicker than the cavern had because he was working with cut stone and thin mortar.

He was almost all the way through the wall when the report of battle horns began to sound in every part of the castle grounds. The battle was underway at the north end of the fortress. The timing was perfect!

Before breaking through into the castle grounds, Creydek called for Astenor, who then moved into the corridor with him to await the opening into the castle compound. Once they determined that the breach was imminent, Astenor went back and made sure that his image of the mountain side continued to obscure the tunnel entrance. He worked some additional magic into the image to ensure that it would hold, then returned to the breach in the wall. Few in any other lands could create such a large, detailed image, which now concealed the tunnel entrance in the canyon wall. He alone, among all his people, had learned the secrets of holding the image for a time without having to be present to control it, a secret that had won him this opportunity. He felt a rush of pride as he went back to watch Creydek complete his task. Creydek quietly removed the first stone, which would break through the inside surface of the wall. Peering out, they saw an empty street, with only an occasional soldier running across it at distant junctions with other streets. The hole was just large enough for Astenor to crawl through, which he did with great agility. It was a little above ground level, so he came out on all fours and quickly established a magical facade to hide the wall's newest door. As Creydek and his crew completed their work, Astenor preserved the image of the inside castle wall so well that no one inside the castle compound was even remotely distracted by it. Fortunately, there were no sensors nearby.

He set that image and returned to the mountain tunnel. "Captain Vance, the castle is yours for the taking," he said with a glint of pride which anticipated a rewarding remark.

"I only wish it was that easy," he whispered as he turned back to face his troops. "This is it!" he shouted. Turning back to Astenor, he said in a taunting tone, "Why don't you grab a sword and join the fun?"

There was less chance of him getting harmed than would be true for most of the others; he could simply disappear in cases of imminent danger, then set somewhere and watch the battle, unseen by its participants. Knowing this, and not wishing to lose face, he pulled out the short sword he carried with him and fell into the formation with the ranks of soldiers, each awaiting his moment of glory.

Back at the north gate of the castle, the battle was fully engaged. Already, the unprepared castle army was mobilizing and heading in force to repel the attackers. A detachment of horsemen was dispatched from the west gate and came around, hoping to flank the attacking army. They met with disaster when a fire master named Oslow began burning them down with white fire as they attacked. Many others were mowed down by a hail of arrows. The remaining few were called into retreat by the commander on the wall, who sounded the horn himself. The horsemen would have all chosen to perish rather than face the commander if they retreated on their own. He made it clear that retreat was treason and had previously announced that any man retreating would be nailed to a wooden rack, hands and feet spread, and then hung on the spikes protruding from the polished metal castle gate to cook to death in the sun.

Oslow turned his attention from the retreating horsemen and mounted an impressive attack against the wall. He moved toward the north gate behind an enormous wall of archers who filled the air with arrows as if the war would only last a few minutes. He and a small band of approached close to the gate with his companions carrying a canopy to protect him from falling or propelled objects coming from the wall. Once he was close enough to use his magic, he focused his attention on the front gate. It was solid metal hung on hinges visible only on the inside of the castle wall. He threw a steady stream of fire against the center of the gate until it began to glow red-hot. Occasionally, he would stop briefly to set a wave of specially prepared arrows on fire as they flew toward the defenders on the wall. This had the effect of creating chaos and panic among the castle dwellers.

Back in the mountain tunnel, Balore had moved to the mouth of the exit tunnel from which he could sense the battle. Being a keen sensor of the use of magic both in type and personal source, he distinctly sensed Oslow's use of fire. The continual use of fire was to be the signal for the attack from within the mountain.

Balore informed Captain Vance that the battle was fully engaged. Vance thanked him and reminded him that Balore was commanded by the king to stay in the tunnel until the castle was secure, a command that Balore deplored but honored.

"Alright, men, this is the moment we've waited for. Let's get that sword!" he shouted as he led the column of soldiers in a regimented jog out of the mountain through the wall and into the city. Astenor accompanied the troops into the city, but Creydek and his men, along with a few soldiers for carrying stones, stayed to reseal the wall after Baylore entered. The first attackers were inside the city before the men on the wall realized what was taking place. Two bands of archers were among the first through the wall. They immediately spread out to engage the few defenders above them. The sentries fell quickly, having virtually no protection from such an attack on the inside of the wall.

The foot soldiers began to round up women and children out of the houses nearest the area of the breach in the wall. A perimeter of men three deep formed around the captives. The outside ring held shields and were supported by the second row of soldiers containing both archers and spearmen. The inside ring stood with swords drawn, facing inward toward the captives. Small bands of soldiers fanned out to collect as many hostages as possible before the defenders, almost all of whom were at the north wall, discovered what was happening.

Captain Vance had given orders that only those who resisted were to be killed, in addition to any men who might present them with trouble. There were a few casualties. The women came, crying and terrified, with children of all ages holding on to them, tears streaming down their faces.

Captain Vance had the soldiers continue to bring hostages until he had a group of several hundred ringed by soldiers and stretching down the street through several intersections.

Vance moved to the front of the hostage parade and began to herd them toward the west gate. Squads of soldiers moved ahead of the group into each intersection they passed to prevent an attack. They met little resistance, most of which perished.

A cry came from one of the lead soldiers that a large group of horsemen were heading toward them from the north wall. Captain Vance quickly moved to intercept them. He ordered that the captives be stopped so they would be clearly visible to the horsemen, then he had the inner perimeter of soldiers face the captives again. This led the captives to scream and cry and huddle close together in the middle of the soldiers.

Captain Vance held up his hand and shouted to the approaching horsemen, who came to a stop. "Your women and children will all die unless you meet my demands. Look for yourselves and see their peril." He gave them just enough time to see but not to talk. "I have only two demands! First, go tell

Lord Falock that he, his troops, and the rest of the inhabitants of the city are to leave the city straightaway, and the hostages will be released. If not, then they will be killed. And finally, the north gate must be opened to allow access for the army waiting there."

One rider was sent back to the North wall with the message. While he was gone, an ever larger group of horsemen and foot soldiers gathered at the back of the original horsemen. They began to shout insults at the invaders, "Come out from behind our women and face us man to man, you cowards!" However, Vance's men held their position without any response at all.

The battle at the front wall stopped when word reached the attackers that Vance's infiltration had been successful. They withdrew from the wall a little further than a crossbow shot and set up a battle line. At about the same time, word reached Falock of their predicament and the consequent demands by the captors.

Falock was a large man who was extremely proud. After a round of cursing and yelling at the regimental commanders with him, he set out on horseback for the meeting with Vance. The mass of soldiers parted like water under a fast-moving cart wheel as Falock passed through to Vance's position.

Falock was full of rage as he dismounted and approached Vance, who was equally his size but slimmer in stature. "Why do you fight like old women and children, you dog?" shouted Falock as he came within striking distance of Vance.

"Your insults will do you no good, Lord Falock. We have your families and will kill them if you resist us. You'll have them back safe and unharmed if you do as I say. It's as simple as that," said Vance in a voice that in no way betrayed the terror he felt inside.

"And what guarantee do we have that you'll do what you say and set them free?" said Falock, hoping that Vance would slip up in some small detail that would give him some advantage.

"You have no guarantee at all," answered Vance coldly, "we have no use for them after you're out of the city. Our only reason for taking them is to spare unnecessary bloodshed. We simply want you outside and us securely inside."

"What's your purpose here? Do you think we'll just sit by and let you live here and move your families in?" said Falock, challenging Vance.

"We have come from Malmoria to claim Fallonrod," he answered without emotion.

Falock and his men began to laugh with almost spasmatic convulsions. "You mean," he said, barely able to control his laughter, "that you've done all this for a sword of legends and wives tales that's magically sealed in a room and which no one has seen in over a hundred years?"

Vance did not display any of the embarrassment he felt at being treated with this contempt, but simply answered, "If the sword is such a laughing matter to you, break open the room and allow us to take the sword with us, and we'll leave with no further incident."

Falock iced up, and his men stopped their mocking laughter. "We will not give you the sword if indeed it actually does rest in the room. You'll have to take it out by yourselves... if you can." Falock turned and consulted with two of his regiment commanders and again faced Vance. "How will this exit take place so that we'll know that you'll honor your word?"

"After you open the north gate, you and your soldiers ensure that the rest of the city's inhabitants leave. After you and your soldiers are a comfortable distance from the gate, we will send the hostages out to you. You must be far enough away to allow us to close the gate safely, or we will not release your families." Vance spoke without emotion, even though his heart was about to pound its way out of his chest. "One more thing, any killing of my men will be met with the death of a hostage, on a one-for-one basis."

The only thing more important to a Pretorian than power was the family. Falock's men advised him that if the stories about the sword were true, there was a good chance that the Malmorians didn't have anyone who could control it. And if the Malmorians had better luck getting through the wall than they had, then a breach would be a welcome benefit. Falock gave in, knowing that whatever happened, help would come as soon as the horsemen he dispatched reached his allies in the other Pretorian castles.

While Falock began complying with Vance's demands, Balore and the remaining men in the tunnel were brought into the city and remained in seclusion until the city was emptied. Creydek began to repair the wall from the outside inward using the original stones which had been moved inside by aids.

It was almost sundown when the last of Falock's men left the city. The incoming soldiers from the north gate made a sweep of the city, searching for any remaining soldiers. Falock was warned that any detachment of soldiers left inside would be cause for the termination of the deal and would certainly assure the destruction of their families. Falock left no one inside.

As the sun set, the only remaining open gate was closed behind the group of freed hostages who ran wailing with tears of joy to their frustrated husbands and fathers.

Long before the gate was closed, Balore, Gredek, and Oslow, having discovered the location of the room containing the sword, went to work on the wall surrounding it. After a thorough search was made of the room's exterior wall, it was determined to be secure and sealed all the way around, even including a secret passage beneath it which had been walled up. By the time the last fortress gate had been secured, Creydek had begun to work his magic on the room's exterior wall from the large east hallway.

Balore and Oslow stood impatiently with about ten armed escorts while Creydek tried over and over to make the stone flow. "It doesn't even heat," he shouted as he pounded on the wall repeatedly with a tightly clenched fist. "I've never seen anything like this...it's been sealed with extremely powerful magic..."

"Does this mean that you're incapable of getting through this stone?" snapped Balore, now completely out of patience.

"I'll try a different mixture of magics and see if that works," answered Creydek with defeat evident in his voice. "I've never met with a stone that I couldn't manage before. It seems to contain a magic that acts against mine," he mumbled to himself as he went back to work on the wall.

Balore moved next to Creydek and began to attempt to manipulate the stone himself. They tried combining their magics against the magic that had bound the stone. Nothing affected the wall at all. They even moved to two other locations to no avail. They returned to the large hallway.

After another frustrating attempt, Balore turned to two of the soldiers and said, "Since the wall won't let us use magic on it, go find some stone working tools. A castle made entirely of stone must have a large supply of them somewhere."

Just as the soldiers were leaving, Captain Vance showed up with Captain Alec, who had led the attack on the front gate.

Balore turned to acknowledge them as they arrived, "Excellent job, you both did very well. How long do you think you can hold them off?"

"Why?" asked Vance, looking alarmed.

"Because we can't get through this wall with magic," he answered. "It looks like we're gonna have to chisel our way through!"

Both captains looked at each other with concern.

"We outnumber them at this point," said Captain Alec, "but we don't know their castle the way they do. If they have some secret passage into the castle grounds, we could be in trouble. If not, we could hold out against them until they get reinforcements from their allies here in Pretoria."

"And how long might that take?" asked Balore, beginning to sound anxious.

The two captains exchanged thoughts between themselves, then Vance answered, "Late afternoon, three days from now, you can count on seeing the first contingents of a sizable army begin to gather outside the walls."

"We should be able to get through this wall in three days, magic or no magic," said Alec, running his hand over the smooth stone. "How hard can stone be?"

Creydek was now totally embarrassed and retreated into the shadows of the hallway, grumbling as he went. Balore looked at the others and back at the silhouette of Creydek disappearing into the darkness and answered, "Very hard, captain, very hard indeed!"

A short time later, a large group of men returned with heavy crushing hammers, a variety of chisels, and tongs to hold the chisels against the stone. In no time, they were pounding on the wall. Every blow rang painfully in the ears of all present in the hallway. Each blow brought a large spark, a small cloud of smoke, and a tiny bit of dust. After many of the men in the hall had taken their turn pounding the wall, only a small indentation was visible to show for their tingling hands, ringing ears, and aching arms.

"Captain Vance," said Balore with raised eyebrows, "It's going to take every bit of the three days to get through this wall. Set up a continuing flow of fresh soldiers to keep the work going. As soon as one tires, the next will step in. We'll work all day and all night until we get through this cursed wall. See if we have some metal smiths among us. Have them set up nearby for sharpening chisels... I don't want anything slowing us down!"

"I'll send the men in by fighting squads of fifty. You handle the rest as you see fit," he said as he turned to find Captain Alec and set up the rotation.

Just before sunrise on the third day, they broke through to the original wall of the room. Creydek was summoned and found that he could mold and flow the stone of the original wall with no trouble. By late morning, they had cleared enough of the magically sealed stone cleared away for a man-sized hole to be finished through the inner wall into the sword chamber. Balore had fallen asleep just before daybreak and had been left to rest until he was needed.

Outside the wall during the night, Lord Welton's horsemen had already begun to arrive from Castle Rock, and the first riders of Lord Linx's army had arrived from Castle Greystone. They had set up a perimeter that left the north gate unguarded. Word had been sent in that if the intruders would leave at once with just their own provisions, they would not be pursued but would be allowed to escape. Otherwise, they would all be destroyed without mercy.

The soldiers from Malmoria grew more and more agitated as they waited for word from the sword room.

The magically sealed stone was about as thick as the length of a tall man's forearm from his elbow to his fingertips. The original wall was only about two-thirds that thick.

Just after noon, Craydek announced, "I'm through!" in a muffled yell from the inside of the narrow crawl space through the walls. Not very long afterward, Creydek crawled out and announced, "It's open now, you can go inside!"

A cheer went up from the large number of people in the hallway who had come to watch, knowing that the opening was complete. Several runners were dispatched to tell the men on the walls that the room was being entered. A successive cheer went up around the castle wall as more and more men received the news. Their spirits rose, and they readied themselves for the fight they knew would come soon, a fight with their powermaster carrying the legendary Fallonrod.

As the now refreshed Balore entered the hall, the cheer rose to a deafening roar. Balore accepted the praise with a broad grin and waved as he walked to the opening in the wall.

"One man has already gone inside to check for traps and has found the room in order with the sword buried in stone just as the legend suggested," said

Captain Vance, having to yell into Balore's ear to get above the noise of cheering and whistling.

"I don't want a lot of people in the room with me, but I think we should have Oslow, Creydek, and you, Captain Vance, accompany me."

By this time, some weary footmen from Castle Rock had begun to arrive but only about half of Castle Greyston's horsemen had yet come. Hearing the cheer go up from the walls of the city, Lord Falock realized that they were inside the room. He summoned Lord Welton and the commander of the detachment from Lord Linx, "We have to attack now, before they can discover how to use the sword. We've rigged the south gate to break down when we hit it with the ram."

The troops were already on the alert and mobilized quickly, having been aroused by the cheering. They did not wait for the remaining reinforcements from Lord Linx.

The battering ram was brought out into full view of the wall. It was the trunk of a large old tree stripped of limbs and bark. It was hung by cables from four posts which were about twice as high as a house top and mounted on a heavy, long wagon. The tree trunk extended in length the distance of a tall man's height beyond the front and back edges of the wagon. There was a plank roof over the top of the wagon extending over the sides to protect those who would maneuver it. Under the roof on the sides of the wagon were rows of beams that protruded from it on each side. Each beam could accommodate three men to push the monstrosity.

A sizable force of archers moved onto the south wall from throughout the castle in preparation for the attack. An even greater number of archers approached the wall from the ground and began the attack while the battering arm was moved into position.

Back in the sword room, Oslow, Creydek, and Captain Vance had all climbed into the room with Balore. The soldier who originally searched the room remained inside at the entrance. He reported to those in the hallway, relaying whatever information he could about the activity taking place in the room.

They quickly found the sword near the fireplace, to the right of the entrance. It was buried in the stone at a slight angle and rested within two handbreadths of the hilt. The entire visible portion of the sword glowed in an eerie greenish-blue hue. They moved closer to the sword using a torch to investigate its position. As they made their initial observations, word came that the battle to retake the castle was beginning.

"Time is not our friend today," muttered Balore under his breath, his heart beating wildly as he remembered the stories about those who tried to master this metal monster in ages past. "We have no more time to waste!" he exclaimed as he handed the torch to Captain Vance and moved resolutely to the sword.

Reaching down to take the glowing handle, he shouted, "For Malmoria! May we reign victorious over our enemies!" With that, he took hold of Fallonrod. There was a bright flash of light that momentarily blinded everyone in the room. There was a crackling sound coming from the sword as light flashed from it. Balore swung the sword over his head and shouted, "I am the master!" The floor underneath him began to glow, then Balore began to glow. Everyone stood transfixed at the sight. Suddenly, Balore caught fire in a brilliant flame which took only an instant to turn him to ash. The sword hit the floor and immediately began to sink into it.

Oslow ran to the sword and grabbed it, pulling it from its new stone sheath. The sword scarcely cleared the floor before he exploded with such force that the guard at the entrance was blown out through the hole in the wall, landing in a dead heap against the opposite corridor wall to the horror of those looking on. Captain Vance and Creydek were both knocked down, and the torch Vance had held was blown out. Only the now much brighter glow of the sword was left to light the room. It took a moment for Creydek's eyes to adjust to the light, but once they did, he was able to assess the damage within the room. Again, the sword was sinking into the floor. This time it was nearly flat with the surface of the stone. The light from the sword was being absorbed quickly by the stone into which it sank. The handle was about to reach the floor when Creydek ran to it, shouting in a crazed voice, "NO! NO! You can't leave." He reached down and grabbed the luminescent handle, still shouting, "We've come too far... risk too much..." he pulled it only partially up out of the floor, screamed in pain, recoiled wildly, and began to jump around the room, shaking his hand and arm. His hand was smoldering, and his shirt sleeve was on fire from the heat of the sword. He ran to the hole in the wall, diving into it headfirst. His large frame was jarred to a painful halt: he quickly squirmed through into the hallway, still screeching with pain. The sword was stationary roughly at the position Creydek had left it.

Captain Vance did not become captain by taking foolish chances. He cursed the sword and followed Creydek through the opening.

The ram swung with earthshaking violence against the south gate. It hit squarely in the center of the doors, and the entire gate simply fell inward, right off the hinges, crushing those who were standing too close. The ram was quickly rolled back, and the attack was on.

Already, many of those inside were being called into retreat toward the north gate, hoping to either find the powermaster in possession of the power sword and make a stand with him, or to escape through the unguarded gate. The best of Pretoria's fighting men were through the gate first and began to inflict heavy casualties. This caused a full-scale retreat among the Malmorians. Once they began to run, the horsemen were brought in to persuade them to keep moving toward the deliberately unattended north gate. Skirmishes in the midst of their retreat left scores of both Malmorians and Pretorians dead at the south gate, but only a handful more died between there and the north gate, and then, only those who chose to stand and fight. Captain Vance made his way to the north gate and stood just outside of it until the last of his fleeing men passed. When he could see no more Malmorians heading for the exit, he followed the retreat at a full run, unpursued.

In this way, Pretoria witnessed the beginning of its greatest challenge in over a hundred years: to secure Fallonrod. A friendly powermaster must be found to wield it for Pretoria, or a way discovered to hide or destroy it.

CHAPTER 3

Ten years had passed since Dalwan had gone to live with his great uncle Shaylan. He had grown to about the height of a full-grown average height man. His normally disheveled dark brown hair touched the collar of the baggy tunic that hung on thin frame. During those years, Dalwan had trained under Shaylan's intensely regimented oversight. It became evident that Dalwan had all of the many magical arts that Shaylan himself possessed and possibly more. Shaylan gave him a broad-based education and training in the use of each magical art that he himself possessed. Dalwan greatly preferred the creative arts of stone molding and wood weaving. It was with these two arts that he spent the majority of his scarce free time. He passively resisted learning to use the arts of war when he could and only grudgingly practiced them when forced to.

Shaylan stood cross-armed with his back to the cabin door, rocking slightly from side to side as he did when he was agitated. This was the first time during the ten years that Dalwan had lived with him that his patience had given in to serious irritation. Dalwan's slender frame slumped in the old high-backed wooden chair that sat near the fireplace. In a dry, teenage I-already-know-everything tone, he said, "I don't want to learn sword fighting and I already know how to control the fire."

"But you've only just begun to learn what you will need…"

"I already know all I need to know. I want to be a stone molder like my father and…"

"…and end up hunted and abducted by some power trader…or even worse!" Shaylan's face was red, and worry plowed his brow with deep wrinkles.

Dalwan sat up and turned slightly to face Shaylan; his tone hardened as his words came faster and with an edge to them that further infuriated Shaylan. "How? How are they going to know what I can do?"

"You know that there are powerful sensors that can distinguish one person's magic from another. They can hunt you down just by tracking your magic."

Dalwan jumped to his feet and began to pace as his voice got even louder. "Then I won't use magic."

"Oh yes, you will! And every time you do, they'll get closer to finding you."

Dalwan stopped at the dining table and, leaning over it on two pencil-thin arms, said mockingly, "Shaylan, do you really believe that someone will actually think that I might be a powermaster...that I could really use that ancient magic sword, Falcon...ereh...?

"Fallonrod?! YES!! That's exactly what I think!" Shaylan walked over, effortlessly pushed the table out from between them, and grabbed Dalwan by the shoulders, as much to steady him as to get his attention. He stared into Dalwan's soul with steel-blue eyes. "Your magic is so powerful now that if we hadn't practiced in the caves, we would have already had visitors. And, like everyone else's, your magic has its own signature to it. Just as voices can be distinguished one from another, your magic is easily recognized… YOU WILL BE FOUND!"

"I can take care of myself, I'll..."

"THEN GO!" shouted Shaylan as he let go of Dalwan and pointed to the cabin door. "Get your things and be gone!" he said, shooing at Dalwan as if trying to get rid of a pesky fly. "Go...now...out with you..."

Dalwan picked up his clothes from the foot of the bed, packed a few other things from nearby shelves into a traveling bag, and headed for the door, bag in hand. "Uncle Shaylan, thanks for helping me get through these years… for the training… I just need to go home… to be normal…"

"Forget *normal* boy! You will never be normal!" Shaylan opened the door to his cabin and motioned with his head for Dalwan to leave. "You know where to find me for now. If I'm not here, I'll be at Castle Crest helping them put things back together after the attack they had."

"Don't be mad at me, Shaylan," he said as he stepped outside.

"When they come after you, boy, it won't be to offer you milk and sweet bread. You need to learn to fight…"

"I promise, I'll come back later and learn…"

Shaylan slammed the cabin door before Dalwan could finish. He stood staring at the closed door, stunned by Shaylan's abruptness, a side of his personality he seldom witnessed. Dalwan's resolve cleared away the emotion of the moment and carried him home.

Dalwan's arrival at home was unexpected.

"It's good to see you again son, and so soon!" exclaimed Kindron as he gave a crushing embrace to his spindly son. "It's only been a few weeks, but I'm sure you've grown another two fingers height since then." He said, laughing as he escorted him into the house. "Reela, guess who's home for a visit?"

Reela peeked around the corner from the kitchen and walked toward him with a quizzical look on her face, "Dalwan, it's good to see you so soon. But why so serious?" she said, tilting her head questioningly.

Kindron started to protest at her dampening effect on the moment, but stopped short when he realized what a troubled look Dalwan now wore. "What is it, son? Is everything OK? Is Shaylan well? What, son? What's wrong?"

"I'm taking a break in my training. I need to be home for a while."

"Had a falling out with Shaylan, did you?" his father said in a manly assessment of the situation.

"Not exactly. I just don't want to learn to fight right now." He said in a dejected tone that begged for understanding and even a little pity.

Kindron and Reela looked at each other with a great deal of concern.

"Dalwan, we can't protect you here," said Kindron, the wrinkles on his face betraying the worry that invades his mind every time he thinks of his very gifted, or else cursed, son."

"And we can't help you learn either," added Reela with sadness that brought her near to tears.

"You don't want me here?" Dalwan was confused and bewildered.

Reela reached out and took both of his hands in hers, "Of course we do… but we are helpless… "

"Helpless and scared… for you and us!" added Kindron, sounding defeated.

"I won't use any magic," Dalwan said desperately. I'll just do the footwork and the back-breaking stuff."

Kindron looked at Reela, and to their individual joy, each was pleading for permission for Dalwan to stay. They broke into laughter and joined Reela, throwing welcome arms around their boy. "We'll make it work, son, don't worry about it. Welcome home, Boy." Smiles turned to tears, and tears begged for hope.

It took him little time to settle in. The very next day, he began to work for his father. Fearing the things Shaylan told him, he used rarely used magic and then only by accident, choosing instead to go into the hills with the wagon and gather the special rocks that his father would use to make the stone wares which he sold in the village market.

****

The Pretorian year was divided into four seasons: The Rising, when crops were planted and trees blossomed; The Ripening, the warm months, when fruit and crops grew and ripened; The Harvesting, when the ripened fruit and remaining crops were harvested and the trees started losing their leaves; The Resting, the cold time when the earth and farmer rested, while plants and trees are dormant and the trees are trimmed. Each season was divided into three phases: Beginning, Mid, and Finish. A particular phase might be written, Mid-Ripening or End-Harvest.

During Mid-Rising, after Dalwan had gone home, a man appeared at the foot of the hill upon which Shaylan's house sat. The man was dressed entirely in black. He wore a heavy, silky-looking black cloak with gilded clasps and a chain holding it fixed at the neck. There were golden braided chains on the shoulders. The belt, which held his sword, was a weave of black leather and gold. He wore golden colored mail over a black leather vest under his cloak. On his head was an odd black hat which was pointed at the front and curled up around the back. It held a single blue black tail feather of the giant fire eagle secured by a delicate gold weave band.

He walked noiselessly to the base of the trail that led up to the house. He paused when Shaylan appeared at the top with a hand raised in challenge. "Stand your ground and state your business."

"You owe me, old man!"

"Be clear with your intentions, dark one, or retrace your steps."

25

"Old man, your mind must be getting weak. You owe me a bird and a mug of ale."

Shaylan's hand came down and pointed toward the black cloaked intruder as he said, "You have a lot of nerve coming here unannounced, you troublemaker!" Blue fire shot from his hand and flashed to the ground directly in front of the intruder. Instantly, there was a gold-handled sword in the man's hand, and his cloak was thrown back over his shoulders like a cape. He moved with startling agility and speed as he advanced upward toward the wizard's position, his face lit with a treacherous grin.

The next fire flew directly at the quickly advancing trespasser… "Your skill has increased, old man," he said as he easily deflected the flame with his sword.

Shaylan stood his ground with balls of fire dancing on his fingertips, each one skillfully dispatched in rapid succession at the attacker, only to have them artfully deflected as if solid.

The sword bearer was only a handful of steps from Shaylan, a broad smile now clearly displaying crooked white teeth, when the wizard suddenly formed a bridge of green fire between his outstretched hands and let it fly like a blazing rope at the feet of his opponent. Like lightning, the swordsman swept down with his sword to deflect this flame, only to have the flame wrap around his sword and feet at the same time, binding them together.

He lunged clumsily forward and rolled headfirst, coming to rest, still bound, at the feet of the wizard.

"Rhem, I am ever so happy we are on the same side. That was nothing short of amazing!" said the wide-eyed wizard as he reached down to dispel the remnant of the dissipating green flame.

"And you, my friend, are more skilled than any I have encountered," answered Rhem as he took the wizard's now outstretched hand and came to his feet.

Both men just stood face to face, powerful grips holding each other's wrists, as the renewed admiration they shared flowed between them. It was as if they shared the same soul. Their lives had been intertwined through adventures and fate. Their care for each other far outweighed that of their own lives.

Breaking the short trance, Shaylan gave Rhem a powerful tug toward the cabin and said gruffly, "Let's not waste time just standing here. Come in, let's catch up with each other. The ale is too warm and the bird is smoked, but both will fill you."

As they entered the cabin, Shaylan said, "I know there's more to your visit than a casual stop or you would doubtless have passed me by again."

"Again?" asked Rhem sheepishly.

"Yes, AGAIN!" answered Shaylan with an obvious taunting edge in his voice.

"How did you know I passed by without stopping?"

"I can sense your presence, Rhem. I sensed your coming yesterday and can sense your concern now."

"How long have you been able to do this?"

"Since last year when you fought the Talon beast…"

Rhem whirled around with a horrified look on his face, "How did you…?"

"I was there!" he said matter-of-factly with a shrug.

"Did you interfere?"

"My friend, there was no need!" Shaylan walked over to Rhem and put his hands on his heavily mailed shoulders. "I would have told you if I had interfered."

"But you were there…"

"I sensed the situation and went. You weren't that far away. But I must confess that it was the trial of my soul to see if I could be there, watch, and not mess it up for you."

"You could watch and not interfere? And leave without a word?" asked Rhem as if questioning a witness at a trial.

Shaylan nodded his head. "Those with you would not have welcomed my presence, as you know."

"Then it's my turn to be tested." Rhem regained his train of thought, "But that's not why I came..."

Shaylan cut him off, "Let's eat before we get too wrapped up in our talk. There'll be plenty of time later to talk about everything that's bothering you."

After eating and laughing through the recounts of past adventures, Rhem became very serious again. "How long ago did you say that Dalwan went back to his parents' house?"

"Let's see...it's full moon now...must have been a few days after the last full moon."

"Did he finish his studies with you?"

Disappointment showed heavily on Shaylan's face, "No. He didn't want to learn any more about fire or fighting ...we only got through the basics...he didn't want to know about swords. He only studied the art of Shadowmaster so he could spy on people without being seen. He wanted to go back home and help his father do stone molding."

"Have you sensed his power in use since then?"

"Briefly...maybe twice or three times, but he said that he wasn't going to use magic except sparingly and then only when forced to. Why?"

"Within the last 20 days or so, I have encountered two groups traveling at night...sensors...I'm sure of it. They must be looking for some single source of power...someone they suspect of being a powermaster or at least close to one."

"But the boy practiced in the caves with me, and he hasn't used his power, well, not hardly at all, since then."

"Have you sensed any other power that might have drawn these two groups to these parts?"

"None at all, but..."

"But they are close by, even now they're searching. Maybe they can sense through the stone of the caves."

"But Dalwan's been gone too many days for them to be looking for him here. Besides, no one can sense through the mountain stone."

"Shaylan, Shaylan! Do I need to remind you how much the rising earth power has changed our abilities...how much your sensing and ability with fire has increased...and my power with the sword is ten times what it was this time last year."

"I doubt they're looking for the boy...it just doesn't make sense."

"Then they're looking for you!" Rhem said with exaggerated candor.

"Everyone knows where to find me, besides, my power is easily recognized and is very distinct from Dalwan's." Shaylan noticed that Rhem was now grinning widely and, realizing that Rhem was toying with him, became flustered... "Will you be serious?"

Rhem regained his composure and his face resumed a respectfully stern posture. "Shaylan, one of these groups had a weapons master with them. He was not at all familiar to me, but from the way he moved, I would say he was very good. It's only a matter of time before Dalwan gets into trouble...he'll show off...or react out of fear, or some fool thing will tempt him to expose his power...then what?"

"What is it exactly you want me to do...kidnap him and hide him in a cave for the rest of his life!?" Shaylan's eyes were wide with frustration, and his voice was icy with sarcasm.

"Come on, Shaylan," Rhem walked over and put his hands on his friend's shoulders, "we both care for Dalwan...you most of all...and you're right, we can't protect or hide him for the rest of his life. But we can get him to understand that he'll eventually have to face the likes of those sensors and weapons master that I saw...you know, there are a handful of kingdoms who would give anything to have one with his power in their court, and who would reward someone handsomely for bringing him to them." Shaylan nodded and put his hands up in surrender.

"You are right...I know everything you've said is true. But what if the boy doesn't want to train?"

"We'll convince him to!"

"Is this why you came?... To train Dalwan?" Shaylan's voice was full of surprise, dipped in suspicion.

"Yes, and I have something of a plan..."

Rhem and Shaylan set out on horseback for Alston, Dalwan's hometown, before dawn the next morning and arrived in the late afternoon. Dalwan's parents' house was a modest stone home with a barn and workshop about fifty paces behind it, all of which sat at the edge of the town on a gently sloping piece of ground dotted with a few small trees.

After a brief time of exchanging greetings and catching up with current family events, Rhem abruptly broke off the pleasantries, "Actually, we're here to speak with Dalwan about his future."

Kindron and Reela exchanged worried looks as Rhem continued, "Dalwan is more powerful than he wants to believe and will be in greater danger than he can now imagine, and time is not his friend in this matter."

Reela stood up and left the room with her hands cupping her tear-covered face. Kindron looked at Dalwan, who sat leaning his simple wooden chair back on the two hind legs. Dalwan's face flushed and he rocked forward with a thud...his eyes begged for help from his father.

"What do you want of us?" asked Kindron, who was himself fighting many emotions at once.

Shaylan stood and walked over to Dalwan and looked back at Kindron, "I think we need some time alone with Dalwan if that meets with your approval?"

"Why don't you go back to the shop...you can be alone there. I'll tend to Reela," he said as he got up and left the room.

"Show us to the shop...," said Shaylan to Dalwan, who was staring at the floor with sagging shoulders. His downcast expression made him look defeated, as if forced to give up his most valuable possession by a gang of bullies. "We only want what's best for you...at least hear us out...then we'll leave if you want."

Dalwan got up and led them out to the shop. It was a quaint and tidy shop, complete with every stone shaping tool you could think of. There were several stone slabs of varying types in piles along the outside wall. The building was split into two parts separated by a wooden wall with large doors. The other side was a stable in which there was a loft with hay, a sturdy wagon, and tack for the animals. The two horses and the mule were out in the fenced yard. After a brief tour, they went back into the shop area where Dalwan sat down on the tallest stack of stone slabs and gave Shaylan and Rhem his apprehensive attention.

Shaylan began, "As you already know, Castle Crest has been attacked by the Malmorians, who hoped to secure Fallonrod for their powermaster. While they did succeed in taking the castle and breaking into the sword room, they failed quite rudely in their attempt to secure the sword."

"You've already told me all of this before." Answered Dalwan in teenage-speak

"But I never told you how you might fit into the consequences of the room being opened and the legends revived."

"I can already tell you how I fit in..." said Dalwan, getting up and walking past them both.

Power comes to only a small handful of people in the world during an entire generation...that means maybe only two or three anywhere at the peak of the earth power surge."

"But if I don't use the power, no one can tell!"

"Not necessarily true," said Shaylan, "the point Rhem was going to make is that during this time of rising power, sensors can sense better and will be discovering new abilities in their art...some can tell your thoughts...there are even legends from the past that some could tell all your gifts even when you weren't using them."

"But that's like knowing your voice without hearing it."

"Not when the earth power grows like it has...a person can no longer assume that simply not using his magic will protect him from being discovered...and this will certainly be true concerning you!"

Dalwan's face turned ashen, his eyes widened, and his mouth dropped open. There was fear and sickness in his words as he spoke, "My dreams...Shaylan...MY DREAMS!!...the fire and the monsters, those walls that trapped me...that hand and the eyes...were they real? Were they some kind of prophetic dreams?"

Dalwan looked so pathetic that Rhem had to turn and face away from him in disgust.

Suddenly, Dalwan's expression changed. His eyes took on a fierce look as he used all the sensing powers he had, "Shaylan, are my dreams real...have you known all along...is this something you hid from me, telling me not to worry that they were just dreams?"

Shaylan debated only an instant how to answer as he felt all his defensive walls being ripped away by the probing powers of the boy. "Yes! Yes, Dalwan, they are your future," he said, looking down with some introspection and regret at having hid this truth from him. Recovering his composure his gaze met full force the searching eyes of Dalwan, "But listen to me boy. They are not events, they are powers and challenges..." his voice turned to a tense harsh whisper, "but you can master those dreams...if you have courage and train... then when the searchers come, you'll be fully prepared."

"But they can't find me here. They have no idea that I even exist," said Dalwan in a defiant tone.

"That may not be as true as you think. Even now, there are sensors in Pretoria...looking...sensing...probing." Shaylan looked over at Rhem, who was displaying some interest in Dalwan's changing attitude and had turned around to watch, "Tell the boy what you saw."

"In recent days, I have encountered two groups of foreign sensors moving under the cover of darkness through Pretoria. One of them had a weapons master with them. I don't believe it to be an accident that they were both near your uncle's village."

Dalwan's face became pale again, and his voice weak and whiny, "But we never practiced outside the caverns... no one could sense our magic through all that rock!" Dalwan's shoulders slumped, and he leaned against the trough again.

Rhem bounded over to him and grabbed him with one hand by the shirt and lifted him onto his toes, dragging the wide-eyed Dalwan nose to nose with him, "Get hold of yourself, boy. You're almost old enough to be a man, act like one!"

Shaylan quickly stepped up and respectfully took hold of Rhem's arm, separating Dalwan from his powerful grip and stepping between them, facing Dalwan. "With the earth's power rising daily, we can't be sure of anything, especially concerning you. The stone should hinder most all sensors who are far enough away, but one close enough...one who is very talented...may pick it up...who's to say how much more ability the earth power could give to a well-practiced sensor?!"

"Then it might be too late. My dreams are coming true, and it's too late!" Dalwan was again wide-eyed until he caught sight of the flash of anger in Rhem's face. He brought his composure under immediate control.

"No boy, NO!" said Shaylan, stepping between Rhem and Dalwan while shooting a chastising look back at his friend, "from the first day we began your training, you've been facing your dreams. In those years when you awoke screaming and I sat with you as you explained to me the fire and the demons, the walls coming from your hands that trapped you,...when you described that awful hand that groped blindly for you out of the darkness and struck out at you,...and the eye that searched for you...through all that time I used all you told me to prepare you to confront the evil symbolized in your dreams."

"Then tell me where the dreams come from. Are they sent to me by someone to scare me, or do they just come from inside me?"

"The dreams are from the magic that dwells in you. The magic connects you with everything else that is of magic in the world. It's neither against you nor for you. It's what you make of it in your life...using your own powers, or being used by others. Do you understand?"

Dalwan stood staring for a moment. He didn't want to think about these things at all and resented Shaylan and Rhem for making him. "I don't know...they still scare me. Sometimes I get afraid that they'll come back...like they used to."

"The reason they don't come is that you have already begun to intuitively understand them."

"Then why am I still scared?" yelled Dalwan as he became even more annoyed.

"You're only afraid of the memory of them. Because they're from the magic inside you, they show you things that can help you face your future and prepare for it."

"How?...dreams can't help you."

"Look back now at your dreams..."

"Here? Now?"

"Go on, boy...close your eyes," Shaylan's voice became melodic as if inducing a trance, "see the fire..."

Dalwan could not resist the wizard's words. His eyes closed and he turned inward...back to the dreams of his childhood.

"See the fire! Where is it?"

"It's surrounding me...flames of all colors...they're all around me and inside me...they come like waves."

"Are they friend or adversary?"

"Neither...they're part of me...I think they protect me..."

"Look for the demons...do you see the little monsters?"

"Yes, they're looking for me...they seem lost...they found me now...they're throwing things at me and yelling, but I can't understand their words...just noise."

"Are they hurting you?"

"They can't get to me through the fire."

"Now the eye. What is the eye doing?"

"It's looking...it gets narrow like squinting then wide like it's seen me...the hand is coming out of the darkness, it seems connected to the eye...it's moving and grasping... jerking and swinging blindly one way then the other...there it goes, back into the darkness...the eye is still looking."

"Enough now, wake up."

Dalwan opened his eyes, and his head was spinning. He would have fallen down but was somehow already sitting on the dirt floor.

Rhem stepped around Shaylan and hoisted Dalwan back to his feet, then stepped back a few paces. "Now that you know what these things mean, you no doubt also realize that you must learn to protect yourself."

Dalwan's eyes came into focus, staring directly into Rhem's steel-eyed stare. "I can protect myself just fine now."

"You may be able to protect yourself from other village kids, but not from a weapons master sent to capture you... and what about the sword...what about Fallonrod? If you are a powermaster, and my guess is that you are, you'll need to know more about the use of a sword than any ordinary swordsman does."

"I don't believe I'm a powermaster! What? You want me to be like the fool that did believe he was? Isn't he a pile of ash and a cloud of smoke in the sword chamber at Castle Crest? So I don't have to learn to use a sword because even if I could, I wouldn't try THAT sword."

Shaylan spoke up in a fit of exasperation, "Fine boy, just fine. Play into the hands of those who want to control you. I'll tell you this, if a sensor discovers your power and finds you untrained and unprepared to resist him, you'll be easy prey for him...yes indeed, easy prey!"

"But it doesn't have to be that way, Dalwan... I could train you, and there would be none who could stand against you." said Rhem with renewed enthusiasm.

"How do you know what that sword will do?" shouted Dalwan defiantly. "Can you tell me for sure that you can train me to use it?" Dalwan walked up to Rhem with that arrogant attitude common among teenagers, "You don't even know what the sword looks like, let alone what it can do. How are you going to train me to use a sword you know nothing about?"

Rhem began to move toward Dalwan in slow, challenging steps causing Dalwan to back track with each advance. "It's a sword, Dalwan," he said menacingly. "And whoever made it did so with the knowledge that it would be used as a sword. If you're going to stone mold or weave wood, you have to practice and practice and then practice some more if you're going to be worth spit...so it is with swordsmanship. A swordsman is a skilled strategist, not a slasher."

Shaylan joined Rhem who continued to speak as they marched shoulder to shoulder, backing Dalwan backward across the floor, "He is cunning and crafty...a worthy opponent of any who dare to stand against him."

"He is trained intuitively, move for move..." said Rhem, thrusting his closed fist toward Dalwan as if holding a sword, which caused Dalwan to flinch, "knowing when and how to attack...when to stand...when to run."

Dalwan was now backed against the stable wall, and they all came to a halt. His expression changed from fear to anger in an instant, "Hold on, you two. What if the sensors aren't looking for me at all? What if I'm not a powermaster? What if the sword can't be mastered by anybody in any way? What if I am skilled enough to protect myself now? What if..."

"WHAT IF..." interrupted Rhem impatiently, speaking loudly over Dalwan's words, "you are a powermaster. What *IF* you are untrained and unprepared when some mercenary sensor stumbles onto you? What *IF* he's able to coerce you into doing his bidding because you're not prepared to resist?"

Dalwan answered in a rage, "Both of you underestimate me...you both take me for some weak child. Shaylan has trained me, and I can take care of myself."

"No, boy! No!" said Shaylan in a disciplinary tone. "I've only set you on the path to mastery. Now you must train to become proficient...all I've done is open your eyes to some of the possibilities you possess."

"But look at what I can do...how many arts I have mastered?!"

"Mastered? Mastered?" said Shaylan in a raspy mocking voice, a voice that Dalwan had never heard this man he called master and friend use on anyone before. "What you practice now is child's play compared to what your true ability is. Your power is greater than mine, but it would take me only moments to reduce you to a groveling, pathetic child."

"I'm not as bad as you think, Shaylan. I've learned your lessons. I can stand my ground!" shouted Dalwan in a peevish rebuttal.

"Then do so now, boy!" shouted Shaylan, raising his hands over his head in challenge.

Rhem yelled as he started toward the wizard, "You fool, not here, not now..." and was cut short by an explosion of green light thrown in his direction by Shaylan. It caught him straight on and sent him flying and dazed him into a pile of straw.

Shaylan lost no time in commencing his attack. Another ball of green flame formed in his hand and shot toward Dalwan, pounding into his chest. Dalwan was slammed backwards into the wall. "Defend yourself, boy!"

He staggered forward and shook his head; tears ran down his cheeks as he tried to catch his breath. He stumbled a few awkward paces toward Shaylan, who backstepped to avoid being run into. Another green ball of flame exploded on Dalwan's feet, sending him to the floor face down. He rolled over with pleading eyes, still unable to regain his breath.

Shaylan stood and watched motionless as Dalwan gasped and again began to breathe. Dalwan struggled to his feet. Again, he was hit by a ball of green flame, which bludgeoned him backwards into the doorway between the shop and stable. He tried to shield himself against the next attack, only to be spun around and knocked through the door onto the stone floor of the shop. Suddenly, the stone began to flow around his ankles, securing him to the floor.

Dalwan's eyes turned dangerous. The stone appeared to melt away, and he sprang to his feet. A ball of red fire shot toward the wizard but was turned away harmlessly. He threw a volley of red fireballs at Shaylan, only to have them turned away with no apparent effect. Dalwan stepped back through the door into the stable.

A huge sheet of green flame formed between Shaylan's hands, which flew toward Dalwan's chest, pinning his hands and arms to his body and knocking him down. Tears filled his eyes again. "It's not fair, master. I've never seen this green fire. I don't know how to fend it off." He rolled over, and as he was getting up, he was hit again but did not fall down.

"Alright...Alright! I'll train. I'll do whatever you say."

Rhem, who had remained sitting on the pile of hay watching, jumped up, "No, you don't, boy. All you're doing is giving up. You don't want to train, you only want Shaylan to leave you alone." Rhem drew his sword and approached the boy.

The wizard stepped back and gave the floor to Rhem.

"What do you want of me?" cried Dalwan in desperation, tears flowing down his cheeks and sobs choking his words.

"Defend yourself," said Rhem with a menacing chill in his voice.

"You want a fight...you want a real fight?... Alright, let's fight!" Turning to vent his anger first against Shaylan, something like a rope of lightning shot out from his hands and wrapped the wizard in a cocoon of light. He turned back to face Rhem a moment too late. Rhem sidestepped him, and the flat side of his sword hit full force in Dalwan's stomach, sending him doubled up onto the floor back through the door into the shop.

He rolled over, still doubled up, and a red ball of flame flew toward Rhem, followed almost immediately by a blue one. The first was deflected, and the second absorbed by the now glowing sword.

Rhem's face wore a broad, wicked grin as he advanced on the crumpled boy, moving through the door like smoke in the wind. He swung his sword toward the boy, stopping only a breath away from his head. He lowered the sword slowly to the ground next to the boy's head and burned the word "TRAIN" into the stone with its tip.

It was then that Dalwan looked back into the stable and saw the glowing ball of lightning rope suspended in the air where he had attacked Shaylan. Panic filled him as he half stumbled, half ran to the place where it hung. Quickly, he sent the light back into the earth. It unwound like a thread from a spool, leaving nothing but open air behind.

Rhem joined him and both of them stood bewildered, staring at the spot where the wizard had been. "But lightning rope only binds, it doesn't destroy...it can hurt but not burn...what happened?"

"Up here, boy," said the wizard with a laugh. "I'm in the loft."

"But how..?"

"Your thoughts betrayed you...So I wasn't there...only my image."

As the wizard climbed down, Dalwan shuffled over to the pile of hay and fell into it, exhausted and sick. His head felt light, and every muscle in his body ached and tingled. He was sure his ribs were broken.

Rhem stood gape-jawed, eyes fixed on Shaylan as he descended the ladder. "I never saw you do it...I missed it totally."

"And you called ME 'Old man'," he said with a dignified chuckle. "I noticed that your sword behaved very properly. Do you like it as well as you liked your old one?"

Rhem still held his sword and walked over to the wizard and handed it to him. "Look at it. Not a scratch."

Shaylan examined it with some interest and a great deal of satisfaction. He mumbled to himself as he carefully searched its finish.

"It appears that you and the metalsmith have created a masterpiece. It not only accepted the power you gave it but continues to grow in power...almost like it's alive." Rhem took it back and began to weave patterns in the air with it. There was still a faint blue glow to the tip of the sword.

"You seem to have mastered it quite well, not even a hint of hesitation or resistance in your swing," said Shaylan with praise in his voice.

"It glides through the air as if riding on sails. It follows my thoughts and moves as if pulling my arm. The more I work with it, the easier it moves."

Dalwan was lying quite still in his agony and was annoyed at being ignored. He coughed to get attention, only to realize that this hurt his stomach and ribs much more than the lack of attention hurt his feelings. He groaned, quite for real.

"Oh mercy!" whispered Shaylan, displaying a placating frown as he turned and, pulling Rhem along by the arm, went and knelt at Dalwan's side. "How do you feel, boy?"

"Like I've been beaten up by adult bullies!" pouted Dalwan, trying to embarrass and shame his tormentors.

Shaylan stood up taking his hand, and pulled Dalwan up with one smooth maneuver. Dalwan stood slightly doubled over for a moment, slowly straightening up to full height. "We must all be on our way now. Our little game here will most certainly have attracted a great deal of attention from any sensors in the vicinity...or, for that matter, anywhere in the land."

"I can't move...I'm sick...I'm broken...I'm not even sure I'll live," answered Dalwan in protest, and obviously suffering from a full dose of humiliation.

Rhem stepped up to him and slapped him solidly on the back, "Boy, if you didn't like our little lesson, which we conducted with great restraint and concern for your safety, then you'd hate the real thing if it found you. You can be sure that the eye of your dreams is wide open and searching for you even as we waste time here talking."

"Rhem, the 'eye' doesn't scare me half as much as you two do," said Dalwan as he began inching toward the door, holding his stomach.

When they reentered the house, Reela had already prepared traveling clothes and was standing at the table packing food for them. Her eyes were puffy and red, her cheeks wet with smeared tears. Kindron appeared in the kitchen doorway carrying a traveling pack...it was his own personal bag.

"Son, your mother and I knew that your coming home couldn't last..." Kindron was interrupted by Reela's renewed sobbing as she stopped preparing their food and leaned with head bowed and fists doubled up tight, knuckles down on the table. Tears dropped onto the table from her cheeks.

Dalwan walked over to her as she recovered, wiped her eyes with the back of her hands, and again began cutting slices of a roast. He put his arms around her waist and gave her a hug from the back, putting his head on her shoulder. She stopped, reached up, and ruffled the hair on the top of his shaggy head. He let go, and she continued the food preparation without turning around or even looking at him.

Kindron continued, "...we knew that your gifts would make it difficult for you to stay with us now. But we know you'll be OK with Shaylan and Rhem."

Dalwan looked back and forth between Rhem and Shaylan, who both looked at the ground as their glances met. "Yeah, I know! They just demonstrated the caretaking skills."

Kindron walked over to Dalwan and handed the pack to him. "I want you to have my pack...it's got some useful things in it...just trinkets to make your life better and to help you remember us by..." he stood for a moment at a loss for words, "...we're sorry you have to leave... we're gonna miss you something awful...but Dalwan, your power is a very rare gift and you could never have been a simple stonemolder or woodweaver...learn to use your gifts well and one day they'll bring you home safely."

Reela turned around and gave Dalwan a long, tearful hug, only whispering, "I love you, son," nothing else.

They wasted no time getting on their way, leaving as soon as Dalwan had finished packing his belongings, which consisted mostly of extra clothes.

****

The men made their way to a small inn near the crossroads at Aldridge Pass, halfway between Alston, Dalwan's home, and Burkeston, Shaylan's home town. Rhem frequented the place because the little tavern there was an excellent listening post for news from the rest of Pretoria and even, on occasion, the outlands. Already, there were stories of foreign sensors looking for a gifted man who shrouds himself in mystery, choosing to move about in secrecy rather than become known. Many with the sensing gift claimed to have sensed his power even recently, "Very distinctive!" they would say. There was much speculation about the reasons for his secrecy.

The next day, they made their way to Burkeston, and from there up the trail to Shaylan's cottage, which sat in the rocky foothills near the caves that overlooked the small town. Rhem and Shaylan had a friend in Burkston, a talented metalsmith by trade and magic. They arranged for Dalwan to apprentice with him as a forger, with the understanding that the boy not practice any magic. The man agreed to take Dalwan on for room and board.

It was Beginning Rising when Dalwan started working for the metalsmith. Rhem commissioned the Metalsmith to make a sword for Dalwan, giving him a special pattern, weight, and balance point for it. Dalwan would go off for about five days at a time, each phase with Shaylan and Rhem to train, especially with his new sword. Then several times each phase he would go off into the wilderness alone and practice what he had learned, obeying Shaylan's instructions: "You must go far enough away from towns and villages that no one could find you quickly, and never practice either too long in one place or more than one time in a row at any one location...go in different directions every time you go out to practice and avoid setting a pattern to your practice time or locations."

This message was strengthened when word came to Shaylan that, within two days of the incident in the barn, men from Castle Crest and Castle Rock had been to Alston at different times. Both had investigated the incident involving the power they had sensed. Because there were no credible sensors in the town from which to gain more information, both groups continued on, looking in nearby villages and even hiked up into the foothills nearby. They had sensed Dalwan's power from the distance of a two-day walk. They left word in each area they visited that they would gladly pay a handsome reward to anyone who would identify the power user they sought.

CHAPTER 4

Dalwan's need for secrecy in his practice of magic took him further and further from Berkeston. Oftentimes, he had to travel for an entire day or more before he would venture to use any magic. In this way, he could avoid being identified with the power he used. He would then quickly pack up and leave before the inevitable seekers would show up. His usual practices consisted of one or more of his magics, which he carefully arranged and designed for maximum exercise of his abilities in a short amount of time. On occasion, when his arts were performed using especially strong magic, he would go some distance away and wait a respectable time. He would then return to observe those who would come in search of the power user. In this way he learned to recognize a few of the people who sought the powermaster so he could avoid them in other settings.

On one such practice excursion, Dalwan's journey took him into the Falcon Mountains east of Middleford Crossing. The lower slopes of the mountain range were grassy, windswept hills on which few trees grew except where there was shelter from the constant blowing of the wind. As Dalwan wandered away from the road that skirted to the south of the range, he made his own trail heading for higher ground. He began his climb into the hills in the evening, heading for some distant rugged crags at the top of the first ridge of mountains. He maintained a strong pace past sunset and stopped only when he was no longer able to pick out a forward path in the dark. He ended up spending the night in a small grove of sheltered oaks growing in a ravine.

The next morning, he rose early and realized that he was already very close to the destination he had set the previous afternoon. He set out almost immediately, eating as he walked. He was anxious to begin his practice and get done with this one, in his now very long series of secret exercises. As he walked along, he felt anger as he thought about all the lonesome excursions... the mandatory silence forced upon him regarding his marvelous powers... about those who hunted him for his power, like thieves for treasure, people with no cause but their own greed. Someday, he knew that he would be free of the need to conceal his power and would no longer find it necessary to live like a fugitive. This familiar line of thought never brought him any peace, so he finally dismissed it and gave attention to his present need, a place to exercise his magic.

By this time, he had reached the base of the crags. They stood like giant sentinels rising high above the piles of rocky debris deposited at their feet by the weathering of countless harsh seasons. He decided to climb over the ridge and practice in whatever valley or canyon existed on the other side. He quickly picked a path for his final ascent. It led up the dry mountainside through a small pass between two high bare rock crags. The higher he went, the more bare it became. Finally, it became so steep that he was forced to climb on all fours.

As he reached the summit, he discovered that the other side was not nearly as steep nor was it barren. Directly in front of him was a tributary gully, a wide, loose-rock dry ravine which started in the gap at the top of the pass. From his position in the pass, he could see a gentle slope which stretched straight ahead, cradling the creek bed that eventually formed the canyon in the valley below. The terrain surrounding the rocky ravine was covered with a sheet of knee-high green grass. It spread out like a welcome mat, which separated the mound of inhospitable rock fragments he was standing on from the forest which filled the canyon below. The trees closest to the leading edge of the wooded valley were short and scraggly. However, the forest grew thicker and the trees taller the further it stretched down the mountain toward a wide valley. At the bottom, it formed a broad, flat, thickly forested canyon floor, large enough to accommodate a small village. A foggy haze hung in the tops of the trees, giving them a ghostly appearance.

Feeling that the small flat area would be the perfect place to practice, Dalwan began to move down the mountain at a jog. As he neared the edge of the forest through the still very wet grass, he was brought to an abrupt halt by a roar the likes of which he had never heard. It was like a combination of the largest lion and the hungriest troll magnified by the echo of a cavern. He heard it again almost immediately, this time accompanied by the cracking of large timbers. Strong magic now filled the air.

Dalwan took off at a run toward the source of the sound. As he approached the leading edge of the heavily wooded area, he realized that what he had at first taken to be swirls of fog were actually columns of steam rising from charred wet grass in a series of locations. Each successive occurrence followed a straight line pathway through the meadow leading toward the trees. Again, he began to jog. Just as he entered the trees, he heard a great crashing and cracking of even larger timbers as if entire trees had been snapped off and sent plunging through the forest. He stood motionless for a moment. Hearing nothing, not even a bird, he again began to move through the trees toward the last location of the sound and magic. He passed several large trunked trees with wisps of smoke twisting upwards from glowing embers on their sides. He followed a path of flattened grass and smashed bushes which looked as if they had been rolled over by a giant boulder. This newly formed pathway led down the gentle slope in the direction of the broader flat area which had been his intended destination for practice.

There was a sustained period of silence that lasted the entire length of time it took him to travel from the leading edge of the forest to the place where the canyon began to widen dramatically and flatten out. As he reached level ground, he could again hear noises, muffled at first, but clearer as he drew closer to their origin.

A distinctly human voice called out. The words were unclear to Dalwan, but their challenging tone was answered almost immediately by a roaring retort that sounded like, "NEVER!"

He could sense fire magic and the deceptive magic of a shadowmaster as he moved closer to the commotion.

He came to a stop in a lightly forested area about a bow shot away from what appeared to be some sort of clearing. Dalwan positioned himself behind a fallen log from which he could see a rather tall, thin man clad in dark green pants and a shirt with a dark brown cape draped over his shoulders, hanging down his back. He was standing amid the smoldering ruins of what had recently been a pristine forest floor and facing away from Dalwan's position at an angle toward his left. His clothes either smoked or steamed, his cape was torn, and one of his boots was ripped from the top to the sole and lay open around his leg.

The man held a staff high in his hand and shouted, "You cannot defeat me, dragon. Save yourself more pain and grant me my request."

Dalwan shifted to peer through the trees in the direction in which the man had spoken. He was still unable to see who or what the man spoke to. Suddenly, out of a huge pile of newly fallen debris at the far end of what was now a clearing, a giant dragon appeared, shaking his head and trying his wings as if checking for damage. He reared up to about four times the height of the man. Smoke came in plumes from his nostrils until he coughed, sending a giant cloud of smoke out toward the man. The cloud obscured his view of him for a moment.

"You will serve me, dragon and do my bidding or perish!" shouted the man, sounding even more arrogant than the last time.

A flaming voice answered, "Never, you human refuse!" as he limped forward several steps and took to the air directly toward the man. The dragon flew upward to tree-top height as he traversed the distance between them in only a few flaps of his mighty wings. Lightning flashed from the man's staff, striking the dragon's right wing and appearing to burn through it. By this time, the dragon was almost directly over the head of the man and was now falling rapidly toward him. A stream of burning fluid fell from the dragon's gaping jaws onto the man who held up his staff and split the river of fire, sending it raining onto the ground around him, hissing and smoldering. His vision had been impaired just long enough for the dragon to drop directly on him. As the dragon landed, there was a brilliant flash of light accompanied by an explosion... then total silence.

Dalwan watched for a short time as smoke rose from the battle site into the air, forming a very slowly drifting cloud just under the tree top level. The dragon lay with his head turned away from Dalwan, revealing only his monstrous profile. There was no movement, no sound anywhere, not even a breeze. Finally, Dalwan moved up to take a closer look. He skirted the area and walked to within a stone's throw of the dragon. After standing very still, being paralyzed with indecision, he sat down on the trunk of a freshly fallen medium-sized tree. He no sooner sat down than the dragon stirred. His eyes came open but did not appear to focus on anything specific. Again, he stirred; this time, his head rose unsteadily, drifting uncontrolled back and forth on his thick neck. He began to lift himself off the pile of smoldering debris, but did not come to full height. He favored his left leg, which had a long, wide-open gash that revealed exposed muscles and tendons, but did not bleed very much. He moved off the debris, revealing the remains of the man, now burned and smashed beyond recognition. But he did not accomplish more than to turn around, stagger sideways toward Dalwan, then fall with a heavy thud that Dalwan felt in the ground under his feet. As he landed, he let out a mournful groan with tones that began as high as the howling of the wind through the trees during a storm and ended as low as the rumble of the ground in an earthquake. Again, everything was quiet. The dragon lay so still that only his shallow breathing betrayed the life that still clung to his badly damaged body.

Dalwan moved slowly toward the dragon, walking toward its right side. He could see burns on the wing that was extended across the forest rubble in his direction. As he approached, the only eye he could see opened groggily and tried to focus, much the same way one does when too much ale has been consumed. The giant head lifted and swung so that it faced Dalwan squarely and stared motionless for a brief moment.

Then, in a deep voice...almost a growl, the dragon called to him, "Kill me, man-child," adding sarcastically, "You can hang my head in one of your little trophy rooms." Smoke curled out of the edges of the gaping, sharp-toothed mouth. Dalwan thought he heard a faint laugh.

This was a truly awkward and certainly much worse introduction to the grand beast than Dalwan would have wished. He hesitated a moment in his reply.

"Get it over with!" rumbled the dragon in a louder, more demanding tone than before. "Or are you afraid of a half-dead anderon?" The dragon lunged slightly toward him in an obvious attempt to scare Dalwan. He only actually moved a small distance.

"Careful or you'll hurt yourself even more!" scolded Dalwan.

"What is this?" said the dragon, mocking him, "a human with compassion for the dying anderon?" The dragon tried to stand and face Dalwan, but just collapsed again, falling with a groan. It was then that Dalwan got a good look at the area of torn flesh on the dragon's stomach. It was about as large an area as Dalwan was tall and about as wide, having burned scale and flesh surrounding it.

After the convulsion of pain subsided, the eyes came open again, but he did not raise his head. "I suppose you have come to save me," this time, Dalwan was sure of the laugh. "Is that it, boy, have you come to save me and perchance make a pet of the 'dragon'?"

"For one so old and so wise, you sure sound stupid to me." Dalwan had closed the distance between them and was now only about four paces from the giant head, where he stood looking directly into his eyes. "If you want me to leave, just say so. I might be able to help you, though...that is...if you want me to stay."

The dragon lay silently, studying this new intruder with some freshly kindled interest, as much as his pain would permit. When he finally spoke, it was quietly like a distinct rumbling, deep and enchanted, "In the generations I have lived, I've never heard of such a thing as I now perceive you to be doing... a human with compassion for an anderon..." A cough caused him to wince in pain and momentarily stop speaking. "I have made many arrangements with men in the past, most out of my need to protect those I watched over. Those encounters tell me not to trust you, manchild."

Dalwan's shoulders dropped, and his face went sad. The dragon studied Dalwan intently for another moment.

"Maybe you are too young to have developed the arrogance so characteristic of your race." Suddenly, a surge of pain rippled through the massive body, putting him in a spasmatic seizure. He let out a mournful cry that brought tears to Dalwan's eyes.

The dragon lay very still with his eyes closed in a moment of confusion brought on by the intensity of the pain. As his mind cleared, he remembered back to his own youth when he had saved a man, a woman, and a child from a pack of carnivorous creatures who thought they had found dinner. After dispersing the rest of the creatures that survived his attack, the man returned the favor by shooting at him with arrows, a gesture that hurt his feelings much more than they could hurt his sturdy scaly body. He again felt the hurt in his heart as the humans rejected his help. He knew now that their legends had blinded them to his intentions, but at that time, he only felt the pain...with a mighty roar, he had left them shaken but none the worse for the experience. Pain again shot through his body like liquid fire, reminding him that his time was short unless something truly amazing happened.

Fighting to regain his open-eyed consciousness, he raised his head... he decided that he would end his life with a great experiment... trust a child of the very creatures that had now almost taken his life from him, "What would you do for me manchild, and what would you ask in return?"

"I'll do whatever I can...whatever you want me to do...I know a lot of magic. If you can tell me what you need or how to help, I'll bet I can surprise you!" He lowered his head for a moment to think and then added, "In return, maybe you'll make me your friend... and maybe you can tell your new friend some stories from your past."

"Is this the reason you have come into my forest?"

"No!" said Dalwan defensively, "I didn't even know there were dragons in this part of the world. How could I know that this was your forest?" Dalwan stood nursing an injured sense of dignity.

He recovered and continued, "Actually, the earthpower is growing and everyone who has magic is getting stronger... You have magic, you must already know that."

"I am aware of this", he said, looking over his shoulder toward the remains of the wizard he fought.

"Well, I have a lot of magic... so much that people search for me and want to catch me or buy my services, so I'll fight and kill for them or some other stupid things that I don't want to be part of. So, I have to practice and learn to use my arts in places where I won't get caught by the sensors that keep looking for me. I have to move around a lot when I use magic... and can't practice too long in one place, or in the same place too soon afterward."

The dragon's eyes widened, "Are you a powermaster, young one?" he asked in a low, unnerving tone.

Dalwan sensed danger in the dragon's voice. He paused to think, then answered carefully, "I don't know. I just want to be left alone by those who want to use me... who just want my power but couldn't care less about what I want... like that wizard you smashed up today."

"Well, young one," said the dragon with a choking chuckle, "I can see that you have been instructed well and are properly cautious. My time is too short to waste any more of it talking. Can you clear a path across this mess toward that large tree over there?" said the dragon, motioning with a directional nod of his head.

"If I clear the way, can you crawl?"

"If you clear the way, I will try."

Dalwan stepped in front of the dragon and raised his hands out to his sides and just above head level. Bright blue flame shot from him, incinerating the brush and debris, burning a path toward the destination on the other side of the opening. Many small trees and several larger trees had been broken off at various levels during the earlier battle. He moved along, clearing sections as long as his flame-throwing would permit. He cleared a space about seven strides wide and twenty long, wide enough for the dragon to move comfortably through. As he went, he left the stumps and larger tree trunks intact, turning to ash everything else that would burn. He used the green flame curtains to knock out the remaining flames at the edge of the path he was making. There were about six such sections needed to cover the entire distance. Over and over, his flame cut through everything in its path. His power seemed to grow in each successive area, taking a shorter and shorter time to disintegrate debris in the path, even some sections of log that obstructed the way. By the time he reached the other side, he was even trying moderate-sized trees with amazing results. The dragon watched for only a brief time before drifting into unconsciousness.

After he had burned everything that was practical to burn, he went back to the other side to check on the dragon. Finding him asleep, he went to the closest tree stump. He had heard stories of wood weavers removing tree stumps by causing the roots to pull them out of the ground.

Because this was to be a new experience for him, he talked himself through the magic by actually speaking out loud to the stump as he placed his hands on its fragmented and splintered top. He spoke in a barely audible tone. As he did so, the stump shuddered. He continued to adjust his magic over and over, causing a variety of effects from the splitting of the trunk to the polishing of jagged fragments. His fascination kept him hard at his concentration until finally, he saw the ground erupt at the base of the stump and a large root cause the stump to heave out of the dirt. It rose about knee high out of the ground before coming to a quivering stop. Dalwan went to the giant surface root which had been first to break out of the soil and put his hands on it, speaking softly again as if to a friend. The root convulsed at his touch and began to pull the stump toward the side of the clearing. When the straining of the root against the other roots began to tear the stump apart, Dalwan stopped and went around to the other side of it and took out his sword. He quickly severed the roots that restricted the stump and held it to the earth. He put away the sword and went back to the other side. He again grasped the large root and began to make it pull the stump toward the sideline. The stump moved along like a ship in a very stormy sea as it made its way to the edge. Its progress was slow but sure. The root would break out of the dark, moist dirt just ahead of the tree and wrap around the stump, rolling it up in a tight coil. Finally, the progressively smaller root broke off, leaving the stump less than a stride from the border of the path. He went to a nearby tree and began to try raising a root near the mobile stump with which to pull it the short distance remaining. Finally, after several roots broke out too far away to help, he raised one close enough to wrap around it and pull it clear.

Dalwan was elated with his newly developed plan. He returned the few paces to check the dragon. He was sleeping fitfully, with rippling spasms that caused his face to distort with pain. Dalwan knew that he had to hurry... soon the magnificent beast might be unable to move to his shelter. He went directly back to work, moving through the intended clearing with a vigorous intensity. His power did not fail nor fade, but instead grew as his concentration and skill improved his technique.

Dalwan was about halfway through the field when the dragon opened his eyes to see what the man-child had accomplished. Something near amazement filled his now much weaker and sickened frame. "If this boy was actually telling the truth about moving around to avoid those who searched for him," thought the dragon, "this exercise would surely attract a great deal of attention, especially in light of the battle fought earlier with the arrogant one!"

Mistrust again filled the dragon's mind, "Does this boy... boy was hardly an appropriate term for this human... does this young man actually wish to somehow persuade an anderon to assist him in attacking this castle containing the sword everyone seems to want. Does he want to steal it like the fool earlier in the day had intended?"

The dragon began to try sensing anew Dalwan's spirit; he knew he had found nothing false before, but possibly pain had blinded his abilities to sense. He had only just begun to try sensing for Dalwan's intentions when suddenly he became aware of another presence, one who was probing... searching... There was unmistakable malice present... out there in the trees... close by. The dragon tried to rise and search the nearby woods. Pain racked him into convulsions as he tried to move his stiffening body.

Somewhere nearby, cold eyes watched. "For months I have tracked you... roaming the hills... sensing your power at work," came a dark whisper from behind a decaying fallen tree. "Every time I would get close, only to have the power vanish... like quicksilver in gravel... leaving me empty-handed again. But not this time, boy...not this time!" There was a faint raspy laugh, "You won't escape me now," he said with malicious glee. He arose from his hiding place, and as he turned, the last thing he saw was the flash of a gilded sword held by a man in black.

Suddenly, the presence was gone... not a trace left. The dragon tried again and again to sense it, but nothing. Could he have been mistaken? Could a greater sensing power, like those of generations ago, have entered the woods disembodied? Was the Earth's power already that great? A jolt of pain distracted him, fogging his thinking. Whatever the case, it did lend credence to the young man's story. More amazing, he could detect nothing deceptive or false about this friendly intruder, turned rescuer. He drifted back into unconsciousness.

Dalwan worked faster and faster as his ability to manipulate his woodweaving magic increased in orders of magnitude. At the very end of the field, even larger tree trunks seemed to move by themselves toward the sidelines as roots from nearby trees wrapped around them like giant snakes dragging their prey into their sanctuary.

With the last obstacle out of the way, Dalwan rushed back to the dragon. "Wake up!" shouted Dalwan directly into his ear. He struggled awake and focused with difficulty on the human form in front of him. "What did you call yourself a while ago?"

"I am an anderon... like you are a man. It is not my name, only my kind," replied the dragon in a dry raspy voice, adding, "...few have ever known my name."

"Then I'm going to call you anderon from now on... unless you don't want me to." He waited for a response by got none. "My name is Dalwan, but you can call me whatever you want," he said with very little emotion. "Are you ready to move?"

"NO!" he answered in a tone that vaguely suggested an attempt at humor...(Dalwan promptly dismissed that possibility)... "I will try, though." The anderon had grown much weaker. He pulled himself along only with great effort, barely able to keep his wound out of the charred and broken up dirt. The pain sickened him, and finally he dropped with a terrible thud and a frail moan, after moving only a distance less than half his length.

Dalwan tried to awaken the anderon again, but he did not even stir. He pulled out his sword and began to collect straight branches and small tree trunks from the remaining forest clutter, cutting off their limbs as he went. He assembled them side by side like a raft. Then, laying his hands on them one by one, he began to cause them to weave together. This was the first time he had worked magic on fresh lumber...that is, wood that hadn't been dried or otherwise cured. It moved with amazing speed, each successive pair of beams weaving themselves into a single piece as if they were actually growing together. After joining them all together, he curved the front end up like a sled. He then made two more layers of small trees and limbs, each going in opposite directions for strength. He joined each beam to the next and each individual layer to the others. It was now dusk.

Dalwan went over and sat down exhausted next to the anderon. He had physically and mentally pushed himself much further than he had ever dreamed possible. His head was pounding, his eyes ached, and burned. He knew that some sensor may well have been able to get to him by now if he had been close enough when Dalwan began his work. But he didn't care... he was too tired to care... besides that, this was the most fulfilling thing he had ever done, magic or not... even in his discomfort and weariness, he felt a sense of exhilaration. This was his finest hour.

His feelings of grandeur were abruptly interrupted by a clear sense that the anderon was slipping away... the ancient life was fading. Dalwan panicked for a moment, trying to think with a clear mind... he knew that some people, very few indeed, could heal certain illnesses and injuries if they understood the nature of the damage. He also knew that death could be rapid and painful for the patient if the art was practiced in error or a misdiagnosis was made.

Dalwan tried to arouse the unconscious beast, "Anderon... anderon... you've gotta wake up... you've gotta get on the sled." He was tugging and pushing on the giant head with little effect. "Don't you dare die, not now... do you hear me! You can't die!" shouted Dalwan in desperation. Tears now flowed down his face freely, though he had sworn to himself that he wasn't going to cry anymore after the battle he had fought with Shaylan and Rhem in the shed. But here he was again, crying... at least no one can see me,' he thought with some small comfort to his pride. Not able to think of any other solution, he shouted, "Wake up! You're gonna die if you stay here like this!" He quickly made his way to the wounded leg, which he then kicked as hard as he could. Suddenly, there was a twitch of movement in the massive head... his brow wrinkled as if trying to stretch tightly closed eyes open. Failing that, it was weakly joined by his monstrous mouth, which yawned open, adding to the effort... then, just as suddenly, all was still again.

"Cursed tears!" he mumbled as he sat down on the ground next to the mangled leg. "What if I can give him some energy... power or something..." Dalwan jumped up and climbed onto the back of his scaly neck and put his hand on top of the motionless head. He did not even know if such a thing was possible... no one ever said it wasn't possible... but then again, no one ever said it was... he had to try something.

He had no idea how to even attempt this... or what sort of magic should be involved. He tried to just give him energy, to send flowing power which would awaken his sleeping patient. He had no idea how to start, so he used his imagination to picture the power passing from him to the anderon. Nothing! After trying several other mental approaches to envisioning power or life force moving from him into his anderon acquaintance with no discernible results, he decided to see if he could sense something from the beast himself that would help find a way to save his life.

He began sensing. His power took him deeper and deeper into the anderon presence, more and more sensitive... probing... searching. As he did, his thoughts became confused as if caught in a fast-moving dream. Visions of other anderon together... talking in growls and hisses... he couldn't understand them... a little anderon jumped and frolicked nearby, he sensed admiration and love... a mammoth cavern with smaller caves in its walls, each having ledges like porches at their entrance. Dalwan was flooded with a feeling of warmth; this was home. The scene shifted to a clearing in a wooded area where a man in a purple robe stood. The view was from up in the air as if in a tree. This man was somehow disgusting and irritating. The man's voice sounded squeaky. Dalwan could sense deception and greed coming from the man. Again, the scene shifted. The view was from high in the air, looking down at a man in a broken-down forest. Lightening shot from the man... pain... danger. Closer and closer came the vision of the man... flame filled with anger went toward the man from Dalwan's vantage point... anger... fear... despair... sorrow... darkness. Then he saw himself walking closer and closer... burned pathway behind him... curiosity... safety... pain... darkness.

Dalwan snapped out of the trance. He realized that he was seeing through the anderon's eyes. Amazement filled him. How could something so big and ugly be so sensitive? Dalwan felt a strange attraction and admiration for the beast. He snapped back to the situation at hand, knowing that nothing he tried had any effect. He was filled with a deep sense of sadness that this magnificent creature, hunted for his power just as Dalwan was, would now die with none able to help... but he would not die alone! Dalwan put his arms around the large, wrinkled, scaly neck. He felt a kinship with him... like the affinity one has for a friend... like the love of a brother. Suddenly, power began to flow through Dalwan into the anderon, feeling like the warmth you experience when you get into a bath of hot water. The anderon's eyes opened, and there was an instant increase in the power as it surged from him into the now aroused giant frame. He stirred as the power began to subside.

"You are amazing, manchild. In my many years, I have never heard of such a thing as that which you have just accomplished."

Dalwan ran to the sled and shouted, "You gotta get on the sled..."

"I know," said the anderon, "I saw it in your mind... the plan is good." He did not waste any more time talking but began pulling himself toward the makeshift sled. It was almost dark by the time the anderon was on the sled, ready to go. The sled was barely large enough to accommodate the massive body, but it kept the belly wound out of the dirt as he pushed the sled along awkwardly with his good leg while gripping the front edges with powerful talons.

Dalwan formed an arch of red fire between his hands, lighting the path for the anderon. The progress was very slow but steady. Finally, they reached the other side of the clearing. The anderon did not stop but kept moving along what appeared to be a path through the trees, off to the left at an angle from the clearing. Dalwan was amazed that he hadn't seen the path before. He quickly ran in front of the still-moving sled and again lit the way.

The path led through the trees a short distance to a giant mound of rock forming a small mountain among the trees. There was a large outcropping of solid rock which jutted up the mountainside, visible in the now unobstructed moonlight. At the base of the outcropping was a large cave entrance. The anderon pushed the sled up to the side of the entrance and slid sideways off of it. At the entrance, the stone was very smooth and level. Dalwan followed him in as he glided over floors polished by generations of wear. Once inside, Dalwan increased the magnitude of the flame he used for lighting so as to see as much of the cave as possible... he recognized it instantly... it was the same cavern he had seen through the anderon's memory. He had only paused for a moment, but that was long enough for the anderon to have slipped into the cave near the entrance and out of sight.

"Hey, where are you?'

"I'm in here, Dalwan," came an amused answer coupled with a gurgly low rumble of a laugh.

Dalwan quickly located the right chamber and found him already curled up on a bed of matted grass, which covered the floor.

"Be careful with your fire in here... my bed is somewhat flammable as you can see," again the anderon uttered a low gurgling laugh that ended in a smoky cough.

Dalwan reduced his flame to a flicker and waited a moment for his eyes to readjust. "I'm sorry."

"Only your sense of humor is sorry..." he rumbled another deep chuckled, "Oh...it hurts to laugh..."

Dalwan couldn't believe that this beast could have a sense of humor, let alone laugh at a time like this. "You'd better take care of yourself or you'll do more damage."

"There is medicine in laughter, my serious young friend... but you're right, I must sleep to heal my wounds. If I survive, I will find you and repay you."

"I don't want you to repay me," answered Dalwan in a wounded tone.

"Then I am free of obligation?" said the anderon with unquestionable interest.

"Yes...eruh...no... I mean, yes. You don't owe me... I was just hoping..."

"Good! Then get out of my cave!" said the anderon demandingly, then abruptly erupted into a spastic combination of laughter and groaning.

Dalwan felt so many different feelings that he didn't know if he was coming or going. He just stood there with his mouth hanging open, feeling quite outclassed.

"Dalwan, if you learn nothing more from this dying anderon, learn to laugh. Life's worst moments can become tolerable if you only learn to laugh a little."

"I'll try, I promise."

The anderon began to lick his wounds and chew at the burnt edges, cleaning debris out. After a few silent moments, he lay his head down again, looking directly at Dalwan. "You must go now so I can sleep."

"Maybe I can help. Maybe I can find a healer who can do amazing things with torn flesh. Let me at least try."

"Perhaps there is another human with your heart. But word of my existence would bring ruin to you and to me if this other person betrayed that confidence, even accidentally."

Knowing he was right, Dalwan went and took hold of the giant head and hugged the anderon as if saying goodbye to his best friend. His mind met the mind of the noble beast as healing power again flowed into the massive body. This time he could feel the pain and sickness the anderon was experiencing and the anderon felt Dalwan's sorrow. The pain and sickness was replaced with a strange growing strength a fierce determination to live. A vision appeared in Dalwan's mind, it was of a boy who grew and changed into a young man, feelings of warmth and friendship filled the vision. This vision was replaced again with determination so strong that Dalwan began to feel that he might explode.

The power stopped, but the vision remained. He could see the cavern entrance... then it just disappeared. Where it had been, there was only a large rock with a majestic tree growing out of it. The vision faded and was replaced with a powerful sense of peace.

Dalwan extended his hand, and a small blue flame lit his pathway back out of the cavern. As he reached the entrance, he saw a bright flash of light as if a fire wielder was throwing flame directly toward him. The flame exploded mid-air into small droplets of fire, which flew in every direction. He could hear angry words coming from someone who sounded far away, but whose voice sounded familiar. Against the vague light coming from the opening, he could see the silhouette of a man holding a sword.

Dalwan moved out through the entrance at the far side from where the man appeared to be striking something invisible in the air. Sparks flew with every swing. The magic of the man was the same as Rhem's... Dalwan could not sense any other magic present except Rhem's.

Once outside the entrance, he saw the shadow with the sword suddenly turn toward him as his sword became a pillar of flame raised in attack position.

"Rhem...don't...it's me, Dalwan."

Rhem's facial features showed surprise and then embarrassment. As he lowered his sword, its flame went out exposing the red-hot metallic glow in the shape of his sword.

"Rhem, what are you doing here?"

"I've been watching you all day. I followed you to the cave and was about to go in when the entrance vanished."

"What...?" Dalwan turned and raised a bright flame to see the entrance... it was gone, replaced by the rock and the tree he had seen in the last vision. "But I just walked through it without trouble..." He touched it and found it as hard as any other rock. "I guess he 'will' sleep undisturbed, won't he?" He looked back at Rhem, "I can't even sense the magic that forms this, can you? Must be old magic... maybe only dragons... or uh, should I say, anderons... have this type of art."

At this point Dalwan noticed that Rhem was only just barely controlling his rage. "Rhem, why'd you come here?"

"You need watching over, young man," he said in a clearly scolding tone.

"No one could've found me this quickly unless..."

Rhem cut in with a rebuking exclamation which got louder as he went, "Unless he was already in this area just waiting and hoping that you would practice nearby this time... just hoping that you would work your magic long enough for him to get a fix on you... and having found you, hoping that your dragon friend would die and make it easy for him to get you!"

"I'm sorry, Rhem!" he felt his cheeks flush and only barely fought back tears. "Did you get hurt or anything?"

"I had to clean my sword, that's all. But it could have been worse... much worse. Dalwan he was a Warminian trained sensor... he had all the magic traps and disguises and doubtless felt sure he could take you safely. He watched your encounter with the dragon..."

"Anderon... he's an anderon.."

"Whatever!" shouted Rhem in irritation. "Will you stick with the topic?! DALWAN, HE WASN'T AFRAID OF YOU!!"

"OK! OK! What do you want me to do... what would you have done? Just leave him there to die?"

Rhem stood silently for a moment. "Every sensor in the ten kingdoms surrounding Pretoria will have sensed some of what took place here today. This whole valley will be crawling with sensors by tomorrow... some will even be here tonight, you can be sure of that! This little trail you made with the sled will be like putting up a sign directing everybody to this place.

"You're right," said Dalwan, surprised that he hadn't thought of that."

Without warning, he turned his fire onto the sled with such intensity that both he and Rhem had to move back and shield themselves from the heat. "There, no one will know where the battle started or where it ended. I'm going to confuse it a little more," he said as he moved off back down the path to the sound of Rhem's loud scolding. He had some roots move a decaying log over the path, caused another small tree to bend over and totally obstruct the path, and placing his hand on several limbs caused them to drop branches and leaves directly on the path.

Rhem went along with him, trying to hurry him up. Finally, he grabbed him by the arm and spun him around, "We can't stay here any longer. Sense the air...what do you feel..."

"A sensor... a strong one... still some distance away..."

"But close enough to find us if we dally around any longer!" Rhem turned and began to head up the trail toward the anderon's cave, "I'm leaving. You can come or stay as you wish."

"OK! I'm comin'"

"No more magic, no fire, no nothing!" shouted Rhem back over his shoulder.

"Alright. But wait up. I can't see in the dark as well as you can." Dalwan stumbled through the dozen or so steps that separated him from Rhem, knowing that Rhem would not let him fall too far behind, but also knowing that this swordsman turned mentor would use every opportunity he could to train Dalwan.

CHAPTER 5

Due to the attack on Castle Crest, it came as no surprise to Shaylan, or Rhem, when three men on horseback arrived from Lord Falock on the eighth day of End Harvest. The men said that they were, "...sent to recruit the services of Shaylan the Wise and Sorhem Amberlain for Pretoria at Castle Crest at the earliest possible opportunity, without concern for convenience..."

"Why don't they just say, ' Shaylan and Rhem, we need your help without delay, thank you!'" muttered Rhem aside to Shaylan after the men had spoken.

"It's a cultural thing, Rhem. Leave them alone," rebuffed Shaylan, barely able to keep his composure and avoid embarrassing the emissaries.

"Come in, sirs, refresh yourselves a bit, and we shall be ready to return with you today. We've been expecting you," said Shaylan as he turned, pushing Rhem politely ahead of him and into the cabin.

"Come in, sirs..." mocked Rhem humorously. "I'd like to tell them what I really think... that this whole affair is out of hand and that we should have been called a long time ago. We've been ready for a phase...just waitin' for them to get around to calling us."

"My, aren't we rude today?!...will you behave yourself!?"

"You'd get bored!"

"Bore me then...at least while we're at the castle."

"I hope their way of talking isn't contagious."

Shaylan stopped and looked back over his shoulder with a cocked eyebrow, chastisement...Rhem returned a "What'd I do?" shrug as both men set about putting the little house in order.

It took them very little time to get their belongings together because they had anticipated the men's arrival for a phase and had remained prepared.

It was midday two days later when they arrived at Castle Crest. Once inside the walls, they were joined by additional escorts so that they now had two in front and four behind them as they walked toward the castle proper.

Everything within the fortress had changed since the failed attempt at the sword. All the merchants had been relocated away from the fortress wall to

make room for the soldiers that camped there. The inner city was now also a
fully occupied military camp. Shops and inns had been turned into
barracks. Armor and supplies were strategically placed throughout the
compound. Piles of wood and barrels of water were piled along walls in case of
a long siege.

As they approached the castle proper inside the fortress walls, they
observed major excavation and construction in progress. Battlements of stone
and iron were being constructed completely surrounding the castle compound
buildings, which were set on a raised, terraced hill. The triple towers of the
castle, evenly spaced at the corners of the hexagonal exterior of the castle itself,
were the highest points in the castle compound. They now served as lookout
towers where soldiers rotated duty throughout the day and night.

As Rhem and Shaylan surveyed the work, they saw many of the greatest
and most talented artisans in Pretoria at work on various projects.

"Looks to me," said Rhem, quietly aside to Shaylan, "that fully half the
resources of the land are here, employed to assist in protecting an object they
can't even use."

"Don't start with it, Rhem," said Shaylan in a rough whisper, trying to
hide the amusement he felt at Rhem's remark and the silly grin he concocted to
embellish it.

"But what if the sword has lost its power?" he continued in a whisper
while Shaylan tried to look as if he wasn't listening. "Then all this elaborate
protection will be just wasted time and money."

"Will you stop... someone's going to hear you..."

"But just stop and think, what if all the stories about the sword are just
fables... greatly exaggerated over the years... and all this is really unnecessary?"

By this time, they had arrived inside the castle compound, and Shaylan
was trying to ignore what Rhem was saying, hoping he would stop
talking. Shaylan sped up his pace to close the distance between them and the
leading escorts, leaving Rhem about a step behind.

Shaylan's reaction caused Rhem to speak a little louder, "Do you realize
that every man, woman, and child in Pretoria will feel the cost of this fancy
work... and all this work will make the castle an even more valuable prize for
some power-hungry king later... that is, after the sword is gone."

Shaylan was sure that their escorts had heard Rhem's remarks because they were giving him very inhospitable looks. Shaylan came to an abrupt halt, spinning around directly into Rhem's path. Rhem had to perform some fancy footwork to keep from running into him. Shaylan grabbed the front of Rhem's cloak as he sidestepped his roadblock and tugged him face-to-face. Speaking while appearing to straighten the cloak and brush it off as if it were soiled, he said softly, "If you don't be good, I'm going to find a way, even if I have to use magic, to make your tongue stick to the roof of your mouth." Both of their eyes screamed with laughter, but the expressions were stern. "I like you, Rhem... so much that I'll even go to one of your earthy taverns and join you in acting the fool if you act properly here... no embarrassing question... no rude remarks... no challenges... just like I said before we left, 'BORE ME'."

Rhem put his head down like a whipped child pouting, "OK, I'll be good... but you owe me again!!" he added with a glint of fiendish humor that Shaylan read instantly to mean, "I'm going to make you wish you didn't keep making these bargains."

The escorts were looking on with irritation at being held up. Shaylan turned and started walking again, "Thank you for waiting, we had some unfinished business to clear up before we meet the Lords... shall we continue?!"

Once in the entryway of the Castle, the escorts were relieved by four mail-clad, heavily armed soldiers and a man known by Shaylan to be a sensor, though not a very good one. They passed one checkpoint after another, all manned with diversely armed warriors, some from each of the three Pretorian castles. Shaylan sensed fear in some of them and near apathy in others.

Finally, they came to the War Room chamber door. The sensor turned and studied the two men a moment, then announced their presence to the door security leader. He entered the chambers and returned a few moments later with a summons for both men.

The three Lords were seated with their backs to a fireplace, all on the same side of a large, heavy table positioned in the room directly opposite the entry door. They watched motionlessly as Shaylan and Rhem were led in, then left standing in front of the table.

Lord Falock, Lord of Castle Crest, spoke first, "I'm glad you have both come. We need your expertise and advice. Do you offer what you have, or are your talents perhaps for sale?"

The question would have seemed insulting at other times, but Shaylan sensed that they were being tested. Knowing that Rhem would be quick to take offense, he took hold of his arm, stopping his advance as he whispered audibly, "This is only a test, my friend." Rhem halted his movement of protest and allowed himself to be pulled the single step back to where he had originally stood with Shaylan.

"My Lord Falock, now, as in times past, our services, arts, and wisdom, however small or great they may be, are yours for the asking, if such service is for the land of Pretoria and for our Lords."

"Does Shaylan speak for you as well, Sorhem Amberlain?"

"My sword has always been in service for our land," said Rhem, speaking boldly and with too much volume for a proper response. "I see no reason..." at that moment, he caught sight of Shaylan through the corner of his eye... he was licking his lips, calling attention to his tongue... Rhem stopped speaking abruptly.

Shaylan's eyebrow raised in question, "...you were saying?"

Rhem adjusted his attention back to the Lords and, speaking appeasingly, "...I see no reason to change my loyalty now or ever..." he finished with a quick glance at Shaylan and then back to the Lords. "I remain in your service and that of Pretoria."

"I hope you will forgive our manners in questioning your loyalty while seeking your assistance, and somehow find it in your soul to forgive this small insult. We needed to be sure of your intentions, although you two are considered among the most loyal protectors of our great land in the entirety of Pretoria. Your abilities and your allegiance to one another have become... shall I say, 'legendary'. By yourselves, you are each formidable. Together, you are an impressive and dangerous force to be reckoned with." Lord Falock paused, glancing toward the sensor who remained in the room. He stepped backward and crossed his arms over his chest, a preset sign indicating safety. "You have both demonstrated your commitment and have been proven now in our eyes. Please excuse our precautions."

"We sympathize with your needs and remain at your service," answered Shaylan.

Lord Welton of Castle Rock spoke next. "We have invested a great amount of time, resources, and manpower into protecting the sword Fallonrod. However, we still do not know the scope of its power. We know that the wall has been breached. We have been told that at least two men perished in spectacular fashion trying to steal the sword. We also have learned that one man suffered a terribly burned hand when he took hold of the cursed weapon, though his life was somehow spared. We want to discover the potential of the sword and then, if possible, how to use it. We want to know if what we are doing is worth the investment since the cost of protecting it will be felt by every man, woman, and child in Pretoria."

Rhem looked at Shaylan with the 'I told you so glance.'

"Don't start!" whispered Shaylan in a quick, rough whisper to the side, which he followed immediately by redirecting his attention back to the Lords, completely recomposed with the appropriately serious expression on his face.

"We certainly understand, Lord Falock. We were speaking of these very things as we entered the compound," said Rhem very seriously, ignoring another warning glance from Shaylan.

Lord Linx of Castle Greystone continued, "If we can know the power it possesses and dangers it presents to the wielder and his opponent, then we may better know how to proceed from this point."

"Are we to infer from the direction of your explanations," inquired Shaylan diplomatically, "that our task is to discover the breadth of the power and the possible uses of the sword Fallonrod?"

"And this additional task," said Lord Falock, "find a way to destroy the sword so that we could safely rid ourselves of it if that becomes necessary."

Realizing that this project would put Shaylan in great danger, Rhem stepped forward, "Lord Falock," he said in a tone which appeared to the Lords to be a protest, "This sword was made for warfare. It's not simply resistant to attack but may even draw power from such activity."

Lord Linx leaned forward in his heavily padded armchair and taunted, "Do you refuse this challenge?"

"Refuse!" shouted Rhem, moving toward the table while speaking with a generous degree of animation. "We have never refused to offer help if such help was ours to give." Shaylan quickly caught up with Rhem and put his hand on his rambunctious friend's shoulder, trying without effect to calm him down. Rhem took hold of Shaylan's forearm and, pulling his hand off his shoulder, jerked him around to his side while continuing to speak, "We have stood together, against outrageous odds on several occasions, willing to perish in defense of the alliance and the people of Pretoria." He now had his arm around Shaylan's shoulder and gestured toward Shaylan as he finished speaking. "If you asked it of us, we would fight an entire invading army ourselves."

Shaylan pulled himself respectfully free from Rhem and leaned over the table directly in front of Lord Falock and said in a quiet, conciliatory tone, "My Lords, we are at your command. We gladly accept your requirement upon our arts and whatever other abilities we may possess."

Shaylan straightened back up, turned, and looked at his red-faced friend. As Rhem looked into the wizard's wise eyes, he immediately recognized the look... Shaylan had a plan... he was confident... all the fuss was for nothing... OOPS!

"I sense some ambivalence in your opinion, Rhem," said Lord Welton, probing the verbal litter left behind by Rhem.

"My Lords," cut in Shaylan, "All this commotion from my companion and long-time friend was out of fear for my safety, not his own. He knows the possibilities presented by a sword of power as well as the dangers that exist for those who trespass or presume upon it imprudently. Rhem's concern is fueled by his personal knowledge of power swords. He wields one."

Rhem's head was down in embarrassment before his friend. He had failed this test. He intervened on Shaylan's behalf without even giving the wizard a chance to speak for himself, and now it appeared that this defense wasn't even necessary.

"He would be no friend at all if he failed to voice his concerns," responded Lord Welton, salvaging Rhem's dignity, "but perhaps a lesson in finesse would be of value to your friend Shaylan." This was followed by a round of laughter from all three Lords and an admonishing grin from Shaylan toward Rhem.

When the noise died back down, Lord Linx continued, "Rhem, we share your concerns; that is precisely why we sent for you two. There are none better in our fair land to handle this task! Indeed, to challenge any others with this task would most likely be a sentence of death upon them."

"I apologize, my Lords."

"Accepted," said Lord Falock, speaking for them all.

After a rest and a meal, the three Lords and their entourages escorted Shaylan and Rhem to the sword chamber, where they introduced them both to the guards and their superiors. Both men were given unconditional access to the chamber and free run of the castle, including the archives.

Lord Falock assigned one of the castle guards to be a guide until they were thoroughly familiar with the castle layout, or he was dismissed by them.

Both Shaylan and Rhem were anxious to enter the chamber and see the sword. The hole in the wall had been enlarged enough for the Lords to enter through... Lord Welton, being the largest in both girth and height, required the expanded entryway. The Lords entered first and were followed by Shaylan and Rhem. There was only one lit torch in the room, and it was held by Lord Linx. Therefore, they would all be able to see the glow in Fallonrod clearly. The room smelled musty as they entered. There was a hint of something burned in the air, like the smell inside a burned-out tree on a damp morning. They observed with interest the setting of the room: the large bookshelf stretching all the way across the wall opposite the entrance; the fireplace to the right with the two stuffed leather chairs pushed back into the corner as if to get them out of the way; the mantel over the fireplace containing several items including some books, vases, a small wooden box, and some elaborate candle holders; the free standing bookshelf positioned near the opening in the wall; and the table and chairs to the left of the opening; and finally, the sword, sticking out of the stone floor about four paces in front of the fire place and to the right of center.

They all gathered around the sword, with none of the group standing closer than about three paces. It was sticking almost straight up with the faint glow throwing a light green hue on the floor around the place where the blade entered the stone floor. Unwilling to touch it or even get close to it, they stood staring uncomfortably at it for only a brief time before Lord Linx turned and walked back to the old rooms' new entrance, saying, "Well, it's certain that you both have a difficult task ahead of you. I, for my part, do not envy you!"

The others joined him one by one, each crawling out through the hole, leaving Shaylan as the last to exit. As he stood there, alone for a brief moment, it took all his personal strength to fight off the urge to go back, just reach out and take hold of the sword. Rhem yelled back through the crawl hole in the wall, "I'll wait for you here in the hall." It was just enough of a distraction to jar Shaylan out of the seditious trance.

"Oh, the trouble we bring upon ourselves..." mumbled Shaylan as he regained his self-control and turned to leave the room, "...it's amazing that we haven't destroyed our entire race already... I guess there's still time enough for that, isn't there?"

"I can't hear a word you're saying, let alone understand you," shouted Rhem back into the room from the hallway.

"Here begins our greatest adventure, Rhem, old friend... and just possibly, our finest."

"And possibly out LAST!" mused Rhem glancing back at Shaylan as he exited the room.

The Lords gave Shaylan and Rhem free run of the castle, including the right to any assistance they wished and the audience of any person they deemed necessary to complete the investigation.

There were no immediate witnesses to the assault on the sword. Several men had ventured into Malmoria, hoping to discover more about the happenings within the sword chamber. One of them, a man called Aldercott, happened onto a group in conversation one night at a tavern, one of whom claimed to have been in the "Room of Terror," as he called it. The palm of his hand was badly marked with fresh sores and scars.

Aldercott reported to Shaylan that the man said their champion, Balore, had taken the sword in hand and been burned with fire from the inside out. Then another man likewise incinerated when he grabbed the sword, which had again become stuck in the stone. Lastly, driven by an irresistible urge, he himself had taken hold of it but got burned so badly by the handle that he released it instantly. He was certain that his quick release was the only reason he survived. Aldercott said the man went on to speculate that since Balore couldn't wield the sword, no one ever would.

While Shaylan interviewed everyone he could who had any knowledge regarding the sword, whether of legend or the recent attempted theft, Rhem headed for the castle archives, hoping to discover as much as he could about the sword, its bearer, and, if possible, its creators. The castle curator, historian, and librarian, a man named Paxly, separated out every book he could find that had anything to do with swords and set them aside in a special reading room for Rhem.

After days of reading, Rhem had discovered only fanciful stories of the sword's magical powers and feats that the sword bearer, Maylore, had accomplished. The older the story, the more odd the recorded feats. The later stories were full of battlefields covered with dead soldiers, and fire that devoured towns and turned stone to ash. But nothing about the character of the wielder or the identity of the sword's creators. The stories varied in content just enough to make most of them believable but not credible.

One evening, while looking through the official archives containing castle documents and agreements, Rhem chanced upon a very old set of parchments, folded and stuck in the back of a very old leather-bound journal. The pages were so old that they cracked when Rhem unfolded them. They contained a set of letters that had been transcribed into a single document detailing a controversy between members of Castle Crest and Castle Graystone. The argument, which actually was more of a debate, was carried back and forth via letters, and occurred about 40 years after Maylore, the original bearer of Fallonrod, had died. It made several references to the book "Epoch". The controversy seemed to revolve around what sort of person should be given power in a kingdom, focusing on what sort of character traits one should have to be a great leader. Judging from the content of the letters, Rhem surmised that they must have been written by the leading ladies of the respective castles.

Rhem inquired of Paxly about the book but had no luck. Paxly was confident that Rhem had been provided every book in the archives that contained significant references to the sword and or Maylore. He could give no hint as to what the mysterious volume might look like or how large it was, or even if it actually existed. The possibility of such a book was the only solid lead Rhem had gotten, other than the letters, so he spent many hours looking for it through every set of books and parchments in the castle. Finally, after two days of searching and countless inquiries, he gave up.

Rhem and Shaylan were invited to share the evening meal with the royal families, a banquet prepared with the sole purpose of breaking the tension in the castle household and especially among the Lord's closest attendants. There was continuous entertainment and more food than twice the number of attendants could consume. Shaylan sat between Lord Falock's wife Annell and Rhem. While Shaylan and Annell spent time in what Shaylan would call "splendid conversation", Rhem sat quietly pouting while peevishly pushing several beans around his plate with a pointed skewer.

After watching his antics around Shaylan's shoulder for a long while, Annell asked Shaylan, "What is the reason your friend behaves like a sulking child?"

"How well put, my lady," said Shaylan, quite amused at her assessment. He glanced at Rhem and decided not to drag him into the conversation, knowing that these moods sometimes bring with them rude remarks or at least, less than courteous responses.

"As you are aware, my Lady, Rhem has been searching through many documents and books which reference the sword Fallonrod. He had little good fortune in obtaining useful information until two days ago, when he chanced upon a document which contained the book title, Epoch. It seems that this book or document contained information regarding the sword, which may be very useful in our investigation. The problem is that no one can find a copy or even be sure that one ever existed."

Lady Annell slipped into a moment of concentrated thought... "Epoch... Epoch.. I remember something..." She abruptly turned to Lady Quellan, who was seated next to her on the other side, and interrupted her, "I'm sorry, my dear Lady Quellan. If I might interrupt..."

"Certainly, My Lady,"

"There was a book that everyone looked for many years ago... it was when we were much younger... remember the ladies all going through the libraries and trunks of books in the archives..."

"I do remember it quite well, they let us go into all those forbidden rooms with our mothers to look for it."

"Yes, that's it. Now, dearie, do you remember the name of it?'

Lady Quellan thought hard for a moment, "..uhm... it's not coming... I should remember... OH yes, it was something about the sword, wasn't it...uh.."

"Possibly Epoch."

"Yes, that's it, I'm sure of it... But it was never found, was it?"

"I don't remember, dearie. But thanks for your help... you're always so helpful."

"Oh, thank you, My Lady."

Turning back to Shaylan, "Did you hear that? It was the very book we searched for when I was a child... tore the castle apart, we did... never found it though."

"Do you remember anything about why you were looking for it or what it was supposed to be about?"

"Only that it had something to do with the sword Fallonrod and, more importantly, with the champion, Maylore, who wielded it."

Rhem seldom missed anything going on close to him and was thoroughly tuned into their conversation by this point. Upon hearing that they had looked before and failed to find it, he abruptly got up and walked out of the room.

Shaylan had been keenly sensing the frustration in his friend for two days, but had resolutely decided not to force comfort on Rhem but instead to wait until Rhem came to him for some consolation. He watched as Rhem slipped away without a word. Shaylan sensed his heaviness but again decided to let him seek his own solace.

Shaylan continued on in high spirited conversation for quite a while, stopping occasionally to see if he could pick up some sense of Rhem, which usually was quite present and very heavy.

It was now late evening, and several of the women began to slip away from the gathering, altogether pleased that their idea for the banquet had proved such a great success. Shaylan's senses were picking up strong sensations of loss and grief from Rhem. "Enough is enough," he thought to himself, "I'll find him since his pride won't permit him to come to me!"

Shaylan picked his way through the castle, stopping at hallways to sense the direction of his companion's presence. Soon he discovered him in the library, sitting slouched down in a large, high-backed, dark leather armchair, with his cloak pulled around him like a blanket. He looked pathetic.

It was such a sight that the wizard had to work hard to keep from laughing, "What's the trouble, Rhem?"

Rhem didn't respond, not even a stir in his position.

"You can't hide your feelings from me, my friend. I could feel them from the banquet room." Shaylan stood silently waiting for some sign of life in Rhem's glassy stare. "I'm concerned about you. I've never sensed defeat in you, not even when you were beaten badly." Shaylan was talking more like a father than a friend now.

Rhem rose to his feet, his tall, strong frame still hidden beneath his cloak. "I've found very little of value in my search of the records. For weeks I've read through books and letters and documents about this cursed sword and found more fantasy... more dreams and illusions than fact. All I have to show for my work is fanciful stories fit for taverns full of boasting drunks."

"I don't recall any promise made by you or by anyone else on your behalf that you would find out everything there is to know about Fallonrod. There was no guarantee that anything of true value even existed here in the archives or in any castle documents. It is possible that nothing of value was ever written about the sword at all. People usually prefer fancy to truth anyway."

Rhem instantly recognized the "I'm going to cheer you up" tone in Shaylan's voice and decided to cut him off, knowing that Shaylan could keep talking for so long that his audience would forget why they were upset, becoming occupied instead with how to get him to stop talking.

"Shaylan!" said Rhem very loudly so as to shock the wizard out of his pep-talk trance. "I believe there is, or was, a book written that contains the information you need."

Shaylan was surprised. "Information I NEED?" he said in a challenge while thinking to himself, "So that's it, he's still worried about my working with the sword in the absence of sufficient information."

"Yes," continued Rhem, now displaying a touch of anger, "The book 'Epoch' that I've been looking for... I'm sure it's exactly what you need... to understand the sword! As I've already explained to you, the letters imply that it was written by a lady of the castle about the leaders in the last great war. It had a part about the sword and Maylore... just the sort of book..."

Shaylan's eyes lit up, "Wait...slow down!" he said as he moved quickly to Rhem, spinning him around and pointing him toward the door. He guided Rhem out of the room at a brisk walk. "When was this book last seen?"

"There was a search for it about 40 years ago... isn't that what Lady Annell said at dinner?" answered Rhem, offering no resistance to being hurried out of the room.

"That's no help... then, when was it written?" asked Shaylan, who now had his arm firmly around Rhem's shoulder and was practically carrying him.

"Can't be sure... but probably during the years right after the end of the wars... probably by someone who actually knew those she wrote about personally,"answered Rhem, noting the strange change in Shaylan's mood. "Where are you taking me, Wizard?"

"To the Sword Chamber!"

"You don't have to push me all the way there, I do know where it's at and I can walk on my own...at least most of the time... and I will go with you."

Shaylan quickly removed his arm from Rhem's shoulder, knowing that he was probably the only person alive who could have gotten away with restricting this weaponsmaster in his movement for any length of time without getting hurt.

The two men passed through a long, dimly lit corridor and up two flights of stairs. Before arriving at the heavily guarded room, they were challenged by several pairs of armed soldiers standing at hallway intersections and one sensor, who recognized them and immediately apologized. At one point, Shaylan faintly sensed the presence of a shadowmaster, but too faint to even get a direction from which it came.

Finally, the two men stood at the entrance to the room. Through the dark opening, they could see the luminescent glow of the sword, the lone light in the room. Shaylan lit an oil lamp using the flame of a burning torch hanging next to the opening in the wall and handed it to Rhem. He then lit another one for himself.

"Why the torch wizard?" asked Rhem curiously. "You can make much better light than these lamps with your magic... or at least you can light the lamps with it!"

"I'm unsure of my magic in the presence of the sword. The closer to the sword I get, the harder it is for me to control the result of my art."

Rhem climbed in first. This was the first time that he and Shaylan had been in the room by themselves. The room itself was obviously a sitting room. The ceiling was almost twice as high as Rhem was tall.

Shaylan hurried over to the wall opposite the hole and started looking through the books on the shelves. There were only about a hundred or so books spread through the shelves.

"You don't actually think..." said Rhem as he moved quickly to join Shaylan in the investigation, "...I never thought of the possibility of Epoch being written before the room was sealed..."

Epoch was not among the books. Shaylan paused to survey the room with one crossed arm, which supported the elbow of the other arm as his chin rested in its hand and his pointing finger tapped on his cheek. His gaze swung around to the mantle over the fireplace, "There... there on the mantle..." he was pointing with an animated wiggle of his finger as he bounded toward the large brick edifice, "...there are some books there."

As he reached the mantle, he held the lamp up ahead of him and somewhat over his head. His light exposed the entire thick wood mantle, complete with various trinkets and personal effects. At the right end, there were five very old books on the mantle shelf, held together by two large carved lion head bookends. In the middle of the small group of books was one that looked more elegant than the rest.

He took the book down and held the cover up to the light he had placed on the mantle. There, in ancient gold embossed letters on the cracked leather cover, was the word, "EPOCH".

Rhem tucked the book inside his cloak, and the two men departed for Shaylan's quarters.

This time it was Rhem leading the way, his countenance renewed to childlike vigor. Once in the room with the door secured, Rhem removed the book for a closer look. The book, like everything else in the room, was amazingly well preserved. The exterior cover was dry and the cracks were shallow and patterned like the bottom of a dry dirt pond. The edges of the pages were slightly yellowed but the rest of each page looked fresh, as if never handled. The date inside the cover proved conclusively that the room had remained open for several years after the death of Maylore.

Shaylan lit another lamp, setting it on a small table around which sat four comfortable chairs. They began reading the book aloud, each taking a turn, first

Shaylan, then alternating back and forth. They frequently stopped to discuss portions as the book brought new revelations. Although some word usage had changed since it was written, its meaning was generally clear.

According to the writer, the sword wielder wasn't a natural warrior after all. His favorite arts were wood weaving and stone molding. By the accounts, Maylore was a gentle and even sensitive man. While his talents and arts were enviable, he was personally despised by many of the military hierarchy because he refused to follow their orders and wield Fallonrod according to their dictates. Early on, one commander, unaware that the sword was a true power sword, tried to kill Maylore, planning afterward to use the sword himself. He perished in that attempt.

Even during the most celebrated period in his life, following his most spectacular victories, Maylore shunned public acclaim, choosing instead to spend time with his few close friends, none of whom seemed to hold him in special regard.

Mention was made in numerous places about the sword itself, including its unusual ability to "help Maylore travel virtually anywhere he wished with no object being able to stand in his way." However, no further description or explanation was given of this phenomenon.

The sword was more diverse in its power than any sword either man had ever heard of. After the last revelation, both men just sat quietly meditating.

"What if this Maylore was himself a powermaster?" asked Rhem. "If he was, no one ever knew it or suspected it."

"But why would a shy powermaster seek a power sword?"

"I can't answer that any more than I can understand why he would have wanted it, powermaster or not...it doesn't fit his character... nevertheless, if he was a powermaster, as the feats of the sword would suggest, and if the sword was forged by a very talented metal forger and charged by an equally extraordinary wizard...?"

"That would make it a devastatingly powerful sword..."

"...and that would explain how it defeated and destroyed every other power sword in the wars of that time..." said Rhem, becoming more concerned with every word. "Could this type of sword ever be wielded by anyone except the one it was conceived for and designed around?"

"You are very premature in your presumption, my friend...all these 'what ifs' and such. Out of all people... it's not at all like you to jump to conclusions from an island of speculation. Neither panic nor defeat wears well on either of us, so pull yourself together and let's deal first with what we find, then we can conjecture together from a position of knowledge."

"Even though you make me sound like an old drunk, I still love it when you talk that way... you really do belong in a royal long-winded court... dazzling them with your..."

"Enough! I say, Enough!!" fussed Shaylan. "I'm through for now, let's get back to the book," he said as he retrieved it from the table and began to read again.

They continued trading off reading for hours. The sun was fully risen now and had broken over the castle wall, flooding its light into the room where they sat. Rhem was reading the end of a chapter after which they planned to break for the morning meal. Neither man felt the least bit tired. The end of the last sentence read, "and this was, of course, a result of the artful crafting of the Deluvian sword."

"STOP!" shouted Shaylan so abruptly that Rhem reflexively sprang to his feet, dropping the book.

"I am... that's the end," answered Rhem, shaking off the start he got from Shaylan's unexpected yell.

"No... I mean, wait!"

"O.K.... what? What is it?"

"Deluvian... what's Deluvian?... why would the writer say that?"

Rhem looked in disbelief at Shaylan... every swordsman knew that the best sword steel was a combination of Dwarven and Elven metals, which they called "Deluvian". "Maybe," he said in a teasing tone, "it's because the sword was made of Deluvian metal?"

"No! No, it can't be!" answered Shaylan, taking so fast and with such intensity that Rhem felt constrained to step back from the table. "The writer said 'Deluvian sword', not a sword made of Deluvian metal!"

"What are you talking about... I think you need some sleep, wizard."

"Just listen, will you? In one of my most ancient books on Dwarven wizardry, the writer calls the use of Dwarven and Elven magic together on metal, 'Deluvian'...don't you see, that would explain the extent of the sword abilities as well as its great power."

"But everyone knows what Deluvian metal is, it's..."

"Not Deluvian metal," cut in Shaylan, sounding very frustrated, "Not a mixture of Dwarven and Elven metals...a mixture of their magics on metal."

"Now look who's jumping to conclusions... at least my speculations were based on current observations, not antique mystic writings."

"That's exactly my point! No one I know would recognize Deluvian as anything but a metal. At the time this book was written, no Dwarf or Elf would have recognized Deluvian as anything but magic on metal. The meaning has changed with time. Maylore would have known the maker and may have slipped in mentioning his sword as a Deluvian sword. The writer picked up that slip and put it in the writing precisely as he said it."

"I hate to steal other people's words, but, shouldn't we wait until we finish the book to jump to conclusions... and after that we can conjecture all we want?"

" Can't argue with the logic in that, can I?"

****

After the morning meal, both men went back to their quarters for a short rest. Both napped restlessly; they tossed and turned, finding it impossible to get "Epoch" off their minds. Rhem finally got up and returned to Shaylan's room to find him awake and sitting on the edge of his bed.

As soon as Rhem entered the room, Shaylan turned, and their eyes met with highly charged intensity. A smile crept across their faces as they rushed to the table in unison for the book. They finished it in the early evening.

Much of the book had nothing to do with the sword directly, but offered a great deal of information about Maylore's personal life and the relationships between leaders of the time. The most helpful fact to surface was that Maylore's love of stone molding and wood weaving had led him to visit the

Dwarves and Elves off and on for many years prior to his mysteriously coming up with the sword. This fact was tied to the arguments of the writer that the Dwarves and Elves had greatly influenced Maylore and therefore, made him a better leading figure than some of the military commanders of their time.

After they finished reading the book, they went to the castle kitchen and brought a plate of cold cuts back with them to the room, avoiding conversation about the book until they were back in the room.

"O.K....suppose you're right," said Rhem after again discussing Shaylan's theory about the sword's origin, "what good is this information to us now?"

"That is a very good question... the possibility seems most likely to be true in light of the discoveries about his association with the other races... but we know that the Dwarves and Elves both hold a great deal of impatience even outright dislike for human activities, especially when Earth power is rising, as it is now... so why would they build a power sword of this magnitude for a man? As far as I know, they have no weapon with this great a power among their own kind, why make one for men?"

"I guess you'll have to ask them", Rhem said cynically.

"That is exactly what I plan to do!" answered Shaylan resolutely and much to Rhem's surprise. "I know that relations between the other races and most of men's kingdoms are cool, but Pretoria has assuredly the closest association with them of any."   "I can just see it now... 'excuse me, my good friend Dwarf, will you please give me the secrets of the sword Fallonrod so I can use it to destroy all my enemies.'"

"Rhem, will you be serious?"

"You think I'm not serious... do you actually believe they'll help us?"

"I know our ways are different..."

"Different is not the word for it... the earth power rises and the Dwarves get together with their friends, the Elves, and they build masterpiece buildings and bridges and all kinds of works of art... men pull away from each other and get jealous, making weapons to destroy each other... friendship vanishes and love turns to mistrust..."

"While that is all true, it was also true then... when the sword was made by them for a man... a regular man..."

"...a man they already knew well... a man they must have trusted."

"Well, whatever the case," said Shaylan, resuming his resolve to meet with them, "they are the only ones who hold the key to these things... one way or the other, we will find out if they are willing to help us...." Shaylan suddenly stopped. There was someone listening, watching... someone with evil intent. The same faint sense he had picked up the night before in the corridor.

The sudden change of countenance caused Rhem to jump to his feet. Before he was fully upright, he held a short sword in his hand. He scanned the room quickly, then glanced at Shaylan for insight."

"A shadowmaster... in the room now... evil..." came Shaylan's words as if solving a riddle piece by piece.

Shaylan continued to search the room with his senses as he spoke. He now spoke in a slow hypnotic cadence, "Show yourself and state your business. If we are forced to expose you, we will show no mercy."

In a series of carefully orchestrated moves, Rhem cut his way through the air with his now glowing sword, ending up directly in front of the door. "I've got the door covered!" he said in a threatening tone that commanded the intruder to surrender.

Shaylan created a blue mist between his hands and, holding it in front of his face like a seeing glass, began to scan the room. As his glance reached the area of the wall next to the fireplace, Shaylan shouted, "There!" pointing it out to Rhem, "standing against the wall."

At that instant, a dagger appeared, flying toward the wizard from the intruder's direction. It disintegrated in a bright blue flash that looked like lightning coming out of the mist in front of Shaylan's face. It was followed immediately by a green flame curtain that shielded the wizard against flying debris from the dagger.

Rhem was bounding from the door on the opposite side of the room when a panel in the wall swung open and closed almost instantly. There was a heavy thud on the other side of the secret entrance. Rhem tried in vain to force it back open. "Blast this door wizard, or he'll get away!" he said, yelling and backing up out of the line of fire.

"It's not worth the risk, Rhem. His magic stopped as soon as he cleared the panel. I can't even tell you which way he went. If he went to all the trouble to conceal himself and have an escape prepared, you can be sure that this malicious fellow had traps laid for any pursuer."

Rhem had returned his sword to it's sheath and was on his way to the door, "We need to alert Lord Falock," he said as he opened it without slowing down. "I'll do it myself. Besides, I want to find out who this shadowmaster is and why he was spying on us." He was still talking as he left the room, followed by Shaylan, who was trying anxiously to keep up with his quickly moving comrade's pace.

With considerable effort, Shaylan caught up with Rhem. "I don't understand how I could have been so careless... how I could miss the presence of a shadowmaster in the same room with us", he said with great frustration. "Caution is the first rule in power conflicts. I had no reason to believe we were at all safe... I must be getting..."

"Will you quit kicking yourself for being human!" cut in Rhem without breaking stride or looking at Shaylan. "You were preoccupied... we were both preoccupied."

He glanced at Shaylan, looking for agreement from the wizard. Shaylan gave up a shrug of the shoulders and a nod of the head that was lost in the bouncing of his jogging step. But his eyes were still turned inward. "Shaylan, our next step must be on solid ground, not some wave in a sea of emotion... I need you to be... to be... yourself!"

Both men became aware of two guards standing at the junction of two hallways. Rhem quickly explained what had happened, and the guards sounded the alarm. They continued on toward Lord Falock's private living quarters, where he was reportedly spending the evening with his family. They had only gone a short distance when Rhem stopped at a door which stood ajar. Pulling his sword, he pushed it open with the point. Just inside the room, lying face down on an oval rug, was a dead guard, his sword missing.

Fearing for Lord Falock's safety, both men broke into a run. They had only just gotten up to speed when they heard an alarm call coming from the area of the castle entrance. They turned and ran for the front door.

When they arrived, they found one guard nearly decapitated, with his sword still in its sheath. The other guard stationed there was still alive but was bleeding badly from a wound going clear through his body just below his ribcage. He said that a man had appeared out of nowhere and killed Jang, his partner, and turned as if in one continuous movement and struck him. The guard had never seen the man before. "He didn't say a word, he just turned around, vanished, and then the door opened..."

Already, there were groups of guards and other Castle officials combing the grounds. Two sensors were led down the hallway from the Lord's sitting room, where they had been, to the wounded guard in hopes of getting some clue about the identity of the intruder. They arrived just before the healer did and were trying to question the man. Shaylan and Rhem physically pulled them away, allowing the healer to get in, and took them aside. After a short session of fact-finding, the two sensors departed to join the search.

There was so much magic being used by so many different people that Shaylan doubted seriously that the sensors would be able to even determine in which direction the intruder had departed.

By this time, Lord Falock had arrived, battle-ready, and joined the others at the entrance. After several brief conversations, each of which he cut off abruptly and very loudly, his attention was directed toward Shaylan and Rhem, who were waiting a respectful distance from him.

He quickly turned and came toward them, pushing several people out of his way as he moved in their direction. He grabbed one of his lieutenants by the arm and dragged him along, shouting as they neared, "Now pay close attention to what you hear... you'll be responsible for following this up."

"Can you two shed some light on what has happened here and why two of my guards have been attacked?" shouted Lord Falock impatiently.

"Three men, sire." Rhem said matter-of-factly. "There is another in a room near your living quarters."

Lord Falock became even more agitated and nearly cut Rhem off, "Will you PLEASE tell me what has happened?"

Shaylan approached the topic cautiously, "Lord Falock, do you by any chance..."

"Cut the formalities, Shaylan, and get to the point!"

"Do you have a shadowmaster in your employ?" answered Shaylan, speaking so quickly that it took Lord Falock a moment to perceive what he had said.

"I have only one real shadowmaster and he's not that good", he answered with the volume in his voice rising at each successive word as his indignation increased over being asked a question instead of being given an answer to his. "NOW TELL ME," he finally shouted without breaking for so much as the hint of a breath after his answer. Everyone in the castle entrance stopped what they were doing and stood looking at the four men, causing Lord Falock to halt mid-sentence and glance briefly around the hall. "Tell me what you know, wizard!" he continued through gritted teeth, a vein standing out prominently from the forehead of his now bright red, flushed face. Before Shaylan could bring himself together to answer, Lord Falock looked around the hall at silent stares and shouted, "Get back to work... go find that intruder!" Instantly, everyone resumed their work.

Shaylan explained about the intruder, the escape, and the room it took place in. Rhem explained about the book and the Elf-Dwarven connection with the sword, and the fact that the intruder heard their entire conversation regarding the discovery.

As soon as he understood how significant the knowledge may be for the intruder, and the relative ease with which he had entered undetected and then escaped, Lord Falock walked out the front entrance, dragging the lieutenant, and yelled at the top of his voice, "FIND THAT MAN! DON'T COME BACK WITHOUT HIM!" He shoved the lieutenant down the steps and commanded him to organize the search and secure the fortress to ensure that the intruder couldn't get out.

Lord Falock sent men to gather his personal advisors and his military cabinet together immediately to discuss their options. Everyone was assembled with remarkable speed. They agreed together that a council of the three Pretorian Lords had to be convened at the earliest possible moment to discuss the intrusion and its possible ramifications. They decided to meet in a central location, in the town of Beorg, so as to facilitate the earliest meeting time. The tightest security was to be set up with sensors to screen each participant.

Somehow, that night, the shadowmaster escaped detection and by morning was out of the castle complex.

Riders were dispatched at first light to the other two castles with urgent requests for an immediate council at Beorg.

The body of the document carried by each rider said:

Of grave importance! Please meet for a security council summit of the three Lords at the earliest possible hour in the town of Beorg. Bring your most trusted and talented negotiators, men familiar with dwarven or elven ways, for a possible delegation of the highest security and delicacy. I will prepare Beorg for your arrival.

LORD FALOCK OF CASTLE CREST

CHAPTER 6

Brandon Keep was known as the castle of magic. It was one of the oldest and at the same time best preserved of the fortress dwellings. Its exterior wall, octagonal in shape, was covered with large, uniform sheets of smooth black stone fit together with precision. It was built on a flat plain at the north end of a narrow valley on the east side of the Greystone mountains.

The castle had been the center of magical arts training in centuries past. Each successive lord of the castle had become wealthier than the previous as over the years they served kings and lords from several lands with talented artisans for hire and loan. Since the last war and the end of the earth power surge, the castle had become more secretive. The number of soldiers employed there had declined significantly during the last 50 years. Rumors had spread that Lord Oakbern, the current Lord of Brandon Keep, was seeking and employing artisans who possessed abilities in the darker magics and paying them extravagant wages.

Lord Oakbern's plan was indeed very ambitious. He was a mystic of sorts, believing so deeply that magic held the answer to every need, strategy, and even the meaning of life itself, that all of his pursuits were wrapped up in obtaining in his employ the best magic wielders in the lands. If he could become satisfied with his power base, he would then begin to pursue dominance over the kingdoms and alliances surrounding him. In this plan was a driving compulsion to own the greatest power sword, Fallonrod, or have one created that could defeat it, if such an advent became necessary. Since the arts and abilities needed to create a true power sword were very scarce, and since his artisans had so far been unable to even create a true power sword, Lord Oakbern decided to seek someone who could control the sword Fallonrod should he somehow gain the opportunity to procure it. This would be a very difficult job because a true powermaster would have to be found, convinced to wield the sword for Lord Oakbern, and then the sword would have to be obtained. All of these pursuits seemed reasonable and were fueled by his personal belief that he possessed the cunning and ability to rule wisely. He was further encouraged by his loyal followers, who zealously persuaded him that he would make a great leader and that his magically endowed attendants would help bring peace, security, and prosperity to all the lands.

He employed two sensors of extraordinary talent. It became their primary mission to locate a powermaster and identify him. One of the sensors

was named Alan. He was a clever man with great discerning and sensing
powers. He had been trained by a Warminian wizard in the ways of deception,
tricks, and traps. The Warminian wizards were among the most feared in the
lands far to the east. Due to their brutality and cruelty, their trades had been
banned from Pretoria and the surrounding areas, although most had someone
who knew one or two more elementary Warminian ploys. Lord Oakbern held a
strong dislike for the Warminian ways but valued Alan's other talents enough to
have sent him out first in hopes of contacting the magic wielder they had sensed
from time to time in Pretoria.

Alan had left Brandon Keep in Mid Rising and sent word from Middle
Shire Crossing that he had settled there because it was the most central location
from which to work. He reported that no one knew who the power wielder
was, nor was anyone even ready to speculate. He set up a modest export trade
in the town, as a cover, and traded mostly in specialty foods, which he exported
back to Brandon Keep. He discovered that there was a pattern to the timing of
the use of power by this mysterious artisan, but no pattern to the location where
he might use his magic next. He had already determined that the power would
materialize within about one day's walk from the town in one direction or
another twice each phase. As quickly as it began, it would vanish without a
residual trace. The wielder was very cautious not to practice very long in one
place. Several times Alan had been, by sheer luck, near the source of the magic
when it began. He would move quickly and almost locate the source only to
have it terminate suddenly and completely, leaving him close enough to have
had the smell of victory in his nose but no taste of its treasure nor glimpse of its
substance. This infuriated him more and more with each near encounter. He
felt keenly that his reputation was at stake and that failure would be
intolerable. After all, Lord Oakbern sent him instead of Eric, showing
conclusively in whom he placed confidence for the job. He vowed to himself
not to fail.

Armed with new vigilance and unusually good luck, which he attributed
to personal genius, he finally sent word that he had discovered the key to the
mysterious power wielder's identity. His last communication was carried back
to Brandon Keep via a courier who visited regularly. It simply stated that he
was going to follow a young blacksmith apprentice from Burkeston, whom he

was sure would lead him conclusively to the identity of the magician he sought. Alan was never heard from again.

****

During the same day on which Alan disappeared, Eric went to Lord Oakbern regarding the enormous power being wielded from the direction of the Pretorian midlands, "Lord Oakbern, I believe that a power of this magnitude may require more than just a clever trap to apprehend."

"Eric of Schrod," answered Lord Oakbern, somewhat amused as this newest round of competition between Alan and Eric surfaced, "Alan will send word if he needs our help. I will grant that his pride is fierce with respect to his ability to secure this elusive power wielder, but he is wise enough to call for assistance rather than risk his own death to satisfy his arrogance."

"My Lord Oakbern, there have been three distinct sources of extraordinary power at work today, all coming from the direction of mid-Pretoria. Each of these sources dwarfs Alan's power as a forest fire dwarfs a candle. If any one of these powers would choose not to accompany him willingly, it is unlikely they would do so by the power of Alan's traps and tricks."

"And you think your abilities are greater and your chances better than a Warminian's?"

"Different...not greater." Eric was getting frustrated with Oakbern's habit of making light of his concerns as if this were just one great big game.

"Let's wait and see what news comes from Alan before we set the two of you up for a confrontation in a foreign town." With that, Lord Oakbern dismissed Eric.

The courier returned to Pretoria on his regular rounds, hoping to obtain new information from Alan. After three days of waiting, he moved on to complete his assigned route and returned again to Brandon Keep. Fully half a phase had passed with no word from Alan nor any sign that he had even returned from his last outing. Indeed, the courier discovered that many of Alan's special tools were also missing. Again, he left, this time returning to report Alan's disappearance.

Lord Oakbern called Eric and dispatched him to Middleford Crossing to investigate. Eric discovered that Alan told his nearest neighbors that he was going out of town on business and asked them to watch after his home while he was away. He never returned. The neighbors confirmed that it was immediately before "The Day of the Great Magics", as it was called by the townsmen, that Alan had left for his trip. Many people had sensed the powerful display, and some had actually found the site of what appeared to have been a battle between great powers.

"Perhaps his tricks and traps cost him his life!" chuckled Eric to himself with a touch of contempt. He never liked Alan and only tolerated him out of professional courtesy and respect for Lord Oakbern, or at least his money.

Eric returned to Brandon Keep and told Lord Oakbern of Alan's disappearance, and suggested that he be allowed to return and complete the mission.

"How do I know that you'll fare better than Alan did?"

"My Lord, I am a weapons master and a sensor. I am not as impatient or in such a hurry that I would expose myself to danger prematurely. I will not be as careless as Alan, but will return with this power wielder."

"My dear Eric, your personal confidence in this matter is reassuring. But you can only speculate as to what happened to Alan. It was, no doubt, a great magic that defeated him. I'm not willing to chance this to you alone. You shall have a partner in this adventure."

Eric's entire body stiffened, and his eyes narrowed to a slit. He was about to react when Lord Oakbern cut right back in, smiling with delight as he spoke, "Her name is Shahandra!"

Eric went from anger to indignation, "But she is only a girl!"

"She's a young lady," cautioned Oakbern, "not a girl. And she has certain powers of persuasion that are extraordinary, as you have witnessed yourself. She can control even those animals which are by nature very frightened of humans."

Eric responded in diplomatic tones as he tried to control his emotions, "Power to control brute beasts and tiny forest creatures is quite different than controlling a powerful magic-wielding man, my Lord. And if the one we seek is truly a powermaster and developed in the arts of sensing, her presence could prove fatal."

"Don't let her scare you, Eric..."

"I'm hardly frightened by her... more like annoyed and ..."

"Eric, Eric, Eric..." Lord Oakbern waited for a moment while the red in Eric's face faded, "I am aware of the dangers you may face as well as you are... and I'm also aware of the distraction an unfamiliar partner could pose... more especially when she is so beautiful."

"That's exactly why I don't want her with me... she'll attract too much attention. A mission of this nature should remain unobtrusive, unencumbered with distraction like ornate baggage..."

"I fully admit that Shahandra is beautiful... why her smile alone, with those perfect white teeth and forest green eyes, is beyond attractive... they're enchanting, even without magic. This type of distraction can be very disarming and even assist you in obtaining entrance to places and access to people you might otherwise not find so easy to secure on your own. Eric, she has an Elven-like charm, I've felt it very keenly, and I know you have."

Eric blushed again as he tried to discern for himself if he was embarrassed or angry.

"I sense even now your feelings warring over her." Lord Oakbern smiled at having unveiled the fact that Eric had fallen victim to her charm just as much as he himself had, even though she was fully 15 years younger than Eric and over 25 years younger than he was.

"I suppose you're right. I'm willing for her to accompany me under certain conditions. First, I am the leader of this expedition, and I shall dictate the plan as I see fit. Second, she will go with me and act the part in every way, as my daughter. Last, I will not be responsible for her safety unless she follows my orders explicitly." Eric had witnessed this girl at work and was not at all sure he could master her or sense all of her manipulations.

"You may have your way up to the point that she is required to take action. Her abilities will have to be in her control, not yours. If she is needed to obtain information or enchant the powermaster, it must be left to her discretion." Oakbern rose from his throne-like stuffed armchair and walked over to Eric. "Oh, and one more thing... she has been raised entirely within my household. Her father and mother were friends of mine and were tragically killed when she was very young. I'm quite fond of her, so don't abandon her needlessly. If she's foolish and jeopardizes her life... then it is in her hands. But do not abandon her in peril simply to teach her a lesson." Lord Oakbern searched Eric's face for some indication of his reaction. Nothing showed, nothing could be read, either positive or negative. "If you agree to these terms, I agree to yours, and you shall be off as soon as possible." Oakbern extended his hand in a gesture of agreement. Eric hesitated a moment, then took hold firmly, confirming the agreement.

"I hope I haven't been enchanted into this deal," answered Eric with a sly searching smile slipping onto his face.

Lord Oakbern laughed a bold belly laugh, "I assure you I would not ... I'm not even capable of such a thing... though it would be handy from time to time when my wife gets into a rage." Both men continued laughing. "Go make whatever preparations you need to for your stay there, and we'll make final arrangements tomorrow."

Eric turned to leave, hesitated, then turned back to Lord Oakbern, who hadn't yet moved. "You know that I don't like working with anyone, much less a girl. But you've shown many times that you have a gift for sensing possibilities and planning for success. I also know that should I... should WE succeed, you will make it worth our while."

"You know how much it would mean to me... to all of us, to have someone who can wield that sword for our cause... yes, you will be rewarded handsomely... both of you!"

"Then you're quite sure the girl will wish to go?"

"I am indeed! The powers of this master you have sensed also intrigue and challenge her. Yes, Eric, she'll go with you." Lord Oakbern smiled to himself as he watched Eric turn confidently and leave, "I wonder who will actually end up leading this expedition when all is said and done?" He chuckled to himself as he pictured Shahandra and Eric in a battle for control, "and she will, no doubt, have her way with you, Eric, as she will also have her way with this power wielder, powermaster or not! After all, this whole expedition was her idea!"

The next two days were busied with preparations and plans for periodic contact with couriers. On the night before their departure, two men arrived at Brandon Keep from Schrod, Eric's hometown. One of the men had been shot in the back with an arrow and was very weak. While his wound was being tended to, the other survivor told of a strange and savage band of raiders that had attacked the town. They had come out of nowhere and killed almost everyone except those few who escaped into the rocky hills at the outset of the attack. The village had been sacked and burned. Then the raiders left as quickly as they had come, seemingly back into nowhere. The leader was a tall man with a crimson cape and a wide-brimmed black hat, curled at the sides. At the end of the raid, he appeared at the entrance to the town and walked down the main road using magic fire to burn every building that faced the street, departing with a roar of laughter after he had set the town ablaze.

This news confirmed what had been speculated by castle sensors, that the power being used in the north and east had been evil. Already, rumors had begun to surface that Danlion, the cruel magician whom Maylore defeated with Fallonrod in the final battles of the Great War, had mastered the magic of life and preserved himself almost 200 years , right up to the present. Up to this time, the stories of his longevity were dismissed as myth and tavern chatter by most sensible folk. Prior to this attack, stories had circulated blaming him for the disappearance of small hamlets and isolated farming groups, but this was the first time that a large village had been attacked in this fashion. Now, true or not, the rumor of his miraculous self-preservation would doubtless grow. Judging from the small number of raiders reported to accompany this man, whoever he was, Lord Oakbern determined that they would not likely try to attack the castle outright at this time, although he conceded that they may try by deceit. Whoever they were, they had become a force to be reckoned with. Sensors were posted at the main gate, and the other gates were sealed as a precaution.

This added urgency to the quest by Eric and Shahandra to find and retrieve a powermaster who could wield the mighty sword Fallonrod.

The circumstances of the ruthless attack on Schrod provided a unique opportunity that Eric and Shahandra could use to gain entrance into Pretoria. They would go as refugees, a perfect cover.

As Eric and Shahandra left Brandon Keep, they were both quiet and introspective. Eric was preoccupied with thoughts of his hometown, Schrod, and all those he had known there. Though he considered the town ingrown and most of the inhabitants shallow in their general interests, he had many in that town he called friend. He wondered about this obscure madman who killed and destroyed seemingly for fun. He personally dismissed the possibility that someone could prolong his life with magic to the extent that Danlion would have had to in order to still be alive. Danlion or not, whoever he was, he would be a force to be reckoned with.

Shahandra's thoughts turned to the magician whose power they sought, and to the magical sword Falonrod. If they could locate him and he really was a powermaster, surely he could be persuaded to lend his powers to the Lord of Brandon Keep. With him in possession of the sword, and Lord Oakbern commanding his army and his magicians, there would be peace in all the civilized lands. Her thinking became fuzzy as she tried to conceive a plan that might give them access to the sword without having to battle for it. And if that wasn't difficult enough by itself, there was now the additional, imminently time sensitive element, of locating the powermaster and convincing him to help them in time to stop the growing band of heartless raiders who were terrorizing the countryside..."...One thing at a time..." she thought to herself, quickly arresting the cascading feeling of being overwhelmed. "First, we locate the powermaster!"

By the time Eric and Shahandra set out, word of the raids by the mysterious army had reached Lord Linx, who consequently set up watch posts and checkpoints along all incoming roads from the outlands. Patrols were sent out routinely to monitor traffic on the roads. Everyone coming into Pretoria was questioned as to purpose and destination. The soldiers at the checkpoints were given the authority to reject entrance to anyone they thought suspicious or who was caught lying in answer to their questions.

Eric and Shahandra came to one of the checkpoints, which was located on the main road leading through the Greystone Mountains into Pretoria. As they approached the soldiers, Eric commanded Shahandra to allow him to handle the soldiers without interruption from her. Eric executed his planned speech about "me and my daughter..." and the raid on his hometown, Schrod. As he did, the soldier interviewing them called another soldier, obviously of higher rank, to listen to Eric's story.

The instant the second soldier arrived, Shahandra spoke up. Her voice seemed to calm the soldiers and reassure them of her sincerity and the truth of their journey. Eric never saw her touch either man as she often had done with animals when she enchanted them by her arts. So well did she accomplish her goal that Eric himself was persuaded to overlook her insubordination as though it had never happened. He was surprised at his own reaction, but was sure it was his idea to be merciful with her and overlook this incident! "After all," he thought to himself, "I know her tricks and could not be trapped by them... besides, she was too busy with the soldiers to have even attempted to enchant him..." Eric froze mid-thought for an instant, ..."then why am I arguing with myself about a decision I made regarding her?"

He no sooner shook off his rationalizing conversation with himself than he heard Shahandra say to one of the soldiers, "I'm a healer and can sense that you have pain. Can I help you with something?" Eric tensed up as the soldier confessed to having a headache, which was making him sick in his stomach.

"Does your neck hurt too?"

"Not as much as my head, but it is stiff."

"Which came first, the headache or the stomach sickness?"

"The headache."

Both the other soldier and Eric watched nervously as Shahandra had the ill soldier remove his helmet, after which she put her hands, one on his neck and the other on his forehead.

After a brief moment, the soldier said, "I feel warmth coming out of her hand... it's filling my head... now my neck... now my chest." Suddenly, he went limp and started to fall.

At the same instant, Shahandra grabbed him to prevent him from falling, and the guard pulled his sword while shouting, "What'd you do to him?"

Before the armed soldier could move, Eric had whipped out a small ball attached to a line, which he used to wrap around the hilt of the sword and pull it from the soldier's hand. Instantly, it was in Eric's hand.

The ill soldier quickly recovered and recognized what was happening, "Malstow, No! She healed me... look... no pain! I'm OK."

Malstow glanced at his healed companion and quickly back at Eric, who was now handing the sword back to him, hilt first. Eric had a broad, friendly grin on his face as the soldier took back his sword, "No hard feelings, I hope," said Eric, maintaining the warmest, almost apologetic smile he could muster. The soldier sheathed his sword while shaking his head side to side, wide-eyed and embarrassed. Suddenly, all four of them burst out in laughter. Several other soldiers were running their way, drawn by the quick movements. Malstow signaled them that everything was under control and released Eric and Shahandra. After a brief thank-you session from the healed soldier, they continued on.

As they walked away, both of them were reflecting on the value of their new partner. Shahandra had only caught Eric's disarming of the soldier through the corner of her eye, but knew that it had been perfectly executed and that he had managed to be diplomatic in the return of the sword. Seeing him in action gave her more confidence in his diplomacy with people, something she had doubted him capable of.

On the other hand, Eric was amazed at Shahandra's ability to manipulate the feelings of alarmed soldiers. More astounding to him and somewhat puzzling was her insistence on healing the ill soldier, "a totally unnecessary exposure," he thought to himself. So he asked her, "Shahandra, why did you heal the soldier?"

Sensing his amazement, she answered, "Would it kill you to tell me that I did a good job... or that you were impressed... or just to say something nice?"

"It's not your power I question, it's your action... your timing, your reasoning."

"Eric, the man was ill and needed help. Why not help him? We weren't going to do battle with him... I didn't give him the magical ability to follow us. I just got rid of his headache." Shahandra was talking to Eric as an equal, and nothing in her tone even suggested that she felt compelled to defend her actions before him. "Besides that, there is always the possibility that someday we may meet in more dangerous circumstances and need the benefit of the doubt to go in our favor."

As she spoke, Eric thought about how naive she was regarding missions of the type they were now on. After a moment in thought, he asked, "Is it wise to let the enemy know your abilities? Isn't it more in keeping with wisdom to protect your abilities from exposure too soon?... to save them for emergencies?... to keep your enemies guessing?"

"I always believed that the best wisdom is to use your power well, not to hide it out of fear and use it only in emergencies."

Eric was becoming more and more irritated, "You're so simple-minded. Don't you know that warfare's a dangerous business? You don't just go around volunteering your power and making yourself vulnerable... it's stupid!"

"Eric, you keep saying 'warfare' and 'enemy'... why do you consider everyone your enemy? All you want on this adventure is to acquire the services of the magician we have sensed working in this country."

Eric didn't know whether to try to explain the realities of the politics of "power" or the techniques of disguise and deception needed when working under cover in someone else's country. "Shahandra, there is no doubt many people looking for this power wielder... people from his own country as well as from other lands. Our presence in this land would not be welcome if they knew our purpose was to convince, persuade, or even delude this person into using his arts for Brandon Keep... they would not welcome our attempts. They'd brand us spies and kill us or hold us in some prison, hoping for a future political advantage that our captivity might provide them."

"Eric, you talk like a thief!" she answered bluntly.

Eric became agitated, "You're a very talented girl. But you're still very young. I was hired for my talents and my ability to stay alive in dangerous circumstances. Remember, our predecessor has vanished. I do not intend to likewise perish. Your ideas about helping everyone and exposing yourself unnecessarily are wasteful and naive. Don't lecture me, Shahandra. I realize I can't control you, but you'll do well to listen to me... it might save your life. I plan to live through this with or without you!"

"Eric, everyone knows you're the best at what you do," answered Shahandra in a shy and compliant voice. "I hope to learn a lot from you. But if we're supposed to be refugees from some terrible raider, if we're pretending to come seeking refuge here, why shouldn't we be thankful and friendly to our new hosts? Wouldn't we attract even more attention if our powers were discovered by some sensor after we had been here for a while and had kept them a secret?"

"You make everything sound so simple...so easy." Eric struggled for an example or way to explain to her the dangers inherent in her way of thinking. It seemed as hard to communicate these delicate matters to her as it would be trying to communicate color to a person born blind. "There are so many complications that can arise when others find out you're a very gifted person. There are very few people anywhere who can heal the way you did today. If you just go around volunteering your art, where it wasn't even asked for, you'll draw much more attention to yourself than is necessary. An army would especially need someone like you to attend to their wounded... they could try to force you into service. And at the very least, you'll be watched more than others for no reason better than mere curiosity."

"But my way could give us a better opportunity of gaining information than if we were sneaky, mysterious people," she answered with so much youthful enthusiasm and confidence that Eric's annoyance level grew to an all-time high.

Eric hated the word "sneaky". It made him think of weird people with shadows on their faces and shifty eyes. "She must know I hate that word," he thought with retaliation in mind.

"We are not being sneaky," he said emphatically. "We're being cautious!" Eric was sure she wasn't listening to him. "You have a point in that we're refugees and as such should be friendly and thankful to our new hosts. But you forget that we have a mission. It requires that we keep our business a secret. If someone becomes suspicious of our actions and knows our abilities, we would be easier to defeat."

Shahandra cut in before Eric could take a breath, "If we've been open with our talents, we won't look suspicious. But if someone does suspect our activities and then discovers our hidden talents, we would become targets of an even greater suspicion."

Eric's voice was raised now to a level that sounded much like an irate parent lecturing an obstinate child, "Shahandra, that's exactly what I was saying. If someone put these things together, we're going to be discovered. They're looking for the power wielder as surely as we are. We dare not become exposed. I'm positive they would frown on our intrusion."

"Then act like their friend and not a hermit or a spy," she said, sounding exasperated and exhausted.

Eric took a deep breath to gain control of his emotions. He hated working with others for exactly this reason. She was even more frustrating than most because she tried to reason with him using childish ideals. He wished it was a battle of strength; he never lost those because he was such an intimidating person... except to this simplistic girl. He let the argument lapse at this point, planning to accomplish the remainder of the job working as much by himself as he could, hoping against hope that she didn't expose them before he got the chance to locate the person they sought.

She could sense his thoughts, and they saddened her. She started to object, but decided to take his advice and not give herself away... maybe there were times for stealth and secrecy. If he got in trouble, she could be close without him knowing it. To her, it was wise to show herself a friend to those of

Pretoria if she ever hoped to convince or charm a Pretorian powermaster to come with them. She couldn't understand how Eric could be so vain as to think he could bargain with or, if necessary, outwit and overcome a powermaster who didn't trust them to begin with. If the one they sought was a true powermaster, he would be a sensor and would assuredly be a very dangerous person when he chose to be. It appears that their predecessor found out just how dangerous. If Eric was going to be secretive, she would devise her own plan independent of him.

They both walked on in silence, wrapped up in their own worlds of thought. Neither seemed to notice their aching feet or the chapped skin under the straps of their backpacks.

Eric and Shahandra decided not to even acknowledge that they had known their predecessor. If the power wielder had killed him, their association with him could put them in jeopardy. Therefore, when they arrived at Middle Shire Crossing, they arrived strictly as refugees from Schrod.

Middle Shire Crossing, or just The Crossings, as the locals called it, was a beautiful rustic town at the beginning of the foothills leading to the Falcon Mountains. Two rivers came together there, the Teaman from the North and the Rockwall from the East. The Teaman was a warm, murky river whose headwaters were near the base of the Dwarvian Mountains, in a broad swamp from which it obtained its name. It runs lazily through the north central plain of Pretoria. The Rockwall is a clear ice ice-cold river that runs from the Eastern side of the Falcon Mountains. The rivers join at The Crossings and continue on together as the Great Landshire River, which flows southward through the rest of Pretoria, eventually passing Castle Rock. There are three bridges at Middleshire crossing, one over each river. The town itself is situated just north of the center of Pretoria, on a plain between two mountain ranges. The town sits on all three banks, with the largest section located on the west bank at the junction. Because it is so centrally located, many travelers stay the night there on their journeys. The majority of the inns and taverns are located on the North side of the junction between the rivers.

Eric and Shahandra investigated several inns and decided on the Oaken Shield Inn for a temporary residence. It was centrally located, near the bridge, and had an active clientele. They made arrangements to stay there for an extended period, telling the innkeeper they were looking to settle in The Crossings. This cover would work nicely until they either succeeded in their mission or were forced to find long-term lodging.

Their first couple of days were spent getting the lay of the land down, exploring the city, and getting a feel for the people. During the evenings, Eric visited some of the rougher taverns, hoping to hear stories or meet someone who might lead him closer to the power wielder. Shahandra was too young to accompany him and was therefore forced to remain at the inn. Out of boredom, she busied herself helping the innkeeper, Ingar, with the chores. In return, Ingar gave her free run of the Inn, including the kitchen.

Ingar was a middle-aged woman of unusually handsome appearance. She had silvering black shiny hair, which she pulled back tastefully into a bun at the back of her head. Her eyes were as dark a blue as a blue-black sword steel. She had a pleasant smile and a manner that put you at ease almost instantly. Her voice was strong but not loud nor shrill. Her speaking had an unheard but definitely felt music in it. She was a good listener, attentive to every word. And although she told entrancing stories, she spoke little of her own personal life.

Shahandra spent several hours with her each night, helping and listening as Ingar told tale after tale of adventures, interesting people, and even of outlanders she had met. Shahandra particularly liked the stories of the outlanders, that is, what the dwarves and elves were called in Pretoria. They fascinated her with their warm, quick-witted humor and their extraordinary use of the magic arts.

On the third night, a fight broke out in one of the rooms directly upstairs from the kitchen, where they were finishing the dishes. Ingar's art of sensing came on so powerfully and suddenly that it startled and frightened Shahandra.

"Wait here, Shahandra," said Ingar in the same calm, reassuring tone that was common to her speech. "Have a slice of pie and I'll be right back... be sure to wait right here in the kitchen for me," she requested in a tone that demanded a response.

"I'll stay right here," she said with a smile to Ingar, who had hesitated long enough to make sure Shahandra promised not to follow, then turned and moved quickly out of the room toward the stairs.

Ingar had only just stepped out of the room when the sound of yelling gave way to that of furniture being shoved around and things breaking.

Shahandra opened up her sensing powers as much as she knew how and quickly picked up the source of the men fighting. One of the men was using the luring power, a magic that confuses and mesmerizes an opponent, on the other in what Shahandra perceived to be a knife fight. Suddenly, she detected that he had stabbed the man. She somehow felt him die, a sensation that she had never sensed without contact with the victim.

Before Shahandra could recover from the shock of the man's death, she heard the other man talk; whether by magic or actual hearing, she could not distinguish, but his words were clear, "What're you doin' here, lady?" Shahandra sensed the presence of Ingar fill the room where the man was. The images in Shahandra's head became clearer than she had ever experienced, as if she was now seeing through Ingar's eyes. The man continued, "This isn't your lucky day, lady." She felt another evil attempt at luring, a sensing magic being used by the man against Ingar. She wished she could scream a warning, but before she could sort out her impulses, she sensed a fire magic followed quickly by a healer's magic. She felt the man die instantly as if he exploded inside. A shock ran through Shahandra as she realized that Ingar used the healing magic to kill. It had been one of her worst nightmares that she would somehow accidentally harm or kill someone by misuse of her healing powers. But to intentionally kill by healing power... this was something she had never considered.

Ingar was no longer using magic, so Shahandra could not sense her activity. Shahandra had been so surprised by what happened that she had no idea whether Ingar had been injured or not. She began to fear for Ingar and searched for her again, using every sensing power she possessed to detect at least some subtle indication of her presence.

Shahandra was concentrating so hard on her sensing that when Ingar appeared very suddenly in the kitchen doorway, it made her jump. Ingar was now the one sensing and discerning, but this time her focus was on Shahandra. "You're very strong for one so young child... earth power dwells in you with great strength and," she said with one eyebrow cocked and a half smile of discovery, "...you use it with practiced skill." Both women stood for a brief moment, senses fixed upon each other, searching for signs of danger or deception, both carefully guarding their inner feelings.

Ingar broke the spell, "Enough of this child. I trust you for now and hope that you have learned to trust me, at least for the present. I need your help now. Will you please go out into the street and look for one of the men who are wearing black leather vests with the Lion seal on them. They are city guards who will come and deal with the dead."

Shahandra stared a moment more, reassessing Ingar and the situation. Then, with a simple, courteous nod of her head, Shahandra left the room and the Inn to search for a guard. She was amazed that she had been so far off in her initial evaluation of Ingar... apparently, so had the man upstairs. Her abilities had surprised Shahandra. Ingar hid them so well... and that had gone in her favor. "Was Eric really right?" she thought to herself. "Do you need to hide your powers?" But then again, she wasn't really sure that Ingar had hidden her powers, the subject hadn't come up, and no situation had previously arisen for their demonstration to become necessary. And yet, she had sensed no use of magic at all in the two previous days. Before she could think about it any more, she came across two guards. She put her thoughts on hold, intending later to ask Ingar how she felt about these things. She quickly located the guards and brought them back to the Inn.

Eric's visits to some of the rougher taverns had provided him with quite a few stories told by travelers from near and far. Of growing regularity had been the stories of raids in the Northeast, beyond the Greystone Mountains, raids led by a man with a crimson cape and wide-brimmed black hat. Some told of atrocities that would chill the soul of all but the stoutest of hearts. Most listened with interest, but others taunted the teller for facts which might somehow verify these as anything but fancy. Then inevitably, the listeners would begin to debate who this mysterious man might be. Most favored the legendary Danlion, the evil magician from the last war, miraculously preserved these many years and back for revenge. Others occasionally speculated that he was a new evil powermaster trying to build a reprobate army with which to invade Pretoria and secure for himself the great sword, Fallonrod, so he could conquer the world for himself. These tales seemed to dominate most taverns where storytelling prevailed over game playing. Eric found little of value about the power wielder he sought since these places usually contained only occupants who were just passing through.

After two nights of tall tales in the North Bank taverns, Eric decided to try the West Bank taverns, where the local folks were more likely to visit. As he had discovered in every other town, each tavern had its own special atmosphere. The first one he entered had only three customers other than himself; two were together, and the other talked with the tavern keeper. They were talking quietly together when Eric came in. As he entered, all eyes turned toward him and stared in silence. He felt as if he had wandered uninvited into a funeral service. He quickly dismissed himself with a smile and a nod of the head, backing out of the door.

He took a little more time before entering the next tavern. He found one where both men and women entered together and from which he could hear music. It was bigger and much more brightly lit than the other had been. As he entered, he saw brilliantly colored banners on the back and one side wall welcoming visitors. The open beam ceiling had colorful glass lamps hanging from the cross joists. Eric stood briefly and looked over the numerous groups of people, studying them carefully, then moved through the room and sat at a table next to the right-hand wall. He leaned his chair back against the wall just under the welcome banner. A small musical group played against the back wall to his right, and he could see the food service area and kitchen door directly across from where he sat.

He sat alone at the table for a short time, it being one of only two empty tables in the entire tavern, before being joined by a short, fat man with bushy white hair and beard, black trousers held up by bright red suspenders over a thick white shirt, and having a very loud voice. The man was overly jolly and had an ale in each hand. "Here ya go, stranger," said the zealously friendly little man. "A little sip of this 'll put a toothy grin on yer face."

Eric didn't like short, fat, overly zealous, too friendly people, but decided that this was indeed the break he needed in order to become acquainted with these people. He had already noticed that this man seemed to know everyone in the tavern.

"Thank you very much, uh..." Eric took the ale and extended his free hand to the man while soliciting his name.

The man took hold of and shook Eric's hand so hard that his fingers throbbed, while announcing loudly, "Borem's my name," with such exuberance that it made Eric cringe. "...and yours?"

"Eric of Schrod," he answered in a pleasant but somewhat sober tone.

The extremely happy-faced little man pulled up a chair and sat down. "Well, Eric of Schrod, what brings ya to the Crossings?" he asked, trying to look sober and attentive but never losing the grin.

Eric explained in some detail that the raid on Schrod and his present desire to make the crossing to his new home.

"What's your art? Or are ya wealthy and without need of one?" Borem now sat forward to hear his answer as if in anticipation of a good story.

"I am not quite sure yet what I'll do. I don't possess any great art of power, but I am a good, strong worker. I've got enough money to tide me over for a while until my daughter and I can find work." Eric was pleased with his answer and the ease of its delivery, especially because he could sense that someone was listening who was attempting to discern by power the truth of his statement. He was certain it was the little fat man.

"Oh, that's a shame, i'tis!" said Borem with childlike disappointment, "I was hopin' you were the powerful sensor we were looking for."

Eric's stomach turned over, and he felt his face flush. "Why on earth do you need a talented sensor?"

Quite a few ears had tuned into their conversation, and several curious people strolled over to the table to listen. About this time, as other conversations ceased and people began to focus on the two of them, Borem stood and, motioning with his hands as if waving with both of them at once, said, "Don't be gettin' yer hopes up. This isn't our man."

There were several disappointed "Oh!"s from various groups of people. Some that had started to walk toward Borem and Eric stopped mid-course and returned to those they had just left, a couple others continued on and joined the small group of curious onlookers who now all crowded around the table.

Borem began to explain, "Well, you see now, Eric of Schrod..."

Eric interrupted him, "Just Eric...call me Eric."

"As you wish, Eric," he continued. "Everyone knows that somewhere in our land, maybe even in our own town, there's a person very powerful and talented in the arts... perhaps even a powermaster." There was a general agreement sounded among those listening. "We have a lady among the friends of this tavern, a lady who can sort o' tell the future of things with some fair accuracy. You see now, our lady friend told us that this very week someone came into our town who can find the powermaster and maybe convince him to come out in the open and perhaps, if possible, even wield the powersword for Pretoria."

Eric didn't trust seers, like this lady, nor did he put much confidence in their assertions, but he was very disturbed by this report. "Tell me, Borem, what sort of person is this sensor supposed to be? Then if I should run into him, I'll know to send him your way."

The little man yelled across the room, "Rennie! Rennie, come tell the stranger about the sensor."

A robust woman with curly red hair stepped out from among a group of men and women. She was wearing an apron and holding empty mugs in both hands. "I don't have time to retell my story every time you meet someone new."

"Oh doll..", he shot back with an ear-to-ear infectious grin, "just one more time and I'll tell it myself after this."

"This is the last time?... You promise?" She was clearly playing with Borem.

"Last time! I promise!" He walked toward her and took her arm as they approached Eric. "Rennie, this is Eric. Eric, Rennie."

Rennie stood for a moment quietly sizing up Eric. He felt as though she stripped his skin off and looked past his thoughts into his tightly concealed and self-controlled motives. Her welcome grin never left her lips, but her eyes were cold and piercing. She began by explaining in short fashion their need for a sensor of exceptional ability. Then she shared what her senses told her, "that someone very honest, someone very strong, someone who can be trusted had entered the town to search for the powermaster." As she finished, her gaze again met his and burned into his soul, "We just want to help this person, that's why all the commotion... everyone hopin' it might've been you." She concluded and pulled away from Borem's hold, speaking over her shoulder as she walked back to the kitchen, "Nice talkin' to you, Eric."

He watched until she disappeared through the door. Eric felt sick. He had blown a perfect chance for help. He would not likely be seen as "honest" or "trustworthy" if they discovered his art now. "Was Shahandra really right?" he thought to himself as his mind raced to assess what was taking place. "But it still seemed crazy to think of just announcing what you're all about to those you don't yet know. Besides, he really wasn't trustworthy." He laughed to himself as he realized that he could not have won in this situation.

Back at the Inn, Ingar had explained the situation to the guards, and a wagon was being fetched to take away the bodies. Shahandra had gone to her room and was lying on her bed when Ingar entered with only a brief knock to announce her presence.

Shahandra didn't sit up or say anything, but moved over away from the edge of the bed to give Ingar an obvious invitation and a place to sit. Ingar saw in Shahandra's eyes the pleading of a confused little girl.

"Child, you are one out of 100,000 in your powers and one of 10 times greater than that in your abilities. Is there more to your visit to our town than merely seeking a new home?"

Shahandra was surprised that Ingar used no sensing power on her, at least none that she could sense. "I'm on a mission to find someone."

"Find someone? Who are you looking for, child?" Ingar's words were quiet and friendly, with just a touch of controlled excitement in them.

Shahandra hesitated for a moment. Her mission was supposed to be a secret. If she told Ingar and Eric found out about it... and he surely would discover such a breach in their cover, she would be in grave trouble and possibly danger. "Ingar, if you had a secret and were supposed to keep it, but you didn't know if it was wise to keep it, how would you decide what to do?"

"Why do you ask me this question? I appear to be the one you are keeping the secret from."

"It's not just you... it's everyone... It's hard to explain with all these mixed-up feelings." Shahandra propped herself up on one elbow so she could look more squarely into Ingar's warm eyes. "I have trusted my senses since I was a little girl. My parents died a long time ago so I lived in a castle full of magicians since then."

"Brandon Keep?"

"Yes! Do you know of it?"

"Everyone who truly practices their arts knows of Brandon Keep."

"I know I can trust you to help me know what to do now. Help me think through this."

Her pleading eyes touched Ingar's maternal feelings so deeply that she wanted to take Shahandra in her arms. "I will do for you what I would wish for myself in your situation."

"I can't ask for more than that, can I?" Shahandra pulled herself up to a cross-legged sitting position and continued. "Well, what would you do if you had a secret and were supposed to keep it but didn't know if you should or not?"

"Why are you keeping the secret?"

"Fear of getting into trouble of some sort."

"Are you doing something illegal?"

"Not really... just not popular."

"Is your mission noble?"

"Yes, of course it is!"

"Is your mission fair to those you keep the secret from?"

Shahandra looked down at the bedspread and sat silently for a brief time before answering. Her words were full of personal condemnation, "Not really... it's not cruel or mean... just kind of sneaky... but it will eventually help everyone."

"You search for the power wielder, don't you?" Ingar's voice was full of unmasked compassion.

Shahandra did not move or look up but uttered a barely audible reply, "Yes...you knew, didn't you?"

"Not 'till this moment, child. Any of us would do the same if we had your ability and talent. We seek this powerful magician ourselves. Our land needs the talents of someone as powerful as this one seems to be... someone who can use so many different magics with such strength."

"What now... you must hate me... I didn't feel bad about it until now... I guess I never thought about it this way." Tears began to run down Shahandra's face, but she didn't cry aloud or even make a noise.

Ingar slid over and gave Shahandra a hug. "Child, I can sense your feelings, you aren't evil... and I don't hate you... as a matter of fact, I quite like you."

Shahandra took hold of Ingar and hung on for a long time, not saying anything, just rocking slightly. She didn't remember her mother but knew that this must be what real mothers were like. As she spoke this time, her voice broke slightly through the tears, "What do I do now... what do I do now? Eric will kill me."

"Eric will be angry, but he certainly won't hurt you, and you know it." Ingar pushed Shahandra back a little and wiped the tears from her eyes with her apron. "I think you should keep looking for the mysterious magician and do so with us."

Not fear, but shock, the kind that comes with loud noises in the dark of night, filled Shahandra. She sat staring at Ingar with her mouth open and eyes wide. Pulling herself together as the excitement of the possibility filled her, "Do you mean it? I mean, do you really want me to help? What about Eric? What do we do when we find the magician?"

"How about one thing at a time, child. Let's go for a walk. I want you to meet some people who I think are waiting anxiously to meet you."

"Meet me... I don't understand... why do they want to meet me?" Ingar stood and pulled Shahandra off the bed and wrapped her in her traveling cloak. "How do they know about me?"

"I'll explain everything as we go... just calm yourself and know that you'll be among friends." There was a warm glow in Ingar's eyes and a tone in her voice that told Shahandra to trust her.

They left the inn at a brisk pace filled with excitement. Ingar began to explain everything she could as they headed for a meeting place with some friends who shared their quest.

Borem quickly broke Eric's train of thought, picking up where Rennie stopped, "You see, many of us here tonight meet secretly together to discuss our findings and to plan new strategies to discover the person or source responsible for the great use of power we sense from time to time around about the Crossings."

Eric was trying to act interested but ignorant, while attempting not to expose the anxiousness he now felt. "What sort of power are you talking about?"

The group standing around them became noticeably quieter. Eric became aware of a lot of very serious stares. Borem was now more serious than

Eric had seen him before. "We'll only tell our information to the person described by Rennie. You don't fit that description. Ya see, I have been watching and studying people for over forty years here as a tavern keeper and have learned to tell a lot about a person by watching them. Let's take you, for instance," Borem said, leaning forward with an intensity that caused every muscle in Eric's body to tighten. "When you walked in, I could sense a tension in you that was not bashfulness nor fear of crowds. You move as a weapons master. You stopped upon entering and observed certain people as if checking for weapons, then assessed the layout of the room. Only a fighter does such things." As Borem spoke, the room became noticeably quiet. There was a sizable crowd gathering at their table. "You came in and took a chair, turning its back to the wall, and sat so that you could see the doors with your back protected. Your foot was tappin' to the music, but your eyes didn't dance... they searched and scrutinized. You are obviously a man of power, but you used none of your arts openly."

Eric gravely underestimated this jolly little socialite. Eric's thoughts raced, "It's hard enough being on a mission of this sort, but it's worse when you have to operate under close scrutiny from the residents. Now I'll surely be watched, and allies will come only with great difficulty."

"Eric of Schrod, you've tried to mislead us. We know that many powerful sensors have come to the Crossings in search of this mysterious person of power. It's safe to say that most of them are not friendly to our land. So far, those who are friendly are incompetent. Unless I missed my guess, you're much more than you would have us believe. Do you wish to set us straight on your purpose here?"

"My business is my own concern," said Eric gruffly as he stood up with his hand disappearing into a fold in his cape.

In an instant, short knives appeared in the hands of most of the men standing near him. "That's too bad, Eric," continued the now significantly more dangerous-looking little man, "We'll be forced to believe that you search for the power wielder with corrupt intent. Stand warned that he is obviously Pretorian... and if he is a true powermaster, we'll see that he remains free to wield his arts for Pretoria!"

"I repeat," said Eric in as menacing a tone as he could muster, "My business is my concern and my choices are my own, not yours. I, like these power wielders of 'YOURS', have a choice as to what I do and who I serve!" At this, he started to move to his right, but no one gave way.

"We give you this warning, Eric," said Borem, noticeably menacing himself, "Leave this area. We'll watch you and not allow you to interfere in our search."

Suddenly, Eric's hand was out with a short sword, "Then you will all disappear, one by one." The women and a few men moved back. Several men stood their ground, forming a perimeter around Eric. "I will not die easily nor alone, Borem." There was a definite challenge in his voice.

As Ingar and Shahandra approached the inn, they both sensed the conflict inside. There was so much magic in the air that it was difficult to sort out what was taking place. Ingar motioned for Shahandra to stop while she looked in. A quick glance revealed Eric holding a short sword and cornered by a group of armed men. She shut the door, "Shahandra, it's Eric, and he's surrounded... everyone's armed.

Shahandra lost no time but burst into the tavern, slamming the door against the wall with a resonant thud, "NO ERIC! NO!"

No eye turned except Eric's. He was shocked to see her and embarrassed that she was intervening for him.

Ingar followed Shahandra, shouting to Borem in a light but excited voice, "Jolly, my dear, I think I found the sensor we seek. Eric there is her traveling companion."

Eric felt all his strength drain out of him. His set-for-battle stance went limp, and his sword hand dropped to his side. Not only was he embarrassed, but he began to fill with rage against Shahandra. It was obvious that she had exposed them, but she had gone even further and apparently joined them. The child had gone too far. He determined to leave her in the hands of these mystics and find the magician on his own. He wished he could just disappear like a shadowmaster could...then they couldn't gloat over his embarrassment.

A barely noticeable signal by Borem caused the men to give way to Eric. Eric sheathed his sword before moving, a gesture he hoped would signal his willingness to leave without violence. None of the others even lowered their knives as they stepped back to make an open pathway leading directly toward the entrance. This gesture humiliated him, but from the first he felt that they had overreacted.

He walked directly to the door without stopping, not even glancing at Ingar and Shahandra as he passed them. He opened the door and paused for a moment to stare at Shahandra. His eyes were filled with anger and bitterness as he spoke, "You're on your own, girl. I release you from your partnership." He turned and left.

"He's sure to be trouble to us, Ingar," said Borem, shaking his head.

"I think he'll always be close by, and at worst, just get in the way. Thank you for trusting me, my friend." There was gratitude and tenderness in Ingar's eyes as she spoke.

"We're all in this together, Ingar. Besides, you probably saved a life or two." A lighter tone was returning to Borem's voice.

Rennie made her way through the clot of people who had moved up to see Shahandra after hearing Ingar's announcement and walked up to her sporting a broad grin. Shahandra stood wide-eyed as Rennie put her hands on her shoulders.

Suddenly, Shahandra felt her consciousness being invaded. Rennie sensed and probed her mind in the most powerful and frightening way she had ever experienced. She felt naked and exposed, as if she had been turned inside out. Fear gripped her, but she did not fight Rennie's search. Just a suddenly as it started, it was over. Before Shahandra could react, Rennie turned toward the crowd in a loud voice, "I never would've believed that the one we sought was a girl." Turning back to Shahandra, she took her by the hand and led her into the middle of the group. She glanced at Ingar and said, "Dearie, will you lock the door, please." Ingar slipped a bolt on the door into the heavy oaken jam.

Turning back again to the group, almost all of whom now wore broad smiles, Rennie said, "I would like you to meet Shahandra of Brandon Keep." There was an instant murmur of surprise and approval that shot through the crowd. "Of all we've met, she has the greatest chance of finding the power user we seek." The group broke into applause mixed with a few controlled cheers.

Shahandra's heart was pounding wildly. Her feelings warred within her. At the same time, she mourned the loss of Eric's partnership and rejoiced over the inroads thrust upon her, which now gave hope of actually finding the one she sought.

Shahandra was struck by the contrast in what she had just experienced with this group as opposed to the relationship she had maintained with

Eric. Both pushed on her through circumstance and need, both very different. She was astounded that this group felt such confidence in her character and ability, much more than she had for herself... indeed, much more than Eric had in her. Now she began to understand something Eric must know instinctively. If you do things for others and they respond to you in the same way, you could become emotionally involved with them, even become friends with them. It might become difficult or even impossible to betray such friendship if such a thing became necessary to fulfill her duty to Lord Oakbern. At that thought, she became even more disturbed. Rennie had known her name and home. She obviously knew her mission. How could Rennie be so sure she would be an ally? Even Shahandra wasn't sure how she herself would act.

Shahandra became confused. "Was this some kind of fate that brought them together? Was Rennie a mystic sensor, seeing the future? Or was this just a group of very well-practiced sensors?"

Shahandra thought it very odd that in all the years she had spent in Oakbern's castle, with magic being used for everything, these people, here in this little tavern, exercised some of the most powerful intuitive magic she had ever witnessed. Here, magic was a very real part of life. In Brandon Keep, it was a distraction from life, an attempt to avoid the difficulties and irritations of daily living.

This brought her to the realization that her magic was not simply a tool to these people. Both her's and their's were very real assets in the attempt to locate this mysterious power wielder, this power so extraordinary that it had drawn the attention of many people from far and wide and caused them to join together in a common effort to locate and secure the services of this evasive person. But more, somehow they searched her heart and mind and determined that she would help them... even though she didn't feel certain of her present convictions... but they seemed confident. This trust and their extension of friendship to her had effectively disarmed her for the present.

The differences between her relationship with Eric and this group began to avalanche upon her. They had bound themselves together as one, with a specific purpose. Each person used his arts for the benefit of everyone and toward the goal of discovering the identity of the power wielder. Pride was set aside, and preference was given to whichever member was master of the art necessary at the moment. That's why Ingar had been so animated when she told the stories of the dwarves and elves; they always operate this way.

How different this was from Brandon Keep, where there was no real purpose or union. Magic was the only glue that held the people there together. They lived to critique each other's performances as they competed with each other for dominance and prestige.

Suddenly, Shahandra realized that someone was speaking to her. She had been standing among them like a shock victim, mouth hanging open and eyes wide with no focus in them. "What? I'm sorry... this is all so different than what I... I mean.... what did you say?"

There was a roar of friendly laughter as everyone listened to her stammer.

Rennie took her arm and guided her to a table, "Sit down, dearie, you're white as a ghost." Rennie helped her into the chair. As she sat down, the others in the room gathered around her at a respectful distance, some bringing their chairs, some moving benches, while others just sat on the floor.

Borem joined Ingar and Rennie at the table with Shahandra and, turning to Rennie, "Is she safe? Are ya confident?"

Rennie smiled broadly and, looking at Shahandra, answered, "She is safe, but she'll need guidance and patience."

Borem nodded in satisfaction. "Then you'd better know a little more about us...I suppose I should leave the history for another time and explain our group as it stands now." Borem received a quick round of cheers and jesting claps, applauding his decision toward brevity.

"Ok! Ok!! We are a group that comes together through a variety of different circumstances, all pledged to find the elusive power wielder with the hope that the person would be a true powermaster and could be convinced to attempt wielding the powersword Fallonrod for the peace and protection of Pretoria."

Borem stared at Shahandra for a moment, "I understand that you were seeking the power wielder yourself, presumably with the hope that he or she could help Brandon Keep. We welcome your help and understand your desire...but you must recognize that we want the wielder to stay in Pretoria...not to work for someone else. But we all recognize that whoever the person is, the choice is ultimately their own. You may join us if you pledge to support the common goals and not to act in opposition to the majority direction."

"I agree...as long as I can at least share my hopes at the appropriate time," said Shahandra. Borem glanced at Rennie and three others in the group, all of whom gave positive nods of their head.

"It's done!" exclaimed Borem with a clap of his hands, which was followed by a volley of clapping and cheers from those gathered around them.

Shahandra felt overwhelmed by their acceptance of her for who she was and for her potential. This was so different from what had just happened when Eric rejected her as a nuisance and presumed liability to his quest. Now she was being welcomed by those who had actually sought her out and now seemed to rejoice in having her in their fellowship because they saw her heart and ability. She flushed with excitement feeling like she found a home and a family.

There was no storyteller like Borem, so he took the responsibility of filling Shahandra in on the history of the power wielder. He explained that the power had come suddenly and had grown with every new exposure. One of the men produced a rough map of Pretoria, which was dotted with sites of the power wielder's outings. Over and over, Borem would say, "and then suddenly the power sprang up in....". He told of times when they had been very close to the source when it mysteriously disappeared... without a trace. He told of times when they found the results of the magic in remote places, but on no occasion was there a distinguishable purpose to its use. Normally, it lasted only a short time before it would disappear. The user left no doubt that secrecy was intentional and anonymity was a priority. The things that could be counted on were: the timing, twice a phase; the location would always be different; the power use would not last long; and the signature was always the same, very identifiable.

One of those present added, "The magic signature is as smooth as oil on a fine honed blade. The magic seems to sing."

After Borem gave the history, Rennie took a turn. "You must be wonderin' how you fit into this picture?" She waited for a moment for Shahandra to acknowledge with the nod of her head, then continued, "During the last phase, our entire group sat together and discussed what sort of arts would be necessary in order to find and, if possible, persuade this power wielder to come out in the open. We determined that, as a group, we possessed all the arts necessary. But we needed someone who possessed several of these arts together. We put the list of essentials together and began a search. If we could successfully locate such a person and find that person to be trustworthy, the group would be complete. Together we would locate the power wielder and then it would be up to the ability of our newest member to persuade the power wielder to come public.

Apprehension began to grow in Shahandra. She realized that these people were looking to her as the final missing link in their plan... the one that would complete their combined ability to discover the source of power they sought. They expected her to personally persuade that powerful magician to become a public figure and even to attempt the most powerful sword in history. They were counting on her to convince a crafty magician of great power to be the champion of Pretoria. What about Brandon Keep? Before she could panic, Rennie reached over and took hold of her hand, "Now child, don't go cold on us. We're all in this together. No part of the team stands alone, no part is more responsible than any other We stand or fall together... succeed or fail together." Turning to the others, "The little dear must get some sleep now her insides are exhausted."

Ingar took her hand and helped her up. The group all bid a friendly good night as they parted to form a pathway to the entrance. Shahandra didn't even remember the walk back to the inn.

CHAPTER 7

When Ingar and Shahandra arrived at the Inn, Eric was gone with all his belongings. Ingar moved Shahandra into her own living quarters, a nicely decorated apartment with two bedrooms and a quaint sitting room.

For the next two days, various members of the group visited Shahandra at the Inn and explained their experiences or gave her information regarding the power wielder. For each one of them, the single greatest occurrence they had sensed and which each related, took place during the last phase, in Midharvest.

In the evening of the second day that Ingar had taken Shahandra in, several group members gathered at Ingar's Inn to share the evening meal. Among them was Borem, Rennie, and Lex, a very powerfully built metalsmith. After the meal, Borem recounted the story of that Midharvest event as clearly as they had been able to reconstruct from the evidence…

"It began with a great power disturbance which had two magic signatures, neither belonging to the 'Source', as we all call the power wielder. It continued with these two significantly different and very powerful magicians working at the same time. The most common description the sensors came up with of the incident was that "It felt like a duel". It started in the morning and continued so long that I had time to make the morning meal and eat before it abruptly ended. Everything was calm for a short period, no magical activity… then suddenly the Source's magic appeared. It continued for the rest of the day, with several arts being used over and over in various arrays. Every sensor that actively followed the progress of the incident ended up in a complete state of exhaustion.

Several members of our group had gone out in search of the Source as soon as they sensed its presence. They prepared packs of provisions ahead of time so they could leave at a moment's notice and stay out for several days if necessary. They traveled for many hours on horseback in the direction of the Falcon Mountains, sensing the power until dusk when it stopped. They spent the night on a hill overlooking a large, thickly forested ravine. The next day, they found evidence of a great battle in that very forest. The Source was not part of the battle but must have been drawn to it by the use of the magic. A search of the area turned up two bodies, one charred beyond recognition, and the other was that of an export merchant who had been in town since Midrising. He was lying some distance from the main scene with his head cut off.

While they were investigating during that day, several other groups of people arrived. One group of three wore the Castle Crest insignia on their tunics, two of them being soldiers, and the other seemed to be a scribe of some sort. They were the second of four groups to arrive. The third to arrive was a man and a boy. The boy turned out to be Dalwan, the son of a stone molder named Kindron from Burkeston, who traded frequently in the crossings. The man traveling with Dalwan was apparently a swordsman of some reputation and a friend of the family.

A fourth group arrived, four men in traveling clothes, obviously not from Pretoria. The two soldiers from Castle Crest challenged them, and the foreigners responded by drawing their weapons. Before they could engage in fighting, the swordsman joined the soldiers. He was dressed in black and drew a sword that turned bright and glowed even in the sunlight. The four foreigners withdrew immediately at a run.

We were not challenged, of course, being known because of our trade in the Crossings. Most of the traveling soldiers stop here from time to time on their frequent visits to Castle Greystone."

After the account of the incident was completed, with as accurate a description of the incident as they had, adding every detail they could think of about the area in which it took place, they decided that Shahandra should visit the battle site personally. The very next day, they set out to give her a first-hand look at the handiwork of the Source. Rennie, Borem, and Lex accompanied Ingar and Shahandra.

They left early in the morning, before daybreak, so they could reach the place by evening. The location had become well known, and there were frequent visitors from all over Pretoria and some from elsewhere. During the many days since the battle, the place had been trampled by the feet of many curious sensors and seekers. When they arrived, the sun had already slipped behind the mountain bordering the ravine. Lex and Ingar sat about making camp while Rennie and Borem took Shahandra for a quick tour. Camp was set up in the long, straight clearing, which was now covered with a velvety coat of tiny blades of emerald colored grass. Their frequent journeys had made them experts at getting quickly established. By the time the other three returned, the camp was in order and the evening meal was cooking.

They were just getting underway when Rennie and Shahandra stopped suddenly, having sensed someone probing them. It was the faintest of sensing, like a whisper in the wind... somewhere close by. Almost as suddenly, Lex and Ingar called out the name, "Lina", to the others. This was a code word for "caution". Rennie answered back, "over her dearie", which signalled that she too was aware of the danger The probing stopped instantly. It had been too faint to identify... too short to locate.

"I think it came from that direction," said Shahandra, pointing in the general direction of a group of trees and brush bordering the opening.

Instantly, Lex and Borem began moving toward the area pointed out by Shahandra. They split up and, with swords drawn, began working the border of the clearing from opposite ends of the area identified by Shahandra. Each man searched the dusk shadows carefully, tree by tree, bush by bush. As Lex approached a large tree with a thicket of tangled vines growing from its base, Dalwan came crawling out, shouting, "Don't hurt me!" He stood up with his hands held high, "I was just afraid, so I tried to sense and tell if you were friendly or dangerous...please don't hurt me!"

Rennie grabbed Shahandra's hand and pulled her toward the commotion. "It's that same boy, Dalwan!" mumbled Rennie to Shahandra with a lot of curiosity in her voice as she drew near enough to get a close look at him. "Are you alone lad?"

"As far as I know, I am," he answered with as much certainty as he could muster. He stood very still with his hands held high over his head and his eyes very wide.

Rennie was fascinated with Dalwan's appearance again in this most unlikely place. But she was even more intrigued by the fact that she could sense no fear or even anxiety in him. "You are very calm for such a young man in a threatening position."

"I sensed you... and I didn't sense anything to be afraid of... and after you used your power, I recognized you from the first time we met... remember when my friend Rhem and his glowing sword scared off the foreigners right over there," answered Dalwan, pointing without putting his hands down very far.

"Relax boy," said Borem with a chuckle. At that, Dalwan put his hands down and stepped clear of the vines. "What brings ya clear out to this place by yourself?"

"I had some time... and I sensed the power wilder before, so I wanted to visit the place again. Every time I come here, I meet new people and hear new stories about him." Dalwan was trying to sound as simple as he could. He could feel that his every word was being sensed for truth.

"Is that the only reason you are here today?" asked Lex with a piercing stare.

"Why all these questions? Everyone has the right to come here, don't they?"

Ingar spoke up in her cheerful tone. "The boy's father is known to all of us. I think we're getting a little too jumpy." Turning to Dalwan, "Come, boy, stay with us tonight, and we'll share some stories too." She had walked toward him with one arm held out, motioning for him to join her. He quickly reached back into the thicket and retrieved his own traveling bag and met her partway. She put her arm around his shoulder and guided him back to the camp.

After a very tasty meal of Rennie's secret recipe venison stew and crock pot bread, which they washed down with some of Borem's best imported elven wine, they all sat down around a comfortable campfire and began to share with Dalwan stories they had heard of this magic wielder. They shared ideas about the nature of the battle and how the "Source" fit into the picture. Dalwan was very quiet during this part of the conversation. As they all talked on and speculated, Dalwan found it more and more difficult to keep his eyes off Shahandra. She was to him the most beautiful girl he had ever seen. Her beauty wasn't just in her elven-like features, her emerald green eyes, or her wide, enchanting smile, or even her silky smooth skin; it was deeper than her looks... it was a beauty deep inside of her, something he could sense without magic. Her eyes seemed to pull him into them. Her smile embraced something deep inside him, an unfamiliar part of him that yearned to break out of its prison and run and jump and shout for joy.

Suddenly, he realized that he had been staring at her and she had become aware of it. She was sensing and probing him, and his daydreaming had caught him unguarded. He became frightened but didn't know how to react. She sensed the fear before he could bring it under rational control. Dalwan felt his face flush with embarrassment, knowing that she must have also sensed his unguarded admiration of her... his immense attraction for her. He shoved all thoughts of his identity deep down, hoping he hadn't recklessly exposed himself to her... hoping that she would sense his fear as simply connected to a hope that his feelings for her had not been clearly discernible.

At that very moment, Shahandra stood up casually and announced that she was going to take a short walk in the moonlight. Her glance shifted quickly around the circle of people until it reached Dalwan. Her eyes fastened onto his soul. With a gentle smile and a very slight movement of her head, she bid him to join her. Her invitation was so powerful that he had difficulty clearing his mind enough to decide if he was even in control of his response.

He stood, shook off the trance, and asked if he could join her. His request was met with a burst of laughter from all those present. Dalwan realized how silly his request must have looked to these people... they are all sensors in their own right... Not one of them missed the smallest part of what had transpired. He was beginning to realize how careful he must be with his thoughts and actions from that point on. For now, at least, they thought he was a simple fellow of modest talents. He promised himself to keep it that way.

Shahandra walked ahead of Dalwan out of the camp a few steps, then turned and extended her hand with a smile. "Come on, let's go." There was tenderness and playfulness mixed with a little bit of "mother" in her voice. She took firm hold of his hand and pulled him strongly along for a few steps until he caught up with and matched her quick pace. Once he was at an even stride with her, he expected her to let go of his hand, but she held on just as tightly as she had at first. His heart raced and his stomach turned over and over and over...

She led him to the upper end of the clearing and then up a barely distinguishable path, one he knew very well. Shahandra stopped right in front of a very large rock with a distinctive tree growing right out of its stone top.

"Isn't it beautiful?" she said as she let go of his hand and started to climb up toward the tree. "Come on! This looks like a wonderful place to sit and talk." She hesitated briefly, looking back through the darkness to see if Dalwan was following, then continued on when she saw him climbing after her.

As Dalwan climbed up, he wondered to himself if the anderon inside could sense their presence. He joined her on a flat spot out from under the branches of the tree and sat down next to her.

She took a deep breath and let it out slowly. "Isn't this view just magic?" Dalwan choked and coughed when she said "Magic", almost laughing out loud. He quickly regained his composure. "Are you alright?" asked Shahandra with genuine concern.

"Sure!" he quickly replied, raspily. "I just choked a little... nervous I guess!" He cleared his throat again, then added, "I like this place a lot. I've been here several times."

"Why do you come?" she asked in a casual tone.

He became aware that even though Shahandra was staring up at the stars, she was sensing him for the truth of his answer.

He decided to give her the truth of his action without the reason. "I come here because I know there was some kind of battle here... and there was a magician here that a lot of people have been looking for... some say he could be a powermaster. I figured that if I came up here from time to time, I could see who was searching for this magician, watch what they do... who knows what I might see or learn. I've met some pretty interesting people."

"Do you ever wish you were a powermaster?"

Dalwan hesitated as he perceived her sensing and probing him, waiting for an answer, but not in a deceptive or malicious way, just being inquisitive. "No, I don't wanna be a powermaster... too much responsibility... too many people would be pulling on you for help and to get favors... and look at us, out here in the middle of nowhere looking for someone who doesn't want to be found... you'd have to hide all the time." He felt confident about the persuasiveness of his answer. "How about you? Do you wish you were a powermaster?"

Dalwan sensed a flood of emotion and turmoil in Shahandra as he asked the question.

Shahandra sat very still, but her mind raced. "Yes!" she thought with powerful emotion. "Yes, and I would wield the great sword courageously and fairly... I would use my power to make a better world..." She came to herself and realized that she was just sitting transfixed and not saying anything out loud. "Oh, Dalwan, I'm sorry, I got lost in my thoughts. It's so hard to know what it would be like... I think I would... but I don't know how I would handle it... I guess it would be exciting."

"What would you do if you were... I mean, if all of a sudden you had the power?" asked Dalwan with amazing intensity.

Dalwan was so serious that it surprised Shahandra. She tried to probe his thoughts further, but was instantly shut out by him. She sat very quietly for a moment, trying to find his soul through his eyes.

"Shahandra, what would you do if you were a powermaster and you knew it for sure?"

"Why are you so serious?"

"Help me understand this mysterious power wielder who roams around doing all these strange things in secret. Why doesn't he let anyone know who he is? Would you hide? How would you act?"

She went deep inside herself for answers. Her eyes glistened in the moonlight. Her features were perfect. Dalwan had to fight back the fierce attraction he felt for her, a fascination so powerful that it could so suddenly and completely distract him. So intense were his feelings that Shahandra became aware of them even in the midst of her moment of intense introspection. Dalwan quickly turned his head away, looking intently at the moon coming up through the trees. Shahandra slipped back into herself, only briefly recognizing what had happened, then dismissing it.

As she thought to herself, she felt sure that she would "work exceptionally hard to master my power. Then I would master the sword. Once in control of the sword, I would... I would... would what?" she said out loud.

"What do you mean, 'would what?'" Dalwan asked softly, much like the whisper of friends telling secrets.

Shahandra's eyes refocused and landed on Dalwan's. She began to speak haltingly, like someone who had seen something terrible and was trying to reconstruct the event from a shock-laden mind, "First... I would...” her eyes glazed over for an instant then she recovered, “…master my power, then learn to use a sword…”she paused again as if strategizing, “…then I would get Fallonrod and... and I..."

"But why go for the sword? interrupted Dalwan. "If you were a powermaster, you wouldn't really need the sword, would you?"

She stared blankly at him for an instant, then suddenly answered with more intensity and clearer focus than he expected, "To protect it from being used by the wrong people for the wrong purposes... to keep it from being used against me!"

Dalwan had thought about the sword over and over in his mind, arguing with himself, weighing his desires and possible motives. Her answer seemed so simple-minded... so childish, "Is that it? Is that the only reason?" There was a hint of laughter in his voice. "You mean you would just want the sword so you could play keep away from the bad guys, whoever they are...not to use it yourself?"

Instantly, Shahandra was on her feet, and Dalwan followed. Her voice began to rise and break as she spoke, "YOU asked me what I'd do and why. Is this some kind of game... did you bring this up just to make fun of me?" She turned and was starting to move off the rock as she spoke. "I'm never going to be a powermaster and I..."

Dalwan caught up to her at the top edge of the rock and grabbed both of her shoulders from behind while shouting, "Shahandra, listen a minute, will you?" Suddenly, a strange power caused him to pull his hands back. She was a weirder - she could control others' instincts and was so quick that she had even caught him off guard. Before he could react mentally, his hands were free of her shoulders. Sensing no danger, only self-defense, he again touched her shoulder with only one hand and very lightly.

"Go ahead, try to explain it away," she said as she turned and faced him, pulling away about a step with a defiant look and a pain in her heart that even she didn't understand. Her posture was combative and had a sobering effect on Dalwan.

The last hint of a smile disappeared from his lips and he spoke with serious sincerity. "Don't you see Shahandra? Don't you understand why I acted the way I did? Everyone else I've ever asked that question to was ready to take the sword and kill half the world with it. They wanted to be powerful and famous and feared... but not you!" Without thinking, he stepped up to her and took her shoulders again. "You were so different... so good, it just made me laugh." At that instant, Shahandra glanced at his right hand on her shoulder. He jerked it back as if he had touched something very hot. "You want to hide this... this... dangerous toy from people who would let it shape and rule their destiny."

Shahandra just stood there staring at him with tears running down her cheeks. It had been a very long time since she had cried, and she wasn't sure why she was crying now. She had too many feelings to sort out. "You've messed up my feelings so much that I don't even know why I'm crying... and you talk like a grownup... are you always this serious?"

"I'm sorry. I was raised by my uncle in Burkeston. I didn't get away from him very often. I'm not much use to talking with girls... and I've never talked with a girl as pretty as you... I didn't even know there were girls as pretty as you." Dalwan felt very awkward. He had seldom been in a situation that was so emotionally charged, and which was his fault. He felt certain that he had done much better with the anderon than he was now doing with this girl. He brushed a tear off of Shahandra's cheek with his thumb as he continued, "Maybe I think about the sword too much. My uncle is a powerful wizard and talks about it a lot... I guess I'm infected with his fears."

"I always think about it...sometimes all day... too much, I guess." Shahandra looked into Dalwan's eyes, and the earlier tenderness returned.

"Maybe that's what this powermaster is planning to do..." said Dalwan, very animated. "Maybe you hit on it... he's gonna take the sword and disappear... and no one will even know where to look for the powersword... that's why he keeps himself so secret." A grin crept across his face, "Is that it? Are you really the powermaster?"

Dalwan was still holding Shahandra's shoulders as she reached up with both her hands and put them on Dalwan's forearms. She spoke with a sad longing, "I wish I were... Oh Dalwan, how I wish I were."

Dalwan's hands slipped off her shoulders, and they stood face to face, holding hands.

"Wouldn't it be wonderful if we could just take it away and lose it forever... no one would ever hurt anyone with it again... innocent people wouldn't get hurt over it?" Shahandra's voice trailed off as she slipped into a reflective trance.

Dalwan was drawn into her dreamlike fantasy with enthusiasm, "Then no one would have to fear that some evil powermaster who hates everyone might get hold of it and use its power to destroy and create fear."

Both stood very quietly, reflecting on the possibilities.

Suddenly, a very uneasy feeling crept over both of them at the same time. Dalwan had a clearer sense of what was happening than Shahandra. He spoke as softly as one might who was leading someone through a very dark passage, "There is danger close by, possibly at the camp. I sense a conflict... emotions and something really evil."

"We've got to get back to the camp, Dalwan, we've got to warn them." The way she spoke reminded Dalwan of his mother, always looking out for everyone else.

"Shahandra," he whispered as he led her by the hand down the face of the rock, "they'll know the danger is present. We've got to be very quiet if we hope to be of any help. Don't use your magic except your sensing, they can't pick up on that very easily, especially with as much magic as they are using now."

They began to move almost noiselessly toward the trail when suddenly two men appeared out of the thicket. Instantly, both Dalwan and Shahandra held short swords.

The largest man, a caped man with a bushy beard and hair pulled back tight against his head and hung in a ponytail, approached them empty-handed. He was a full head taller than Dalwan. He spoke very loudly, "These are but children, Dak. Doesn't it seem like bad manners for children to pull swords on guests?"

Dak was shorter than Dalwan by half a head and resembled a tall meaty dwarf. He spoke with a deep gruff voice, "Be careful Bane, you fool, the girl is powerful and very frightened."

Dak put his hands out in a feigned apology as if to try to calm down their sense of alarm. "We could not help hearing your conversation, with the air being cool and calm and all... we are looking for this mysterious power wilder just like you. Our land is being raided by a madman, and we need someone powerful to stand up to him. We're willing to pay handsomely."

Both Dalwan and Shahandra knew he was lying, but counted heavily on the others' ability to perceive this. Dalwan put his sword away and said, "I guess everyone wants a piece of him, don't they?" He walked toward Bane and glanced back at Shahandra, "Come on, they're not going to hurt us."

Shahandra was shocked by Dalwan's absolute confidence in what he said. She stood her ground, thinking to herself, "How can he believe for a moment that these guys were even remotely better than the shadow of death itself." She watched without budging as Dalwan reached out and grasped Bane's monstrous hand, "My name is Dalwan, I'm from the Crossing." He looked back over his shoulder at Shahandra.

At that moment, Dak said, "Come on now, young lady, trust your friend." There was unmistakable deception in the man's voice. "Keep your sword out if it'll make you feel safer," he finished with a smile that was lost in the shadows to all but himself.

Dak continued, "We have been traveling for quite some time to reach the place where the battle took place and where the powermaster performed his work. We arrived after the sun set tonight in this little forest, knowing that we must be close to the place we were lookin' for. That's when we saw the campfire and the horses. While our three companions went to talk with the others in your group, Bane and I decided to explore and see if there were others 'round about. We heard you talkin' just before you came off the rock." What he said was so mixed with truths and lies that it made Dalwan and Shahandra very nervous for the others at the camp.

"Let's get back to the camp, and we can talk a little more there," said Shahandra, moving ahead of the group with her sword still drawn. "How many are traveling in your group?"

"There are just five of us," answered Dak in a matter-of-fact tone that even an ungifted person could tell was a lie.

Bane and Dalwan followed Shahandra, and Dak followed them.

As they approached the camp, they saw two men seated on one side of the fire with a third man standing behind them, wrapped up completely in a traveling cape, hands and arms hidden from view. As they entered the camp, no one seemed surprised to see them. Lex and Ingar stood, one on each side of Rennie and Borem, across the fire from the strangers.

Shahandra addressed Rennie as they arrived, using a subtle magic with certain words as she spoke, "'Mother', this is Bane, and this is Dak," she said, pointing to each in turn. "They are traveling companions of the men you have already met. The 'five' of them are traveling together and are also looking for the power wielder, only they intend to 'hire' him."

As Rennie answered, "That's nice, dear..." and began to introduce the other men, Dalwan realized that Shahandra had communicated the lies that the men had told. He wondered if the guests would pick it up. They appeared to miss it.

The two seated men remained seated through the introductions. The older, tall, thin man on the right appeared to be the little group's leader. The young red-haired man seated next to him appeared to be a sensor, periodically giving signals or whispering to the leader as members of Ingar's group spoke.

Both groups were careful with questions and answers, couching their words precisely like emissaries at a round table council. Even with the great care exercised, there was sufficient mistrust brewing to make all present uncomfortable.

Borem was by far the best at sensing deception and making deductions from conversational clues. It was he who brought the situation to a head. "So tell me, if you will, why it is that you want the powermaster dead?"

Swords appeared in almost everyone's hands. The leader shouted, "Kill them!". All four of his men rushed at Borem's group. The man behind the leader pushed between his seated comrades and leapt over the fire toward Borem. As he landed blue fire shot from Ingar's fingertips, striking the man in the eyes. An instant later, Borem dropped him with a single thrust of his blade. The red-haired man had scarcely taken a step before a heavy knife, thrown by Lex, buried itself in his forehead, sending him to the ground twitching. The leader quickly retreated behind Bane and Dak, who had been moving toward Dalwan and Shahandra, but halted about four paces away. Everyone had stopped moving except Dalwan, who stepped between the three men and Shahandra with his sword on guard. Very suddenly, a cord wrapped around his sword, and it was gone and lying at Bane's feet. At that same instant, an arrow zipped out of the darkness from the edge of the clearing and found its mark in Lex's left shoulder.

The momentary distraction gave Dak enough time to bound toward Dalwan and grab him, putting a knife to his throat. "Back off or I'll kill the boy!"

Dalwan looked at Borem and said, "It's OK Dad, I'll be alright. Just do what they say."

As this took place, Ingar slipped into the shadows and out of the camp. The thin man realized this and said, "Woman - Ingar, show yourself or the boy dies."

There was a small flash of light and the short scream of a man out in the darkness. He sounded as if he had died of a terrifying pain.

The leader was now next to Dalwan with his own knife next to the boy's throat. "Show yourself now, or he dies." Bane stood about two strides away, facing Borem and swinging a bolo over his head.

A dark form appeared at the edge of the clearing and walked into the light. She smiled as she approached the men, stopping a safe distance away. If you so much as hurt the boy, she said in a tone that gave Dalwan the shivers, "you will all die as your friend did."

"No one moves," said the tall, thin man as the three of them backed out of the light and into the darkness. "If I even feel threatened, I'll kill him... I won't die alone... do you hear me?" The man broke out in a mocking laugh, but terror filled his voice.

Rennie sensed Shahandra's intentions to follow and attempt a rescue, so she moved next to her as the men drifted from sight. Shahandra started to follow as soon as she heard the men turn and run, but Rennie grabbed her. "We need you here now. Lex is bleeding badly, and we need you to tend him."

Shahandra hesitated, then turned to see Borem kneeling over Lex. His entire tunic was blood-soaked. She looked at Rennie with amazement while moving toward Lex, "How did you know I could heal?"

"Why, dearie, you told me in the tavern," she said with an infectious laugh.

Shahandra was still thinking about Rennie's ability when she reached Lex. He had apparently torn the arrow out himself while no one was looking and had made the wound much worse than it had originally been. The arrow has a slightly spiral tip. The tear was horrible and made Shahandra queasy as she began to cut away the shirt over the wound. "Let me see the arrow." She took it and was able to tell how deep the wound was from the blood stains on it and what damage she might expect inside his arm. She placed her hands directly on the wound and began to whisper, softly and methodically. After a very long time of concentration, there was barely a scar present where the wound had been.

"I can't be sure it won't give you trouble later," said Shahandra, sounding like a mother as she wiped the dried blood off his arm, "or maybe even bleed a little inside. Take care of it and move easily for a while." She got up and moved back a step. "Does it hurt very much?"

Lex was weak and felt dizzy, so he quickly abandoned his attempt to stand. He tried to move it and gave a groan that told everyone that it still hurt. Shahandra knelt back down and began to work her magic again. This time she took even longer, testing the arm over and over, trying to work the pain out. Finally, it stopped very suddenly and very completely.

"You've done it, little lady... thanks!" said Lex in a baritone whisper.

As Shahandra got back up, she noticed Ingar and Borem standing at the edge of the camp, their keen sensing powers cutting away the darkness... something in Dalwan's confidence had persuaded them that he would indeed be 'OK'.

CHAPTER 8

As soon as the three men, with Dalwan in tow, reached the other side of the clearing, they went south about 200 paces, being led through the darkness by their leader, the tall, thin man. After they were completely out of sight from the camp, the leader held his right hand up, and a ball of yellow flame appeared in it, which he used as light with which to guide them. This amazed Dalwan because the man had not used his fire in the fight at the camp.

Dalwan remembered Shaylan telling him that fire was one of the most difficult arts to develop without getting hurt by it. "Some just never learn to control it!" Shaylan would say, shaking his head in disgust. "Maybe," Dalwan thought to himself, "this man never learned to use it well and just held the art loosely." He would at least have to be cautious if he had to confront him. A slap in the face from a tree branch released by Dak brought Dalwan painfully back to his present situation.

He used the incident to begin to slow down, playing the "injured and awkward" game with Bane. This forced Bane to work harder to hold on to Dalwan and to fall a little behind with every step. Dalwan knew that if he could get loose from Bane's powerful grip, he would be able to easily outrun them all. By the time they reached a small clearing about thirty running strides across, Bane was noticeably tiring. As he and Dalwan entered the clearing, the leader and Dak were leaving it on the other side. About half way through it Bane shouted for the others to wait up. Dalwan used the distraction of Bane's irritation with his comrades to break free. He turned and ran toward the path from which they had just come. He was almost to the edge of the clearing when he felt a cord wrap around his legs from both sides, followed instantly by the punishing blows of the bolo balls attached to it. Dalwan fell with tremendous force, hurting both of his wrists and arms.

He lay agonizing for only a short time before Bane stood over him, "I almost killed you with your own sword, boy... and I would have gladly, except you may be useful to us alive." Bane reached down and grabbed one of the bolo balls and gave it a hard upward jerk. The cords cut into Dalwan's legs, causing him to yell out in pain. "Next time, you die, boy!" said Bane as he unwrapped the cords roughly from Dalwan's legs.

At that moment, the other two men entered the clearing from the other side, leading horses toward them. As they approached, Bane yelled angrily toward them, "Mallon! Why are we running?"

"Because they are not just another group of sightseers. There was power there that, if used together, could challenge the powermaster himself. If we had fought them, every one of us would be dead."

"Some of them would be too!" shouted Bane back, still irritated.

"And what would you be fighting and dying for... because they found out our motives... because they might go tell someone? There is no one they could tell who'd be more dangerous than them... and all they wanted to do was to stop us from hunting the powermaster." Mallon stood staring at Bane as Bane tried to sort out what he had said. "You still don't understand, do you? If you're going to die for something, die for something better than a 'good fight' or your stupid pride."

Dalwan just lay in the grass while Bane and Mallon shouted at each other. As Mallon finished insulting him, Bane reached down and jerked Dalwan up by the tunic. He then grabbed the reins of one of the horses and commanded Dalwan to mount it. Dalwan was sure his legs were cut from the bolo cord because he could feel the wet sticky blood on his pant legs. His wrists throbbed as he pulled himself up onto the horse.

As he sat on the horse, the three men talked in whispered tones. He heard both Dak and Bane argue to kill him, with Bane finishing, "He's more trouble than he's worth, what do we need him for now?"

"Just wait until we are out of these woods and we can be sure we aren't being followed," said Mallon in a harsh whisper. "I tell you both, the people we met are among the most dangerous I have ever encountered... I can't believe they won't follow us... if they do, the boy will be good insurance."

"If they're that dangerous," said Dak, "let's ambush them."

"Where were you a little while ago?... didn't we try that... aren't we missing a few companions?" Mallon's eyes flashed in the light of the fire he held high in his hand. Both men looked at each other, then turned to mount their horses without another word.

As they mounted, Dak shouted to Mallon, "What if the boy gives us away? What if he signals them somehow?"

"Can't you persuade him to cooperate?" said Mallon with a laugh.

"Why don't you persuade him, Mallon?" There was defiance in Dak's voice, but Dalwan sensed fear in him. He rode up to Dalwan's horse and looked him square in the eyes, "I say, kill him now or let him go, but don't take him with us."

"If he uses magic to signal them or gives you any more trouble, you can kill him. OK?" shouted Mallon, obviously playing with Dak.

"If anyone gets to kill him...I DO!" shouted Bane as he looked with contempt at Dak. "If I have to pull him through the forest, and capture him when he tries to escape and tie his horse to mine... I GET TO KILL HIM!"

Mallon sat still on his horse, obviously sensing the area. "We have no pursuers," he said as he rode over to Dalwan. "If you so much as move wrong, I'll kill you myself." He sensed Dalwan for a moment, "You are a fool not to fear me, boy!" he said with such intensity that both Dak and Bane held their breath.

At that, Mallon rode off at a gallop with Bane pulling Dalwan and Dak bringing up the rear, mumbling curses as he rode. They soon slowed to a steady walk through the woods. Mallon lit the way through those thickly forested areas where the trees blocked out the moonlight.

It was beginning to get light, and Dalwan's wrists and legs were now very sore. He began to attempt to heal them himself, using only the slightest whisper of magic so as not to attract attention. Only once before had he attempted to heal himself of an injury like the one he now had in his wrist, and it had taken a long time for him to get it right. Now he had to work with slight enough power so that even if one of the men sensed him, they could not identify his power print. They would only be able to tell that he was the one using magic.

He had only just begun when Mallon suddenly straightened and tensed up. Only an instant later, he wheeled around and shouted, "What are you doing, boy?"

"I'm fixing my hurt wrist."

"Stop or I'll kill you this instant." Mallon's sword was in his hand, and he was riding back toward Dalwan. Bane and Dak stopped and stared expectantly.

With one last tiny pulse of power, he stopped. "What's the harm to you if I stop my pain?"

"And draw attention to our location... I'm not a stupid boy." Mallon sat a moment, he was sensing again. "There is someone searching for us... not one of the other group. Let's make camp here in this clearing and invite them to breakfast." He looked intently into Dalwan's eyes and pointed his sword at his face in warning without saying a word, then sheathed it and dismounted his horse.

They set up camp, and Mallon made a small fire by casting fire into a hastily gathered pile of twigs and dry leaves. It burned violently for an instant, then dwindled into a small campfire.

Dak kept watch perched high in an oak tree that overlooked the camp. He blended in very well. He took a long bow with him and several long, thin knives.

Bane tied Dalwan's hands behind his back and then secured them with another piece of rope to a small tree. He left enough loose rope so that Dalwan could lie down on his side. He then tied Dalwan's feet to the tree in a similar fashion.

With a stern look and a tone of voice that was anything but friendly, Bane said, "Sleep boy... get rested so you won't give me trouble later on and make me kill you."

Dalwan's legs still hurt from the bolo injury, and he wanted to bring them relief but knew that any use of magic would end up forcing him into mortal battle. He was sure it would come to that sooner or later, but had two things mitigating for later rather than sooner. First, he had never knowingly or deliberately killed anyone. Secondly, he felt a compelling need to know more about these men. Who were they? What was their reason for coming to Pretoria? Why did they run so far away from the area where they kidnapped him? And most importantly, if their purpose truly was as Borem suggested, to kill the power master, how did they plan to accomplish it?

He knew he would have to fight for his life unless something truly strange happened. As he considered what kind of men he was dealing with, he decided that he was ready to kill if necessary. Whatever the case, the wait would be worth the while. He decided to sleep. It came easily in spite of his discomfort and the morning chill.

When he awoke, it was fully light. Bane and Dak were both asleep. He felt a deep chill in his bones. His right side was damp from the dew, and his left side was numb. His neck was sore and stiff as he raised up slightly to assess the situation. He tried to maneuver into a sitting position but found that impossible, especially with his left arm and leg completely incapacitated.

As he lay still looking around, he couldn't see or hear Mallon. He became aware of a presence very near him, a very evil presence. He looked around quickly, trying not to look panicked or draw unnecessary attention to himself.

Suddenly, Mallon appeared out of thin air, standing only about on stride from his head. "So, boy, you can sense too?!" The air was filled with malice. "You can heal and you can sense," Mallon crouched down and whispered tauntingly, "What else does our mystery boy do?"

At that moment, both men became aware of another presence. Someone sensing, probing... silently announcing his presence.

With a nasty sneer, Mallon said, "I'll deal with you later, boy. Right now we have to welcome our visitor." Mallon stood and took about three steps toward Bane and Dak, then disappeared. He heard Mallon kick Bane and shout at Dak. Both men were amazingly quick to rise. Both came up with swords in hand, looking around.

Mallon spoke from a point directly next to Bane, "Are you awake now?"

It made Bane jump and Dak laugh. Bane cursed Mallon, "I hate it when you do that...someday..." there was violence in Bane's voice.

"Someday? Someday you'll get yourself killed, fool!" answered the seemingly vacant space now directly in front of him. "Now get ready, you two, there's a visitor coming, and when you see who it is you'll want to make him feel especially welcome."

"You do your part and we'll do ours," shot back Dak as he put away his sword while heading to the now smoldering fire. Dak and Bane rekindled to full flame while Mallon stayed invisible.

After a short time, a black caped man appeared at the edge of the camp area. "Where is Mallon?" asked the man with a raspy voice. The man appeared to scan the camp area, coming to rest on a spot under the tree that Dak had been in earlier. Mallon appeared standing at its base.

"What do you want, Shaner?" Mallon walked toward the man with purpose in his step. "Bane, Dak...you remember Shaner, he's one of Danlion's personal attendants." There was marked distaste in his tone.

At the name "Lord Danlion," Dalwan gasped.

"That's right, boy, the legend lives!" Mallon laughed at the surprised look on Dalwan's face.

"Where are the other three, Mallon? Danlion has sent me to retrieve you and the Whiz for another project."

"Whiz is dead, as are Lark and Sam. We've had a setback." Mallon tried to hide the embarrassment he felt from Shaner.

"And who is this Mallon, the powermaster, hog-tied to a tree with magic ropes!" Shaner's laugh was louder and more taunting than even Mallon's had been. Mallon did not like being taunted.

"He's just a boy we borrowed as insurance for safe passage."

"A hostage!" His laughter was almost hoarse by now..."Mallon had to take a hostage..."

As this talk went on, Dalwan took advantage of the distraction to begin loosening the ropes that bound him. His magic caused the cords to begin separating and unwrapping from his feet and hands... slowly... one at a time. As the men continued to exchange meaningless insults in the midst of Mallon's attempt to explain his present circumstances, Dalwan finished loosening the ropes and began to bring his numb side back to life.

By this time, Bane had walked over to Shaner and grabbed him by the cloak, "If you've got some orders for us, GIVE 'EM. If not, GET OUT OF OUR CAMP!"

"The orders are for the Whiz and Mallon. You can come or not as you wish. I suggest you come through. I sensed that you are being followed by an angry old woman." His grin was infuriating, and he seemed undaunted by Bane's rough treatment. "If you stay, she might kill the rest of you!" Shaner continued chuckling to himself as Bane lifted him off the ground.

Mallon walked over to Shaner, now firmly suspended in mid-air and still bearing a hideous grin. "Put Shaner down before he breaths on you and gives you some vile disease," he said with near hatred in his voice. Bane drooped him with a bit of a shove backwards. Shaner landed much more gracefully than any of them expected.

"Now Shaner, what does Lord Danlion want of us?"

"He's planning to make Brandon Keep his home," answered Shaner in a very haughty tone. "From there, he plans to launch an attack against Castle Crest and secure the sword Fallonrod. After that, it won't matter one way or another whether the powermaster lives or not." Shaner's grin was even more taunting than it had been before. "Then your whole little expedition will have been for nothing."

Bane hit Shaner in the stomach with a quick undercut. Shaner absorbed the blow without losing his composure.

"Bane, I shall look forward to killing you later," he said with only minor distress in his voice. "But for now we must be on our way to meet with Lord Danlion." His calm, cool manner was unnerving, and his grin remained infuriating.

"Shaner, we've lost three companions, all of whom we liked. You need to remember that when you taunt us. We might forget your exalted position and just rip your face off and spit in it." Mallon was as cold as ice when he spoke. The hint of a smile touched his lips.

Shaner's smile diminished, and he replied with noticeably less antagonism, "We need to be on our way. I assume all three of you are coming." He paused to look at each man for some sign of agreement. Receiving some observable positive indication, he continued, "We must get going if we're to meet Lord Danlion at the rendezvous."

Shaner looked over at Dalwan and back at Mallon, "I doubt he will be of any further use to you. Our path is northward."

Mallon glanced at Dak and laughed, then motioned to Bane with a jerk of his head toward Dalwan while running his index finger across his throat in a slashing motion. Dak spat at Mallon's feet as Bane turned toward Dalwan. Bane had a faint smile on his face as he walked toward him.

Dalwan's heart was pounding wildly, but his head was amazingly clear. His wait had paid off; he knew what they were about and a rough sketch of Lord Danlion's plan. He knew this would be his moment of truth. He had both dreaded it and courted it. He was angry that it would come when he was outnumbered four to one, and at that, by magic-wielding fighting men and mercenaries. He had to act now, without a clear plan, and trust his instincts.

Bane started to kneel down next to Dalwan's head with a skinning knife in his hand and a squint-eyed, mean-spirited grin on his face. Dalwan had filled his right hand with dirt as Bane approached. He hit Bane in the eyes with the dirt as he rolled quickly out of his reach. Bane cursed loudly, drawing the attention of the other three. Dalwan had taken a knife out of the back of Bane's belt and only narrowly missed being slashed across his chest by a blind swing from Bane. Dak now ran toward them with a short sword in his hand. The other two just stood watching. He had hoped to draw them all closer, but it had not worked, so he ran toward the trees away from Dak's approach. His legs were still sore from the bolo injury, causing him to hobble much like limping on both legs. Dak closed in on him as he neared the trees at the edge of the clearing. Sensing that Dak had almost reached him, he dropped suddenly and rolled with his knife held up to block Dak's inevitable thrust at him. Dak was too close behind him to stop, so he went directly over him. In outmaneuvering Dak, Dalwan managed to fend off his awkward swordsmanship and send him rolling on the ground with a painful leg wound. This sight brought laughter from the two observers who appeared to be enjoying the fight.

As Dalwan regained his feet, Bane was closing in quickly, still blinking dirt out of his eyes. Dalwan found himself between Bane and Dak. He adjusted his position with a feigned a stumble so as to facilitate and necessitate his only escape route being toward Mallon and Shaner.

Meanwhile, Shaner had taken to taunting Bane and Dak, who "together couldn't kill a village boy" and, "…who need to get going because their woman pursuer was getting closer." Mallon had been laughing but now grew annoyed with Shaner's harassment.

Dalwan ran several paces toward the stationary men while looking back at Bane. He then faced forward and appeared to see Mallon and Shaner for the first time. Dalwan adjusted his path away from the two men at an angle between them and Bane, hoping to draw them all together, if the other men would move to cut him off. It worked.

Mallon, now thoroughly agitated at Shaner's verbal abuse, reached out and gave Shaner a powerful shove in the direction necessary to cut off Dalwan's escape. "Enough of this show! Let's get this over with and get going."

Both men began to jog so they could intercept Dalwan. At the same instant, they both disappeared. He had not considered that possibility. He ran a couple of steps farther and then threw the knife toward the place he thought they would end up. His judgement was good and his aim was perfect. An invisible sword knocked the knife from its course.

Dalwan instantly lit the entire area in front of him with the most intense fire he could muster. One figure burst into flame with a scream. A second leapt sideways, burned but not down.

He stopped instantly and turned to see Bane throwing the bolo toward him from about 5 long strides. No sooner had the bolo left Bane's hand than fire leapt from Dalwan's left hand, incinerating the cords that bound the heavy balls. His right hand let go with the largest green flame curtain he had ever thrown. It completely obscured his view of Bane, pounding into him so hard that it lifted him off the ground and slammed him into a tree across the clearing, another 10 paces further. He grabbed the only bolo ball that wasn't swept away with the green flame, as it rolled past him. Dak had stopped at the first sight of fire and now turned and ran back in the direction he had come from. Dalwan quickly took the ball in his right hand and lit it as he threw it at Dak. It left Dalwan's hand engulfed in a brilliant blast of flame, which appeared to accelerate it as it moved toward the quickly retreating Dak. It hit him in the small of the back and burned through him without stopping. Dak fell motionless on his face.

Sensing danger, Dalwan disappeared and dropped instinctively to his face. A small, gleaming ball appeared out of nowhere and sliced the air where his head had been. Again, Dalwan spread fire across the area from which the flame had come. He missed!

He jumped quickly to his feet and moved a few paces, trying to gather concentration. It was very difficult to remain invisible and throw fire at the same time. He released the fire powers and began to sense the area from movement. Suddenly, a small fireball came directly at him from the center of the clearing. He shielded himself with his arm, from which he threw a green flame curtain. It was weak because of the haste in changing powers. The fireball was partially dissipated by the curtain but still broke through, and hit him on the left shoulder, where it exploded, singeing his clothing and giving him a flash burn on the face. He was momentarily visible. He held the protective green flame curtain and strengthened it. He then turned the curtain into a flying wall. It made a loud noise like a gale-forced wind as it rushed toward the spot where his assailant had stood only an instant before. It rushed through the clearing and hit a small tree, where it burst into pieces as it ripped bark off the trunk and showered the ground with leaves and twigs.

He quickly changed positions, moving to within a stride of the smoldering corpse he identified as Shaner. As he moved, Mallon appeared at the edge of the clearing near the place where Dak lay face down. Dalwan was using his sensing powers as keenly as he was able. He realized that what he was seeing was not Mallon but his image. He also knew that Mallon would be using all the concentration he possessed to remain invisible and project the image at the same time. His sensing powers would be hampered and ineffectual.

Still invisible, Dalwan moved quickly to the place where the image stood and took a position in the middle of it. It then took him only a short time to locate Mallon by sensing. He knew that to sense his presence, Mallon would have to let the image vanish.

It didn't take Mallon long to realize that his illusion had failed. The instant that let go of it, Dalwan shot white fire directly at him from the midst of the vanishing image. The air itself seemed to explode as the blinding light of the fire entered the invisible body. It was the most disgusting thing Dalwan had ever witnessed. Mallon's body was blown into a shower of burning, sizzling fragments.

Suddenly, Dalwan was overcome by the sight, which was now accompanied by his awareness of the smell of Shaner's still smoldering body. His stomach convulsed, and he fell to his knees, retching. After a brief spell of dry heaves, he put his forehead on the ground in front of his knees, and with arms wrapped around himself. Dalwan began to sob.

His body began to shake violently, with every muscle tensing and cramping. He remained in the same position, periodically rocking back and forth as he sobbed. He was glad to be alive, but there was no pride in what he had done. Victory was not sweet, even against the likes of these men.

As his stomach stopped turning over and his nerves calmed, Dalwan got up and looked around. He was still lightheaded and noticed that his face had a burning sensation, like a bad sunburn. Small flames burned here and there in the dew-dampened brush and grass. His eyes came to rest on Bane, who sat motionless in an upright position against a tree. Blood had run out of his mouth, nose, and ears. His face looked bruised. Dalwan began to wander around the camp without any discernible pattern, putting out the small fires that continued burning and smoldering. He finished next to the tree whose bark had been blown off by the green flame curtain. He stood motionless for an extended time, staring at beads of sap that oozed from the freshly exposed splintered wood.

He went back to the tree under which the supplies sat and began to pick through the charred remains. Virtually everything had been touched by fire. He found some bread and jerky that were still edible and began to pick at them.

As he sat eating and sipping water from a blackened skin, he began to consciously survey the damage done in and around the little clearing. The little wisps of smoke trailing upward here and there began to dissipate in the gentle breeze that was arising. It blew the smells of the fire and burned flesh away from him. This experience was all he thought it would be, and exactly why he didn't want to be known as a powermaster. How many more people were there who would seek his services? They would court him and lavish him with gifts so that he would kill and destroy for them.

As he glanced at the scattered remains of Mallon, he was overcome with the enormity of what had happened. The powerful impact of the green flame curtains he had twice thrown again astonished him. And the bright white fire... where had that come from?... he had never even made white fire... it was the single most destructive magic he had ever used.

He went deeper into himself as he contemplated the ramifications of the fight. "If I did all this to these powerful men," he thought in a whirlpool of emotion, "what would I be able to do with the sword?" His mind went wild with visions of castle walls vaporizing before him and armies vanishing at the point of his blazing sword... evil, arrogant wizards turning to ash, totally dismayed in their last conscious moment...

He shook himself out of the enticing trance. All that he feared most was encompassed in that horrible vision of unlimited power. Indeed, would he own the sword or the sword own him? "What if," he thought, again drifting into daydream, "I could use the sword in a fantastic and terrifying display of power that would force men to quit fighting or suffer the consequences... quit fighting or...or..." he glanced around the camp again at the battle remains coming finally to rest on Mallon's dismantled-beyond-recognition body, "...or perish in ash!?" He was filled with a deep despair, an inward aching that nothing seemed to quench. This was too much responsibility, too many decisions, too much at stake.

As Dalwan sat thinking over these matters for quite some time, he became aware that he was being watched. He felt Shahandra's presence and someone else he could not identify.

"It's safe, you can come in," said Dalwan in a loud but strikingly monotone voice.

A moment later, Ingar and Shahandra entered the clearing from the same place Shaner had. They stopped as soon as they cleared the tree line and surveyed the area, both with a sense of astonishment that each face mirrored in its own peculiar fashion.

"Dalwan, did you do this?" Shahandra's voice had a quiver in it as she spoke.

"The powermaster was here Shahandra," he still sounded devoid of emotion, although his voice was clear and distinct. "He saved my life."

"Are you hurt, Dalwan?" Ingar moved to his side and examined the burned area of his face. She then took a cloth from a pocket inside her cape and wet it from the skin Dalwan still held. She began to wipe carefully around the injured area.

Dalwan winced as the now mildly blistering skin was touched.

She stroked the singed hair on the side of his head with the rag as if dusting it, "You said that the powermaster was here. Did you see him?" She was testing him with a very gentle but direct sensing.

"You had to have sensed his presence... you already know he was here... why are you testing me?" Dalwan gently pushed her hand away in a pouting gesture. "Leave me alone if all you're gonna do is test me."

"OK...OK... I promise! No more tests. I just wondered why he would do all this and then simply disappear?" She wiped his face again and examined his burns closely.

Dalwan did not resist. He felt a strong need for her tenderness now. "He doesn't want anyone knowing who he is."

"Well, that is certainly true to his form up to now, isn't it?" said Ingar as she turned to find out where Shahandra was. "Shahandra, take a look at these burns. Can you help him?"

Shahandra had wandered over to where Dak lay and was staring with her mouth hanging open at the massive hole burned through him. She did not respond to Ingar's request.

Ingar saw what was happening and called a little louder, "Shahandra." Her head snapped around and stopped, looking directly at Ingar. Her face was white as snow and her mouth still hung open. "Shahandra dear, come help Dalwan. He needs you now."

At that, Shahandra's mouth closed, and she began to walk toward Dalwan and Ingar. Her color returned, and she became a little more focused as she approached them.

"You'd better sit down too, dearie," said Ingar, who stood to take her hand as she approached. Dalwan sensed that Ingar had used some kind of healing art on Shahandra as she helped her sit down. After a few moments, Shahandra seemed to feel better.

"You heal him, Ingar. You can do it so much better than I can. Besides, I don't trust myself right now." Her deep green eyes pleaded with Ingar.

"Shahandra, Dalwan needs more than physical healing right now." She took Dalwan's hand and put it in Shahandra's, then got up and walked back in the direction from which they had entered the clearing.

Dalwan flushed with embarrassment. He started to pull back his hand, but Shahandra held on.

"It's OK, Dalwan. I really do want to help... I just feel so...so..."

"Numb?"

"Yes...numb...I feel like you sound."

That brought a brief, slight laugh from Shahandra and a faint hint of a smile to Dalwan.

Shahandra began to touch Dalwan's face ever so softly. As she did, she sang in delicate, low tones. The heat began to leave his face, being replaced by a soothing cool feeling. The blurring and sting in his eye were relieved as if lifted off by invisible fingers. She touched his forehead with two fingers of each hand

and, after a moment, said, "You are injured somewhere else. Where?" Her face was full of compassion, and he sensed true concern.

He pulled up his pant legs, revealing horizontal rope burns and several bruises. She immediately began to work again. Her musical voice calmed his spirit as her songs filled his head.

"I can't make your hair grow back now, I don't do well with that yet." There was a sincere apology in her voice.

"Don't worry about it... it'll grow back... thanks for helping me."

"How do you feel now...I mean...are you still scared?"

"They were going to kill me, Shahandra... he was coming to slit my throat." Tears welled up in his eyes as he spoke, and his voice cracked as he tried to fight back the urge to cry.

Ingar led three horses into the clearing as Dalwan and Shahandra spoke. She tied them to a tree and returned to kneel down next to Dalwan. "What were these men about? Did you hear their plans, or did they tell you what they wanted?"

"They are from Danlion's camp."

Both Ingar and Shahandra showed signs of shock on their face. Ingar put her hand on his shoulder and looked searchingly into his eyes. "Are you sure, Dalwan? Maybe this was some kind of trick..."

"Ingar!..." he cut her off mid-sentence, "...they talked openly... they were going to kill me... they didn't care what I saw or heard..." tears again filled his eyes.

"OK...OK..." Ingar stroked his back with her hand. "I believe you. We both do," she said, looking at Shahandra for agreement. She nodded.

"Danlion is planning to make Brandon Keep his home, then attack Castle Crest and secure the sword so no one else can use it against him."

Shahandra felt as if she had been hit by a hammer blow. Her head spun. I've got to warn Lord Oakbern so he can be prepared," she said, looking for support from Ingar. She felt overwhelmed, and her eyes filled with tears. She needed Eric now. She didn't want to try the trip on her own and knew that her new friends would be pledging their support and arts to the defense of Pretoria. This was the first time she had ever questioned the wisdom of the Oakberns in their refusal to make an alliance with Pretoria. If they had, help could be expected. Now, however, they would be on their own. If

Danlion could actually capture Brandon Keep it would give him a power base to work from and a degree of legitimacy that would attract small power-hungry kingdoms into alliance. She remembered hearing Lord Oakbern suggest such things about other castles. She concluded that she would do whatever it took to warn Lord Oakbern, even if it meant traveling alone..."But..." she thought to herself, "...it sure would be perfect if the powermaster would go with her."

"Dalwan," her green eyes pierced his soul, "Do you think the powermaster would help us... I mean... Lord Oakbern?"

Before he could answer, Ingar asked him point-blank, "Dalwan, do you know the power wielder?"

"Yes, Ingar, I know who he is now." He stood up and walked a few paces before turning around to address them further. "He knows everything that Danlion is going to try and I'm sure he plans to do something on his own... or maybe with a few friends... who knows. But I don't think he'll expose himself just yet."

"I hate it..." exploded Shahandra with tears running down her face. "I just hate it that all those fighter types think they have to hide their identity... always being secretive and sneaking around... disappearing before anyone sees them." She turned and shouted in the direction of the trees, "I think you're a coward...I think you'd better stay hidden...you...you..." her tears choked her words so much that she had to stop.

"Coward?..." shouted Dalwan, "...COWARD? Look around you... look at these men... they were mercenaries of some reputation."

You should have seen them fight. He took on all four of them and saved my life! That's not a coward!" Dalwan's intensity startled both of his companions.

"Then why does he hide?... even from us, he hides." Ingar's frustration showed in the wrinkles on her brow. Never before had she been so close... so very close and yet still didn't get to talk with him... to reason with him...

"Maybe he feels that he can move about more freely as an unknown. Maybe the element of surprise will help him do what he has to do." Dalwan walked over to Shahandra, reached out, and touched her shoulder as he spoke. "I'm sure he'll let everyone know who he is soon enough. But for now, everyone will have to wait."

A sense of deep loss settled in on both Ingar and Shahandra. No one spoke for a few long moments. Ingar silently stood up and joined the others. Dalwan still stood with his hand on Shahandra's shoulder.

Dalwan broke the silence, "Will you search for your friend, eh?..."

"Eric."

"Yes, Eric?"

"If Eric were anywhere close, he would find us. He's one of the best sensors anywhere. What happened here today will attract a lot of attention." Shahandra made the mistake of looking back around at the battle scene. The sun was now warming the air, and flies were beginning to swarm on what was left of Mallon. Her stomach gave a violent heave. Both Ingar and Dalwan took hold of opposite arms and led her out of the clearing to an area behind some bushes, out of sight of the battle remains.

Dalwan went back over to the area where Bane had piled the things he had removed from the horses earlier. He sorted through them and found his sword. He slipped it back in its scabbard as he turned to head back to Shahandra and Ingar. He had only taken a few steps when a man appeared at the precise place where Shahandra and Ingar had entered the clearing.

"If you're looking for the powermaster, you won't find him here," said Dalwan loudly enough to alert the others to the man's presence.

"May I ask what happened here and what part you played in this?" the man asked politely but with more than passing interest.

Upon hearing the voice of the newcomer, Shahandra yelled, "Eric! Oh Eric. We've got terrible news!" She was now running towards him from the bushes and talking as fast as she was running. "Danlion is alive and he's planning to make Brandon Keep his home base..."

Eric grabbed her by both shoulders and shook her once, "Shahandra!" his voice overflowed with command. "Slow down!"

Shahandra took a deep breath and started again. "Danlion is still alive!" She paused and stared at Eric, waiting for a response.

Eric prodded her on with a nod of his head, "Go on...just talk slowly."

"Danlion is planning to capture Brandon Keep and make it his home base." She fought back tears as she spoke. "Then he plans to take Castle Crest and secure the power sword Falonrod so that no powermaster can ever use it against him."

"How did you come by this information?"

"These dead men were talking about it when the powermaster destroyed them. Dalwan heard the whole thing. Just as they were going to kill him, the powermaster himself showed up and saved him."

"And then just disappeared?"

Shahandra looked toward Dalwan for help.

"He saved my life. The only reason he even got involved was to save my life."

"Why, you boy?" Eric asked in a decidedly sinister tone. This was the break he had been waiting for. His spirit swelled with anticipation, and his voice filled with demand, "Do you know him?"

He moved past Ingar, a step closer to Dalwan, his eyes narrowing to a slit.

Before Dalwan could answer, Ingar reached out and touched Eric's shoulder and moved toward him as if to whisper something in his ear. He leaned sideways to listen without losing eye contact with Dalwan. She cupped her hand to shield her words from Dalwan, and as she touched the side of his head, he fell over unconscious.

Shahandra's eyes fill with terror. Ingar reacted quickly, raising her hand in a calming gesture and speaking softly, "He's only asleep, dear. Let him sleep a couple of hours before you wake him. I sensed, as I'm sure you did, that he was going to harm Dalwan to get what he wanted. Convince him not to follow us. He'll be very susceptible to your suggestions while he's sleeping." Ingar finished with a wink and a smile. "You must give us plenty of time to get away." Ingar went back to the horses, which were tied at the edge of the clearing, took the supplies off one of them, and brought them to Shahandra. "These should get you and Eric to a place where you can buy what you need. Good luck, dear. And know that my home is always open to you. But next time, bring along better company." When she finished, she gave Shahandra a hug. As she let Shahandra go, she glanced at Dalwan, "Say goodbye, Dalwan, I'll wait for you with the horses." She looked back and forth at the two with an animated motherly smile that made both of them blush, then turned and walked back to the horses.

They stood staring at each other, overcome with awkwardness. Dalwan spoke first, "Don't worry, the powermaster knows Danlion's plan, and won't let the sword be taken by him."

"I know..." she said, but her voice betrayed doubt. "Good luck, Dalwan." She reached out and took his hand.

His heart leapt inside. He didn't know what to do... run away? or take her in his arms?... so he just stood there with her hand in his as he gazed mesmerized into her eyes. "You're so beautiful...I hope I'll see you again... I mean, I hope we both live through this."

His feelings were so strong that Shahandra blushed. Even though she liked Dalwan, it was hard for her not to feel superior to him. She just couldn't help thinking of him as a simple, innocent boy. Her thoughts drifted to the one she was waiting for, "a hero to ride into battle with... a champion to go on quests with... someone who equaled her in power and vision." But not wanting to hurt Dalwan, she said, "We will make it...both of us... and we'll see each other again... I promise." At that, she gave him a quick hug. As she let go of the embrace, she took hold of his arm and led him over to where Ingar was waiting.

He read her feelings perfectly, even though she thought she had covered them from him. He mounted his horse and sat for an instant with a sad-eyed stare, then whispered, "Goodbye, Shahandra," turned, and rode off without Ingar. Intuitively, he knew that this wasn't the time or place to reveal his identity, but everything inside him wanted to let her know. Anger flared as he realized that once again that who he was had cheated him out of something he wanted.

"He'll be OK, dear. It'll just take some time." As she turned to follow Dalwan, she glanced back, "Be careful, and trust your instincts... they're very keen." At that, she galloped off to catch up with Dalwan.

Ingar quickly caught up with Dalwan. They rode back to the camp at an easy gallop. It was a bright sunny day. A gentle breeze blew through the tree tops. It was the kind of day that puts energy and courage into important undertakings.

They arrived back at the clearing to find that Borem and Renne had broken camp, and Lex was still asleep. Although he was healed from the injury, his blood loss had left him weak.

Dalwan recounted the battle as they finished the last bit of preparations to leave. They woke Lex and sat out for the Crossings. They had decided to drop off Lex, get fresh supplies, and go to Castle Crest with the news of the possible invasion by Danlion.

They left in the late afternoon and rode all night at a steady but leisurely pace. They knew that they could not afford to waste time, but also knew that their animals would need to be fresh enough to continue on to Castle Crest.

The night was like the day had been, clear and warm. There was an exhilaration in the air as they rode and talked together. They planned and brainstormed and strategized their intentions with an intensity that invigorated them all. From time to time, they would lament that the powermaster did not make himself known and join them.

They arrived at the Crossings with the first rays of the sun's light. They parted ways, agreeing to meet in the tavern at midday with fresh supplies.

CHAPTER 9

Dalwan had only been back for a short time, having left so he could pack and rendezvous as soon as possible. He had washed off, changed into fresh clothes, and was putting together some supplies for his trip when Rhem suddenly appeared in the doorway to the kitchen. Rhem was dressed in black with none of his customary gold trim.

It startled Dalwan so much that he had formed and held a green flame shield up and was about to pound Rhem with it when he realized who it was. Dalwan spun the shield off at the floor, where it broke up with a heavy thud, producing a concussion effect on both of them. Dalwan had taken a deep breath when he first noticed Rhem, and only after dispensing with the flame shield did he let it out. His face showed embarrassment and fatigue. Rhem stood and studied him for a moment before speaking. There was a marked difference in Dalwan's countenance. More than that, Rhem had never seen him so reactionary; he was usually slow and methodical. "What happened to you? Why so jumpy?"

Dalwan collected his wits and recounted, in short order, the events of the past few days, including his battle, his attraction for Shahandra, her feelings about him, and her current destination with Eric.

"Most of this will be of value at the Council. You've got to come with me, and we've got to leave now."

"What Council?"

"With the three lords, at Beorg. I'll explain as we ride."

"But I at least need to tell the others I won't be going with them."

"Are they going to Castle Crest?"

"Yes... to warn them about Danlion."

"O.K.. But you can't tell them about the Council. Just tell them that Lord Falock will contact them when he arrives back at Castle Crest in a couple of days."

Dalwan nodded in understanding and finished packing. They left together in a hurry.

Rhem stayed outside the tavern with the horses as Dalwan went in to find Ingar and Borem. They listened patiently as he told them he couldn't go with them with only the sketchiest details for an explanation. Before they could question him, he turned and headed for the door to the sound of their immediate protests. As he opened the door, he stopped and looked back, only to find that they were right behind him. "I promise to fill you in as soon as I can," he said with sincerity and apology in his voice.

Ingar and Borem watched as Rhem and Dalwan rode off at a gallop.

"I tell you, Ingar, there's more to that boy than meets the senses."

Ingar stood silently for a moment, contemplating everything she could put together about Dalwan and Rhem. "What purpose could one such as Rhem have that is so urgent and requires Dalwan's attendance? Is it possible that Rhem, this swordsman called Amberlain, is actually the powermaster?"

"Now that you mention it, Rhem and the boy were together at the first battleground."

"But Borem, there didn't appear to have been any sword fighting at all in the last battle, only fire... lots and lots of fire!"

"Sounds like a good cover to me."

Rhem led the way, riding briskly until they were out of sight of the town, then slowed to a steady walk.

Dalwan listened as Rhem explained all that they had discovered about the sword Fallonrod and its strange origin. There was still a great deal of anger and frustration in Rhem's voice as he told about the escape of the shadow master spy.

At Rhem's insistence, Dalwan again recounted in entirety the events of the past days, starting with his reasoning for going back to the anderon's forest. Rhem listened patiently, interrupting occasionally for clarification. Dalwan knew instinctively that Rhem was evaluating his actions and seeking to discern if Dalwan might have given away some clue about his true identity.

They rode a long way as Dalwan gave a detail-laden narrative of everything he could remember. Finally, Rhem decided to stop and water the horses as they passed a stream.

"It looks as if you've handled yourself well. I would've done a few things differently, but I may have died, and you didn't. What's more, you managed to hide your identity. Can't argue with success!" Rhem's eyes displayed approval and, to Dalwan's surprise, admiration.

They ate as they rode from there toward Beorg. Dalwan began to tell Rhem more and more about Shahandra. Off and on for a long time, Dalwan shared about Shahandra's intelligence, Shahandra's arts, Shahandra's passions, Shahandra's beautiful elven-like features... Finally, Rhem became so annoyed that he stopped his horse and brought Dalwan's to a stop.

"You've gotta snap outta this love-sick trance you're in. We've got some very serious business ahead of us, and you must keep yourself alert... no more girls for now... O.K.?" Rhem's eyes burned a path into Dalwan's consciousness.

This stung Dalwan. He hadn't noticed the irritation he had caused Rhem. His embarrassment radiated in red hues from his face. He sensed that this was no ordinary excursion they were taking, but had somehow missed the intensity of the present danger that Rhem seemed to feel. He knew Rhem to be a man of action, so he had not taken seriously enough the definite and purposeful way that Rhem had come for him. "Rhem always operates this way," he thought to himself, feeling defeated and incompetent.

"I'm sorry, Rhem," said Dalwan, quite embarrassed by his obvious lack of perception.

"Apologies aren't necessary. You must be alert from now on. Dalwan, you'll need to be a man. You're now my comrade and will cease to be my disciple. You'll need everything you've learned and maybe much more."

Rhem's words were sobering to Dalwan. Many times, he had told Dalwan that the day would come when he would call him comrade. Before, Dalwan had expected to feel proud and strong... confident! Now, though, his stomach swelled and his jaw tightened as his mouth began to water. He felt very nervous.

Rhem saw the reaction in Dalwan. "How can you be afraid? I've never seen or even heard of anyone facing a dragon the way you did. I've watched you practice your arts, and you're the best I've ever seen at what you do. And add to all this, yesterday you fought for your life with seasoned men of war and won! HOW can you be AFRAID?"

Dalwan thought about it for a moment, not fully understanding what he felt. "Rhem, I don't know why I feel this way," he answered, sounding confused. He paused, turning his thoughts inward, looking for insight. Suddenly, he blurted out, "You scared me!"

Rhem's face took on a disgusted look. But before he could speak, Dalwan went on.

"Why does everything have to be so dramatic? You seem to WANT to scare me... with unsolvable problems and invisible enemies. You sound like we're already surrounded and are sure to perish if we miss a wink. You act like we don't stand a chance of survival, let alone real victory."

Rhem was spurring his horse forward again, acting as though he wasn't listening.

"Rhem, when I faced the anderon, I did so because I wanted to. I saw the end of the fight and thought I would try to help the beast. I was in control... figuring out what to do as I went. In my practice, I'm in control. Even in the battle I fought, I controlled it. In this adventure you're leading me into, we'll both use everything we have to help Pretoria. I know it'll probably be dangerous. But let's take every danger one at a time and control them as best we can."

Rhem rode very silently atop Phlanx as he listened to Dalwan. "If only I had his power..." he thought as he tried to drown out Dalwan's words, "I wouldn't need to sit and listen to this overly sensitive and too philosophical young man work through his emotional problems." Rhem had waited long enough after Dalwan's question to create an uncomfortable period of silence before answering, "Alright, Dalwan, one danger at a time." He managed a forced smile to placate him before slipping back into thought. He knew that he had to bring Dalwan, but wondered what would become of this young, inexperienced, and overconfident power wielder in the coming, certain-to-be life and death struggle. Rhem knew that sooner or later, Dalwan would be put to the test on terms not of his own choosing, whether he liked it or not. And chances were that Dalwan would not end up in control, nor even find himself ready. Better that it happen with him and Shaylan close by than somewhere alone...again. Besides that, there was another question that had plagued him about the shadow master who had escaped, "Did he overhear something that would lead him to Dalwan or warn him of the young man's power, while at Castle Crest?"

They rode on in silence for some time, with Rhem thinking strategically about the extraordinary powers that Dalwan possessed. "If Dalwan were to live through this, he would certainly be a hero, perhaps even if he didn't live through it. But most certainly, he would be a reluctant hero. He had practiced day after day, diligently developing his arts, guided by Rhem and Shaylan as far as they knew how to take him. From there, he had worked on arts that Rhem had only heard of in tall stories over many mugs of ale. If only he had spent more time developing his fighting ability. He was a decent swordsman now and could hold his own in a civilized contest against almost anyone... but war isn't civilized! At least now he had used his abilities to kill. Only a few times in the past had he found it necessary or even practical to use those powers for anything but practice. From now on, he would be playing for keeps. Hopefully, his recent battle wouldn't give him a false sense of security."

It was late afternoon, the fourth day after the shadow master escaped from Castle Crest, when the meeting convened. Present in the meeting hall were the three Lords: Falock, Linx, and Welton, a pair of scribes for each, their defense ministers, a sensor each and a historian each. Witnesses included primarily Rhem and Shaylan, but also the shadow master from Falock's castle and the injured guard from the palace entrance.

Dalwan had arrived at Beorg earlier with Rhem and registered as the attendant and apprentice of Shaylan and Rhem. As such, he was given free run of the inner perimeter and, for the most part, ignored. Rhem and Shaylan both warned Dalwan not to expose his power because some of the most sensitive sensors in Pretoria were present, "...some who had searched the central area of Pretoria for the one who would display great power from time to time and then simply vanish!" said Shaylan with his eyebrows raised, wearing a wide-eyed smile. "You might know of such a one, mightn't you, Dalwan?! And the print of his magic will be keenly etched in each of their minds." Shaylan did allow him to practice his sensing ability and to use a small amount of fire magic, "if and only if called on to demonstrate the art that would be expected from an apprentice, of men such as Shaylan and Rhem." "A small amount," he concluded, "would be of insufficient power to identify the magic's print and associate it the any one particular person, like a whisper is difficult to identify in speech." So it was that Dalwan was left to fend for himself while Rhem and Shaylan attended to state matters.

The meeting hall was a large room twice as long as it was wide. It would easily hold two hundred people at a social event. It had a high, open vaulted ceiling with huge hand-hewn beams crisscrossing it. Scenic carvings decorated the lowest beams, which ran across the width of the building. Fireplaces of polished stone stood at either end of the hall. Each firepit was three strides across and about two-thirds as high. On each side of the pit, there was an oven for cooking or baking. There was a large, thick, ornately decorated mantle running across the entire width of each fireplace. In front of each was a step hearth of polished stone. Along each wall were three narrow high windows, each with a half-round stained glass mosaic at the top. There were two sets of double doors evenly spaced between the windows, with one set being much larger than the others and obviously the formal entrance. On each side of the thin windows hung a beautiful woven tapestry, twelve in all, each representing leading families in Pretoria. The floor was carefully laid flagstone on each end near the fireplaces, with the remainder being heavy plank oak running across the width of the room and held down with pegs.

There were two guards at each door and a scribe at the entrance. As the participants entered, each had their name, position, and the Lord they represented recorded.

There were three large heavy heavy-bodied tables set up, pushed together end to end across the opposite end of the hall from the entrance. High back leather chairs sat on the fireplace side of each table to accommodate the lord and his staff. On the auditorium side of the table, about 5 paces back were two rows of 12 chairs each, which contained the remainder of the attendants and entourages of the lords.

The meeting had one precondition to be met before officially commencing. Two sensors were dispatched, one each from Lord Linx and Lord Welton, to check the hall for the possible presence of a shadow master and to discern the intent of the participants. This was an obvious sign of mistrust toward Lord Falock. His face became red, but he didn't object, knowing how sensitive both lords were to the events which had transpired. Any confrontation could jeopardize their union, and Falock knew the great degree of cooperation that would be needed between them in this venture and even more so if war became a reality.

As the sensors worked their way back toward the head table, one stopped in front of Shaylan, Rhem, and Dalwan, all of whom sat together on the left side of the front row of chairs. He exchanged greetings with Shaylan and Rhem and voiced praise for their mastery of their respective arts. When he arrived at Dalwan, he turned to Lord Falock and asked, "Lord Falock, do you know this boy and why he is present in such a meeting as this?" As he finished speaking, he quickly looked back at Dalwan, focusing all his powers of sensing on him. Dalwan sat perfectly still, trying to blank his mind and calm his emotions. The sensor discerned a control of extraordinary proportion in the young man's ability to turn off his emotions and mask his thoughts.

Suddenly, Shaylan shot out of his chair with such abruptness that several guards drew their swords. The sensor's trance was interrupted. Shaylan instantly motioned, with his hands held straight out, waving back and forth, and a very strained smile, that his intentions were not hostile. "My lords. May I be allowed to explain the presence of my nephew and apprentice, Dalwan?" The word "nephew" rippled through the group present.

Lord Welton answered, "Yes, Shaylan. You may speak on the boy's behalf."

Shaylan looked back at the sensor, then to the head table. Lord Welton called the sensor, "Calon, you may return later and question the boy if we deem it necessary."

"As you wish, my Lord," said Calon, taking a step backward and turning to resume his place at the head table.

As he walked away, Dalwan heard him say in his mind, "I know you from somewhere... I'll remember..." Dalwan was amazed that he had read the sensor's thoughts and debated briefly as to the authenticity of his perception before having his concentration interrupted by Shaylan's defense.

"If this meeting goes as I suspect it will, I will need the assistance of my nephew. He is my apprentice as well as Rhem's. He is a good sensor himself and has remarkable powers of observation. Rhem has been training him in swordsmanship, and I in the arts of a wizard. He is loyal to Pretoria and to me. After our initial business, he has an adventure to share that will make this meeting even more important. If you trust me, please allow him to stay." Shaylan worked very hard to control his thoughts and feelings so as not to alarm the sensors.

Calon spoke up immediately, "My lords, everything he says is true, but I suspect there is more..." his gaze turned back directly at Shaylan, "...much more!"

"There is no need for indictment," answered Shaylan pleasantly toward the lords. "As I have already intimated, there is indeed much more," concluded Shaylan, returning Calon's insinuating glance with a chastising glare.

Rhem was already on his feet by the time Shaylan finished speaking, and barely gave him a chance to finish talking, "Calon, do you challenge our loyalty or our motives?"

The tension was thick in the air. Lord Falock knew that if this confrontation continued, the meeting would be lost for the benefit of all. "If there is anyone who has a charge or suspicion of disloyalty or treachery regarding these three men, speak now. If not, we must get to the business for which we have come."

Falock glanced from sensor to sensor at the table, each one gesturing and shaking their head, indicating no charge against them.

Turning to the other lord, "Does the boy stay or not?"

"Stays," said Linx approvingly with a brush of his hand.

"Fine, let him stay and let's get down to business," answered Welton with a tone of concession in his voice.

Everyone sat down except Rhem, who stood with his eyes fixed on Calon. Before anyone could react, Shaylan took hold of Rhem's shoulder and pulled him into the waiting chair, "Patience, my friend. Everything in its time," he whispered.

Whispering loudly, Rhem replied, "He challenged your integrity."

"Am I too old or too weak to stand up for myself?" Shaylan wore a smile which immediately reminded him of the same look his mother often wore when she caught him in some little mischief.

"Sorry, I..." Rhem was cut short by a shout from the head table.

"This meeting is now called to order. Let the record reflect that the three lords of Pretoria are all present." The loud little man speaking was the scribe of Lord Linx. He was a curious little man with a pot belly, stick legs, and a bald head. His greatest claim to fame was that he had developed a technique of writing that enabled him to take down every word spoken, a valuable person at meetings such as this.

The lords listened intently as Rhem explained his search through the archives, leading to the discovery of the letter. The Shaylan discussed the things learned from the magic books. Then both men took turns recounting what they had learned from the book "Epoch", when they had taken turns reading aloud to each other at Castle Crest.

From time to time, they were interrupted by one of the lords for clarification.

Finally, they virtually reenacted the discovery of the shadow master they had discovered in the room with them and how Shaylan had sensed him earlier near the sword chamber.

When they finished, Lord Linx began to criticize Lord Falock for his "...poorly organized security... that would let a shadow master roam the halls undetected," and his "...inability to catch one fleeing man with a whole army..." He was joined by Lord Welton with the two of them continuing in a highly emotional tone to chide Lord Falock for some time.

Lord Falock listened in silence and frustration. After the tirade failed to wane after an acceptable time, his patience wore so thin that he feared he would react rashly if they continued on even one more moment. He suddenly stood and said in a conciliatory tone, "I do not deny responsibility for these troubles. But our purpose here is to decide how to proceed from this point on, not to determine who's made the greatest errors or been the biggest fool."

Everyone quieted down and gave their attention to Lord Falock.

"We now know that the secrets of the sword lie with the Dwarves and Elves, if indeed they are still known or understood at all. We also know that this shadow master has discovered these things and will most likely deliver the information to someone who is obviously interested in the sword and is not friendly to us." Lord Falock looked around the room at faces full of disgust and irritation at the state of affairs dealt them. He continued, "If this were not enough, our problem is compounded because the dwarves and elves hold great contempt for our conflicts. They're not likely to help us without some agreement, which will unduly complicate the use of the knowledge they give us. Yet without that knowledge, we may be doomed to spend our lives and resources protecting something we can't use and can't throw away. We're even left without the option to destroy it because we don't know how!"

Lord Linx objected loudly, "Is our only alternative to go to the dwarves and elves for help? How do we know that no one can wield the sword without their help? I've heard several accounts by credible sensors of a great power at work in central Pretoria... what has been done to secure his services?"

Dalwan's heart felt like it would burst inside of him, pounding wildly. Immediately, he brought it under control, and the tightness in his chest and throat eased. But two of the sensors at the front table were already searching the faces of those sitting near Dalwan for the source of the emotional upheaval. Shaylan also sensed Dalwan's response and reacted immediately by standing up as if the reaction was his own. "Yes, Lord Linx, I have sensed the presence of a person with great control and diversity of power myself, even very recently. However, I have also found it true that this magic wielder doesn't stay in one place long enough to be discovered."

Lord Linx became more excited as he heard this. Looking directly at Shaylan, he asked, "Could this person be somehow apprehended and convinced to wield the sword?" He had the tone of one who might hunt a great trophy animal for sport. He was now leaning so far forward on the table that it looked as though he would climb right over it.

"My lords," said Shaylan in his scholarly voice, "even if such a person were...shall we say, 'apprehended', then even if we could convince him to attempt to wield the sword, there is no guarantee that he won't perish just as the others have done who have tried on their own. We do not know for sure that the sword can ever be wielded by anyone."

Linx leaned back into his chair with a look of disgust on his face. "Where is the sense of adventure?... the challenge of winning at great opposing odds?... the daring to go where others have already failed? We're fighting for our land, or at least we will be if this beast in the North continues his conquest. Shall we just give in to him?"

Shaylan replied quickly as he walked toward the head table, "This is precisely why we must proceed carefully and seek the wisdom that created the sword in order to instruct the one who might try to wield it." He had walked up to the table and now leaned over it, palms down, with his arms fully extended. In a low, deep tone, glancing from face to face with eyes wide, he said, "Otherwise, we very well may take all of our most significant and useful power wielders and turn them one by one into ash in the sword chamber!" Shaylan hoped this would put a damper on the idea and distract everyone enough to make them believe that he had been responsible for the intense reaction Dalwan had suffered.

Lord Falock seized the opportunity provided by Shaylan, "Our people are our greatest asset... we can't risk them on clearly destructive uncertainties."

"Then destroy the cursed thing and let's be done with it once and for all!" shouted Lord Welton, pounding on the table as he finished.

"We don't know how!! Besides that, why destroy it before we discover whether or not we can use it. It brought peace once before, I say let's give it a chance again!" answered Lord Falock with contempt.

"Chance?...CHANCE?.." said Welton shrewdly, "First you say we can't take a chance with the people and now you ask us to take even bigger chances... a chance that we'll discover from the dwarves and elves some useful way to exercise the sword's power... a chance that we'll find someone who will wield this most powerful sword for Pretoria without being seduced by its power... a chance that it will not fall into some hand that is clearly set in opposition to Pretoria. Is this what you mean when you say 'chance'?"

"You're starting to sound like my mother, Lord Welton," answered Lord Falock. "We take a chance, whatever we do... keep it or destroy it. The chance I was speaking of means that we investigate the possibilities of using the sword. If we find that it is to our advantage to try its use, then we will. If not, we may at that point choose to attempt to destroy it... something we aren't even certain is possible. At least after the consultation with the other races, we may have a better idea. But let's not just act rashly and possibly destroy a source of security before we even know what our options are or what possibilities may exist for us."

"Lord Falock, we seek the best for all, just as you do," Welton's voice was calm as he spoke dryly. "I'm sure you have no personal desire to control the wielder and through him to exalt yourself..."

Lord Falock jumped up out of his chair cutting off Lord Falock shouting as he stepped toward Lord Welton, "Dare you accuse me of self-interest. I'm the one who called this meeting. If this was personal power I sought, I would have sent these men to the dwarves already, and without your knowledge or consent!"

Linx got up and moved quickly between the two men before they could physically reach each other. "Listen to me... both of you!" He was looking back and forth between the men after having restrained Falock with an outstretched hand on his shoulder. "We need each other. Falock, you need us to help you protect the sword. Welton, if the sword is lost to some other people, it would likely spell the end for us and our people. We can't let this become personal. Falock has the sword and is committed to its use for Pretoria. Let's find out what can be done. He said by insinuation that our vote counts toward its fate."

Shaylan entered the conversation again very carefully, having waited for a pause. "Lords of Pretoria, my magic is very strong, yet it distorts greatly in the presence of the sword. I do not believe we can destroy it or even attempt it without great risk to our lives. Let us go to the dwarves and elves to learn as much as they will teach us about it. We may learn enough to help someone wield it or even to destroy it. We may discover that they no longer have knowledge of the sword or its craft. One way or another, we will then be in a position to make a proper decision."

All three lords stood exactly where they were, eyes locked on each other, without moving or even acknowledging Shaylan's words.

Falock backed up a step and looked toward Shaylan, "What do you require from us?"

"First, I, or shall I say we..." he gestured toward Rhem and Dalwan, "will need signed and sealed notification to the dwarves and elves that we speak for Pretoria and our contracts with them will be binding on the three lords and those under their jurisdiction."

Secondly, we need secrecy among those present with us here. This news must not get out and compromise our mission in any way.

Lastly, we reserve the right to have final say on our traveling companions."

Lord Welton was first to answer, "If I agree to any such plan, it will be with the stipulation that one of my people accompany you and have a voice in any decision made that binds us in responsibility or agreement with the dwarves and elves."

The lords were still exchanging glances   of hostility and mistrust as they again returned to their chairs while Lord Welton finished speaking.

Lord Linx turned his attention back to Shaylan after the other two men were seated. He sat back down in his chair as he addressed the group in general and to a lesser degree, Shaylan, "I too will demand representation in such an adventure, should it come to pass.. The choice of my delegate will rest with me and will be final," he said, then turning his gaze toward Shaylan, "and not you! I will entertain objections should they arise, but final approval will be mine, and my representative will have an equal vote in any agreement, or my realm will not participate."

"I will also send a representative," said Falock. "Each of us will send someone to speak for our realms. Let Shaylan be the spokesman for the group and carry a vote as well as those from each of our castles. If there come a deadlock occurs in the decision, no bargain may be struck."

"Then a simple majority will hold the lords to the decision?" asked Welton.

"I would propose that be the binding rule," answered Falock in a sigh that evidenced the fatigue brought on him by the events of two very long days.

"This means that it takes at least three representatives from among the lords to pass a binding resolution?" asked Lord Linx.

"That's correct," answered Falock.

"We need assurance that we will be represented from a position of strength, not weakness," said Welton. "The dwarves and elves know very well that if we are defeated by some outside force, like this renegade fighting in the outlands, they would not be spared. They need to be reminded of this."

"I agree!" said Linx, slapping his open hand on the table. "In the past, when they have needed help, we've never refused them. They need to be reminded of this fact also. It's their turn!"

Again, Shaylan spoke up, this time a little more boldly. "My lords, I am committed to Pretoria. I also understand the feelings of the dwarves and elves regarding our wars. We must do what we can to maximize our benefit and to appease their convictions. You must choose men who understand the dwarves and elves, their customs and mannerisms. This will enable us to work out a solution suitable for all involved."

Finally, the men all agreed to send a delegation for the purpose of gaining as much understanding as possible about the sword. After hours of deliberation and private meetings, they also decided whether the size of the group should be very small or very large, a handful or an army. Since the army was needed at home and a small party might go relatively unnoticed, they decided on seven because a group of this size could move freely and be ready for departure fully provisioned, almost immediately.

Shaylan, Rhem, and Dalwan were to accompany the 3 envoys, one from each lord's domain, along with a skilled linguist and scribe who was to draw up any agreement and ensure proper expressive wording.

From Falock's camp, Malan was chosen. He was shorter than most of the others by half a head. He had thick black hair, which was straight and shiny. He was a heavy bodied man with dark skin and a thick beard with a bushy mustache. He had grown up near the border of the rocky highlands where several clans of dwarves lived. His father was a trader in metal work with the dwarves and quite an artisan with metal himself. Malan was also gifted in metalwork. He carried as a weapon a short handled broad axe which the dwarves had made for him and had taught him to use correctly. He was in Lord Falock's security cabinet.

Lord Linx chose Draymoor. He was the tallest of the group and a very quiet man. He had wavy brown hair, which he held in place with a woven headband. He was thin but very strong. He moved as though he were a vapor being blown along by the breeze, making scarcely a noise as he walked. He carried a long bow and short sword as well as several small special weapons, which he made for close combat or for stealth. He was Lord Linx's cousin on his mother's side. Draymoor was a student of elven ways from his youth.

Attleman was Welton's choice. He was older than the others, being well into his fifties. He had strong upper-body features and skinny legs. He carried a sling and a regular fighting sword. He kept his hair cut very short, almost shaved, because he was bald on top. He was the Lord's strategist in domestic affairs and was a keen observer. He had been an ambassador of trade to the elves for three years, until the post was abolished by the elves.

Lastly, there was Draxyl. He was a medium-height man with a pot belly. He moved a little awkwardly. He carried a short sword but did not know how to use it well. He apparently had some power to work with wood, but had never developed it. He was, however, very skilled in the trade language of the dwarves and that of the elves. He was also very meticulous and a prolific writer and scribe. Lord Linx volunteered his services... Draxyl went along very grudgingly.

After this decision was made firm and all the traveling companions, except Draxyl, were satisfied with the delegation, Rhem brought Dalwan up to the head table and announced the need for an audience.

It was now evening, the delegation was set to leave early the next morning, and the lords were exhausted.

The lords each agreed to hear Dalwan on the condition that he be brief and to the point.

Dalwan could not resist the temptation to do exactly what was asked of him. "Lords of Pretoria, Danlion lives. He's the raider of the North lands. As we meet, he plans to attack Brandon Keep and make it his stronghold for the conquest of Pretoria, beginning with Castle Crest, where he hopes to secure the sword Fallonrod from ever again being used against him."

By the time Dalwan had completed his short speech, every ear in the room was tuned to his voice. As he finished, sensors whispered words of perception into the hungry and anxious ears of the three lords.

"Why is your knowledge of these facts so clear and your confidence in their authenticity so unwavering?" asked Welton, who now sat on the edge of his chair leaning hard on the table.

Every person in the room was either leaning forward or sitting on the edge of their seat as Dalwan explained the incident, including how the powermaster saved him from death.

After he finished with his story, everyone sat in silence for a moment. Lord Linx spoke up. "Shaylan, the boy obviously believes these things with alarming certainty. He's your relative. Give us your sense of his story."

"I can only tell you that I have complete confidence that what he has told you is indeed what took place."

"Very well then," looking back and forth between the other two lords, "and you're very sure that contact with the powermaster would not be possible?"

"He is firmly committed to secrecy, but he told me he was committed to Pretoria and that he would make himself known at the right time," finished Dalwan with an apologetic shrug.

"Seems to me that now would be fine... just fine," said Linx dejectedly.

Lord Welton stood up, "There is not much more we can accomplish here... it's up to you now," he said, gesturing with a slight bow to the delegation, who were all standing together near Dalwan. "We'd better call this meeting to an end and let these men get prepared for their early departure tomorrow. They have a long night ahead of them."

CHAPTER 10

After successfully escaping from Castle Crest, the shadow master, Jarmin Andros, a thief and fugitive from almost everywhere, made his way to a cave high in the rocky crags that stood behind the Castle. There he met his partner, Drummond. Drummond was a thin, weasely-looking man. He was the agent through whom Jarmin fenced his stolen goods. He was a very cold-blooded, hard-dealing, squint-eyed, intellectual crook. Each man was the only one the other trusted. For over 10 years, they had been an inseparable pair. In all that time, Drummond had never revealed the name of his partner without full prearranged consent, even when pressed hard for such information.

Jarmin spent the remainder of the night writing out what he had learned from Shaylan and Rhem about the Sword. After explaining everything carefully to Drummond, he went to sleep briefly until sunrise. He then set out for Thamerlain, the Dwarven high counsel seat and center of all Dwarven culture, to see if he could discover the secrets of the sword's power or how to destroy it. Drummond was charged with getting the information to Lord Danlion and bringing back whatever orders or strategies Danlion may have for them. They determined to meet at the upper junction of the Mountain Highway and the Central Pretorian Highway in 12 days.

Jarmin did not like traveling alone. He much preferred the company of Drummond, even though the two men operated much differently. However, having discussed the possibilities thoroughly, he and Drummond decided that the knowledge he had discovered was important enough by itself to merit communication to Lord Danlion as soon as possible. Should Jarmin's mission fail and he be killed or detained, the information could become invaluable and its loss prove disastrous to their goals.

Jarmin reached Thamerlain in the evening of his second day of travel. He hid at the outskirts of town until he could get the lay of the city.

Thamerlain was built at the base of the Emerald Mountains in a heavily forested area. The main part of the city, where the majority of the shops and industries were located, was situated on a terraced area that jutted southward between the mountains into the valley. The terraces were fortified by ornate rock walls designed and fabricated by some of the most talented stone molders in the Dwarven community to protect the city from erosion by the river Dhall, which flowed from the north around its perimeter toward the valley. The city

businesses were situated quaintly around the central park, which contained the
Dwarven High Council Meeting grounds and the city gardens. From there
everything else around the city was uphill. Many roads and trails led into the
hills immediately surrounding the city where groups of dwellings, each of
marvelously unique design, housed the inhabitants of Thamerlain. Some were
built of rock and others of wood, each with its own character reflecting the
personality of its creator. On occasion, only an entrance leading into the
mountainside evidenced a dwelling at all. Many of the largest trees had been
preserved, and a few even contained homes which had been carefully hewn out
of the center without damaging the living part of the trunk. Carefully
constructed and concealed aqueducts provided water to the city dwellers.

Jarmin noticed very little of this artistry because he was preoccupied with
making a plan for finding one of the dwarves who might know of the power
sword's origin or power. It would be very difficult to learn who among the
Dwarves might have knowledge of such old magics, if indeed any of them still
had the knowledge. If anyone would possess such ancient wisdom, it would
surely be one of the great Dwarven wizards. Getting restricted information
from any Dwarf would be, at best, very difficult, and from one of great status,
nearly unfathomable.

"No human would be given any information that could be useful for
killing or harming any other living soul," he thought to himself, "...this is going
to be very tricky business."

He sat in the deepening shadows running through countless plans,
dismissing them one after another. "If only I were a dwarf," he thought in
frustration. This led him back to one option that he had already dismissed at
least three times. "I'll have to try being a dwarf!" Unlike Elven magic, it is
immediately discernible as distinct from all other magics; dwarven magic was
similar enough to human that it required a very discerning sensor to distinguish
it from that which was human, based solely on the magic. He felt sure that he
could carry off the deception if he could find a way to keep his talking part to a
minimum. He knew the dwarven language well from living among them with
his merchant father for many years prior to becoming a professional thief. He
had a terrible accent that would immediately alarm the dwarves. If he could
convince them he was from a small, isolated tribe, he might get away with it.
Jarmin was convinced that it was his only viable option. Changing his

appearance into that of a dwarf was simple, but only the illusion he could make would be small; his actual size would not change. He realized that he would need to be very careful.

He disguised himself as a wounded Dwarf and entered a tavern at the leading edge of the plateau. As he entered, he noticed a large number, perhaps fifty, dwarves sitting around heavy wooden tables, some in deep discussion, some laughing and joking. He stumbled to the floor as soon as the door closed behind him and recovered his footing feebly. Several dwarves from the nearest tables immediately came toward him with genuinely concerned looks on their faces. He held them back with outstretched hands. Speaking hoarsely in broken sentences, he asked for an urgent meeting with a "worthy wizard" on a "secret matter of deepest need."

His shirt appeared torn and blood-stained, and he walked with a visible limp. The dwarves wanted to attend to his wounds before leading him to a wizard, but he steadfastly refused help until his mission was complete. He knew that in the dwarven community, his honor-bound countenance would command respect. The other activity in the tavern came to a halt, and they all gathered around him. Jarmin became worried about being discovered, so he turned and headed for the door, asking for someone to lead him on now, "...while I can still walk!" A quick discussion led to a unanimous decision by those in the tavern as to who should lead him and which qualified dwarven wizard should attend to his needs.

He was led to a cabin at the base of a rocky outcropping not very far from the tavern. Jarmin insisted that he walk unassisted to the wizard's home.

As they approached the cabin, two of the accompanying dwarves ran ahead and alerted the wizard. They had briefly discussed the matter prior to Jarmin's arrival. Sensing deception, the wizard asked two stout dwarves to remain and sent the others away.

The wizard introduced himself as "Lanterlain" and invited Jarmin and his two new companions inside. Jarmin, still disguising himself as wounded, sat between his dwarven escorts, both of whom remained standing, one just behind each shoulder.

"Where have you come from and why have you come here?" the wizard's words were not compassionate, nor did they beckon for a rambling answer.

"I have come from Castle Crest of the humans, with a power sword I have stolen at near cost of my life," came the answer in halting words with raspy tones. "I need to see someone who can explain the prize I have taken from those destructive and mindless beasts!" The act was perfectly executed, but the wizard wasn't buying it.

"My senses tell me you are full of lies. Let me see the sword," came the demand from the steel-hard voice of the wizard.

Jarmin pulled his sword and, working with all his powers of concentration at their maximum effort, gave it the appearance of the sword he had seen in the protected chamber at Castle Crest. He handed it to the wizard without speaking.

The wizard's eyes widened as he received it. He glanced quickly back at Jarmin, trying to sense him, then back at the sword. "This looks like a dwarven forged sword, but its magic seems as though it could be human... hard to tell," again he scrutinized Jarmin, sensing and watching.

Jarmin just held his breath and waited.

"Here's your trophy," said Lanterlain, handing the sword back to Jarmin without releasing his gaze. "Darric will know about its origin better than any. I'll take you there tomorrow if you can still travel," he motioned to Jarmin's wounds.

Jarmin put away the sword. "Just tell me the way, I'll find it myself. Time is most important to me." He sounded very determined.

All three of the dwarves laughed aloud. "Will you now?" said Lanterlain, coughing through a laugh. "You'll just head out into the darkness, weak, wounded, and foreign to this terrain, and find Darric!" they all laughed even harder.

"My need is greater than you know," Jarmin was trying to sound noble and desperate.

"I think you're out of your mind," answered Lanterlain, trying to control himself and become responsive to his guest. "He lives at the top of the mountain, which we are now setting at the base of. It's almost impossible to climb in the daylight, but only a total fool would attempt it at night." Lanterlain was now just grinning widely and shaking his head back and forth. "It'll surely cost you your life for this trinket of yours."

Jarmin stood up to leave. As he started turning to leave, Lanterlain asked, "From which family do you come, and where are your people so we can send them word and rite of your death?" grinning ear to ear but obviously waiting for an answer.

Jarmin's concentration broke for an instant, and his illusion faded... he had planned a name, a town, a trade, but not a family - he was exposed.

As fast as lightning, he pulled a knife from between his shoulders and threw it at the wizard. It stuck in his throat. At the same instant, he disappeared and dove for the floor, shaking off the powerful grasp of one of the dwarves at his shoulder. The other dwarf was already at the side of the fallen wizard.

Jarmin rolled over onto his feet, still invisible, and drew his sword. The dwarf that had grabbed him never saw the sword coming that went threw his heart. He fell dead instantly. At that, the other dwarf began to yell loudly while he pulled his own sword and began to flail wildly at the air with it. Jarmin side-stepped any danger and hit the dwarf across the back of his neck, felling him with a single blow.

Hearing voices coming, he slipped invisibly out of the cabin and headed up the mountain.

Lanterlain lived long enough to scribble out a brief account of the "man... his magic... and the sword", before he choked to death on his own blood.

Jarmin had hoped to escape extra attention, beyond his initial contact, and to be able to move on to his next visit without complication. His carelessness had cost him that luxury. With three dead dwarves in his wake, he would need to move quickly and hopefully beat the news to the top of the mountain.

As he moved up a steeply sloping train, barely visible in the still moonless sky, he thought back to the encounter he had just experienced. Using the illusive disguise of being a wounded dwarf had only narrowly missed being discovered in the tavern. Lanterlain had correctly sensed the deception, but was unable to locate it or just didn't make the effort needed to expose it. The next interview would not likely be so lucky. He needed a better plan this time.

The path vanished into the darkness, and Jarmin found himself at the leading edge of a steep, loose rockslide. It was like ground-up granite gravel with numerous larger rocks and boulders mixed in sparingly. Progress was difficult before reaching this point, but it became nearly impossible now with the lack of light and the instability of the slide. At least he was out of the trees now and could make out some vague landmarks and distinctions in the terrain. He began to work his way around the base of the rockslide, moving to his right, periodically slipping and falling in the loose rock. He had cut and scraped his hands several times and was aware of a small foreign object lodged in the heel of his left palm. In spite of picking at it several times, he did not get it out, and there was insufficient light to try digging it out with a knife. He reached the top edge of the slide and found a rock ledge leading upward. He began to climb, hoping that his luck would change. After climbing upward at an aggressive rate for about a hundred difficult paces, the entire ledge gave way, sending him crashing down the now virtually sheer mountainside. He fell away from the side of the rock wall for a brief moment, bounced hard... then darkness.

When he awoke, his head was pounding and his hands were stiff and throbbing. He was aware of distant voices. He sat up with some difficulty because his left leg was asleep from the hip down. The half crescent moon had risen, and the side of the mountain was now much more visible. He felt sick... very sick and dizzy. He tried to move, but his leg was totally limp. He began to rub it briskly, becoming painfully aware again of the object stuck in his hand. He reflected on his situation as he worked his leg... "Why all this work and danger for a man who would doubtless kill him on a whim?" He knew that his lifestyle of stealing and killing had made him a wanted man in just about every neighborhood. He also knew that only such a man as Danlion would welcome, let alone accept, his service. He enjoyed being a thief in the society he'd grown up in. "But, if Danlion prevails, that society will perish... lawlessness would become law!"

As he sat for a moment reflecting on these things, he became aware of approaching voices. He could now catch an occasional glimpse of distant moving torches through the trees. Doubtless, they would have heard the ledge break and fall, and at least some of them would come to investigate.

His leg was waking up now and felt as if it was wrapped with cactus. As he stood up, the "little man with a sledgehammer" pounding in his head forced him to move slowly.

Jarmin was not accustomed to self-pity but began to indulge a bit, "Why do these powerful types always live high on some mountain or out in some monster haunted forest?" His pain caused him to refocus before continuing his thoughts, "Why couldn't this one have just lived down the road a little in a nice cabin?" Jarmin laughed briefly to himself, having the humor again tempered by the sensitivity of his throbbing head. "The reason they don't is because some fool or another would always be bothering them or attempting to harm them... I guess I'd do the same thing."

He began to move up the mountain again, very slowly this time. He knew he was no match for the wizard when he was well and fully operational. Now the best he could do was hide. Even if he did get the information he desired, how would he get away now? All too soon, the news of his deeds in town would be known to the wizard. "Maybe," he thought to himself, "if I simply hid again...just disappeared... like in Castle Crest, where I learned so much from Rhem and Shaylan?" He knew that sooner or later Pretoria would send a delegation to seek the information... "but would they come to this wizard?...even if they did, the head start, and all the advantages that meant would be lost..." He knew none of this would work now, now that they would be watching for his magic.

He decided not to go back up the way from which he had fallen. Instead, he set out to try and find a way up on the side of the mountain that would remain the most clearly lit by the moon's light throughout the night. As he worked his way around the mountain, he always moved to his right, away from the town and his pursuers. Because most of the ground he was moving across was barren of trees, having only occasional waste high brush, he realized that he would be very visible and would surely be apprehended by the dwarves if he was seen. This motivated him to fight against the pain and move quickly. But, as he did, his sickness increased and his dizziness began to affect his ability to walk straight.

He knew that any use of magic would attract immediate attention to his position. He also knew that he would not be able to keep moving very long before his body gave way. He came to a place where the hill slanted upward slowly toward some rocky crags. Jarmin decided to try and make it to the base of the crags with a plan to find shelter there and sleep until morning.

The pain in his head swelled with every heartbeat, bringing with it powerful waves of nausea. He had to stop several times from weakness... twice he nearly lost consciousness. By the time he reached the base of the crags, he was so sick that he felt sure he was dying. "The head wound must be worse than I thought," he mused as he sat down leaning against a vertical rock wall between two large boulders. Hopelessness flooded his entire being... injured, hunted, lost... and without any clear plan. He knew that everything he had suffered would mean nothing to Danlion unless it obtained the proper results.

Sitting down was the only ingredient that had been missing in the recipe for unconsciousness. Before he could decide whether to keep sitting, lie down, or look for a better place to sleep, he was out.

He awoke suddenly with a heavy sense of dread upon him. His entire body ached now, including his neck, because his head had fallen forward on his chest as he slept. To make things worse, in the suddenness of his awakening, he had jerked his head up and caused an even more severe sharp pain in his neck muscles. He sat very still, sensing and trying to open and focus his eyes that seemed to be forced shut by the pounding in his head... his eyes did not open wider than a slit nor clear beyond a blur.

After his eyes got as good as they were going to, he looked around, just barely moving his head. He realized that the sky reflected the approaching dawn and that there was a dwarf with a heavy coat on, holding a long, thick stick in his hand, and standing only about a single stride away, directly in front of him. Neither spoke for a long time. Only the dwarf moved, and that was to shuffle back and forth from foot to foot as if cold.

Finally, the dwarf mumbled something, and a faint greenish glow formed around the hand in which he held the stick. The dwarf pointed the stick at Jarmin, and suddenly the glow streaked down to its point and leapt from there, to hit Jarmin mid-body. He tried to avoid it, but accomplished little more than a jerky twitching of muscles. Energy filled his body momentarily, along with an odd warmth, like being a little drunk. His vision cleared.

"Ya awake now, stranger?" came a pleasant but decidedly mature inquiry from the dwarf.

"As much as I can be," he answered with each word pounding pain into his head. "I don't think I can move."

"Then ya better just sit there," came the reply, accompanied by a low chuckle. "Why are ya here?" The question had that familiar tone of a father who caught his child somewhere that was known to be off limits.

Jarmin's thoughts were too racked with the consciousness of pain for him to reason clearly enough to be clever. "I'm looking for the dwarf wizard that lives on this mountain."

"Why might ya be doin' such a thing?"

Jarmin hesitated..."Information."

"What type of information?"

"About a sword." Jarmin felt sure that this entire line of questioning would just get him killed, but he didn't care anymore, so he just told the truth.

"What sword might that be?"

"The dwarven forged sword at Castle Crest in Pretoria."

"Now why might ya be thinkin' that the sword is of dwarven origin?"

"I heard the magician and the swordsman at Castle Crest talking when they figured it out... discovered that it was made by dwarves and elves."

"I see... did the sword look like this?" The dwarf reached his arms out, palms up, and formed a lighted illusion of a sword in the air between them.

It was perfect... "That means," thought Jarmin to himself, "that this fun little dwarf is most probably the wizard, has most certainly somehow discerned his business and was now toying with him... he also most likely knows of the deaths."

"Yes, just exactly like that!" answered Jarmin, now resigned to dying soon. At least it would relieve him from his pain and sickness, which were both escalating again. "Just kill me and get this over with," said Jarmin with as much force as he could muster.

The dwarf laughed, "Oh, no, no, no! That won't do! No, that simply won't do." The dwarf raised his hand above his head, and several other dwarves joined them almost immediately, appearing seemingly from nowhere.

"Let's get him into the lower cave for the rest of the night. We'll tend him there, then move him up later," he said as he directed four of the dwarves to carry him.

One of them protested quite adamantly, "Now, Darric, why take him anywhere? He killed Lanterlain, Lox, and Fumbit. He'll kill again, he will! Just give him the chance." The others joined in approval.

"If my suspicions are correct, he is more valuable to us alive than dead." Darric was trying to calm their emotions.

"Not likely he feels the same about you!" shot back another of the dwarves, with the others chiming in again.

Darric moved up next to Jarmin and asked, "What's your name, stranger?"

"Jarmin."

"Jarmin, why did you kill our friends?"

"They exposed my disguise and would have killed or captured me."

"But Jarmin, why did you kill our friends?"

"I was afraid."

"Are you going to kill us too?"

"I hope not. I don't like to kill. It makes me feel bad."

At that, one of the dwarves cut in almost shouting, "...makes YOU feel bad?! How about those you kill? How about their families?!"

One of the others joined in immediately, "Darric, how can you believe this man. Lying is second language of most humans!?"

"Because, Brankx, I charmed him, he has to tell the truth, "came Darric's words with his characteristic intelligent chuckle.

"Last question for now, Jarmin. Who do ya work for in this matter? Who's payin' for the information ya so recklessly seek?"

There was a moment of silence while Jarmin fought back the powerful urge to speak. Finally, he just blurted out, "Lord Danlion" so loud that the pain from his head caused him to pass out.

When he awoke, Darric was removing an amulet on a chain from around his neck. He was lying on a bedroll, which was on the floor near a window in a quaint wood-paneled room with an open-beam ceiling. He was much longer than the bed that he lay next to. The sun shone in unfiltered through the open window, causing him to squint as he tried to open his eyes. His eyes did not focus well, and he had a total-body ache, especially in his head. He still felt sick. He tried to sit up, but the room felt like it was spinning... this complicated his feeling of nausea.

"How do ya feel?" was Darric's warm-sounding inquiry.

"I feel awful!" whispered Jarmin in a hoarse voice.

"Ya look even worse," came the reply with a chuckle attached. "Just lie back an' I'll try the amulet again."

Darric took the same amulet he had just removed and placed it around Jarmin's neck. He felt an addicting warmth creep slowly through his body. His head began to clear a little, and his eyes started to focus.

"What is this thing?"

"It's an Elven healing necklace."

"How does it work?"

"Elven magic!" answered Darric with a smile. "It draws power from the earth as long as the body has enough structure to heal or at least stay alive. It works slowly, though, because there is no mind guiding it. It is especially effective when healers can't determine the cause of an ailment and therefore can't use their magic safely. If it feels warm to you, your body still wants to heal. If the power is cold... icy... your body is too tired to heal. Then it will only work to sustain life as long as the body holds it."

"It made me feel almost well."

"Ya might feel that way lying there, but if ya took off the necklace, ya would quickly sink back nearly to yer past state of injury. This is one of only four amulets that have this power. They can actually help ya heal while ya work. They were made for Elven and Dwarven leaders at a great cost. They would wear them in times of crisis like wars and such, bein' enabled by their magic to perform required duties for days on end without resting. Each one is passed down from one leader to another with the succession of responsibility. They are to be used in times of great need and then only for as long as is absolutely necessary. I am one of the leaders privileged to possess one."

"Why are you using it up on me?"

"Oh...no, no, no!" chuckled Darric, "Ya can't use up the necklace. It's magic is of another age and kind. It works permanently, unless the amulet is damaged... then it will simply cease to work." Darric studied Jarmin's thoughts, a trick easy for him to do. "As for why I use it on ya, which was actually what ya intended to ask, I need ya well for carry'n a message back ta Danlion when I return from Castle Crest. After I've ensured that the proper man has use of the sword, I'll send a message through ya to yer evil task master." Darric studied Jarmin again, "I advise ya to put yer intentions of stealing the necklace away. Let it heal ya, and after that just put it out of yer mind. If ya take it, it'll likely cost ya yer life!" The dwarf now wore a stern look and spoke as a wise old grandfather might to his grandson.

Jarmin was mystified by Darric. He sensed nothing extraordinary about him but his countenance carried such confidence and sure-footed emotional control that everything inside him longed to test this aged dwarf magician.

Darric kept watch from a room directly across a well-lit hallway from Jarmin's room for the rest of that day. Dwarves came and went. Some brought scrolls & books, others carried cloth bags which contained delicate things requiring careful handling. Jarmin watched as much as he could see with great interest.

When evening came, several dwarves accompanied Darric into the room where Jarmin was being kept. Jarmin surmised that they were some sort of military types, army or constables or some such office. One sketched a picture of him that was remarkable in detail. They discussed him in hushed tones and in a dwarven dialect he was unfamiliar with. He tried to use his sensing power on them, but for some reason was unable to enact the necessary magic. During one such attempt, Darric looked over at him with bushy eyebrows raised and shook his head back and forth while scolding with his pointing finger, both signaling, "NO! NO! NO!" Then with a friendly smile, he added, "Save yer strength for healin'. These Dwarves need only ta get a good look at ya. They're not plannin' to harm you." All the other dwarves, who had stopped talking and joined in staring at him during the brief caution from Darric, turned passively back toward Darric and continued the conversation.

"This Darric is no one to trifle with," he thought to himself. "He's just plain scary!" He lay for a while reflecting on the difference between Darric and Danlion. Everyone addressed Danlion as "Lord Danlion". If the proper respect was not shown, the offender was usually chastised painfully... or, if the offense was great enough... was turned into something quite dead and most often disgustingly gruesome. This dwarf, however, had no airs, no pomp, no demand of respect. Everyone did show some sign of respect, but if disagreement arose, he was actually patient and conciliatory. Jarmin became convinced that it would be certain death for the dwarf if he ever faced Danlion. "The dwarf was too nice for his own good!"

Just as the dwarves were preparing to leave, a guard came in with a beautiful cup in his hand. He stopped briefly and spoke to Darric, who took the cup from him and brought it to Jarmin. It was filled with a clear orange colored drink that smelled like fruit blossoms.

He handed the cup to Jarmin, "Now drink all of this and it'll help ya heal while ya sleep." Darric was not asking him "if" he wanted to drink this; there was a clear tone of command in his voice. "No need ta worry. I'll leave the necklace on ya every night from now on while the drink works ta heal ya also."

He took one taste of the drink and found it very pleasant but a little too sweet. As he finished it, he could feel warmth filling his body. Just as suddenly, he began to feel lightheaded....

When he next awoke, the sun was up. He was weak, but the pain in his head was minor. The necklace was gone. He tried to sit up, but the combination of weakness and resurgent headache stopped him cold.

There was a dwarf guarding him who got up out of his chair and walked briskly over to him. A much gruffer voice than Darric's announced, "Now ya just lay still and stop tryin' to move. You're gonna make yourself worse if ya don't just be still!" Jarmin closed his eyes again, partly in pain and partly in defeat.

During the rest of the day, he spent most of his time sleeping, being awakened periodically for food or to be assisted, at his request, with other vital necessities. At one point, he realized that his left hand was totally bandaged, as were his knees and head. He did not remember any of it taking place. This bothered him immensely. His body was very weak, and almost every joint was stiff and ached with something near severity. Only when he wore the necklace did he remember the pain totally leaving.

He asked several of those who attended him if he could wear the necklace for just a little while "...to get some relief from the pain...". They all, in turn, informed him that it wasn't good for him to wear it too long at one time unless in the greatest of need. They did, however, give him a bitter drink that killed a substantial amount of the pain temporarily.

At night, Darric would bring the necklace with the amulet on it and place it around his neck as he drank the special healing potion. The warmth of the amulet's power would join with that of the drink, and he would again drift off to the most peaceful sleep he had ever experienced.

This routine went on for three more days. During that time, Jarmin discovered that the drink was a common, well-liked dwarven sweet brew that the guards would add medicine to each night. Darric kept the necklace all day, only using it when the medicine knocked Jarmin out at night and removing it early in the morning for the daylight hours.

The next day, Darric was sitting in a chair next to Jarmin when he awoke. Darric removed the necklace from Jarmin's neck and placed it in a box with a small lock at the top. He called the guard over and had him lock the box onto his own belt. Darric instructed him, in Jarmin's presence, to only allow it to be worn at night, and then only under the influence of the healing drink.

Darric explained that he was going to have some visitors from Pretoria later that day and would likely leave with them within a few days to Castle Crest. "When I return, I'll have a special message for ya to carry. Hopefully ya'll be well enough ta travel by then." Jarmin felt defeated. Let alone did he not get the information he needed, but probably the only dwarf in the land with that crucial knowledge was slipping away with the competitor to reveal the secrets and make things even worse. And there was nothing he could do to stop it.

CHAPTER 11

The seven men were up and packed while it was still very dark. There was a marked sense of camaraderie among them, all of them that is, except Draxyl. No attempt by any of the others succeeded in breaking him out of his self-pitying depression... he did not like adventures, invisible enemies, or negotiating with those other crafty races. Quite apart from that, he didn't like traveling on horseback. "So what's to like?" he would say to each member who tried one after the other to cheer him up with such encouraging declarations like, "Come on Draxly, this is bound to be a historical adventure..." and "Just think, your skills in writing will create a permanent record of our negotiations, you're going to play a central role!" With each attempt, his mood grew darker. Finally, the others grew tired of trying and let him wallow in his own personal mire.

As soon as their gear was packed on the horses, they were treated to a breakfast prepared under the direction of Mersalin, the chief chef of Lord Welton's castle and envy of all chefs who taste his food. After the meal, they were each supplied with traveling food, courtesy of Lord Falock (who was prepared for the advent of such an adventure). Their rations contained small bread rolls, dried and smoked meat, dried fruit, nuts, and a skin of his best wine. The provisions had been carefully wrapped in water resistant satchels with each foodstuff separately packaged.

With all this accomplished, they set out just before daybreak. The sky was again clear, with only a slight chill in it and not even the hint of a breeze. The members of the council were all present to bid a farewell as they rode out of the Beorg camp.

They decided to travel through the Crossings and up the Pretorian highway, which skirts the Teaman Swamp on the way to Thamerlain, capital city of the dwarven confederation and seat of the Supreme, their leader. They didn't feel that the much longer "Ridge Road", a road which provides more cover for moving in stealth, would be advisable because, if their mission had become known to Danlion, they would need to get to Thamerlain as quickly as possible. The Pretorian Highway was built as a commerce road and therefore put on the flattest part of the Marlton Plain. On this road, however, travelers could be seen a great distance away, making them vulnerable to ambush. To protect the Pretorian merchants, traders, and other travelers against these attacks, the three lords had assigned 21 groups of eight men each to patrol the road. They also acted as escorts for Pretorian trade caravans. The combined group of soldiers took on the name "Pretorian Rangers". They had special uniforms that would be readily recognizable and which were distinct from other soldiers who might from time to time travel the road.

The men rode with determination. Even their horses seemed to feel it, sometimes breaking into a spontaneous gallop that had to be reigned in by their riders. They arrived at the Crossing early in the midday and decided not to stop, but just to stick to the highway all the way through town. Dalwan did not even look from side to side as he rode through town, hoping that no one he knew would see or recognize him.

With the Crossings behind them, they continued straight up the highway. They now rode in silence, contemplating the mission, each man feeling that somehow destiny had brought them to this place and time. If the other races held the keys of knowledge of the sword, this trip could prove to be the most significant event in what was sure to be a tumultuous struggle for dominance among men. It was even possible that the knowledge they would discover would be sufficient to allow the powermaster to wield the sword, if he could be identified. But dark clouds of uncertainty hung over their journey. Would they be received favorably by the other races? Would Danlion somehow discover their mission and try to stop them? If they were given knowledge, would it even be useful to them, or just some trick that would prevent them from using the sword ever again? These thoughts and many more, thoughts of loved ones left behind, terrible acts of warfare, and mystical beasts of past wars all danced in their minds as they headed toward Thamerlain.

They rode until dusk before setting up camp their first night out. They stopped alongside the road where a creek ran under a small bridge. The bridge was magnificently constructed, obviously the work of a powerful and talented stone molder of the past. Its arches and supports appeared seamless in the dimming light of the day.

The excitement of the day had left its mark of fatigue on them all. They quickly decided on a rotation of watch through the night, and after a quick, quiet, cold meal, all but the first watch went off to sleep.

The night went by very quietly. The only activity was that involved in the changing of the watch, the howl of distant coyotes, and a couple of deer which wandered unwary into camp only to be startled by Draymoor's cough, who watched them gracefully bound away over the flat grassland in the bright moonlight.

Shaylan had the last watch and took advantage of the opportunity to awaken Dalwan and warn him further about showing his power. After he woke the rest of the camp, he took a small pan that he carried with him and heated some water for those who wanted a hot drink with their breakfast. He used his fire art to heat the water in the pan. Their four traveling companions had all seen the fire art practiced, but none of them had ever seen it used to cook anything. And certainly, none had ever tasted drink heated with magic fire. There was something of a side-show atmosphere at breakfast.

This was the first time in the journey that the men began to get to know each other. Some were known by reputation to everyone, like Rhem, Shaylan, and Attleman. Everyone seemed in high spirits as they shared about their adventures and their responsibilities, everyone except Draxyl. He did not appreciate the great outdoors, hated cold food, dirt, and especially sleeping on the ground. He remained withdrawn and sullen in spite of Malan's repeated attempts to cheer him up and draw him into the group. Draymoor was quieter than the others but listened with intense interest as the others spoke, often smiling broadly at the jesting which continued between Malan and Attleman, who thoroughly enjoyed each other's company.

The talk continued even as they rode along. They were now on the Marlton Plain, and because it was so flat and the road so wide, they could all ride abreast of each other and talk without interruption.

Draxyl rode about five lengths behind the others, alone for a good part of the morning, even though several attempts were made to draw him in. Finally, Dalwan dropped back and rode silently with him until late afternoon, when they stopped to water the horses. They were nearing the southern edge of the Teaman Swamp and therefore needed to make a decision about where to spend the night.

As the horses drank their fill from a small, shallow creek, the men began to recount stories purporting the Teaman Swamp to be the haunt of a family of dragons and supposedly the home of a few dark beasts of vague and terrible description that roamed in packs and ate every living thing they found, including people. "It was most likely," speculated Attleman in a whisper which caused everyone to lean a little toward him to hear, "that those few people who were known to have vanished from the road while traveling in or near the swamp, had been the victims of much more devious and deceptive beasts...bandits!"

The truth of this did not stop the much needed laughter that broke the tension which had been created by the storytelling and speculation. There had been no recent reports of disappearing travelers, not since the establishment of the patrols.

The men here were not superstitious nor timid, with the notable exception of Draxyl. But they were wise and realized that, at one point at least, they would be very vulnerable to attack should Lord Danlion somehow become aware of the activity. That would be when they went through the swamp itself. The road bordered the swamp for most of the way around the southeast side of it. But at one point, it went directly across a narrow strip about an hour's ride through. The road was built generations ago of dirt and stone fill and was bordered by a swamp on both sides. If they were being hunted, that would be an ideal place for their adversaries to force a confrontation. Even without evil beasts, the swamp was no place to be on foot, off the road.

After some discussion, they decided to spend the night on the south side of the place where the road entered the swamp and to pass through in the morning. The sun had set and dusk was dimming the features of the land when they set up camp within eyesight of the road's entrance into the swamp. They quickly decided to follow the same watch rotation they had used the night before. Though they were not overly superstitious, they knew that few people had ever camped so close to the swamp. Most travelers camped far enough away that once they started again in the morning, they would make it to the swamp crossing area in the early afternoon. But the urgency of their mission made it important for them to push ahead and camp close.

By the time they were situated and ready to go to sleep, a mist-like fog had risen from the swamp and obscured their vision of its tree-lined border. Before they lay down, they all stood together at the edge of camp, staring at the wall of swamp fog. Then, with little talking, each went to their bedroll, hoping to find there a much-needed restful sleep.

A few hours into the night, during Attleman's watch, there came through the fog a muffled scream. It was hard to tell how far away it was or from what manner of beast it came. All the men woke up and came out of the night rolls armed. They stood silently staring into the night toward the swamp fog, which was now much closer than before. The moon lit the entire area, making an erie scene which looked as if someone had painted earth and sky and left a gray, smudged band across the middle. Suddenly, there came a series of roars each followed by the scream of another beast. The roar was deep and reminded them of thunder. They could not determine at first if the scream was from fear and pain or an act of intimidation. The noises began to move across the landscape... noises without bodies. The roar was obviously stalking the scream. There was a brief period of quiet, which was broken by the two much closer sounds. They grew closer and closer until the men began to get anxious, pacing and watching, white knuckle grips on their weapons. Finally, the long-anticipated battle took place very near the leading edge of the fog bank, not far from their camp. The moments that the fight lasted seemed like an eternity to the watchers. It ended when a roar of obvious pain was followed immediately by the scream as it retreated at a high rate of speed toward the swamp. It also sounded injured. This was followed in turn by the heavy thuds of the pursuer moving and protesting after it at a much slower rate until finally only a faint reminder remained of the horror they had experienced while the invisible foes fought.

After a few minutes of fog-shrouded silence, the men began to return to their beds. Those who could sleep, did so fitfully, with visions of demons & beasts invading their dreams. None of them had ever heard the likes of these two disembodied inhuman voices except Dalwan and Rhem, who quietly agreed that the roar resembled that of the anderon.

The men arose with the first vague hint of dawn's approach and made a fire around which they waited for sunrise. They had not slept well, and the cold they felt went clear through them, a cold the source of which was more than the intolerably damp air, and went deeper than mere flesh and bone could feel. As the warmth of the fire melted their outer chill, the dancing flames presented fleeting images, bodies with which to surround the sounds now etched in their minds from the night's noisy battle. None ventured away from the fire's light until the light of the coming dawn began to dissolve the night shadows, and the landscape became clearly discernible. And none of them admitted, even to themselves, anything other than the need for the fire's comforting warmth.

As soon as the sun's rays began to penetrate the wet air, the men prepared to set out for the swamp crossing. They packed and mounted their equally tired and quite spooked horses, setting out in pairs. The still hazy air was full of the odor of decaying plant life. A hint of movement in the air was seen in the wisps of misty vapors that whirled upward in long, thin spiraling shafts as they rose from the marshy soil. The road they traveled was becoming more distinctive from its surroundings as it rose about the height of a wagon wheel above the grassland it passed through and became wide enough for two wagons to pass each other comfortably. It was crowned in the center with a gentle slope to each side. The top surface was a hardpack mortar-like combination of clay and sand, which had been carefully applied over a bed of crushed rock. The engineering of the road was carried out by the Dwarves and was especially effective in the wetlands. The dwarves sent crews to tend the road surface twice a year.

As they approached the edge of the swamp forest, the fog still veiled in gloomy grey all but the very tops of the tallest trees. At the edge of the swamp forest, they entered the cloud where they had only a very limited amount of visibility. The front riders appeared only as misty forms to those in the rear.

Once they entered the tree line, the misty fog turned into a haze that seemed to dull everything and suck out its color. The sun above was trying to melt away the grayness, but only an occasional shaft of light broke through the thickly cloaked forest canopy. Each rider shivered in his saddle as the cold-saturated air penetrated clear to their bones. The odor of decay was more pungent, and the air so heavy that even sounds were absorbed into it, much like the effect in a snow flurry.

The men rode on in silence, each very glad that there was only a short distance to be traveled before they cleared this cheerless place. That distance was made irritatingly longer to the men due to the fact that the dwarves had not cut the road straight through the swamp but had woven it through the trees, avoiding the largest ones and skirting tight clusters of trees that they called families.

They had ridden about halfway through when Dalwan sensed the presence of others ahead of them. He was giving thought to announcing his perceptions when Shaylan stopped the column and warned them of imminent contact. Attleman had also sensed their approach and further warned the men that he feared there was danger in the coming meeting, but couldn't identify what prompted his feeling.

The group reorganized, with Rhem and Attleman taking up the lead, Shaylan and Dalwan next, Draxyl by himself, and Malan with Draymoor in the rear. Attleman was designated the spokesman for the group.

The road skirted a thick grove of Cypress trees and revealed a long straightaway on the other side. As they cleared the bend, they could make out the forms of eight riders coming toward them. When they were about 100 strides away, it became clear that they were all men dressed in uniforms. As soon as he was sure, Attleman announced that they wore the uniforms of the Pretorian Rangers. Both groups continued to approach at a casual rate. Only a short distance had elapsed between them when Attleman suddenly turned in his saddle and yelled, "IMPOSTORS!"

At that instant, the Rangers' horses broke into a full run toward them. The delegation reigned up to a stop. The first two oncoming riders fired crossbows, which appeared to be attached to their saddles by a cord. With lightning speed, Rhem deflected one arrow into the trees while the other hit Attleman's horse in the neck. The horse whirled wildly, throwing Attleman onto the ground. It then stumbled off the road in convulsions and fell into the swamp. Rhem dismounted as did the others and formed a hasty barrier, laying Rhem, Shaylan, and Dalwan's horses across the road end to end. Malan and Draymoor formed a second line behind them, and Draxyl retreated to the rear of the group. About 30 strides from this temporary barrier, four of the riders broke off their attack and four continued on in pairs, putting about three lengths between them.

Attleman joined Rhem, Shaylan, and Dalwan, standing behind their horses on the front line. As the first two riders approached, they pulled swords and held them high, yelling as they rode.

"Duck as they jump the horses," shouted Attleman. Then, turning back to Draymoor and Malan, "The first wave is yours."

As the first two neared the front line, they shifted to the left so as to engage only Shaylan and Dalwan. The riders behind them adjusted to take on Attleman and Rhem. As soon as they began their jump, both Shaylan and Rhem feigned a defensive posture, then suddenly dropped to their backs with swords up to protect against the rider's swing. This threw off both riders, and their initial blows were easily deflected.

Malan jumped over his horse toward the rider closest to the center of the road. As his horse landed and the rider was thrown forward, Malan threw all his weight into a broad axe swing that hit the rider in his side, throwing him to the ground with the axe still embedded. Malan was spun around and fell, sprawled face down on the road.

Draymoor took on the other rider as he jumped the second line of
horses. He firmly planted his feet and held his sword firmly with both
hands. The rider swung powerfully as his horse landed. Draymoor moved as if
made of smoke, totally avoiding contact with the attacker's broadsword. This
threw the rider off balance momentarily, but he quickly regained his composure
and pulled his horse to a stop. But before he could even adjust in his saddle to
turn the horse, Draymoor had cleared the distance between them and jumped
up behind the rider. Having abandoned his sword on the road, he grabbed the
rider's hair and pulled his head back, slitting his throat with a sheath knife he
now held.

The second wave of horses was already jumping over the first line,
having moved to the right side to engage Rhem, near the middle of the road,
and Attleman on the far right. Dalwan was close to Rhem, and as the rider
jumped between them over the line of horses, Dalwan, who was still lying
down, stuck his sword into the horse's belly from the side. At the same time,
Rhem delivered a powerful blow to the rider's oncoming sword. The horse
landed lamely and rolled forward directly over its rider, narrowly missing Malan,
who was only just then gaining his feet after recovering from his first
engagement.

Attleman tried to deflect the blow of the rider who attacked him, but his
fall had left him injured. His sword was hit squarely by the rider and knocked
into the swamp. The rider reigned hard, virtually turning his horse in midair to
reengage Attleman before he could recover. He was barely moving back toward
him when Rhem attacked from the other side of his horse. The combat was
very short, ending with the crack of a whip at which time the rider, drug by the
neck, fell backwards off his horse at Draymoor's feet... he never even caught his
breath.

No sooner was this finished than a volley of arrows split the air from the
four remaining horseman who stood side by side in front of their horses. One
arrow hit Draymoor's mail shirt on the left shoulder, making a painful
bruise. The other arrows all narrowly missed their intended but alert targets. In
a heartbeat, Rhem and Draymoor were running toward the archers. The
extended time required to load a crossbow proved too long to prevent
swordplay. Rhem was a formidable match for any two good swordsman... these
were not good swordsman. Draymoor drew the other two away from Rhem

and was able to hold his own ground against them. Then, to Draymoor's surprise, they suddenly dropped their swords and held up their hand at the approach of Malan, Shaylan, and, to their astonishment, Rhem. The two men were quickly apprehended and tied up with leather cords.

Shaylan questioned them as Attleman and Dalwan used their sensing powers to determine the truth of their answers. The men were made to kneel down in the middle of the group, sitting on their legs, which were crossed at the ankles. Attleman and Dalwan stood behind the men who faced Shaylan.

"Where do you come from?" asked Shaylan, sounding much like a prosecutor.

"From my mother!" said one of the men sarcastically.

Malan gave him a slap to the back of his head and received for it a vicious look.

Turning to the other man, "Where do you come from?"

"Why should I tell you anything... you're going to kill us anyway?"

"Not if I can discover a way to keep you from interfering... but most certainly if you don't cooperate!"

The man was obviously not blessed with the art of sensing, so he studied the Shaylan's expressionless face for a moment before answering. "We were sent by Lord Danlion to stop any representatives from Pretoria from inquiring about the sword from the dwarves and elves... he said it would only be necessary for a short time."

The other man spat at his partner and received a second slap on the back of the head, which seemed to bring him near insanity with rage.

"What good is it to keep slapping him?" asked Shaylan with little tolerance for such methods.

"'Cause he irritates me... 'sides, we only need one of 'em to get answers from... 'n this one seems tired of livin'," answered Malan in a caustic tone.

"They are quite subdued for now, so let's get on with our questioning... and civilly please," said Shaylan with one eyebrow raised in Malan's direction.

Shaylan looked at the belligerent man, who returned a defiant look, "If you don't cooperate, I'm going to give you to him," he said, motioning toward Malan.

Malan stepped to the man's side and looked him in the eyes, taunting him with an ear to ear menacing grin.

"Are you talking about the legendary Danlion?" he asked the other man, returning to the questioning.

"Yes."

"What sword are you talking about, and why does Danlion think someone will come from Pretoria to ask the Dwarves about it?"

"I don't know for sure... we only got here yesterday... we were woke up in the middle of the night a couple of days ago and sent here with no preparation or warning. We were told to stop anybody from getting to the dwarves and elves from Pretoria until he got a message from someone. The sword must be some powersword... maybe Fallonrod from the last earth wars."

Shaylan looked to Dalwan and Attleman for the truth of it and received the nod.

"How many of you were sent?"

"About 20 in all..."

While he was speaking, both Attleman and Dalwan shook their heads.

"Hold right there!" Shaylan said, interrupting him with an insightful chuckle. "Staying alive depends upon you telling the truth as well as you know it... and you know that isn't true. You want to try again?"

The man turned pale for a moment. "O.K... O.K... there are two bands, each about 25 strong, out looking for those who should be coming from Pretoria. One is heading for the road from Castle Crest, and we are part of the other group."

"And you were simply going to kill everyone coming from Pretoria to Thamerlain?"

"No, No... each group has..." he stopped briefly and looked at the body of one of the men Rhem killed, "...HAD a good sensor who was supposed to be able to tell us when we had the right group."

"Why did you attack us?"

"Atna, our sensor..." he said, motioning toward the body, "said there was possible danger close... and then one of your group shouted 'imposter' so we just attacked."

"How did you kill the rangers?"

"They thought we were merchants traveling from the south on the mountain highway. We were such a large group that they never considered us bandits, so they let their guard down. We set a signal, and when it was given, we struck them... even then, they killed two of us and wounded two more. That was last night, just south of Balorton."

"Where is the rest of your band?"

The other man yelled, "Don't tell them, you fool... we'll both be dead men..." Malan cut him off with a backhand to the mouth.

Shaylan returned his attention to the original speaker without further comment or question.

"Most of them are waiting at the junction of the Central Pretorian Highway and the Mountain Highway. A small band... three or four... went down the Mountain Highway scouting out travelers, same as us... only without uniforms."

"I'll kill you myself if we get out of this alive," shouted the man's companion, with blood all over his teeth and running down his mouth from the blow Malan gave him.

Attleman walked over to him and crouched down face to face with the man, "We don't usually kill prisoners, unless they come to trial and are convicted. In this case, you both would already be dead if your partner hadn't talked. He will most certainly live now... you're making a question out of yourself."

After a brief consultation, it was decided that it was too risky to take the prisoners with them. And in light of the threats against the one who talked, it was determined that he would be untied and given a sheath knife, and the other man would be left tied. Both men were given their horses and sent south on the highway. It would take them far too long to get back around the swamp to be of any danger.

"Your fate is now in the hands of the man you threatened," said Draymoor, still nursing his injured shoulder. "Your mouth has jeopardized your future due to your ignorance of civilized behavior. You owe him your life."

"Well, all this fair play stuff doesn't sit well with me when I see the likes of you," said Malan, staring at the belligerent captive now tied to the mount of his horse. "If it was up to me, I just a'soon killed you and been done with it." He looked at his companions for a reaction but received, at most, a few amused grins. "I suppose you all think they would let us ride south if they had won?"

Attleman walked over to him and slapped him on the shoulder, "Come on, friend, they can't be of hurt to us now... besides, you wouldn't be able to sleep with yourself if you killed a bound man under these circumstances... and the rest of us have to live with our consciences too."

Malan turned and slapped the man's horse on the rump so hard that it took off at a run down the road to the curses of the bound man. He got a laugh out of it and looked over at the other man, "Take good care of him for me?" The man nodded and rode off slowly, knowing that he'd catch up sooner or later.

Attleman grabbed Malan by the upper arm, "Come on an' give me a hand gettin' my things off my horse... most of them are probably soaked by now." They both went back together, and Attleman waded out into the swamp and handed his belongings back up to Malan, who collected them and spread them out to let them drain, while Attleman stripped the riding gear from his dead horse.

Dalwan rounded up the remaining living horses and brought them to Attleman so he could choose one for himself.

It was only after this that they realized that none of them had seen, or even missed, Draxyl. Dalwan mounted his horse and set out back down the road to look for him. As he rounded the curve that skirted the grove of cypress trees, he noticed a muddy water trail leading out into the center of the grove from the road. He stopped and called out, wondering if it was Draxly's or the man they tied to the horse. He sat still for a moment, not hearing anything but a faint splashing of water. He called again and then saw Draxyl riding slowly out, slumped shoulders forward in his saddle. As he approached, Dalwan could see that his eyes were puffy and red, and there were tear stains on his cheeks.

Dalwan took some water from his water skin and wet a cloth he carried in his pocket, and handed it to Draxyl, "Wipe off your face, Draxyl, and let's get back. I'll ride with you until we get out of the swamp."

Draxyl didn't say a thing but took the cloth and cleaned himself up. They rejoined the others who were already mounted and ready to ride.

They all rode hard from there until they cleared the swamp. Once they were completely away from the swamp, they regrouped and decided to ride through the junction as fast as they could in a group. Draxyl was placed in the middle of the group and told to ride as hard as he could, keep his head down, and stay with them this time.

As they approached the junction, those with the art of sensing rode a ways ahead of the others and tried to sense what they might encounter. They all sensed danger, but no magic. "They must not be expecting anyone," said Shaylan, "...still, there is something unsettling about this..."

Attleman cut in, "I'm sure we're being watched... I can feel their eyes... but I share your misgivings about the situation... something strange."

They returned to the others and decided that since they were so close to Thamerlain, they could chance using magic if they had to, to escape whatever was waiting for them in the junction.

The junction was the coming together of two roads, the Mid Pretorian Highway met the Mountain Highway in a fork, combining to form the Thamerlain Highway. They met in the rocky slopes of the Emerald Mountains, which separated Pretoria from the dwarven and elven lands to the North. The Thamerlain Highway went on through the pass to Thamerlain, the dwarven capital city. The actual junction was where two rock walled paths joined, with rolling granite on both sides, sloping steeply upward from the roads.

When the group reached the bottom of the rock formation that formed the Junction and the outlet to the pass through the Emerald mountains, they started a wild charge. They rode as hard as their horses would allow, heads down, hearts pounding. As they rounded the rock-walled curve taking them into the heart of the junction, they encountered a wall of dwarves, the first ranks of which were standing with crossbows leveled at the oncoming riders. They broke off their charge abruptly and found themselves surrounded immediately. The barren rocks were now covered with stout-bodied archers, while broad axe-wielding dwarves circled each horseman.

No hostilities were exchanged. However, they did notice a significant pile of human bodies a little further up the road.

The sea of surrounding dwarves parted to permit a clean-shaven dwarf wearing a mail coat and helmet to approach the captive party. "What is your business?" he said in a gruff voice.

Shaylan was closest to him and therefore spoke for the group. "We are an official delegation from Pretoria come to seek official counsel and assistance from your wise leaders."

"What help do you seek?" said the dwarf who was as short on words as he was in height, and whose tone was impatient and irritated.

Sensing hostility from the dwarves and this one in particular, Shaylan chanced to tell the truth. "We need insight on matters concerning a power sword forged by the Dwarves many...uh..er..." As soon as he said "sword," the dwarven spokesman quit listening and made an arm gesture which triggered an echoing response from various dwarves in the army outward and up into the rocky surroundings. Before the last words and murmurs were out of his mouth, the sea of dwarves was moving up the road, and he was completely drowned out.

"Follow me!" shouted the dwarf as he turned and headed up the road.

"A little shorter and to the point will probably suit these folks just fine!" shouted Rhem with a broad smile and slap to Shaylan's thigh as he rode by. Shaylan's face shown red with embarrassment, which no one noticed except Rhem, who did so with unrestrained glee. "Shaylan. These are my kind of folks!" he shouted back as he took the lead, staying as close to the dwarf as possible.

"They can have you!" shouted Shaylan, shaking his head and trying not to become further entwined in Rhem's humorous web.

Rhem responded with a laugh that even brought smiles to the dwarves who escorted them.

CHAPTER 12

Most of the Dwarves were on foot, but some rode small horses, and a few rode in wagons. As those with transportation began to separate from those on foot, Attleman approached the leader of the dwarves about the men who were supposed to have been hiding in ambush on the road between Thamerlain and Castle Crest. The Dwarf, who identified himself as Westle, dispatched the foot soldiers and one wagon to investigate, promising the officer in charge that the others would catch up after they had escorted the "guests" safely to Thamerlain.

Very little was communicated to the little band of Ambassadors by their "escorts". They kept up a hard pace for the entire morning. By late morning, the hardest climb seemed to be behind them, and the sparse forest of hardwoods gave way little by little to towering pine trees. The further they went, the larger the trees became, with some so large that a single tree would have built a small village of houses.

By early afternoon, the road again began to climb significantly, this time in a zigzag pattern, which took them above the tree line and over the pass through the mountain range. By late afternoon, they were approaching a beautiful city that was laid out in the midst of the woods at the edge of a river in the valley below. As they approached the city, they saw what appeared to be hamlets, artfully spread throughout the countryside. Most of those in Thamerlain lived in one of these little settlements. The walled city was particularly small considering the number of people living around it. They crossed a magnificent bridge, which appeared to be a single log of uniform circumference supported by a latticework of stone arches and wood braces. The top and sides of the bridge were decorated with rows of various-shaped windows and skylights. Once inside, they discovered the carved murals that lined the inside corridor.

Shaylan asked Westle about the carvings.

"They're depictin' some of the greatest dwarves and the events which brought them fame," he said with a reverence that bordered on religious.

After hearing the explanation, the men paid special attention to the content of the carvings. Each man in turn became keenly aware that very few of the scenes related in any way to war or battles. Most were acts of civic service, kindness, self-sacrifice in assisting others, or somehow related to works of art.

After they crossed the river, they were led to the inner city. Its walls were thick and ornate, built by precision stone masons, no doubt with the assistance of copious amounts of well-developed magic. An aqueduct system ran through the walls. They noticed that the bridges, gates, walls, and exterior aqueducts had markings distinctive of both dwarves and elves. Without prompting, Westle explained that when their magic arts would grow in strength during the earth power swells, the dwarves and elves got together and joined their magics in cooperative ventures. They completed many projects of architectural excellence, showing remarkable synergism. Together, they turned each other's cities into works of art.

In Midcity, the majority of their escort party took a different road from the one they continued to follow. Westle and about 30 of his companions continued on with the delegates. Right in the center of town, they entered a beautiful park. There were large open areas of lawn with patches of flowers, clumps of bushes, and small groves of trees. Located in the middle of the grounds was a cluster of buildings that varied in size and design. The dwarves stopped at the leading edge of the lawn area, and Westle requested that Shaylan and his companions give up their weapons for the time of the upcoming meeting. All relinquished them without question or complaint. Their ease and willingness to comply seemed to defuse an underlying tension that pervaded the dwarf's countenance up to that time. Westle courteously promised to see that they were returned promptly after the meetings. Throughout the entire contact they had with him, his voice remained calm and controlled, and he had been polite and professional. But emotion filled his eyes. Both Attleman and Shaylan sensed a great conflict taking place within him, as if he wanted to strike out at them, yet at the same time felt pity for them.

Another dwarf joined Westle. He was dressed in a very stately manner. After a brief discussion, Westle explained that after they cleaned up a bit from their ride, they would meet briefly with some of the leadership as a welcoming gesture. Westle explained that he was required to report on his activities and therefore, found it necessary to take leave of them. He turned them over to the care of the nicely dressed dwarf who, in turn, led them to one of the smaller buildings in the complex. There, they were given provisions to wash with and offered assistance for any wounds or injuries they may have incurred.

After a brief rest, they cleaned up and dressed in appropriate clothing for their first meeting. They were no sooner ready than their escort arrived and guided them to the large central building in the complex. The principal room in the building was a meeting hall. It was, quite simply, a work of art. There were sculptured overhead joists, delicate wood and glass work in the arched windows, intricately designed and crafted stone floors, masterfully woven tapestries on the walls, massive carved doors and mantles, beautiful tables and chairs, each a separate work of art, and finally, the lamps, dazzling blends of polished metal, cut and stained glass, crystal, and mirrors. The spectrum of the room was as if it were a museum of the finest works their artisans had to offer, each built to be used, not simply gawked at.

As they entered, they were escorted to an area where refreshments were served. There were many dwarves present, each wearing festive clothing. They were served from tables, each of which contained a variety of finger foods. Everyone ate standing up and wandered from group to group. This gave the men time to look over the building as they ate, drank, and exchanged greetings. As they all ate, several of the attending dwarves introduced themselves to the men, but avoided giving up their official identity, only mentioning their first names.

After a time of eating and informal chatting, which was obviously and quite deliberately limited to pleasantries, a simple reception line was formed by the dwarves. This made for an easy transition between refreshments and the introduction of the purpose. The line formed in a manner that led the men directly to a table at the far end of the hall, where the formalities were to commence.

As the men went along the line of Dwarves, they were given a name and a position in the Dwarven community. The last six in the line were the only ones who were going to attend the actual meeting. As they introduced themselves, they reported their position and the function they would serve in the meeting. This party included the leader of Thamerlain itself, Frone; next, a lawyer, Honslan; next, a historian, Faux; then a military advisor, Anxler; then the magician, Darric, who introduced himself as the keeper of antiquities and advisor to the Supreme; and last, a dwarven cabinet member and representative of the Supreme, Lanamir.

It didn't take a sensor to discern that several of these dwarves were very uncomfortable at the meeting and most assuredly came only out of a sense of duty to their office. There was something present in their countenance which was deeper than their normal, simple distaste for human tendencies, including their proclivity toward violence and destructive activity. This was personal! Though each member had been officially courteous to the men, they were markedly guarded in the content of their greetings and scope of their discussions, and all appeared emotionally cool.

Dalwan was the last in the delegation of men to traverse the reception line. Throughout the entire encounter, he had been working hard to read the dwarves. There was a common thread running through their emotions... something... possibly an incident or a person. He studied each of them with his senses fully alert in each encounter. It was a combination of Anxler, the military advisor, and Lanamir who gave him the answer. He noticed that Anxler used sensing on him to determine if he had knowledge of some incident, searching for a hint of recognition in the "youngest man". This was the first time Dalwan had ever knowingly understood the complete content of a sensing probe by another person, having known in the past when he was being sensed but never the specific target. The next dwarf was Darric, the magician, who took hold of his hand and continued to shake it as he looked deeply into Dalwan's eyes without perceptible sensing, which made Dalwan very cautious. He could read nothing in that Dwarf. The final dwarf in the line was Lanamir, who was not himself a sensor, and who made no attempt to guard his thoughts against a possible sensing intrusion. He was grieving for a lost friend and wondered if the "man-child" had knowledge of his death.

As the emotionally intense introduction period was ending and everyone was taking a seat at the large round table, Dalwan quickly recounted what he had sensed to Shaylan. He only barely finished when Frone stood and made a brave attempt at a welcoming speech, trying to sound warm and official.

Shaylan stood in response, "Good Dwarves of Thamerlain, thank you for receiving us at such short notice. Before I share anything of our intent and need, I wish to inquire about an incident that my nephew and apprentice have sensed in his meetings during the reception. He told me that his senses revealed to him a deep grief among your delegates for an esteemed member of your society, a member who he perceived to have been recently killed by a man." He watched for a response and needed no magical powers to read them. "I take it from your countenance that such is indeed the case?"

Darric stood and explained, "Four days ago, a man came ta us in disguise as a dwarf. He was lookin' for information on the sword Fallonrod, a power sword of the last power wars of mankind. He had some information that the sword was of dwarven an' elven origin. He was caught in his deception an' those who caught him paid for their discovery with their lives. The man's name is Jarmin an' he appears ta be a professional thief in the employ of the ancient Danlion. We learned of his source of information an' therefore knew that a delegation would be sent ta us soon. This quest has already brought bloodshed ta our land and'll doubtless bring even greater bloodshed ta yer land. All these things, we as dwarves an' elves, detest. That is why ya sense the apprehension an' coolness in us... not our usual countenance when hostin' visitors."

Shaylan stood again, "Good dwarves of Thamerlain, we share your sorrow and must express our shock at such an atrocity against your people. Further, it is our deepest sadness that our problem has caused you this grief. Jarmin is indeed a legendary thief, but is not one in our council or company, nor one that we would entertain on any level. Our sympathy goes out to their families and loved ones."

A murmur went through the delegation of dwarves present, giving Shaylan the sad realization that his words were being perceived as nothing more than mere diplomacy. He hoped that at least one of them was gifted enough in sensing to discern his own personal grief.

Shaylan was still thinking about the murmur of reaction when Rhem stood up with emotion in his eyes and a hint of a tremor in his voice. "I can tell that you think this is just some sort of diplomacy used in these formal occasions by my partner..." he said as he pushed his chair away from the table and walked around to Shaylan's chair two spaces away. "This is more than personal to us," he said as he put his hand on the shoulder of his still standing and quite shocked companion, "...you see... we... Shaylan and I... were the two that discovered the truth of the sword's origin... and it was we who didn't perceive the presence of this Jarmin as we talked..." Rhem paused and looked at Shaylan silently for a brief moment, then spoke again, this time much softer, "...and it was us who didn't stop him... we are personally responsible for the death of not only your friends but of several men at Castle Crest... and we really do share your sadness." He looked from dwarf to dwarf around the table, making strong eye contact with each one before returning to his seat.

Shaylan, still stunned by Rhem's address, just sat down with no further comment. The other members of the delegation from Pretoria were now reassessing the feelings they had formed about the reception they received from the dwarves. Everything made sense now... the army; the escort; the fact that dwarves were waiting for them at all; the much cooler than expected emotional tenor from the officials. Each man knew that the dwarves were very clannish and no lost friend is "just a casualty of war", especially when the war is among men, not dwarves! Now they sat watching for the dwarven reaction to Rhem's words. Apparently, they too were doing some reassessment of their own.

No one spoke for a few very long moments.

Finally, Lanamir stood, "We may have much ta relearn about each other's races. We'll give careful thought ta yer words an' the meaning of 'responsible', Rhem. For now, I'll tell ya what ya must by this time have deduced for yerself, that Jarmin's visit was responsible for our anticipation of your arrival, including the waiting army, escort, our cooler than normal reception an' even the intention of yer visit. As ya know, dwarves and elves hold man's violent tendencies an' war centered society ta be detestable. We feel that yer race holds much promise for the future, after ya have learned ta put yer desire for dominance of other ta rest. This desire for dominance seems ta be centered in yer greed and pride. Yer tendency toward violence makes those with war related arts more valuable than those who possess constructive art. Power for dominance is at the center of yer directives, with greed and pride its motivatin' factors. For these reasons, we da not generally feel that yer race is ta be trusted. We do make the concession that this disease is not so obvious among yer masses but becomes universally evident in yer leaders and their servants."

Attleman leaned forward in his plush chair, putting his hands on the uncomfortably low table, "Isn't it possible that there are other motivations in man other than those you mention? Perhaps fear of being dominated may be a better analysis."

"Our opinion is only a considered analysis of yer society at large," said Lanamir casually. "The fact that there is such fear indicates that someone else desires dominance. We've observed in the past that when the fortunes of one of yer tiny kingdoms change, they begin to attempt dominance over those who once dominated them. In short, their fear changes ta aggression. This is especially true when one of yer power giants arises who can be controlled politically."

"There are good men in every land... men who share and use their arts to help others," said Attleman. "We are here to try and ensure that the power sword is not taken by someone who would use it maliciously against the civilized kingdoms."

"We too have a stake in the security of the sword," answered Darric. "That's why we've agreed ta meet with ya. But ya must understand at the outset what our perspective is. Armed with that understandin', ya can deal effectively with our skepticism, hesitation, and outright mistrust of yer race and yer proposals."

Lanamir then stood, "We do have several conditions which I'll now present," he said looking at Draxyl to ensure that he took them down properly. "First, only those absolutely necessary ta the proceedin's will attend - a list 'ill be submitted in the morning by each side for approval or question; second, either side may call a recess at any time; third, either side may discontinue the talks at any time. Each side 'ill select a spokesman who'll be responsible for presentin' considered opinions an' makin' official statements for presentation. Any decisions made and sworn at this counsel 'ill be bindin' on those lands represented by the attendin' delegates. Sensors 'ill be given opportunity ta cross examine or question any delegate regardin' matters directly connected with the official talks. Finally, we'll need ta see the official document from yer land an' have time ta examine its content an' make any clarifications before beginnin' the discussions tomorrow. We'll have official documentation of the conditions an' sanctioned attendees prepared tomorrow for signature prior ta continuin' the content of the talks."

Draymoor had been charged with carrying the document and presented it, in its unopened wax sealed leather-bound pouch, personally to Lanamir. Lanamir handed it to Honslan the lawyer and Faux the historian, who checked the signet seals for authenticity. While this was underway, Brent, the dwarvan sensor and personal attendant to the Supreme, walked over to Draymoor and asked, "Is this document an official and bindin' introduction from Pretoria for those with ya here present so far as ya know?"

"Yes, it is." His answer was very courteous and even had in it a hint of kindness and respect, a hint the dwarf did not miss. He smiled as he turned and walked back to Honslan and Faux. It was the first sincere smile Draymoor had seen. The dwarves conferred among themselves in hushed tones for a moment, and then Lanamir stood again. "Yer papers and yer honor all seem ta in order. Yer credentials are officially accepted. Do ya have any questions of us or stipulations ya wish to request at this time?"

After a very brief conference, Shaylan stood and answered for the men, "We have very little to offer you and, being in great need, are at your mercy. We are grateful that you have given consideration to meeting with us."

"Very well! A list of yer intended meeting representatives and their respective roles is required at the evening meal tonight. Please provide it to me personally. Our response 'ill be forthcomin' before nights end. Tomorrow 'ill be the first official meetin'. We'll extend a list of our delegates, their titles, and rolls in the negotiations. Any one of them may or may not be present in the upcomin' or any possible subsequent meetin's until the termination or resolution of our negotiations." The entire dwarven delegation stood up.

Shaylan stood motioning for the others to follow, which they did immediately. Frone escorted the men back out to the building they had freshened up in earlier. He told them how much time they had left until dinner, offered them the hospitality of Thamerlain, and left, promising to have them escorted back to the hall at the proper time.

Draxyl began immediately to prepare the required document while the others held a quick meeting to fix formal definitions to the duties of each member of the delegation for presentation to the dwarves.

After the formalities were dispensed with, the group gathered around Malan for some insight into the dwarven ways with respect to counsel and important conferences. Malan was the most knowledgeable about dwarven protocol and proceedings of meetings such as the one they had just attended. He assured them that everything had gone well up to that point and there was nothing out of the ordinary to be concerned about. The only advice he could give was for the group to be very honest and conciliatory. "If some point of content in the negotiations is not absolutely necessary to our purpose, give preference to their requirement or suggestion. This'll be seen by them to be a gesture of good faith, not weakness."

Frone showed up at the exact appointed time and personally led the delegation to the dining hall. As soon as Draxyl arrived, he exchanged his list of proposed delegates for the dwarven list of prospective attenders.

CHAPTER 13

That same night, Jarmin waited in painful expectation for the guard to bring the wonderful Elven necklace. He knew the hour was close because the evening lamp lighter was making his rounds, having lit the hanging lantern near the door only a moment earlier. His day time guard was growing noticeably restless, pacing back and forth, walking out to the door, and looking down the hallway, and then walking back to his chair, which he did not sit in. Like clockwork, the guard with the little box on his belt came in holding two mugs of dwarven sweet brew. He set one down near the door and brought the other to Jarmin. The dwarf set the mug down on a small side table and removed the necklace from the little box with a key that the day guard provided. He placed the necklace carefully around Jarmin's neck. At that, the day guard bid the other a good watch and headed out the door. The amulet began to work its magic almost instantly. His pain was dimming, and his eyes began to unfog. He could feel strength returning. The dwarf reclosed the little box and handed the mug to Jarmin when they heard a cry from down the hallway, "Fire! Fire!" It was the day guard's voice shouting, "Begoran, the lamp is a'broken and the wall's on fire!"

"Begoran" (that was the first time he had heard the guard's name) turned to run out of the room, yelling back at Jarmin as he did, "Don't drink that brew yet, I da not wanna carry ya out if thar's a need." He stopped to pick up the wash basin of water as he ran out the door.

Jarmin realized that this was surely the only chance he would get to escape. He had only dreamed of such an occasion, having already conceived a plan for several different possibilities... and this was one of them. He arose quickly and switched the mugs. When the dwarf came back, he would sleep, not Jarmin. That would give him all night to get down the mountain before being discovered. The amulet would protect him should he become injured any further. He was back on his bed when both dwarves reappeared in the doorway a couple of minutes later. Both entered the door with swords in hand. Seeing Jarmin still in bed, they put away their swords, and Begoran walked over to the bed. "Sorry ta come in on ya like this... but with the power of the necklace an' all... we jus' didn't know what ta expect."

He picked up the mug again and handed it to Jarmin. "Drink it up now. My partner here is gonna stay 'till ya sleep the healin' sleep." Jarmin drank it straight down.

Having gone through this several times already, it was easy to feign the expected reaction. In a short time, he appeared to be fast asleep.

He could hear the guards walk back to the door. Begoran announced, "Looks like it worked just fine, ya can go now ma friend."

Jarmin heard the other dwarf walk away and then the sound of the creaking of Begoran's chair as he sat down.

His hearing seemed intensified. He concentrated on hearing the sound of the mug being placed on the table. He waited and waited... nothing. He was just about to chance a look when he heard something fall onto the floor with an accompanying splash. He did not move. No sound followed. He opened one eye very slowly and found the dwarf fast asleep in the chair. The mug was on the floor.

Jarmin arose quickly and quietly moved to the dwarf's side. He was amazed that he didn't have even the faintest dizziness that he had experienced when he originally got up to switch mugs. From the size of the splash near the mug, Jarmin surmised that the dwarf must have consumed about half the sweetbrew. He looked for some rope or cord to tie the dwarf up with, but found none. He gently removed Begoran's sword from its scabbard and cut a thin strip of cloth from his bedding. He took the strip and tied the dwarf securely to the chair and put a gag in his mouth.

Not wanting to chance a confrontation in the house, Jarmin went to the window and opened a small one next to the large fixed one. A cool breeze blew into the room and seemed to invigorate him even more. Looking out, he could see that he was on the second floor of the house, with the ground slanting downward from the side of the house he was presently in. To reach the ground from where he was would require a drop of an entire floor, plus a distance roughly equal to his height, too far to risk. He didn't want to use bedding tied together as a rope to get down with, because it would attract attention if someone were to see it from the outside. There was a ledge that paralleled the floor line on the outside wall between the two stories of the house. If he could work his way down to the corner of the house, he could easily climb to the rock mountain side that the house was built into. The outside of the house was faced with stone slabs, like flagstone, in irregular shapes. He planned to use the joints between the slabs as finger holds while he worked his way along the ledge. He glanced over the terrain from the window, trying to get a good grasp of the layout of the grounds. There was a well-kept stone-paved pathway cut into the steeply slanting mountainside leading from the house down the hill and around a large outcropping of rocks about a long bow shot from the house. He decided that was to be his escape route.

When he was confident that there were no dwarves on the grounds, he climbed out the window. He closed the window from the outside and began to inch his way down the wall. The window ledge and frame were his most difficult obstacles. Because they stuck out about a hand's breadth from the wall, he was forced to move in an off-balance shuffle around them. Once past the window, there was only about the distance of five large strides to the corner of the house where it met the rock wall. He had gone only about one of those strides when he heard whistling. He looked around to see a young dwarf walking out from the house area down the stone pathway in the direction he planned to use in his escape. He had a lamp lighter in his hand. Because it happened so fast and there was no place for him to hide, he chanced using his magic and disappeared. He slid his feet along the rough ledge a tiny bit at a time as he hugged the stone facade to keep his balance, all the while trying to keep his eye on the lamplighter dwarf.

Jarmin began to panic, knowing that his magic would soon give him away. He tried to slide along the ledge a little more quickly so he could get out of sight and release his magic cover. As he did, his leading foot hit a loose, large knot in the wooden ledge, and it gave way, causing him to lose his footing and fall. He grabbed the ledge as he fell past it, scraping open old wounds. He was sure he had become visible for at least a brief portion of his fall and recovery. He hung motionless for a moment, watching breathlessly over his shoulder to see if the dwarf had seen or heard the incident. He did not appear to have noticed. Once again, Jarmin was working his way toward the rock wall, this time letting his fingers do the walking for him... painful, tormented hands began to inch their way toward safety. Soon, he was at the rock wall and found it easy to climb onto it and down to the ground. His chosen profession had prepared him well for such adventures, but he still did not enjoy them until they were finished.

Dusk was well set in now, and distant objects were becoming a blur. The stone pathway was lit about every 20 strides with a hanging lantern on an ornate metal pole. This seemed like a real waste of oil unless it meant that night travelers were expected. He chose not to use any further magic, remembering the look on the dwarf magician's face and his word of caution when Jarmin had tried to use magic to sense their conversation. He moved cautiously toward the outcropping of rock, forced by the steep terrain to stay on the pathway.

He felt amazingly good and noticed that his hand no longer hurt and had stopped bleeding. The amulet warmed his chest, its power working miracles in his body. His visit had indeed been fruitful. But unlike other trophies, this would remain his. No amount of money or reward would pry it from him. He determined to keep his presence a complete secret, even from Drummond.

He encountered no one on the pathway leading to the outcropping of rocks. Once around the rocks, he saw a large flat landing which marked the entrance of a cave in the mountain. He hid among some of the rocks as he waited for the lamplighter to return. He continued to hide long enough for it to get seriously dark outside. Finally, he got too nervous waiting and entered the cave even though the young dwarf had not returned. The initial entrance was like a small cavernous chamber at the leading edge of a passageway and was lit by a beautiful hanging lantern. He moved into the corridor and stopped to listen, holding his breath. All he could hear was the slight blowing of the wind through the opening. It created a strong breeze in his face, blowing from the inside of the cave as he entered. Once inside, he walked only a short distance until he was in a much larger cave. He was immediately struck by the immensity of the cavern in which he stood. He moved into the pathway leading downward, lit by small lanterns. From time to time, the path turned into a stairway of tiny steps, uncomfortable for his feet and legs. Sometimes there was a banister or rope that paralleled the descending pathway to protect travelers. There were places where the path became a long tunnel, obviously carved through the stone. There were giant stalactites and stalagmites in undisturbed galleries, sometimes lit by well-placed lanterns. On occasion, he saw beautiful pools of water with crystal-lined bottoms and other perfectly flat mineral floors, again lighted fortuitously to show off their best features. In places, the cavern was so large that the lights seemed to vanish before reaching the opposite walls. At times, he could hear the wind blowing in howling tones, several times heard running water. There were many landings with tables and chairs or benches. By the time he was far down the pathway, he had passed two doorways, one of which was locked, and the other, much larger, was unlocked but apparently shuttered another cavern entrance. A brief look convinced him that it must be there only as a barrier to keep visitors from getting lost. Being interested in getting out of the mountain, not exploring it, he did not waste much time on either one. As he came upon a third door and was about to pass it by without any thought of investigation, he heard the sound of someone singing. He knew that he would be seen if he just waited, and if he used magic, he might be discovered, so he decided to try the door. To his amazement, it was open and swung effortlessly into the inside of a room. He stepped quickly into its total darkness. The door had opened and now closed noiselessly, with the only sound being that of the latch when it secured the door as he pushed it closed.

Jarmin leaned hard against the door, trying to hear when and if the happy little traveler would pass. Seconds seemed like hours, especially because Jarmin's imagination was wild with visions of inhospitable inhabitants that might lurk in the room in which he now stood. He did not know for sure how large the room was, but from the way the sound had traveled in it when he shut the door, he thought it to be no larger than a good sized pantry. It was in this darkness that he noticed a pale green glow coming through his tunic. He pulled the amulet out, holding it by the tiny chain, and to his amazement, it was the source of a greenish light which now gave a vague definition to the room. But before he could get enough of a look to determine what he was seeing, the light in the amulet went out. He felt weakness begin to invade his body, so he quickly put it back in touch with his skin. Immediately, the weakness faded, and the feeling of vitality again filled him.

When he put his ear back to the door, the jubilant voice was just approaching. He heard it get louder and then quickly taper off. He waited for a brief time before stepping back out of the room to ensure that the dwarf was out of eye and earshot. He stepped out and pulled the lit lantern from near the door, and went back into the room. The walls were cut out of stone, forming a square about 4 strides in each direction. It had no ceiling, looking like the inside of a giant erratic smokestack going upward into the pitch darkness. The room was filled with weapons, most of which hung neatly on the walls, segregated by type. There were crossbows, swords, knives, and broad axes. There were even two types of shields. There were between five and ten of each item. Jarmin took a crossbow and slung it over his shoulder along with a quiver of arrows. The Crossbow and arrows, like the steps on the stairways, were not a comfortable size. However, like the stairs, they would serve the need. He then helped himself to a sheath knife and slipped it under his tunic using his belt to secure it in place.

He moved out again into the passageway and stopped initially to listen for any sounds of the company. He could hear nothing but the distant sound of running water. He continued on for a distance roughly equal to that which he had already traveled, and finally exited a long tunnel and came to a halt at the edge of a swinging footbridge, about 25 strides across, which spanned a very deep, dark chasm. He could see another short tunnel on the other side of the chasm, which appeared to open into a well-lit room. The dome ceiling high overhead was covered with giant stalactites looking like teeth waiting to devour unsuspecting travelers. He rested for a few moments and listened, trying to determine if anyone was in the upcoming cave. It was difficult to hear over the low moan from the cavernous trench below.

After gathering his composure, he worked his way slowly and quietly across the swinging bridge. The mammoth opening he was crossing felt like a giant mouth poised open to receive some tender morsel dispatched by the teeth above. Sound and light disappeared into its depths. A slight but icy draft chilled him to the bone as it swirled around the inside of the cavernous dome through which this bridge hung. It was coldest and strongest at the center of the bridge, tapering off at the edges where the bridge had its landings.

He glided silently to the opening of the tunnel. He could now see through the corridor into the lit cavern much better than before, having a straighter shot at it now. It was not like any of the caverns he had already traversed. It was a well-decorated and furnished room. He moved toward the room down the artfully excavated tunnel, which was wider and higher by half than any he had traveled through to this point. Every step revealed more details about the room. He began to make out the relief scenes carved in the wall opposite the hallway he was in. Then he caught sight of three multicolored glass chandeliers hanging evenly spaced across the length of the room from a naturally vaulted ceiling. This gave him a chill. This place was going to be full of dwarves he thought. The top of the ceiling appeared to be a shaft going out at an angle from the far wall. He got to the entrance and from there could see that the room was laid out in an unsymmetrical octagon, with the center wall about twice as long as the end walls. The walls were about twice his height and were cut into the cavern rock. This design left an overhang of irregular form jutting out around the entire room. Intricate tapestries hung on each of the three walls opposite the doorway through which he now stood. The room was furnished much like a meeting hall, only with varying sizes of furniture. All of the chairs and tables were draped with custom-made covers, and all sat in perfect order.

There was a large door jam fitted into the hallway entrance, which gave Jarmin some measure of cover from which to investigate the room for occupants. The hallway approached the cavern at an angle to the right end wall, which gave him a clear view of all except the far right corner of the room. As he stood surveying the room, he could for the first time hear voices talking and laughing from time to time. The immensity of the room and its furnishings had apparently absorbed their sounds well enough for him to miss them until now. He could see other doors leading through the long wall opposite him, but they were all closed. He chanced a look back to his right along the side he was standing on, and there, at a table in front of a very large set of double doors, sat four dwarves apparently playing some sort of game.

Not wanting to wait on the chance that they would just up and leave, he decided to use magic just one more time and attempt to sneak by them... after all, how many sensors could this dwarven community have?! The longer he waited, the more chance he had of being discovered, because he knew that sooner or later there would be an alarm from up on top.

He unslung the little crossbow which he had already set and silently nocked a shaft. He cradled it in his left arm, finger on the trigger, while he walked as quietly as he could into the room. After he took a couple of steps, he instinctively glanced back. The door he had come through was gone. The wall appeared solid there. Realizing that it must be hidden by some sort of magic, he began again to head for the double doors. He had traversed about half the necessary distance when one of the dwarves announced, "I sense human magic."

The others stopped talking and all of them stood, then froze. They remained stationary, not making any noise or even moving.

"Protect the door!" shouted the same dwarf who had spoken first.

Before Jarmin's disappointment could set in, he saw all four break into a run toward his position. He braced himself to fight but realized that they were not running exactly for him but only in his direction. He quietly put his back against the wall and watched them run past him to the exact place he had come through the wall.

He hesitated for a moment while two of them went through the magic door, and the other two began to search the floor through the tables and chairs with their eyes. It was then that Jarmin realized they were guarding the magic door, not the front entrance, so he began to make his way toward the double doors, moving backwards so he could observe their activity. It amused him to watch them guarding the wrong door, and at that from the wrong side.

As he neared the entrance, he turned and watched over his shoulder as he continued to move as quietly as he could. He was only a few steps away when the dwarf sensor reappeared through the magic door, shouting again.

"The magic is in this room!" He ran a few steps and used his power to isolate the source of human magic. "I don't seem to be able to pinpoint the intruder," he shouted. He then turned to one of the others and shouted, "Bergan, the horn!... SOUND THE HORN!"

"I left it at the table," he shouted back as he broke into a run toward it.

"Get it! GET IT!" yelled the sensor as he, too, began to run for the table. "Remember what that one upstairs did in town when he turned invisible... watch each other."

Jarmin was at the entrance, glancing quickly at the table to see if he could identify the horn they sought. When he heard the last remark, he fell victim to something relatively uncommon to him... conscience... real grief at what he had done. He immediately turned and ran out into the cave entrance without the horn, not wishing to chance another bloody confrontation. It actually made him feel good to have been so generous.

As he exited the cave, he stopped to check the area for the presence of other dwarves. His survey was cut short by an exceedingly loud blast of a horn, so loud that he could feel its vibrations in his entire body. He ran full speed down a sloping open area dotted with patches of waist high brush. He had not gone far when he realized that he was crossing the same terrain where he had been captured.

With his memory now jogged a little, a few details of his journey to that place returned in vivid recollection, so he decided to leave by another route and avoid completely the town itself. He was not sure whether or not these dwarves would be able to pick out his trail immediately, so he continued to move invisibly. He could hear the shouts of the dwarves from the cave fading in the background. He was amazed that he could run so well. "The amulet must have been increasing my endurance," he thought as he jumped through some brush in his path without losing stride. He felt the power of the elven magic filling him with strength long after fatigue should have set in.

After an extended period of fast footwork, he felt safe enough to stop. He was breathing hard but was not at all fatigued or exhausted. The only true discomfort he felt was that his mouth was extremely dry. He listened intently in an attempt to hear water running, but could only hear the pounding of his heart in his ears. As he held his breath in an attempt to enhance his listening ability, the glow of the amulet became even more visible through his shirt. He pulled it out from his tunic again, this time holding it in his hand. It glowed bright with the green color of new grass on a hillside after the rains. It felt very warm to his touch, and he could feel power running through his arm into his body. Its light was bright enough to reflect off a nearby tree. His heart filled with a childlike wonder. He had always had a restless desire inside, a craving that could not be quenched. He had stolen some fancy treasures trying to satisfy it, but he had never experienced fulfillment from any of them until now. True enough, he had very much admired several of these treasures, but none of them had captured his heart as this ancient elven amulet. He had often thought, "If I could only know what would truly satisfy me, I'd get it and settle down for good!" At this moment, he realized that he had obtained the prize for which he had always searched. It was as if it had become part of him.

He dropped it back under his tunic and set out to find some water and the road. He knew he could travel safely on the road at night as long as he used no more magic. In the still of night, he would easily hear any approaching horses and would be able to conceal himself before they could get close enough to detect his presence.

CHAPTER 14

The occasion was designated a State dinner and was hosted by Frone, complete with the best foods and very professional entertainment. The Pretorian delegation was amazed at the hospitality of the dwarves, especially knowing how much distaste they held for the men's business. This was compounded by the fact that the dwarves knew there was precious little the men had to offer them in return for any help the humans might receive.

However, the dwarves' hospitality far exceeded any expectations the men held. They prepared a long table of elegant main dishes, side dishes and a variety of breads and spreads arranged in designs and combinations that staggered the imagination. Although there were elegantly prepared precut meats, master chefs stood prepared to recommend additional possibilities or to carve various bulk meats to the specifications of any person's palate who might wish a special cut to accompany one of the many sauces and dips made to embellish them.

A cart laden with various drinks was circulated continuously through the tables, catering to the whims of every guest. There was dwarven sweet brew, water, ale (dark and light), numerous fruit juice mixtures, and several varieties of wine.

There were over one hundred invited guests in all, including wives of delegates and other officials, plus several elves. The elves and the men were provided with larger chairs to accommodate their obviously taller stature. There were higher tables available, but to sit at them would have isolated the men from the rest of those attending the meal. Following the lead of the elves, the men joined the dwarves at their tables, splitting up in groups of two and three to mix better.

The entertainment was tastefully apportioned throughout the meal, giving ample time for the diners to converse and make acquaintances. The evening was a blend of talent and magical arts, both elegant and enchanting. The last performer was introduced as Clank, the Director of Public Works. He was praised as one of the most profoundly dedicated administrators the dwarven community had ever had the privilege of being served by. Clank gave a magical performance using smoke and lights that was nothing short of astonishing.

In the midst of the slowly rising smoke emanating from a special pot on the raised entertainment platform, Clank brought visions of animals to lifelike animation. He made creatures with beautifully colored eyes and intricate designs in their skin, move gracefully through swirls of color. Some would dance, others just moved about in seemingly routine activity.

In his finale, a green forest materialized in the smoke, as if viewed from above it, looking down at the treetops from a distance. A dark spot appeared on the horizon and moved toward the viewers. It was an anderon, gliding gracefully along just above the treetops. It came closer and closer, and the total size of the vision grew larger and larger, filling the entire stage area. The perspective shifted from in front of the anderon to its side as if now seen by someone flying next to it. The anderon turned abruptly and headed directly toward the audience, scales glistening and eyes flashing, coming closer and closer. Its body began to fill the entire vision. When it seemed that it would fly out into the audience itself, its giant jaws opened and it spewed a multicolored jewel-like flame directly at the awestruck watchers - there was a universal gasp, then laughter followed by loud applause.

Dalwan remembered Shahandra's description of the arts practiced at Lord Oakbern's castle. These arts are limited to the magician's imagination, skill, and ability to reproduce intricate details. "This dwarf accomplished, on a grand scale, what those in Oakbern's cast could only do in minutia." Dalwan laughed to himself, "If Shahandra were here now, she would most assuredly be amazed, especially when she learned that his magic was only a hobby to him!"

At the close of the meal, after a fabulous dessert, Lanamir and Honslan requested a brief meeting with the entire delegation. Everyone was rounded up and met in a small room adjoining the banquet hall.

"We have called you here to discuss the prospective lists of delegates to the council," announced Lanamir. "Everyone on the list from among the dwarves is there as a requirement and condition ta the meetin' taking place. We'll accept nothin' less!" The men were not surprised to find the names of several representatives from the elven community also among those required delegates to the sessions.

Honslan delivered the accepted list of Pretorian delegates. All the delegates were accepted except Dalwan.

"Dalwan is simply too young an' inexperienced ta be a member o' this negotiatin' party," explained Honslan with a tone that left no room for argument.

Rhem and Shaylan exchanged glances of concern, feeling strongly that his attendance would be very important. Shaylan was first to speak, "He's come so far and fought with us. His arts could be very useful..."

"He isn't even allowed by our own Pretorian rulers to count for a vote," said Malan, cutting off Shaylan. "Let's not jeopardize the meeting for the sake of Dalwan's attendance."

"His arts 'ill be more useful later on," added Draymoor, "and it's likely that the Dwarves are more sensitive to this than even we are! Personally, I think this is little more than an attempt to test our sincerity."

"It's possible..." said Malan, jumping on Draymoor's thoughts, "just possible that by eliminating the least necessary member of the team and then watching our reactions, they're testing our willingness to bend. I say we give in without objection."

After a few moments of silent soul searching and with no further argument, they unanimously agreed to approve the list without dissent.

Shaylan answered for the group, "We humbly thank you for your hospitality tonight and for agreeing to meet with us on a topic of such distaste to you. We find your requirements quite well reasoned and hereby agree to them."

"Well done," said Honslan, wearing a satisfied look. "We shall convene tomorrow at midday in the room where the earlier reception was held. We'll send an escort for ya at the proper time."

With that, the meeting concluded.

As the delegation was being led to their sleeping quarters, Dalwan walked alone, carefully avoiding contact with any of the others. His sense of disappointment was just about to overwhelm him when Shaylan dropped back in the procession and put his hand firmly on his shoulder.

"Dalwan, did you sense any strange magic during the night... maybe a man's magic..."

It took Dalwan a moment to snap out of his personal pity party and begin to focus on the words coming from Shaylan. "What...uh... what're you talkin' about?"

"Tonight at the party... magic... some sort of strange magic..."

"There was lots of magic toni..."

"NO NO!" cut in Shaylan, losing his patience but trying to keep quiet so as not to draw attention to them. "Not Dwarven magic... man's magic... it was somehow vaguely familiar... I just can't remember where... there was too much distraction for me to focus on it."

Dalwan's eyes lit up, "Yes, now that you mention it, I do remember something... it was about the end of the dinner... I sensed the strong use of human magic. I glanced at Darric and saw him sensing the air... probing for a direction and a content. I was distracted watching Darric. He didn't seem alarmed, so I ignored it."

"What kind of magic was it? Could you tell?"

Dalwan thought a moment. "It was the strangest magic... like ancient magic but like a shadowmaster... like scrambled magic... like two people singing together, one with a beautiful voice and the other untrained... that's why I looked to Darric."

"That's it! That is most surely it... the shadowmaster from Castle Crest. He must be here somewhere. We must find Darric, NOW!" Shaylan grabbed one of the escorts by the arm and alarmed him so much that he sent an attendant on the run to find Darric.

Darric had barely gotten out of the meeting hall when he was met by four dwarves, all of them quite excited.

"Darric, i'tall happened jus' as ya said i'twould... every part o'vit... everyone top side is OK, they answered the horn."

"Thank you, Tully," answered Darric with a chuckle, "I knew I could count on yer sensing powers. Ya were all very brave."

Tully smiled with embarrassment.

Turning to the other three, "All of ya were very courageous ta trust my estimation and then act it out."

The dwarf with the horn, Bergan, jumped in, "I'twas easy actually... Tully knew where Jarmin was all the time and arranged hand signals to help us stay out of his way... he drilled us over an' over while we waited... all we had ta do was follow his coachin'."

"Yea," cut in one of the other two, "I almost felt like I could see him maself." He then got a quizzical smile on his face, "Tell us how the rascal got away up top without hurtin' anyone."

Darric's eyes danced with simple glee, "I'twas a simple matter! Since Jarmin was use ta gettin' his sleepin' medicine in sweet brew, they created a believable distraction just after two mugs were brought inta the room... one supposedly containing the sleepin' potion was handed ta Jarmin by Begoran. Begoran kept the other for himself. Begoran, by far the bravest of all, went out of the room in a feigned emergency for enough time so Jarmin could switch the mugs. When he came back in, Jarmin drank the brew an' pretended to be asleep. When Begoran saw him pretending to be asleep, knowing that there was no sleeping potion in the mug, he knew that the trick had worked. He then pretended to fall asleep and Jarmin escaped leavin' Begoran supposedly sleepin' in his place!"

"An' now he's on his way," said Bergan with a faraway look in his eyes. "I hope it works."

"Now remember, my brothers," Darric's smile was still beaming, but the tone in his voice had caution in it, "no one can know about this for a while. Go ahead and talk carefully among yourselves, but ta no one else... I'll tell ya when it's safe ta share the adventure."

They had scarcely finished this conversation when the runner found them and requested that Darric accompany him back to the visitor's housing quarters. Darric followed without objection.

Upon arrival, he discovered that Shaylan was quite excited... more excited than he would have thought possible of this seemingly seasoned self-controlled fire warrior. Shaylan was shuffling nervously back and forth in front of the quarters, staring squint-eyed into the darkness from the lighted porch, waiting for Darric. "Thank you for coming with such dispatch," said Shaylan, speaking so fast that the dwarf was forced to fight back the urge to laugh, and had to work hard to maintain a respectful countenance and listen carefully to Shaylan. "We have a matter of great concern to inquire about. We've kept our suspicions to ourselves until we could confirm them with you."

Sensing that Shaylan considered this to be truly a serious matter, Darric took them aside to a large open field in which was set a sunken stone-lined firepit. Darric walked up to it, picked up a stick from the partially burned wood debris in the pit, and, using it to quickly push several other pieces together, he touched it to the new stack, and it immediately caught fire. They did not see any flame jump from his hand, only the wood began to burn in a controlled fire.

"Now, Shaylan, why have ya sent fer me?"

Shaylan was visibly upset and spoke with hesitation in his words, "We sensed the presence of human magic tonight... magic mixed with another unfamiliar magic... magic designed to deceive. I'm most certain it came from the same person who overheard our discussion at Castle Crest and presumably the same one who came here and disrupted your lives."

"Are you sure you sensed him tonight?" asked Darric with unnerving calm.

"Yes, but not very close... not on the grounds... but most likely in the area."

Darric smiled and invited the others to join him on a bench near the fireplace. "Ya're correct in yer sensing. Jarmin was allowed to escape tonight."

Shaylan began to object but was cut short with a firm but friendly hand gesture, "We're a followin' him ta Lord Danlion's residence."

"But we already know where he is," blurted Dalwan in a chastising tone laced with defeat, "...he is laying siege to Brandon Keep... probably already took it by now!"

Darric used his hands again, this time to calm Dalwan down. "Jarmin is delivering a prize to Danlion that will allow us to find him no matter where he goes."

"The 'old magic'!" said Dalwan as he began to piece it all together.

"Yes. I'tis an ancient Elven magic. 'Tis a healing necklace. A very special amulet that can heal an' bring great endurance. 'Twill also lead us straight to him."

"But what if Danlion himself gets hold of the necklace?" asked Shaylan in slow, deliberate words with eyebrows scrunched together over his eyes in a look of disapproval.

"If he did, wouldn't he become almost indestructible?" added Dalwan, feeling that there must be some other factor in the equation which at this point looked like a child's plan with an obvious flaw.

The look on Shaylan's face changed from chastisement to bewilderment when Darric retorted, "And hopefully, he will gain possession of the treasure personally."

Still chuckling, he continued, "This amulet has a very special magic in it. It'll make its wearer feel vigorous... even youthful. However, its power is addictin'... soon if the holder of the treasure is not careful, the amulet will own him. If the owner wears the amulet long enough, he will become in danger of collapse when he eventually removes it, a fact he no doubt will discover too late. I predict that human nature will prevail in all ways an' the amulet 'ill be Danlion's undoin'! At the very least, it 'ill be a beacon ta guide us straight to 'im."

Shaylan had recovered from his emotional wild rapids ride, and, regaining his composure, asked, "Why are you so sure he will use it?"

"As I inferred already, 'tis deduction of the evidence from yer race that leads me ta believe such a thing. He must 'ave been weak from the injuries he suffered so many generations ago. If he'd been able ta assert dominance prior ta this time ya know he would o' already tried. I surmise that only recently has he recovered enough strength ta wage battle. And even at that, he still ails to some great extent."

"Is that really the reason you believe he'll put on the necklace?" said Shaylan, not doing very well at hiding his impatience for a suitable answer.

"Well, ma good Shaylan, what would ya do if i'twere you who found this beautiful amulet, all aglow with ancient magic?" said Darric, eyebrows raised with a teasing smile on his round face.

Shaylan didn't answer, so Darric kept going, "Danlion 'ill most certainly sense the elven magic and easily identify it. He'll simply demand it from Jarmin, who'll most assuredly be compelled ta part with it. Its beauty and glow will seduce him to touch it... its power will then sweep through his ailing body upon first contact, bringing a renewed sense of vitality. He'll not wish ta put it aside after that."

"It all sounds so simple... but why risk losing the amulet while taking a chance that he might somehow alter its magic or by it become even stronger?" asked the flustered Shaylan.

"Because this elven magic can be sensed at a great distance and through a variety of obstacles, by a trained elven sensor. Aside from that, the magic in the amulet will not respond favorably ta tamperin' from any other source, dwarven or human. Besides, why would Danlion want ta chance destroyin' the source of magic that's providin' the thing he needs most, health? Yes indeed, human nature 'ill take its course an' Danlion 'ill possess the amulet!"

"Not all men are greedy and power hungry and selfish," said Dalwan, becoming offended at the insinuations against human nature being made by Darric. "Some are kind and noble like Shaylan... and brave like Rhem."

"Yes indeed, ma young friend. There 'ave been many such among yer people. But even some o' those who were most noble fell to the baser nature of mankind and could be counted on ta follow in step with their depraved ways. One such as Danlion is certainly no exception. As a matter of fact, in this situation, Danlion is a picture-perfect representation of all that can be disgustin' and dangerous of yer race." Darric now leaned toward Dalwan, the smile left his face, and the laughter disappeared from his voice. With his stubby finger pointed right at Dalwan, his voice both questioning and challenging, he asked, "And how will one such as you guard yer way? How 'ill ya become heir ta the qualities ya seem ta admire in yer companions? Do ya have a plan ta protect yerself from the temptations common ta yer people?" his voice now turned hard, "...or do ya think that somehow ya're too special to become prey for the arrogant twin beasts called Pride and Lust that 're at the root o' all this evil?" His eyes were wide, and his face shone bright against the flickering flames of the fire.

Darric's words burned deep into Dalwan's consciousness. His thoughts were frantic. He didn't have a plan! "I don't need a plan," he thought in self-defence. "I'll take one day at a time," he continued, as his thoughts confirmed his pattern of life, "...I fully intend to be my own master... doing good... doing what's right... after all, Shaylan has drilled me over and over about responsibility for my actions and accountability for their results..."

Shaylan broke Dalwan's trance, "I'm sure your warning will be of great value, Darric. But he's still just a boy. He has much to learn before such temptation will be of much danger to him."

"I'm surprised ta hear ya say such a thing, Shaylan. You've instructed him in responsibility an' accountability yet you yerself have come here somehow feeling that the death of our friends was your fault."

Shaylan was not the least prepared for this personal confrontation. The shock and confusion it produced was shown on his bewildered face when his bearded mouth dropped open.

"Shaylan, do ya think us dwarves so poor of common sense that only one such as yerself could 'ave saved us this loss? If only ya had been a little keener on yer sensin' this tragedy may never have happened... Is that what you think?" Darric gave a moment for some sort of response. He could sense that Shaylan was wounded in his spirit and felt that his honor was being drug through the mud. He could also tell that Shaylan's pride constrained him not to speak until he had heard the dwarf's last word.

Darric got up and walked over to Shaylan, who remained seated. Putting his hand on Shaylan's shoulder, he continued, "No ma noble friend, ya take yerself far too seriously. 'Tis these common failings that bind us together. The pride o' man points an accusin' finger of guilt, either ta himself or some other unfortunate person... shouldn't be that way. The elf and the dwarf know, understand, and respect the failin's o' their country folk an' the other races. 'Tis the very thin' that binds us together. If the boy is ever ta be anythin' of value ta himself or others, he must learn mutual dependance... not independence, 'cause that's the pride that separates and destroys." Darric became more serious yet, speaking in a passionate near whisper, "One day he may find himself in a position ta take himself too seriously also... an' perhaps on that day thar 'ill be no other person present to warn him from his error... or worse... no one he'll listen to!"

Shaylan assumed diplomatic tones as he answered, "I'm sure all of these thoughts have been carefully constructed. I'll give considerable attention to your perceptions as we work through our negotiations with your delegates. This should prove invaluable. I'll also give consideration to your words in assisting my nephew and apprentice in these matters. Thank you for your thoughts and for easing our minds on the situation surrounding Jarmin's escape."

Disappointment... now disgust, covered Darric's face with wrinkles. He took a step back, assessing this odd reaction by Shaylan and spoke only after an uncomfortable moment of silence, "Vary well then... but be sure ya make no mention of the escape nor reasons i'twas allowed," he said in a commanding but respectful tone. "Should the reasons get out 'twould prove a great loss for us!"

As soon as Shaylan and Dalwan agreed, Darric turned and walked off, leaving them both sitting on the bench. Dalwan was so taxed by the conversation that he was left numb, and Shaylan was left without words.

****

The next day, the Pretorian delegation prepared all morning for their meeting with the dwarven and elven delegations. Dalwan listened carefully to their discussions and even added some very helpful suggestions. But even in the intensity of the discussions, they were still keenly aware of the deep disappointment he felt about being excluded from the conference. At times, his emotion became so powerful that it made him physically shake. He felt that he belonged at the meeting as much or even more than some of the others. After all, out of all the people in Pretoria, it was probable that only he would have the ability to wield the sword... and that if he couldn't, maybe no one could. As the morning wore on toward midday, he became more and more bitter and disillusioned.

As he rationalized these things, it hit him that he was letting his pride run away with his emotions. "Was the dwarf right last night?" The thought kindled a smoldering fear inside him. "But I am the 'powermaster' everyone is looking for!... or at least I might be a powermaster... I'm not taking myself too seriously... this IS SERIOUS!" He could feel the conflict rage inside of him growing stronger and stronger.

Suddenly it struck him that he was becoming exactly the kind of person he despised... arrogant... self-centered, self important. He began to rapidly introspect like a condemned man with only a moment of life left to argue his case, "I didn't even want to train. I didn't want to be the one who had a chance to wield the stupid sword. Now I'm pouting about being kept away from a meeting by people who, for the most part, have no idea who I really am... if I'm really anything at all... a meeting that I really don't want to attend... a meeting that I probably would wish I hadn't gone to if I had gotten to go." His mind continued to race at a mad pace in an ambivalent direction. "Who am I mad at anyway? Why am I mad if I didn't want to be in this position in the first place... a place I worked hard for? What would I do there at the meeting that would be so important, make myself known as the savior of the races, the sword bearer? I don't really know if I'm a powermaster at all... I feel sick again! How did I get like this? I hate what's happening to me."

He was wallowing deep in his thoughts when the host arrived to lead the men to the meeting. Dalwan was informed that a courier was going to bring him a delightful meal and some challenging companionship shortly.

Dalwan thanked the host and slumped sulkingly back into a large, heavily padded armchair to wait for company to arrive. He was still depressed, and his emotions lay close to the surface. He went back and forth between wanting to be the sword bearer and wanting to run away. He could feel the drive within him to be independent from everyone, to use his power as he chose when and where he chose... "just like Darric warned!" The magic inside him was now beginning to rule his life. He could feel reason being replaced with passion, which had its roots in an obsession with his powers and the possibility of obtaining the sword.

He was so distracted with his thoughts that he did not notice that Darric had entered and was standing near the door, motionless. Dalwan finally noticed him and jumped to his feet like a child caught in some mischief, "Sorry, I was just thinking."

"'Tis not yer power or possession of the sword that'll make ya great," came Darric's words, resonating peacefully with a powerful conviction that again hammered at Dalwan's consciousness. "Bein' savior or destroyer 'ill be determined by yer character... that is, by who ya are!" There was a kind look on Darric's face as he watched and listened with invisible eyes and ears that pierced deep into Dalwan's soul. Dalwan had the sensation of being naked before this intruder dwarf. "What ya are inside 'ill determine how ya use what powers ya possess. How ya use them... an' why ya use them 'ill determine yer greatness."

"Why are you telling me all this? What am I supposed to do with it?" Dalwan's voice was challenging, and there was fear in it.

"I was listening to your thoughts," came the reply in a rather matter-of-fact tone. "I heard yer battles... battles I recognize well 'cause I fought 'em too... fought 'em an' won!"

"What difference does it make what I think? I don't have your power, so my battles aren't like yours."

"Indeed!? Do ya think me a blind fool? Does it not puzzle ya in the tiniest that I'm here with you instead of at the BIG meetin'?" Darric walked over to Dalwan and handed him a covered dinner plate. "I sensed the power in ya at our first meetin'. I tested it by givin' ya the chance ta pick my mind for the deeds of Jarmin. Ya did... perfectly!"

"If you knew this, why did you wait until now to talk to me?"

"Because I sensed that only Shaylan an' perhaps Rhem know yer strength, so I wanted privacy. What better cover than makin' the others think they're at the important meetin' while I meet with ya here."

Dalwan's mouth was hanging open in surprise; his heart swelled with pride and a little apprehension. "So what do you want with me?"

"Only ta find out what sort of stuff y'ar made o'"

"You mean I've got to pass some sort of test or something before you'll really talk to me... even though you already know my power?"

"Power does not greatness make! An' great power, such as yers, is dangerous. For every ten thousand men that can stand victoriously through poverty of substance an' power, there's but one who can survive unscathed o' soul the ravages of abundant wealth or great power!"

"Everyone else would say that if you have great power or lots of wealth, you're already victorious."

"Power and wealth 're only tools. Victory comes from the wise use o' those tools. Any good tool can turn to ruinous activity in the hand of a fool." Darric watched patiently as Dalwan digested his words without speaking a reply. After the short silence, he continued, "Mark ma words well, lad, no one truly escapes bein' changed by wealth 'r power. They'll change the life of whoever they touch. The key is in how the change comes! Does the nature o' the wealth or the nature o' the power change ya? 'R does yer character dominate the use o' the wealth or power, makin' them yer soul's charge?"

"Then I'll fight it... it won't get me... I'll keep my power from dominating my life," said Dalwan with deadly determination.

"It already dominates yer life!" shot back Darric in a strong fatherly tone. "Yer power 'twill be a determinant factor in most every decision you'll make from now on... you'll not likely escape it... might as well master it while ya have help!"

Dalwan's defenses came up full strength, "I don't need help... I have to conquer this myself..."

"Vary well!" said Darric, turning and heading for the door.

"Wait!... wait, Darric."

Darric stopped.

"Darric... I don't even know how to think about this... I don't have any idea how to go about this..."

"Would ya be askin' for assistance?"

Dalwan was very frustrated and confused, "What do you want of me? What am I supposed to be like to pass your test? An' what happens if I do take it, I don't even know what happens if I pass? I'm not even sure I want to pass... how do I know if I even want to be part of this whole thing... whatever it is?" Dalwan just stopped talking and stood, feeling very awkward and tongue-tied.

"I understand yer feelin', I..."

Dalwan cut Darric off, "They said I have to learn to use a sword," he complained in a slight whine, "I didn't even like swords... they said people would come after me and try to make me use the sword for them. They made me practice and train and study. Darric, I don't even know for sure if I really am a powermaster. I don't even know how to find out. I'm not even sure I want to know."

Dalwan sounded on the edge of tears when the aged Dwarf walked over, took his arm, and led him gently back to the chair he had been in and eased him back into it. "Rest yer mind, young one. Ya have already passed my test."

Dalwan sat perfectly still, not reacting to Darric's statement.

"As fer ya bein' a power master 'r not I'll help ya find out fer sure this vary day!"

"Is it really possible to know for sure?" Dalwan was using his sensing power to detect deception by Darric.

"O'course i'tis!" It made Darric chuckle to see Dalwan so anxious. "But then if ya would rather not know..."

"Don't toy with me! You know how much I want to know... to find out one way or another... I want to get on with my life!"

"OK, Dalwan. I'll take ya ta the Elven test stones. They'll determine which powers an' potentials ya have."

"But will I really know for sure?"

"Yes, and the test 'ill reveal whether 'r not I'm ta tell ya the secrets of the sword!" He was becoming more animated with every word. "Come, lad. We may as well go now and have the truth of it." Darric turned and walked toward the door without looking back to see if Dalwan was following. He could sense the rising turmoil and conflict in the young man. Dalwan was clearly afraid to discover the truth, whatever it was.

Dalwan stood up but did not move toward the door. He remained motionless, transfixed with a glazed eye stare... heart pounding, breath shallow, stomach turning over and over...

Darric opened the door and called back as he walked out, "You'll not be able to get on with yer life proper 'till ya know fer sure. Come lad, we're a wastin' time."

Dalwan refocused on the short stout figure walking out the door. He couldn't feel his body; his feet seemed stuck to the floor. Slowly, as if out of a dream, visions began forming in his mind... there was Shahandra, sword in hand, fighting a half dozen men. She called his name. He had to help! But he wasn't there! The vision changed. It was the anderon. He was taking to the air in a rain of arrows, fire spewing wildly from his mouth. Their minds touched for an instant, but he seemed too far away to understand the anderon's thoughts. The vision changed again. He saw himself standing next to a battlefield where two armies were locked in fierce hand-to-hand fighting. He felt his heart aching with the desperate hope that his friends would win. At first, the warriors were faceless men in a dusty cloud, fighting for their lives. The scene cleared, and Shaylan was there with Rhem and Attleman nearby. They looked gaunt and exhausted. Suddenly, he saw, in vivid detail, the body of Mallon exploding directly in front of him... the shock of it brought him out of his trance. He turned to see Darric standing outside the door, looking back at him with penetrating eyes.

"Come, lad, we have a long journey ahead of us and I want ta have ya back before the dinner ends tonight. If we get a movin', yer companions 'ill not get suspicious of yer activity today."

Dalwan began to drift toward the door. He felt as though he was moving in slow motion, floating through a sea of chaotic emotion.

Darric grabbed the back of his arm and pulled him through the threshold, "Get 'hold o' yerself, lad! No matter what the outcome today, yer life 'ill have adventure aplenty." Darric shut the door behind them and half pulled Dalwan, as they hurried off at a quicker pace than his short legs should have allowed.

Dalwan began to come to his senses. He became more aware of his surroundings as they left the grounds. He had been too dazed to observe the two dwarf centuries run off when he first exited the room. Darric had dispatched them to their designated duties with an almost imperceptible motion of his hand. As soon as Darric and Dalwan had cleared the conference grounds, they were rejoined by the two centuries. They had two horses hooked up to a small wagon, a basket of food, and two dark green with black trim capes, complete with hoods.

"Thank ya, ma friends," Darric said to the dwarves as he climbed up into the wagon. Dalwan was now back to himself and could clearly see that these two were very fond of the old dwarven magician.

There was laughter in his voice and a special sparkle in his eye as he told Dalwan, "Hop aboard lad an' hold on tight!"

Dalwan was about to learn that this particular dwarf didn't make idle suggestions... he really meant what he said.

With a crack of the reins, the horses were off and running. Even though the road was well-engineered and cared for, the speed at which they traveled made it necessary to hold on for dear life. The dwarf very obviously enjoyed this race against time. Dalwan found it odd that this great magician could enjoy so profoundly such a simple thing, and at that, display his pleasure in so animated a manner; laughing, talking loudly to the horses as if they were having as much fun as he, and moving about the floor board and seat as if dancing with his love at a festival. Dalwan never saw Shaylan or Rhem, or for that matter any of those gifted and therefore very serious types, ever seem to have so much fun doing anything... let alone something as simple as driving a wagon like a crazy person. As soon as they were out of town, Darric slowed to a steady but gentle trot. It only struck Dalwan afterwards that they had not encountered any traffic on the road... no other wagons, horses, or even pedestrians.

Darric guided them along the road up the gently sloping valley, which was studded with a few small but ornate farm complexes. After a long straight stretch, the road began to follow the river, which flowed through the now-narrowing canyon. The road through the canyon was well maintained, and there were signs along the way indicating that a sort of resort or park called a Canta was just up ahead. After riding about as far into the canyon as they had already traveled to get to the canyon, they arrived at the Canta.   It was immaculately maintained. There were many groups of small cottages nestled among groves of trees or set in carefully designed gardens with flowers and bushes, and rocks as decoration. Each group had some theme or other which dominated its landscape. There were small creeks of trickling water dividing the groups one from another. Between each group, there was a sturdy but very ornate bridge. In a central location among each group of cottages was situated a fire pit, barbecue pit with spit, and tables in keeping with the area motif.

There were several groups of dwarves using the grounds, and Dalwan found himself staring at them as they passed each occupied set of cabins.

"Do they own these houses?"

"No, Dalwan, these cabins are fer any of the dwarves ta use who want to. They simply sign up with the director of public works and set aside a time they wish. As long as there are openings, they can come stay here."

"Does it cost very much?"

"No! No!" laughed Darric, "Thar's no charge. Each of us who uses the grounds 'ill commit about one day for each five days that we use them. We employ whatever craft or art we possess ta maintain or enhance the grounds. If their particular talent is not needed for a specific task, they simply help wherever they find a need. I'tis the groundskeeper's job ta know where the greatest need is an' maintain proper raw material... even some tools for the work, although most dwarves bring their own tools." There was immense pride in Darric's voice as he spoke. His tone changed to something between scolding and taunting, "Don't suppose ya have anythin' in yer own land like this do ya?" There was the unmistakable hint of a smile on his face as he watched out of the corner of his eye for a reaction from Dalwan.

"No, Darric," conceded Dalwan, "we don't do this kind of thing. I'm not so sure we ever even thought about it. Someone would wreck it or steal it or charge people to stay in them. Then only the rich would be able to afford it." He became aware that he was being sensed on a deep level... someone probing deeper than just his thoughts... he felt unnerved. "Darric, was that you?... I mean, were you..."

"Ya're very safe here, lad. No cause fer alarm." Darric's voice was like medicine to his soul. A calm flooded over him like the feeling you get when you lie down on a soft, comfortable bed after a long, hard day of physical labor.

"How'd you do that?" asked Dalwan in surprise. "How'd you calm my feelings like that?"

"Thar's more than one type of healin' lad. Thar's body healin' and thar's the healin' of mind and soul. 'Twas you who allowed me to do it. You let me right past your defenses into yer mind.

"This is too mystical for me, Darric. But thanks just the same." Dalwan's words didn't hide from Darric the reservations that he felt. Dalwan realized that whatever Darric had really done to him, the truth was that he had a reckless trust for this dwarf.

They finally came to a halt at the upper end of the Conta, where a waterfall plunges into a beautiful, large pond, which itself dumps into the river. They stopped there and parked the wagon. Several feeding and water troughs were situated near the place where the wagon was parked. Darric dispatched Dalwan to the pond with two large buckets for water while he fetched some meal from a nearby shed.

When Dalwan returned with the water, Darric sent him back to the feed shed with the empty bucket and two coins to put in the slotted box by the door.

"You mean you take whatever you want and pay whatever you like for the grain?" asked Dalwan in astonishment.

Darric found himself laughing at Dalwan's question, which had so much of "man" in it. "Not exactly, lad. Ya can take as much as ya need and pay whate'r ya think it 'ill take ta replace it."   Darric was very pleased that these incidents were bearing so much fruit so quickly. "The lad is more observant and may be better equipped than I dared hope," he thought with a sense of anticipation and destiny, "...now to make sure!"

CHAPTER 15

Dalwan and Ingar had been gone for quite a while. Eric lay very still for a long time while Shahandra kept vigil over him among the remains of the men the power wielder had destroyed. As Shahandra kept watch, she sensed the approach of several animals. They were close by... moving cautiously. Almost without a sound, and nearly invisible in its natural camouflage, a large cat appeared near the spot where Dak's body lay. It was an immense thick-bodied cat, with erratic black lines on a tan fur, and stood about waist high to an average man. It stopped as soon as it caught sight of Shahandra and stood frozen in its tracks.   It stared motionlessly at her through large dark green eyes. After a moment, the end of the cat's tail swished back and forth several times while it continued to intensely study Shahandra and Eric.

"You must have been drawn by the smell of blood... is that why you came? Because of the dead?"

The large cat shook its head violently as if trying to rid itself of some pesky flies or shake off the effects of a blow.

"You're hungry, aren't you?" It appalled Shahandra to think of animals eating the remains of the dead men, but she had no tools with which to bury them. Even if she did have the tools, she knew there wasn't time to dig deep enough to keep them from being unearthed by hungry and quite determined forest creatures.

"Come here." Her voice was charged with the art that had brought so much pleasure to her in the years she spent with Lord Oakbern at Brandon Keep. She could communicate with almost every type of animal. She used her ability to sense their feelings, desires, and even moods.   Then she would use that insight to communicate and even, at times, control them. She learned that if she projected a feeling to an animal according to its particular inherent nature, it would often reciprocate. If, after she had worked with a particular type of animal long enough to become familiar with its patterns of thought and emotional responses, she could project an image of a desired action, and the creature would fulfill that stimulation if it was able to do so. Each animal was different in its level of emotional sophistication and ability to respond. Some would respond quickly, while others would take extra convincing. She found the greatest satisfaction in calming the fears of various beasts and befriending them. With one large cat that lived in the neighborhood of Brandon Keep, she had forged a bond so close that she believed the cat fancied her as its cub. Whenever it came to her beckoning, it had strong maternal feelings which demonstrated themselves in snuggling and an extended session of preening with a large rough tongue. Encounters of this type were the highlight of her young life. Often, the smaller creatures would require a more primal feeling or vision before they would understand and respond. Often it would require many visitations with an animal before she knew how it would react and which feelings it could receive and respond to.

The cat again shook its head. "It's OK," she said as she projected affection and safety to the majestic beast. It moved toward her, slowly at first, with each step full of hesitation. Then, as it got nearer, its apprehension melted away, and it walked uninhibited directly to her. As it arrived, only a step away, it stopped, extended its head toward Shahandra, and began to sniff her. She raised her hand and held it out with fingers pointing upward and an open palm facing toward the large cat's probing nose.   Again, it sniffed and then moved a step closer, smelling her hair and cloak. It was a he. She sensed something like affection coming from the beast, immediately followed by several strong licks across her cloak. She stroked the giant head and scratched behind his ears. His giant eyes closed as he tilted the back of his head towards her. His purr was almost as loud as a growl.

After a moment, he walked to the other side of her and, standing between them, sniffed Eric.

"He's mine. You don't want him... I'm sure he's bitter." She laughed at the thought, and the big cat stuck its tongue out several times as if trying to push something out of its mouth... something distasteful. Shahandra laughed again, which in turn caused the cat to shake its head.

She stoked the velvety fur on his side a few times and received a lick to the side of her face from a dry, rough tongue fully the width of her head.

Since the situation was not going to be manageable in any other way, she gave the beast leave to take Dak. As he turned to walk away, he looked back and gently nuzzled Shahandra, face to face, with only a hint of a lick. Shahandra returned the gesture with a hug around his giant neck.

Without looking back again, he trotted directly to Dak and, with a brief growl, dragged him off by the arm.

"It's not like he was a nice man," she thought. "Besides, what else could I do about it with the small time I had?" Her guilt feelings subsided.

A little while after the large cat left the clearing, several smaller animals entered, sniffing and rummaging. She also became aware that there were vultures in the tree tops. While she knew that this was inevitable, she didn't want to watch it. She used her art to project the vision of the large cat as if it were again present. Instantly, the animals scurried off, and the vulture's talk stopped. She held the vision for a few moments to give her time to get Eric up so they could be on their way before the creature banquet began.

Fearing a confrontation with Eric over Dalwan and remembering the hint that Ingar had given about him being susceptible to suggestion while unconscious, she decided to work on persuading him to move quickly toward Brandon Keep. She touched his brow and began to use her art on his thoughts, much in the same way she had with the cat. She projected thoughts of Dalwan being a victim and lucky to be alive. She projected Dalwan as being very frightened and hiding during the powermaster's battle. She suggested that the powermaster may even now be going ahead of them to Brandon Keep.

After this, she began to awaken him. She used her healing art to bring him back to consciousness.

"Are you alright?" she asked in a soothing tone that evidenced concern.

Eric stirred, then sat up. "What happened to me?"

"You fell over!"

"It was that woman. She did something to me. Why was she protecting the boy?"

"He's not important. He's just a scared boy. The dead men here took him for safe passage and intended to kill him. He was only a bystander. Forget him." Her voice was very calm and reassuring.

"I guess you're right. Maybe this powermaster will head for Brandon Keep..." he said, still sitting with his head hanging down, "...since he knows what's going on, he might just be heading there now."

"Let's get going then. You've been asleep for a long time." Shahandra stood up and brushed off her clothing.

Eric followed but was very clumsy as he tried to recover his footing. His head spun, and his muscles felt weak. For a moment, he was motionless on his hands and knees with his head still hanging down. Finally, he stood up but was very wobbly on his feet. He staggered a few steps to a nearby tree and leaned against it, one arm wrapped around the trunk and one holding his forehead.

Shahandra stood a respectful distance away and watched. "Does anything hurt... is your head in pain?"

"No, I'm just lightheaded... like getting up after being sick in bed for a while."

"Can you ride?"

"I think I'll get better as we go. If you get the horses, I'll try... I don't think we have time to waste.... to waste waiting for me to get better." He spoke slowly, searching for each word and even after finding them had to concentrate to keep them in proper order.

Shahandra gave a short whistle, and her horse, which had wandered off while she attended Eric, came trotting to her. She then closed her eyes and concentrated on Eric's horse. Her mind quickly found him and silently called him. He soon joined them, coming directly to her, not Eric. She put out her hand and tenderly touched the horse's forehead, stoking it gently.

Seeing what had happened, Eric called his horse. It did not respond at all. He called again... same results.

Shahandra removed her hand and said, "You shouldn't be so impatient, Eric. Call him again, but don't scold him. My magic held him not his will."

Again, Eric called. This time, the horse wheeled around directly and went straight to Eric unhesitatingly. Eric glanced at Shahandra for a moment, boiling a mixture of jealousy, anger, and admiration, all of which she was able to read instantly and with remarkable clarity.

"Why do you look so surprised, Eric? You know that I can do these things, and that I love animals."

"That's not it at all. I know of your abilities. But you're still playing power and control games with me. You called my horse with magic and then prevented him from obeying me. You were even tender and caring for the horse, but have not even offered to help me..."

Shahandra turned and, with a childlike teasing smile, cut in, "Oh, Eric, Eric!" she said, shaking her head back and forth. "You officially broke our relationship, embarrassing me in front of a lot of people, people who were very nice to me. Now you show up and immediately threaten one of my new friends, a friend who risked his life for me, and as a result, you get hurt. Then you expect me to run to you and offer unsolicited help! You're quite the arrogant one, aren't you?"

"What do you want from me, girl? I'm only doing what I've been commissioned to do. I don't have time for your games. I need your help, and you're unwilling to lend a hand." At that moment, he looked around at the corpses, intending to use them somehow in an unkind and grewsome illustration. Noticing that Dak's body was missing, he asked, "What'd you do, bring the one with the hole in him back to life and let him go?"

"No, Eric," her face became theatrically reflective, "I had a visit from a very large, hungry cat. He wanted something to eat. Actually, he preferred you over Dak. I was forced to make a choice, so, after some considerable thought, I gave him Dak." She finished with an animated matter-of-fact shrug of her shoulders.

"Another game!" said Eric, visibly angry. He stepped weakly to the side of his horse and swung awkwardly into the saddle. Instantly, he slumped over sideways and almost fell off. He managed to stabilize himself and immediately pull himself forward, where he finally lay flat against the horse's back. "What do I have to do to get some help from you?" he shouted in a weak, horse voice.

"Just ask nicely," she replied as she stood resolutely, arms crossed with wide eyes fixed on him and a taunting smile decorating her face.

"We're losing precious time, girl." His voice was now almost a whisper.

"I know." She still didn't move.

"OK! OK!" He said, still in the prone position, now with one arm hanging limp at the side of the horse's neck and a very pale look on his face. Then, in a weak, dry voice, "Shahandra, will you please help me?"

Shahandra uncrossed her arms and started towards him, "Yes, Eric... I'd be glad to help... thought you'd never ask."

She reached him and touched the side of his face with her left hand, and put her right hand on top of his head. He just watched her without speaking, as she worked her magic. After a short time, she let go and stepped away from the horse.

Eric sat up and just stared at her, still without uttering a word. He was physically restored but had no idea how to deal with Shahandra. She made him furious, yet at the same time, he was grateful. He thought her foolish for taking advantage of his momentary weakness to force her proud, childish notions upon him. With that thought, he recovered his emotional stability. "Indeed, the problem was simple," he thought to himself, "she really is just a proud child playing games which are childishly inappropriate at this time, or for that matter, anytime." He resolved to simply let the matter drop and get on with the truly important business at hand, warning Brandon Keep!

Leaning forward and speaking with clear condescension, "Shahandra, there's no time for any more of your little games, OK? Get on your horse. We've got a very hard ride ahead of us."

Shahandra hesitated, then, with a shrug of her shoulders, obeyed.

They returned to their village to collect their things, including Eric's special weapons. They packed light for a faster ride back. Early the next morning, they were on their way before first light.

They rode hard for the rest of that day, stopping only to water the horses and refresh themselves. At dusk, they camped next to the creek, which flowed through the valley they were traveling up. They ate their own provisions without bothering to light a fire.

With the twilight of dawn, they were up again. Eric believed that the dead men they left the day before must have been important to Danlion's plan of attack against Brandon Keep. Their delay in returning would give Eric and Shahandra time to warn Lord Oakbern. This motivation kept them going strong for the entire day. They climbed out of the valley in which they had camped and followed a narrow road that cut through the mountains toward a high pass. They reached the summit by nightfall. At the summit of the pass, they were well above the timber line and it was late End Harvest, there were patches of snow scattered around in sheltered areas. The pass itself was fairly narrow with a sheer rock wall on the north side and a broken, steep rocky slope on the other. A stone stairway led a zig zag path up to a small, crude travelers' shack which sat on a large flat rock sheltered by an overhang from the north canyon wall. They found the single room empty except for six piles of dry grass, apparently used as beds. At the end of the shack, opposite the door, was a small fireplace made of stone fragments and mortar. Along the south wall was the only window, under which was a single board about half a hand thick and two hands wide and as long as Eric was tall. It was supported on both ends by piles of flat stones. In the fireplace were the two charred ends of what had been a fair-sized log.

It was very cold that night. They utilized most of the grass for their beds. Each bedroll was placed on a separate pile of grass, and then another pile of grass was placed on top, sandwich style. Even with this arrangement, they were cold all night. Eric splintered up the remains of the charred log and, towards morning, made a small fire using some of the grass from the bed piles as kindling.

As soon as they could see well enough to travel, they moved out, having decided to wait until it was warmer before eating. They were able to cover ground much more quickly going downhill than they had the day before on their ascent to the pass. As the sun came up, the cold stiffness in their muscles and joints began to wear off. They ate without stopping and did not slow their pace until midday when they arrived at the bottom of their descent. There, they discovered the beginning of the road that traverses the entire valley. From there, it would be about one hard day's ride to Brandon Keep. Where the road began, there was a grassy meadow bordered by forest. They took time to feed the horses and stretch their stiff muscles. Eric had gone down to the creek for a drink and was on the way back up the rocky bank when he sensed the use of magic. It was nearby and weak, very weak! Shahandra had also sensed it and was looking toward the edge of the meadow on the same side of the creek that they were on.

"Eric!"

"I know. I sensed it too." Eric had jogged over to the place where Shahandra stood, and they both scoured the tree line for some sign of the magic's source.

"It seemed to come from over there," she said, pointing to an area almost directly perpendicular to the creek from the place where they now stood.

It happened again, this time Shahandra became very excited, "It WAS from there! It is a healing art... I'm almost certain of it!"

"If it is a healing art, it is a poor practitioner who uses it... that or he's almost dead himself." Eric made no overture of going to investigate or assist. Seeing the pleading look on her face, he said, "Let's take a look as we leave... get your horse and let's go." His voice echoed with irritation at this interruption to his schedule.

Shahandra was sure that he would have ridden off without so much as a second thought if she had not been with him. Given his feelings for her and his obvious disenchantment with the potential disruption provided by this excursion, she wondered why he even allowed it to occur. She only hoped it was some latent hidden concern for the possible plight of an unfortunate that had led him to consider this diversion from their course. Whatever the reason, she would take it and probably would have gone anyway, whether he did or not.

As they rode up to the place from which the magic had come, they became aware that some sort of activity had taken place all around the immediate area. The grass had been flattened in erratic patterns, and the earth was torn in several places. About twenty paces from the leading edge of the forest, they came across a freshly killed horse with an arrow sticking out of its neck and flank. Eric dismounted, drew his sword, and advanced the rest of the way on foot. Shahandra also dismounted and was walking parallel to Eric about ten paces away.

"Eric, there's a man dead here... his head is almost cut off from the back." Shahandra continued her approach with all of her senses fully engaged.

"There are two more here... and another horse," said Eric, almost without emotion. "These men are too mutilated to have used magic recently... There must be someone else nearby."

They stopped before entering the woods and made their horses lie flat in the grass. They then entered the trees about twenty paces apart, searching and sensing. The undergrowth was so thick when Eric entered that he put away his sword and pulled out a knife. Shahandra held no weapons.

"Eric, I sense someone close to me. His life is slipping away." There was enough urgency that Eric instinctively ran the distance between them, kicking and shoving his way through the brush and low limbs until he cleared them just short of her position.

Within a short space, they located a man setting down leaning against a tree facing away from the meadow. His left leg was badly broken, and he had lost a lot of blood from a wound near his right temple and another in his chest. His eyes were barely open and unfocused, even though he made an effort to look at them.

"We won't hurt you," said Shahandra as she knelt down to get a closer look at his wounds.

"I'm already hurt... beyond fixin'," came a raspy gurgly reply followed by a weak cough.

Shahandra began to explore his most visible wounds as Eric bent down on one knee to question the man.

"What happened to you and your companions? Who were you fighting and why?"

The man tried to focus on Eric before speaking, but finally closed his eyes as he answered almost in a whisper, "All they wanted was our weapons... they just wanted our weapons." the man drifted off.

"Who did?" Eric asked in a demanding tone, sounding like an avenger.

"Let him rest a moment, Eric."

"There's no time left for him, he's dying." Eric reached out and shook the man. "Who did this? How many were there?"

Shahandra pushed in on Eric, trying to get between them and pressure him to move back from the man, "Eric, he can't..."

"Shahandra!" shouted Eric as he physically shoved her back away, "This information may keep us alive. Now keep him alive... work your magic girl!"

"He's lost too much blood, I can't..."

Eric took hold of the man's shoulders and gently shook him while speaking very loudly, "What did these men look like? How many were there?"

"If you shake me again..." the man whispered, "I won't talk to you at all." He managed to get one eye open, "...for the girl's sake..."

"OK, for the girl's sake! Tell me." He let go of the man and sat back on his heels.

"Six of 'em... one with... wounded hand... big one has green cloak..." his open eye crossed, then closed, and his mouth dropped open. His breathing was shallow, labored, and gurgling.

"Let me try to help him, Eric." Shahandra moved back to the man's side.

Eric got up and started back toward the clearing, "He can't live, and you know it!"

"But I can't just leave him here... I can't let him just stay here to die alone."

"Then stay with him until he dies if that pleases you." Looking back over his shoulder, he talked progressively louder as he walked away, "I'm leaving now. If you pity him, put him out of his misery."

A flash of anger filled Shahandra. How quickly Eric had forgotten his plea for help now that the victim was someone else. Her thoughts returned to the man. Touching the side of his face, she spoke softly, "What's your name?"

After a brief delay, she saw him weakly lick his lips and form the word "Osmond," barely loud enough to understand.

She took his hand and spoke again, "Osmond, what can I do for you?"

He struggled to form the words, slow, halting with each one, "let me...die...thank you..."

"Do you hurt?"

His lips formed "No," but no sound came out.

Shahandra became aware that Eric had been yelling something, but she ignored him. She heard him ride away.

She gently touched his head and whispered, "Sleep well, Osmond... sleep well."

His shallow breathing stopped, and there was a brief twitch at the corner of his mouth. Then he was still.

She arose and walked back to her horse, which was still obediently lying in the grass. "Up, lady."

She felt a deep sadness. These men had died at the hands of other men for their weapons... that's all, just for their weapons. A strong dislike for men seemed to grow with each interaction she experienced. And yet at the same time, there was a desire for romance germinating within her. The conflict took her by surprise. It seemed strange to her to think of romance now... now with war close... now with people dying... now while she traveled with a predictably disappointing man... a man like so many other men she had known... now when her future was so unsure. Yet maybe this was the very time romance was made for... a time when everything you know hangs in the balance... a time when the only thing you might have, indeed the only thing you might wish for, was someone to love you, someone you could love and respect.

As she mounted her horse, she put her thoughts to rest with a promise to herself not to lump all men together in her current narrow category, at least not yet. She had met some clever and seemingly sincere men, but had not gotten to know them well enough to assess their potential in such matters...

"and there is Dalwan," she thought to herself. "Too bad he's so... so... limited & simple." She dismissed him as nice but not nearly challenging enough for the kind of relationship she envisioned for herself.

As she rode off, she sensed the area for signs of magic. Eric was nowhere in sight. She set out at a gallop, hoping to overtake him. She was sure he would be only a short distance ahead of her. While riding, she thought about the fact that he had left her again; that she had helped him recover, and he still had no consideration for her; that he cared nothing for the dying man except to get some information from him before he died, intending nothing more than to discard his life like a note received and thrown into a fire. She slowed her horse down to a walk as resentment and a deeper distaste for Eric grew. She remembered his antics with Borem at the inn and decided against even trying to rejoin him. She wanted to see what he'd do if she hung back, whether he would wait for her somewhere, come back for her, or just go on without her.

Quite suddenly, there was the distinct awareness that she was being sensed by someone... or was it? It seemed to be just the pure magic of sensing... magic with no print on it. It stayed with her only briefly, then vanished again. I felt eerie but didn't frighten her. She decided to ignore it for now, especially since there was nothing she could do about it.

Shahandra had traveled alone before in difficult circumstances. "So I'll do it again!" she thought to herself. "I'll be just fine...perhaps even better without him!" She sat still on her horse and continued her discussion out loud to herself, "If I need help, I'll call on the animals. I'll prove that I'm his equal... that's right, equal to His Majesty, Lord Arrogance."

She became aware that the sensing was back... it seemed to be listening to her conversation... just as quickly, it was gone. This time, she had tried to sense which direction it came from... it felt like it came from everywhere around her. Again, it had no print on it, as if magic itself was listening in on her. This time, as before, it left her with no feeling of dread or fear.

Eric continued at a strong pace for quite a while. His horse could easily keep up a walk of this speed almost all day if required. He was irritated that Shahandra was so sentimental. "Why," he thought to himself, "did she dally around when time was so precious?" He was glad that she had chosen to stay behind because she would just get in the way if something truly dangerous confronted him and would surely slow him down. Besides that was the fact that it would be much easier for him to remain undetected if she were not with him. He was still annoyed with Oakbern, that he had deemed it necessary to send her with him on a mission of such import and potential danger. She had accomplished nothing more than the infernal complicating of the entire affair! Her alliances had proven to be the death of the only good chance he encountered of discovering the identity of the powermaster. "Besides," he finished his rationalization, "if she gets in trouble, I'll sense her magic and go back and help... then maybe she'll value my company!"

Eric rode on stewing in a bath of emotion, which eventually turned back to a consideration of her as a person. "Actually," he thought, "she would probably be a fair companion, in less perilous times, for someone who was not as serious about life as he was." The more he thought along these lines, the more convinced he became that she would be well suited as a wife and mother, someone to come home to. She could wipe away the day's troubles and soothe a vexed soul.

The road down the valley seemed to stay parallel to the river. Shahandra left the road and began to travel on a deer trail that followed close to the riverbank. She had never been this far up the valley and was therefore not acquainted with the lay of the land. She was, however, almost certain that the road remained relatively close to the river throughout its journey down the valley. She would stay on the trail as long as was practical, hoping to avoid contact with the likes of those who had killed the men earlier. She felt that this would be a strategic advantage since no one would be expecting anyone to travel along the river when there was a perfectly good road nearby.

There was a thick line of vegetation and trees that grew along the bank of the river between the road and the trail she was on. For long stretches, it would conceal her from anyone who might be on the road. For the rest of the day, she traveled the river trail, often changing sides of the river and several times being forced to move right down the river bed itself for a considerable distance.

When darkness began to set in, she started looking for a safe place to spend the night. After finding nothing very suitable down by the water, she decided to search the area on the opposite side of the river from the road.

After a brief search, she happened on a place where the stream flattened out considerably and a point bar was formed on the inside of a large bend. On the roadside of the river was a high sheer wall where the stream had cut deep into the side of the hill, on top of which was the road. On the point bar side of the river was a stand of trees that appeared to be very old. There was a thick growth of small trunked trees near the river, which appeared to give way to bigger and more widely spaced trees the further into the plateau she looked. Finally, the tallest, most spaciously oriented trees were clearly visible, towering over the rest of this small forest, toward the back center of the bend.

Shahandra headed directly for the tallest trees. At first, she traveled up a slight incline through the bordering slender trees. The ground was initially rough with river rocks, but gradually gave way to gravel and finally sand near the top. The further up she went, the harder-packed the ground became and the more littered with needles and debris from the trees. She swung down from her horse and began to lead it through the thicket. The trees at first were very close together, which caused her to constantly search for a path clear enough to pass through and to protect herself from low limbs. The further in she went, the wider the spacing between the trees and the higher the limbs were from the heavily matted ground. It became noticeably cooler and darker the deeper she penetrated into the grove. As she neared the center of the grove, she became aware of old magic, very strong, very old magic. Only once before had she sensed this type of magic, but she would never forget its feel. The further she went, the more powerful the sensations became until finally it became so strong that she stopped to see if its source could be determined. She could see a faint glow coming from the center of a circle of trees just beyond her. Still, there was no discernible definition to the magic, no sign of any others present, and no fluctuations of any sort in its strength.

She left it Lady, her horse, standing next to a large tree as she cautiously worked her way a few steps closer to the light. She realized that the magic was so strong now that there was no need to consciously use her sensing art to detect it... it permeated her. The magic seemed neutral and uncommonly stable... a steady source of magic. Her growing apprehension began to affect her horse, which in turn began to fidget and whimper. She turned and looked in its direction, and it immediately settled down. She was surprised that her magic worked with such a small effort exerted on her part... maybe it was her horse's ability to perceive that was enhanced.

The glow was now brighter than the darkening sky and silhouetted the massive trunks of the trees, which seemed to circle it.

Again, she stood frozen in her tracks, trying to sense the magic's source. Fear and exhilaration filled her. Her heart pounded so wildly that she felt sure some nearby ear would hear its rapid beating and detect her presence. Still nothing moved. There was no sound, no sense of danger or caution. Her experience told her not to trust it...

Realizing that just standing there, paralyzed all night, wasn't an option, she began to advance slowly, hiding behind tree after tree as she got closer, squinting into the hazy light, trying to see some greater definition. Still, she sensed no danger and no change in the magic. Step by step, she moved closer to the inner ring of immense trees. Extreme peace began to flood her being as if she had somehow come to the safest home in the entire world, to be loved, cared for, and sheltered by the strongest and most loving parents. It was intoxicating. She was now near enough to see clearly into its glowing center. Through the hazy light which filled the center of the huge ring of trees, Shahandra could see that apart from a single large bush, there was nothing in there, just light. She moved through the ring of trees that bordered this shining meadow and immediately stepped into glowing grass. It was about a hand breath deep and was a transparent green, like the purest jade, and was as soft as goose down to the touch. The hazy air over the grass seemed to radiate light. The air itself felt comfortably cool, but there was a warmth about the place that permeated her entire body. The magic meadow was about as large as the ballroom floor at Brandon Keep.

The feeling was so wonderful that she began to laugh, first just a chuckle, then more and more until finally she was rolling in the beautiful grass with full unrestrained laughter. The marvelous trees that surrounded her now seemed more like a circle of loving friends reveling in the moment with her.

She had already traveled far and knew that she was fatigued, but she could feel none of her weariness. She finally stopped laughing, but the exhilaration didn't fade. She lay still at the edge of the circle, looking up through perfectly formed trees whose tops appeared to brush the stars.

She wondered how this place came to be and even more, what sort of place it really was. She had never even heard tales of such a wondrous work as this in which she lay.

She was sure that this entire place was intertwined in magic, but could not pinpoint a source. In fact, the magic did not appear to have a source. It simply was magic. She wondered if the elves had somehow found a way to create a magic forest garden. It was certain that no man would have had the magic or ability to have done such a thing. And, as strong as the magic was at the place where she now lay, she was amazed that it was not perceptible from the river, or from the pass, for that matter. What type of magic was this that the trees could totally capture it and shield it from escaping?

She sat up and looked around, remembering the bush she had seen earlier. She rolled to her feet and, as she strolled toward it, she stopped over and over to turn around and fully take in the panorama of the glowing meadow and its giant guardians. There was no hurry. When she finally got to the bush, she found that it was a bundleberry bush comfortably covered with ripe clusters of plump berries. To her amazement, she also found berry blossom buds, full blooms, and other clusters in various stages of maturity. How could such a bush exist? Stranger than that, why hadn't the forest creatures eaten all the ripest berries already? And why hadn't someone come along and homesteaded this forested wonder, unless, for some strange reason, not everyone was able to get into this place? Or worse, it was guarded by some loathsome caretaker?

Shahandra reached out and plucked a nice-sized cluster of berries and held them up to her nose to see if they smelled like those she had eaten elsewhere. She realized at this point that her sense of smell was heightened. The berries had the same tantalizing smell as others she had eaten, only sweeter and more intense. The fragrance filled the air as she mashed one of them between her fingers. The rich, dark red-violet syrupy juice ran all over her hand. She put the entire remainder of the cluster, about five or six berries, into her mouth. There was an explosion of sweet aromatic flavor. She savored it, sucking the essence out of the berries slowly and purposefully. The sensations were at once extremely arousing and so intense that she became self-conscious of her reaction. With eyes wide, blushing with embarrassment, she looked around the area quickly while sensing the possible presence of some hitherto unseen watcher. There was not even the slightest hint of anyone else. Her embarrassment turned to laughter as she grabbed another cluster of berries and began to bathe her mouth in their exquisite quintessence, delighting herself in them one by one. There was no hurry. She walked back to the place where she had left her horse as she savored the remaining berry from her last bunch. It was much darker now and harder to see in the thick woods surrounding the open circle. The radiance from the clearing seemed much brighter now and cut through the trees in swaths of diffused light. As she reached her horse and began to guide it back toward the clearing, she noticed that the places on her fingers where the juice had run glowed in the dark. She turned away from the inner circle to shield her hand from the light and get a better look... it really glowed. She turned back to her horse and said, "Look, Lady, my hand is glowing!" Then reached out with it, touched her horse's head, and soothed the last hint of fear away. She sensed peace fill her.

As she walked back toward the inner circle, this time with the horse, she was struck with a deep sense of reverence for the entire area. It was as if this place was actually the source of all magic, like a wellspring of ancient magic, pure and secured by a ring of protectors, keepers of the magic. Every one of her senses affirmed this growing notion. As she reached the edge of the circle, she took all the riding tack off her horse and let her go into the circle unrestricted. She entered slowly, looked around for a moment, and began to eat; slowly, purposefully, there was no hurry.

Shahandra went back and pulled off one more cluster of berries to eat with her evening meal. She unwrapped some bread and smoked fish and ate them both with the berries. The meal was wonderful. She ate slowly, relishing each bite, chewing a little longer than usual. There wasn't any hurry.

After her meal, she spread out her blankets and lay on the top of them. As she stared off toward the tree tops surrounded by stars, she thought how wonderful it would have been if her parents could have lived to experience this incredible place. It had been many years since she could clearly recall what her parents looked like. As she tried to recall them, the light around her swelled as if in a wave that rolled toward her and heaped up over her, growing dramatically in brightness and power. She was so greatly distracted by this amazing display that she sat up quickly, looking around, attempting to grasp its meaning. The swell vanished like a ripple in a pond, diminishing the light as it went. She couldn't sense or see anything out of the ordinary... that is, out of the ordinary for this place.

Without lying back down, she again returned her thoughts to her parents, trying to recall their image. The light swelled into a giant mound over her again. An image began to appear in the light. It was in the form of a woman, a beautiful well-formed woman with shimmering, radiant hair. The face began to take shape. It started with the eyes and continued to develop with incredible detail until it was fully fashioned. It was her mother. Then came the man... slender and strong. He was moving, walking toward the woman with gliding strides. His face began to form, starting with his eye... he was an elf... and he was her father. Shock and amazement filled her. She was half elven! "Yes", she thought, "that's it... that's why I feel the way I do about so many things... I'm half elf!" She was so pleased that a broad smile broke out all over her face.

Both images looked directly at her. "Hello, mother. Hello father. I wish you were really here to see this with me." A flood of emotion filled her as she stared wide-eyed into the vision.

"We love you very much, Shahandra," came a reply she never expected to hear. It was spoken by her father with a voice full of music.

"Can you hear me? Are you really here?" shouted Shahandra as she jumped to her feet.

There was no real answer, only a statement by her mother, "Just remember, sweet Shahandra, we'll always be with you, in your heart and in your mind." As she spoke, Shahandra suddenly remembered in the most minute of detail the circumstances that surrounded the things she was seeing and hearing.

Her ability to recall things about her parents seemed to expand with each new vision of them she saw, even though she had been so very young when they were killed. It was unclear how much time passed as she watched one scenario after another unwind and play itself out. Sometimes they were close, sometimes far away. At times, she was being held by them and saw the vision from that very odd perspective, giving her a strange visual sensation.

Finally, of her own choice, she halted the vision. She had taken all the time she needed and experienced everything in full. It was like finishing a good meal with plenty of food. She had enjoyed every part but was filled to capacity.

Next, she thought back on her parting with Ingar. She wished Ingar could experience this with her. As quickly as her thoughts turned to Ingar, the vision appeared. It was that awful battleground. All the sensations and smells returned to her. She blanked out the image with its intensities. She wondered if Ingar and Dalwan had made it back safely.

Suddenly, Ingar's form appeared, only it was a different color than before. She saw Ingar in Borem's Inn. The image and surroundings were vivid. There was a bright blue aura around her. Borem was there. He also had an aura that seemed to swirl with yellow and red colors. They were talking. Their voices were unusually clear... as if they were actually present. Shahandra listened in to see what sort of vision this was, something out of the past or maybe even the present. She picked up Ingar mid-sentence,

"...n't think he's as uninvolved with the incidents of the past as he has led us to believe... something about him puzzles me and intrigues me..."

"He has turned up in the most unexpected places," laughed Borem.

"Yes, but he always travels alone... and yet seems so timid and so shy..." said Ingar, now facing away from Shahandra. Shahandra wished she could see Ingar's face, and the vision shifted positions, obeying her desire. She was now looking directly into Ingar's face.

"And what do ya suppose that the likes of Rhem and Shaylan see in the lad?" asked Borem more seriously than he had been at the start.

"I'm surprised at you, Borem. You know very well that he's Shaylan's nephew, even if he has powers greater than we think, he's never made use of them when they could be detected… and don't you think he would have at least done something when we had to fight that night?"

"I'm sure you must be right." But a hint of doubt still hung in his mind.

Shahandra paused to reflect on the conversation, and the images vanished in the misty radiance of the meadow. "What about this Dalwan?" her thoughts turned to her own estimations of him. "He was such a nice boy... but Ingar was right about him being too timid. He would have been a nice friend for a quiet time... an easy, relaxing time." She recalled his image in detail and wondered almost aloud where he was. His vision arose. She was startled to see a very large aura about him. It was a veritable shimmering rainbow of color that frothed and boiled all around him. He was with a very distinguished-looking older man whose aura was a swirl of crimson and aqua blue. There were soldiers stationed at the entrances and others moving about, conversing in a well lit room. Some of the soldiers had faint auras, with one particularly tall one having a fairly substantial yellow, blue, and green one. Among those who milled about the room was one with a strong aura that reminded her of the glow of the moon. He seemed to be looking directly at her. It gave her a strange sensation, so she avoided watching him.

She returned her attention to Dalwan and his companion and listened in on their conversation to see if she could determine what place they were at and at what time. They were discussing the sword Fallonrod. The older, distinguished-looking man seemed to have discovered its origin. Dalwan listened with intensity as the man explained about a shadow master and someone named Rhem. The old man was a good story teller, but got too carried away with details for Shahandra. She got distracted and began to look around the room in which the two were talking. It was crowded with people, most of whom had some sort of aura. It was then she realized that the auras around the old man and Dalwan were larger and more intense than any of the others in the room, with some being difficult to detect at all. While she was scanning the crowd, a man came in an entrance on the far side of the room. He was dressed in black with a gold chain securing a cape that flowed about him as he walked. A royal blue aura swirled around him with visible wisps of forest green at the edges of it. He left a vapor-like trail behind him as he walked. His appearance was so striking that she watched him without even blinking from the time he entered the room and worked his way through the crowd, finally stopping right in front of Dalwan and the older man. Upon arrival, he addressed the older man as "Shaylan".

Shaylan acknowledged him with a respectful nod and finished what he was saying, "...so tomorrow I will introduce you as my apprentice... but don't practice any of your magic here..." with that, all three men laughed. Shahandra had moved the vision in close to get a better feel for facial expressions and to see what else she could catch... it was only when they laughed that she noticed their combined aura. The three auras had joined into a frothing pyramid of lights with Dalwan's side dominating. Shahandra moved the vision off to a distance so she could study this. It was then that she noticed the man with the moonlight aura looking in her direction again. As she moved her vantage point of view, his eyes followed. It again gave her a strange feeling, this time persuading her to let the vision vanish.

Her thoughts turned to Danlion. She wondered if she could see someone she had never met. She tried to picture him, recalling descriptions given by those who had survived attacks by him and his heartless band. The misty light swirled, but no image appeared. She had several times in the past sensed a power of considerable magnitude, the source of which she was never able to identify. It seemed to coincidentally correspond with the destruction of certain outlying villages. Chancing that Danlion was the power source, she brought to memory the print of that magic along with the mental image she had concocted of him. The light in the magic meadow intensified past normal daytime brightness, making Shahandra squint. The power swelled as the radiant mist about her rose to twice her standing height.

A hard day's ride on a good horse away, Danlion paced the floor in the living room of a house that he borrowed from a nice man who coincidentally incinerated at their initial meeting. He stopped his pacing quite suddenly to the absolute horror of those attending him in the room. (This type of sudden halt often ended with the premature and quite permanent dissolution of a relationship with someone close by.) Nothing happened, no one vanished into a pile of ash, no charred or mutilated bodies to remove. He just stopped and stood staring at the floor... sensing, probing, trying to locate or at least identify the huge swell of power he was detecting. It seemed to come from everywhere.

"To your posts!" he yelled in a voice charged with command and anticipation. Everyone who was able to move was in motion for the various doorways before the sound of his order finished echoing through the room.

Still, he did not move. He began an intense sensing, again probing... hoping to locate the source of this incredible and hitherto unknown power.

In the meadow, Shahandra recalled more and more about the magic of the ancient man turned demon. Oddly aided by the magic, her memory continued to build a clear image of that power source, which she immediately set as the center of focus for her search. She again joined the improved power print together with the mental image she had of his physical identity. Her thoughts rapidly solidified. With explosive speed, the image formed in the mist, complete in every minute detail.

Suddenly, Danlion's head snapped up. "I've got you now! Who are you and what do you want?"

At that same instant, Shahandra saw and heard Danlion with amazing clarity. His aura was dark red and violet. His image and power were now indelibly etched in her mind. She tried to answer, but the words stuck in her suddenly dry throat.

Shahandra began to move her point of focus, an activity which seemed to confuse Danlion. He tried to identify which direction the power was emanating from. He turned this way and that, menacing eyes squinting cold as ice and lips pursed in a sneer, "What are you? Show yourself, coward... FOOL!" Suddenly, he looked straight at her, like the man in the ballroom had done, and began to sense with intensity she could feel.

It was at that instant she realized he couldn't see her... only sense her power. She immediately shut down the vision.

Instantly, the source vanished, and Danlion cursed and writhed as if in pain. "There must be two powermasters. I must find this other source... this invader of my presence... he will pay for his games with his life!"

He called his attendants and quizzed them as to which had sensed the power. Only one other had sensed it, and he was not nearly the most competent sensor in Danlion's employ. He was, however, the only sensor present at this occasion. Danlion grabbed him by the sleeve and headed out of the house while yelling orders over his shoulder, "Dorslin, you will accompany Mornic here on an urgent quest. Take your most powerful weapons. You will doubtless need them." He was exiting the front door at a good clip as he finished the orders.

In the living room, a powerful looking man dressed in tight fitting green pants, a coarse weave brown pullover shirt, and a tan leather cape stood and walked undaunted, unhurried toward the door in response to Danlion's request.

Back in the meadow, Shahandra lay down in the cool grass. She was flushed and frightened. Her heart beat so hard that she felt as though it would pound its way out of her chest. Danlion's ability to perceive her probing made her realize how dangerous this sinister, "would-be overlord of the world", really was. There had been no indication that the others she sought out had any perception of invasion, except possibly the man in the ballroom. But Danlion went so far as to verbally challenge her presence. As fear and hopelessness began to drag her down very quickly, she realized that her reactions to all these things were very exaggerated. She sat up and sought to clear her mind. The fear and despair subsided rapidly, giving way again to the peace she had experienced earlier.

This magic meadow seemed to empower and greatly enlarge her arts and even enhance her emotions. She wondered if everything she had seen was trustworthy or just an apparition of her thoughts. She wondered what, if any, permanent effects this place may have on her. Although the place itself seemed to be neutral and all incidents and experiences had been affected by her own desires, she was now respectfully wary of the power present in the meadow.

Knowing that Eric would be somewhere close by, she decided to look in on him. If she could find him and he was in an appropriate setting, then it would lend credence to the other experiences of the evening. She first cleared her mind and then made a mental image of him, complete with his magic. His image came quickly into focus. The light in the area of the vision dimmed, and she saw him lying on a bedroll in a dark meadow. His moonlight aura silhouetted his body as he slept. Nearby, she could see the forms of three men moving very slowly through the grass toward Eric. Two of the men had small crimson auras with a touch of yellow. The other had a larger aura of blue and red. She could sense the imminent danger to Eric. The men were still far enough away that if awakened now, he would be able to defend himself. In a panic, Shahandra screamed, "Eric! Watch Out! Errriccc! Wake UP!" Suddenly, Eric sat up and, in the blink of an eye, the men were running at him with swords drawn.

Again Shahandra screamed, "NO! NOOOO!"

She sprang to her feet and called her horse, who was lying down. She responded in an instant. She saddled her with speed and agility that amazed even her. She mounted her horse and realized that she had no idea which way she needed to ride to reach Eric.

She concentrated on him, and his vision appeared immediately. He was fighting with two men. She began to summon as many forest animals as her powers could locate and send them to Eric's aid. She located a bear and a mountain lion, both near enough to Eric's position to help. She gave them the image that Eric was one of their young and under attack.

She then turned the horse around, trying to decide which way she had to ride to reach the river. Frustration rapidly became tears, and she closed her eyes, wishing that she could find a clear pathway to Eric. A bright flash that she could see through her eyelids occurred, and when she opened her eyes, there was a clear pathway leading out of the forest about a quarter way around the circle to her left. Her horse broke into a full run for the path. Light flowed like a river from the circle out into the corridor ahead of her, as if a dam had broken. She followed the glowing pathway out of the magic forest. The light dimmed as she approached the outer parameter of trees. She picked out a vague landmark in the starlit distance to keep her on track as she left the forest, breaking for the river down the bank at a gallop.

CHAPTER 16

Darric led Dalwan up a zig zag path that worked its way to the top of the falls. From there, the path branched, one part heading for an observation platform overlooking the falls and the other up the creek that fed the falls.

Darric headed up the creek without even looking back to see if Dalwan was following. This old dwarf, like most other dwarves, was a powerful climber. For one having such short legs, he was amazingly quick and easily kept ahead of Dalwan. Though Dalwan was an avid hiker, it wasn't too long before he was working very hard just to keep up. Dalwan kept expecting Darric to settle into a more reasonable pace, but the dwarf showed no signs of tiring or slowing. The path was in good repair but obviously not often used. It was steep and covered with leaves and debris from the trees. As the dwarf continued on without breaking his punishing stride, Dalwan's best efforts weren't enough to keep from falling behind. "Darric,... Darric!... I can't... keep up with... you!" he was so winded that his words came out in gasps.

"Do yer best lad," came the disgustingly strong reply, "we don't have much further ta go...but it's gettin' late!"

Darric suddenly left the path at a small bridge and headed up a rocky dry creek bed that it spanned. The middle of the creek was a smooth bedrock with pockets of gravel and was littered with large granite boulders from place to place. It was fairly steep to begin with, but turned very steep as it headed up the canyon wall. There were places where it was so steep that the climbers had to use tree roots protruding from the banks and overhanging branches as handholds for support.

Darric got so far ahead of Dalwan that he was no longer in sight. Soon, he could not even hear the dwarf. He knew the dwarf was up to something. It was his firm suspicion that this was part of the test being conducted by the dwarf and that somehow he was being watched, so he determined not to give up.

After a short time of climbing in solitude without so much as a hint of the dwarf's presence or whereabouts, the terrain began to flatten out, and Dalwan found himself at the base of the sheer rock cliffs which formed the walls around a narrowing gorge which ended, opposite his position, in a dry waterfall. There was a somewhat flat floor to the arrowhead-shaped gorge with the cut of a wet weather stream in the middle. The walls were virtually straight up, maybe ten times higher than the tallest fir trees in the mountains. Darric was nowhere in sight. Dalwan listened for some sign of the dwarf's movement... nothing!

He began to sense for him, but knew that this would be fruitless unless Darric was using his magic... still nothing! The cliffs were too high for the dwarf to have climbed in such a short time, if such a thing was even possible.

He began to feel panic setting in... he didn't know what he was supposed to do. He stopped and calmed himself, then tried to think back to see if there had been any hint given earlier that could give him guidance now. He was sure he was being taken to a place where he could find out for sure if he was a powermaster. It had something to do with Elven magic. He remembered the "old magic" that he sensed last night, magic which had turned out to be elven. He began to search his memory for the exact print of the elven magic for comparison... if he could sense elven magic here, then he may be able to locate Darric. He started forward from the base of the cliffs, moving purposefully from left to right. He walked away from the actual cliff walls because he could make faster time on the flatter surface. He was using his sensing power at its maximum, searching for even the slightest hint of elven magic. He had passed the falls at the far end of the gorge and was heading back up the other side when he sensed it... a faint source of elven magic. It seemed to come from the rock wall of the cliff, up above him... possibly inside the rock itself. There was loose rock debris at the base of the cliffs, a pile of granite fragments that was as difficult to walk on as a hill of dry sand. He worked slowly through it toward the direction from which the elven magic was proceeding. He could barely keep his footing without sliding back down the steeply sloping pile, as every successive step gave way under his feet. He saw a place where there appeared to be a stone ledge just above the pile. It seemed to be protected from accumulating the irritating rubble. With some difficulty, Dalwan climbed up onto it just so he could gain a solid footing for a moment and get his bearings on the magic source.

From that perch, he studied the rock wall and his options. He began to sense. The magic seemed to be coming at him from every direction. "That must be it..." he mumbled, "this must be some sort of entrance, maybe with a magically sealed stone facade or door of some sort." His mind raced forward in search of a solution to his dilemma. Was he supposed to be patient? "No, not enough time!" Was he supposed to be inventive? "Probably! At least he was supposed to think through the situation." Was he supposed to be powerful and try to blow a hole in the rock? "The dwarf didn't have to, so he shouldn't either."

He was a decent stone molder, so he decided to use his art on the rock in front of him to see if it was shallow or solid. He began by touching the rock and decided that he should chance using full power due to lack of time, even though he risked attracting attention from any nearby sensors. Nothing happened. He was astonished. He tried again. Same results. He reached down and took a stone fragment from the ground and tried his art on it. It molded like cheese, quickly and surely, just as he intended it to. He was puzzled. This rock wall wasn't strong enough to withstand the kind of power he had used... not strong enough unless... "Of course!", he laughed to himself, "...this was an illusion like that protecting the entrance to the anderon's cave." But how to find out... and how to get in, if it really was a magical wall.

He pressed against it... hard as rock... just like the anderon's illusion.

He had never tried to control this type of magic from another source. Indeed, he hadn't ever experienced anything like it before except at the anderon's den. He was not even sure what kind of magic he was dealing with. He tried to replace it or push it away with magic. All that happened was that an area of the wall changed color from granite gray to white. He then tried matching the sensed elven power with his own power and to cause it to vanish using the same magic one would use to create an illusion. As he did this, the wall began to shimmer and for a moment he could see in... the substance of the wall remaining intact but the visible image vanished. He saw Darric looking out at him and a taller person, possibly an elf, standing next to Darric. He could not hold the magic and communicate with the dwarf, so he let it go. He leaned against the door again with his hands as if trying to push it open while he talked directly into it.

"It's too hard, Darric. I can't figure it out this quickly," he said, shouting, hoping that they could hear him through it. "If time is important, why don't you just open up and let me in?"

At that very instant, the wall disappeared, and Dalwan came tumbling through, landing at the feet of Darric and the elf.

"That's all ya ever needed ta do lad...just ask. We would 'ave let ya in straightaway!"

Darric reached out his hand and helped Dalwan to his feet. Once up, he brushed off his clothes while repairing his wounded pride.

"Allow me ta introduce ya ta Fallwyn." Darric turned to Fallwyn with a slight bow, "Fallwyn, this is Dalwan."

Fallwyn had a glint of good humor in his eyes and a touch of laughter in his voice as he extended his hand toward Dalwan and spoke, "Greetings, child of man and son of magic." His voice was different from that of men and dwarves. It sounded like wind being blown through reed pipes. It was at once much higher than a man's voice, but somehow carried another deeper tone simultaneously. His, was a voice of music. It was in some unexplainable way familiar to him, but he couldn't place it.

Dalwan reached out his hand to take Fallwyn's, but found himself holding his wrist instead. Before he had time to react to that, he felt as though his entire body and soul were being invaded. Fallwyn was somehow inside of him. He lost control of his breathing, feeling as if he was going to suffocate. He no sooner regained his breath than his eyesight failed. He started to cry out when a bright light filled his mind. It was a light filled with emotion. As the light quickly dimmed and turned a pale green, he was filled with thoughts of beautiful places and people... no, they were elves. He saw faces that were accompanied by deep emotion, some joyous, some deeply respectful, some almost erotically sensual. Then he saw an anderon and his heart leapt inside. The dim light changed to a light blue. He realized now that he could feel Fallwyn's body as if it were all mixed in with his and could even see himself through the elf's eyes, a circumstance that caused him to close his mouth and correct the silly, shocked expression on his face. This, in turn, caused both of them to share a laugh inside.

He now realized that he was seeing things from his own past. The images came randomly and were often incomplete or cut short as Dalwan recognized them. After a brief time of erratic mental images, he began to understand how to control his thoughts and how to bring important things into focus. He brought up memories of Shaylan and Rhem... how they trained him, things they did that impressed him... his respect for Rhem and love from Shaylan. He brought up the memory of the wounded anderon and felt pain from the elf for it. He brought memories of his battles and the gruesome extent of the power he had used.

At that instant, the light turned greenish again, and he felt a questioning probe into his emotional being commence. For a moment, the visions were gone. The color changed back and forth between blue to green in shifting hues which varied in intensity as they moved together in swirling mixtures dominated alternately by one or the other. Suddenly, he felt fear invade his consciousness as he saw anew his childhood nightmare etched in his vision... the eye... probing... searching... then out of the darkness flashed those terrible hands that grasped blindly at him. As suddenly as the vision had come, it vanished, leaving relief in its wake. The next emotion he felt was pride. He saw, as if reliving it again, the short battle between him, Shaylan, and Rhem in the shed. The pride turned to despair, then it too disappeared. Pride again filled him; this time, he was by himself, pouting about being left out of the conference. He tried unsuccessfully to block the thoughts and emotions that he had felt, but the damage was done, and he became ashamed. This was quickly replaced by a feeling of respect and reverence. Shaylan and Rhem came to focus. He saw them standing at the council, presenting their cases. The scene changed to the fight at the Teaman swamp crossing. Next, Darric came into focus, then quickly vanished being replaced with a scene of the magnificent dwarven forests in Thamerlain, then in turn the beautiful Falcon Mountains. At that instant, he felt the elf's heart jump, and the color went all greenish. He saw majestic trees that seemed to have halos about them. Then he saw a cave with a strange rainbow of lights in the walls, and last came the view of a land from high in the air. It was a view that looked almost straight down and seemed to be moving slowly. The sense of respect was intense. Then it disappeared.

The colors mixed again, and he felt love invade his insides so intensely that his stomach knotted. Faces flashed before his mind, parents, Shaylan, Rhem, the dwarf people, and suddenly stopped on Shahandra. The vision turned greenish. The elf reflected the love for Shahandra, and the vision suddenly broke.

Dalwan came to his senses as Fallwyn was releasing his wrist. His eyes had a bright spot in front of them as if he had glanced at the sun. Before he could pull his thoughts together enough to react, he heard Fallwyn say, "It's fortunate that he is so young. He shows great promise."

"Promise for what?" Dalwan asked, still dazed. "What happened? How?..."

"It was my way of saying hello." Fallwyn had that laughter back in his voice. "An in-vision is worth an hour of talk. You share well!"

"I know you feel that this is somehow your right since I need your knowledge. But don't you ever ask first? I feel like you stole my soul." Dalwan sounded so wounded that the other two looked at each other with raised eyebrows... no smiles.

"Dalwan, what happened was not my right; it was my requirement. What we did was necessary in order for me to make a decision on which course of action to take regarding our association. What has taken place is far more significant than you know. I am a leader among my folk. I exposed my soul to you. We are now very strongly linked and will likely remain so for quite some time. I trusted Darric's assessment of you and acted on his confidence. I joined our beings in what we call soul-link, an in-vision. What you saw clearly is only part of what you will discover that you know about me. That would make you a deadly enemy should you follow the course of most of your leaders."

Dalwan became aware of another sense he now had. He could also somehow feel the elf's emotion. He knew that what this elf had done was at great peril to himself and his folk. He also understood that this was as much an unsolicited gift as it had been a test.

"A radical attitude adjustment is in order", he thought to himself. Then addressing Fallwyn, "Well!? What do you think? What are my chances of doing this right?"

"Very good if you can hold on to your heart and not let your magic rule you. We'll help you if you choose, and even more if you prove to be a true powermaster."

Both Fallwyn and Darric turned and faced back toward the mouth of the cave. Fallwyn put up his hands, and the entrance darkened in a shimmering blackness. At the same time, Darric moved his hand in a sweeping motion across the opening, from right to left. As he did, a wave-like motion followed his hand's movement across the shimmering darkness, replacing it with solid definition resembling gray granite.

Fallwyn motioned toward another opening at the back of the well-lit cavern in which they stood. It was a thin door-sized opening which was pitch black. "To the test, Dalwan!"

Dalwan's heart began to pound with considerable force, and his face flushed warm. His thoughts raced, "This is it... now I'll know for sure... But what if I'm not...?" His legs went weak, his feet and hands began to tingle as he followed the other two toward the opening.

"You must go in alone, Dalwan," came the familiar voice of the dwarf.

Dalwan stopped a few paces from the narrow opening in the cave wall. "Is there anything I need to know? Should I take something in with me?" His mind was moving at a near panic pace now, but his voice was almost under control, revealing only a little of the apprehension which gripped him. "What am I supposed to do in there?"

Reading his anxiety, Darric broke out in a belly laugh. "Lad, this 'ill be the best part o' the whole day fer ya. There's nothin' a'tall ta fear. You'll doubtless enjoy this greatly. Fallwyn 'ill instruct ya step by step."

"Is he... I mean..." looking back at Fallwyn, "are you coming in too?"

"No lad!" answered Darric, looking at Fallwyn as they both broke out in laughter... "can ya even imagine what that'd be like!?" Eye to eye, both of them laughed again. He continued, barely able to control his laughter, "Go ahead in lad, you'll like this!"

Dalwan looked back and forth between the two faces, each with unmistakable amusement on it, then turned and stepped through the entrance into the darkness.

"Sense the area as you enter." Fallwyn's words echoed like harmonic music from the walls.

Dalwan began to sense the area. A glow became visible from the wall opposite the entrance. As the glow brightened, he could see that he was standing in a long chamber with a low ceiling. It was like a hallway, wide enough for at least three people to walk comfortably side by side. As his eyes adjusted further, he could see doorways all along the corridor leading away from his position.

Dalwan's attention was drawn back to the glowing spot in the wall. There was a luminous object situated on a wooden counter attached to the bare stone wall of the hallway. As he got closer to it, he noticed that it was an odd-shaped crystal with many unsymmetrical but polished facets, altogether about as large as a big goose egg.

"Pick up the stone, Dalwan."

He obeyed Fallwyn's instructions, and as his hand touched the stone, it brightened into a rainbow of colors. The flickering inside it was as if the crystal were on fire inside. He wrapped his right hand around it and removed it from the shelf. The light suddenly jumped in arcs of colored light between his free hand and the hand holding the crystal. The color in each beam of light drifted through the spectrum in a clear, bright display. He began to shift the crystal from hand to hand to avoid the very warm sensation coming from it, and as he did, the colored arcs continued forming in shafts between the finger tips of his free hand and the hand holding the stone. His art of sensing was greatly increased. He could sense old magic all around him. He could feel the elements, wood and metal, and stone. He could sense water, something he had not done before. He had never even considered using magic on water. His hands finally became accustomed to the heat of the crystal. It even began to give him a pleasant sensation, like holding a pet or something you cherish. As he studied the stone, he became aware of new light sources as light began to shine through some of the open doorways further down the corridor.

"What do you see, Dalwan?" came the musical voice which broke his spell of fascination.

"I see other light coming from other doorways down the hallway. What am I supposed to do now?"

"Keep the first stone and walk down the passageway toward the other compartments. Stop at the first one, it'll be on your sword's hand side, about six strong strides from your present position.

Dalwan began to walk slowly toward the second compartment. He was mesmerized by the changing brilliance of the stone he held. It seemed to pulse with his heartbeat.

As he got closer to the upcoming compartment, the glow from inside it increased. He stopped short of the doorway and peered around the corner. The compartment looked much like a closet without a door. It was cut into the wall of the corridor with the ceiling about a handbreadth over his head (just enough space to accommodate a tall elf) and was about two regular strides deep and three wide.

He rounded the corner of the little room and was greeted by a brilliant flash of light which formed a steady white beam between a source in the middle of the back wall and the stone in his hand. The light appeared as a clearly defined beam with rigid definition near his hand and became fuzzier as it approached the source on the wall.

"Dalwan, the stone you see in front of you is a fire crystal. Pick it up in your left hand. Do not allow it to touch the other stone."

He stepped to the back wall and saw the fire stone. It was also irregular in shape but flatter, and had larger facets.

"After you pick it up, tell me what you see."

Being extra careful to follow Fallwyn's instructions and heed the warning, he stood sideways to the wall and held his right hand out toward the door. He then gently picked the stone up with his left hand fully extended. The light beam continued unchanged, flowing right in front of him, until the instant he touched the fire stone. Suddenly, the light in the beam began to move in waves of color. The waves got closer and closer together, going faster and faster, moving in one direction through the spectrum over and over, until it was finally a steady stream of pulsating color. Then it would begin to reverse the process in the other direction, fast short waves giving way to wider, slower waves. This process continued on through several complete cycles without Dalwan speaking.

"Dalwan! You still there?" asked Fallwyn with a good-humored laugh.

"It sends waves of colored light back and forth between the stones." Dalwan sounded like a small child explaining his adventure to his father.

"Dalwan, prepare your mind to use white fire."

Dalwan's thoughts shifted to that terrifying moment when he had actually used this fire on another human. He hesitated.

"It's OK, Dalwan, you need not use it, only PREPARE yourself to use it," said Fallwyn with reassurance in his voice.

Dalwan set his mind in motion, and instantly light came to the stone from the walls of the small room. It was like bright mist that came from all directions. It grew in intensity, some of it passing through him and all of it being sucked into the crystal. He stood for a moment transfixed by the sight and stunned by the swell of emotional power it created. He felt as though he was about to explode. Then he became aware of the voice yelling to him, "PUT

THE STONE DOWN, DALWAN! DALWAN!! PUT IT BACK ON THE SHELF!"

He hurried and put it back on the shelf, breaking the intensifying impact of the crystal on his consciousness. As he did, he could hear Darric and Fallwyn shouting and applauding in approval of his power.

"Quite an experience eh lad!?" shouted Darric.

Dalwan returned to the corridor and stood facing the entrance. "What are these things? What are they doing to me?" asked Dalwan, his voice cracking with their infectious laughter.

Fallwyn answered, "They're source stones, Dalwan. They only imagine what you already possess. They put your art and power into images of light."

Darric cut in, "..no art, no light! Art and no power, dim light."

"But," continued Fallwyn, "Art and great power...what a display." The approval in the elf's voice made Dalwan's confidence take a giant leap.

With his apprehension all but gone, Dalwan got anxious to get on with the test. "What do I do now?"

"Go to the next opening and repeat the process."

"What stone is it?"

"It is the molders' stone."

As Dalwan entered the little room, the stone glowed brightly. He picked it up. It was flat with irregular sides. A misty aura formed between the stones he held. It was thicker on his hands, surrounding them both like puffy gloves, and thinned between them. Its intensity did not change as he moved them further apart or closer together. The glow did, however, change colors in gradually shifting hues, which went from bright red to light orange. As he put his mind to the art, the room exploded in flashes of this same misty light in a form which resembled funnel clouds having their base on the rock with their tails dancing across his body. Each of these funnels would last only a short time, vanishing when tiny but distinct flashes of light, like lightning, sparked between the rock and his body. The flashes of light would then snake across the top of his clothes to the molders' source stone. Sometimes only one of these would hit him, but for most of the time, there were three or four working in various stages, each appearing from different locations on the walls or ceiling. Finally, one formed between the ceiling and his face and temporarily blinded him with intense red light before he had time to close his eyes. He reached to protect his face with both hands and almost touched the stones together. This caused even a brighter flash of light to continue flowing directly to his head. The misty cloud intensified, spreading across the ceiling and down the walls. Spider-like flashes of light traveled along the stone walls from all over the room, creeping through the rapidly forming misty red radiance, all finding their way to Dalwan's face. He tried to peep out past his hands but was totally engulfed in blinding light.

Finally, Dalwan realized what had happened and quickly separated his hands, bringing his concentration on the art to an end. The misty light faded back to its original, much more manageable form, and the radiance disappeared like steam.

"Are ya alright, lad?"

"What happened, Dalwan?"

"I don't know...there were lights coming at me from all over the room...then one hit me in the eyes...I think I got my hands too close together."

"Put the stone back and rest yer eyes a spell before ya move on." The laughter was gone, but Dalwan could still hear the humor in both of their voices.

In the next chamber, he found the wood weavers' stone, a thinner version of the molders' crystal. This stone behaved much like the molders' stone, except the misty light was yellow to a greenish blue in hue. Dalwan was careful to keep his hands away from his head and keep them well apart. He could sense the approval of the elf as he went through the exercise of the weaver's magic.

As Dalwan replaced the weaver's stone on its pedestal, he could hear Fallwyn speaking loudly from down the corridor, "We're much alike in our love of these arts, Dalwan. I, too, love the weaver's art most of all." It was reassuring for Dalwan to hear that one with such great power as Fallwyn loved most of all what others would call the simple arts.

As he found the next chamber in the dark corridor, he realized that he could see no light coming from it. Other chambers still glowed enough for him to see from where he stood in the dark doorway. He felt a creeping fear cross his mind. His confidence faltered.

"Dalwan!" The sweet music of Fallwyn's voice snapped his descent into premature depression. "Dalwan, you can't despair until you have tried...the stone is already responding to you...I can feel it from here."

Dalwan stepped into the little room and stood for a moment, focusing on the darkness. Very suddenly, out of the corner of his eye, he caught the image of a very faint, clear white light, so faint in fact that he had to continue to focus just to the side of it to be certain that it was there at all. It was so vague that its definition and size were also unclear until he picked it up. It was a smooth crystal that felt like a slightly flattened egg.

"I found it...what is this one...I can't even get a fix on the magic that it responds to."

"It's called the water walkers stone...the name's a little misleading."

"It's barely glowing and doesn't seem to be responding at all."

"Dalwan, think of the water in a river you know well...picture it flowing...feel its coolness."

Dawlan began to bring up the image in his mind.

"Good!...now feel its movement...Good! Now set your mind to make the water move as you would stone....Excellent! Now hold that image."

Dalwan chanced a look at the crystal. A glowing, white misty misty-looking light covered both his hands and followed a path along his arms and across his chest, connecting the stones.

Fallwyn continued, "Now, in your thoughts, touch the water and make it hard, hard like the ice of a mountain lake in deepest winter."

As Dalwan did this, the entire room filled with sparkling white misty light which drifted to his body from the walls like whiffs of smoke being drawn up a chimney.

"Ya did it, lad. That was wonderful!" came what could only be defined as a cheer from Darric. As Dalwan set the crystal down and exited the little chamber, the misty light swirled around him and trailed him into the corridor like smoke, then dissipated into the darkness.

In the next chamber, he found a glowing crystal which looked and felt like the molders' stone. It glowed with the same colors as the molders' stone.

"Hey, Fallwyn, this looks like the molders' stone...it acts that way too."

"They are very similar, Dalwan. You must have the molders' magic to wield the metal welders' magic. But the reverse is not true."

"Why is that?"

"I don't know for sure...it must have something to do with both metal and stone coming from the ground...I don't know anyone who is sure...it's the way of the magic. Who can explain magic!?"

With the blinding light of the molders' magic still fresh in his mind, he made sure to keep his hands far apart. As he set his mind on the metal welder's magic, the same phenomenon occurred with the funnel-shaped bursts of light, except that they all went from the wall directly to the welder's stone in his hand. Some of those which came from behind him would wrap around his body but would remain intact, with the tiny lightning-like fingers sparking right to the stone. As he replaced the stone crystal on its shelf, he wondered how many metal workers knew that they could also work stone and how many more stone molders had no idea that they possessed the more prestigious art of metal welding.

As he entered the next chamber, his senses told him that the stone here was that of illusion. It was already glowing brightly as he entered. It was a misshapen cluster of crystals. As he took hold of it, a cloud of light, like white fog, formed around his hands in large balls which changed size as he moved his hands closer or further away. The cloud always encompassed his hands, no matter how close or far apart they were. The exterior of the ball always appeared to be fixed with a definite boundary around its surface on which waves of light moved like ripples in a pond.

As he watched, Fallwyn's voice broke through, "Dalwan, what do you see?"

"A large ball of foggy light."

"Set your mind on making an image appear."

As Dalwan set his mind to the art and began to mentally run through several alternatives, he saw the ball quiver and began to reshape with each new thought. He thought of Shahandra and saw the image of a woman form from the ball of light. The definitions formed more and more clearly until he felt constrained to let the image go. The ball quickly reshaped.

"Good Dalwan. Now set your mind to make something disappear."

As he did, the stone changed colors to a crimson glow, and the ball disappeared except for a fine line visible around its edges, which consisted of extremely tiny, faint pulsating waves of light moving together in erratic patterns as if connected. The vague definition the waves gave of the exterior of what had been the ball of light was now the only part of it that was visible. When this change took place, he lost his concentration on the images he had prepared to make disappear. Because he wasn't accustomed to making things disappear that weren't really there to begin with, he decided to try a different approach. He chose himself as the object of illusion. Suddenly, he saw his own image inside the ball. It grew and grew until it pushed out the sides of the ball, leaving only a crimson-light portrait in his own likeness. He released the image and watched it shrink away to a pinpoint again, leaving only the faint outline of the ball.

He put the stone back without being told to. He felt that the art of illusion was somehow dirty...a cheat. He never liked to use it, although he had frequently employed it when on his practice journeys. Of all the arts, he felt that this was the one which would be most likely to distract him into evil or tempt him toward activity apt to warp his personality.

"Dalwan," came Fallwyn's interruption into Dalwan's introspection, "no art is evil in and of itself. It is the manner of use and the character of the user that determines its ultimate moral content."

"It makes me feel ugly inside, like some sort of criminal, when I use it," answered Dalwan, stepping back into the hall.

"Then guard your heart before and during its use."

"What's next?" asked Dalwan, obviously changing the subject.

"The life stone. It's for the healing art!"

Dalwan could see the glow coming from the room even before he entered. As he rounded the corner and started in, the stone began to radiate a light which swirled gently from the stone like irregular whiffs of smoke from a smoldering coal and flowed toward him, gaining speed as it got closer to his body. The intensity of the light grew with every step he took toward the stone, and the speed of the light between him and the stone increased until it was a racing blur of irregular, flowing light as if blown by an unseen, violent wind. The light blanketed the entire front of his body until the moment he picked up the almost perfectly round stone. Then suddenly the flowing light stopped and he began to glow...all over him... his clothes, his hair... and his exposed skin glowed much brighter than anything else.

"Dalwan! Dalwan, can you hear me?" shouted Fallwyn excitedly.

"Yes, Fallwyn...I can hear you fine...what's the matter?"

"Your power in this art exceeds the boundaries of the test. You seem to have magic in this art that neither of us has seen before."

"How can you tell...what makes you know that?"

"The stone has already responded to you completely and gone beyond what I have ever seen in an elf or dwarf. Dalwan, prepare to heal with the same magic you used in your very last encounter."

Dalwan tried to think back on any significant healing he had done, knowing very well that he had never had the nerve to try anything drastic, deferring to those more practiced than himself. "I can't think of anything very spectacular that I've ever done... at least not knowingly," said Dalwan with enough indecisiveness that Fallwyn was rendered speechless for a time.

"Lad, let yer mind go for a moment. Let the magic o' the sense stone guide yer thoughts toward the magic of healing," said Darric in a flash of inspiration.

"That's perfect!" said Fallwyn, slapping Darric on the back, "that should show him his art."

Dalwan's mind went blank for a time and began to drift back through many incidents where he had dared to use his art on himself. Suddenly, he drifted back to the forest on the day he first met the anderon. He again sensed the magic flowing into the giant beast..."

"That's it! That's it, Dalwan! You somehow healed not only our monstrous friend's body but his magic as well. You healed the anderon's magic!" Both Darric and Fallwyn were ecstatic.

Dalwan put the stone back down, reentered the corridor, and stood there staring back toward his two coaches with a fearful respect for Fallwyn. "How do you keep knowing what I think?..and how I feel?..and how can you sense my past?.."

Darric cut in, "Dalwan, what's that in yer hand, lad?"

"It's the sense stone...you told me to keep it..." Dalwan froze mid-sentence, "is this it?... is this stone helping you do this weird stuff to me?"

Fallwyn was laughing heartily by this time and took a moment to recover, "Yes, Dalwan, it is! That plus an art you must now prove yourself. It's in the next chamber...go ahead in."

Dalwan walked to the next chamber and peered into coal black nothingness. "Is there a stone in here?"

"It is there, Dalwan. You must search for it with your soul, not your intellect," said Fallwyn in a tone that had turned very serious.

"What is this stone?...and how do I search with my soul?" Dalwan's confidence was waning, and disappointment crept through his countenance like an armed thief through an unlocked house. He felt powerless to control it. His mind raced again as he reflected on his situation, "Why hadn't Shaylan told him about water?...was it possible that Shaylan didn't know?...highly unlikely!...and what was this new test, this challenge to his soul?"

"Dalwan, can you hear me?" shouted Fallwyn. Dalwan pulled himself out of the emotional quicksand and answered, "Yes. Go ahead...I'm listening."

"This is the separation stone. The art it reflects is that which allows you to know the thoughts of others and see or find them at great distances. It's as if your soul goes out to them."

"How do I manifest it?" said Dalwan as he climbed out of his self-imposed emotional pit and began to feel a trace of encouragement.

"Think of Shahandra," shouted Fallwyn, "Let your mind go to her." His voice had that soul-healing music in it again.

"How did you know about Shahandra?"

"It was in your mind... you shared it with me during the in-vision."

Dalwan no sooner began to think about Shahandra, wondering where she was... what she was doing, than a faint glow crept into the stone. From the door, he could see a large cluster of crystals sitting on a pedestal that rested on the now familiar-shaped shelf located at the rear of each little room. Only one set of crystals in the cluster glowed. As he walked to the shelf, he searched for her with his heart; the other clusters began to glow. He reached down and picked it up.

His searching for her turned to longing, and quickly his mind fogged with emotions and thoughts of their past short encounters. The light in the crystal went out.

"No Dalwan!" came a friendly admonishment from down the corridor, "Search for her where she is now, not in your memory of the past."

Dalwan cleared away old thoughts and again set his mind on finding her.

"Go ahead, lad. Once ya find her, go ta her," shouted Darric.

This time, he saw her. She was surrounded by heavily armed men. At the same instant, he became aware that the intensity of the light from the separation crystals in his hand was throwing prisms on the walls and ceiling.

"She's in some sort of battle or something... I sense that she feels danger!" Dalwan abruptly stopped the vision, replaced the crystal, and ran back toward the entrance where Darric and Fallwyn stood.

Dalwan was at the door of the corridor before Darric and Fallwyn had a chance to get his attention. "Is this real? Is what I saw really happening?"

Darric held out his hand and stopped Dalwan before he could step out of the corridor, "Hold on, lad... listen up fer just a moment."

Dalwan calmed down almost instantly as Fallwyn began to speak, "It's hard for us to be absolutely sure about the when of what you saw... it could be the past or the present... it is most likely that what you saw was her present."

There was unspeakable sadness and helplessness in Dalwan's face. His heart screamed for some hope or word of encouragement, but none could be given. They all stood silently as Dalwan's eyes searched the darkness for Darric and Fallwyn without receiving comfort.

"Dalwan, there's nothing you can do to help her... her own skills will save her, or she'll be rescued by those she fights with if she is to survive. One way or another, you must finish the task at hand. She's probably days from here, and if she is fighting, her battles will certainly be over and her fate determined long before you could get to her. If you are the powermaster we can help you obtain a weapon that can assist you in preventing this senseless cruelty from continuing." Fallwyn pointed back into the corridor, "Shall we continue?!"

Dalwan stood torn by emotion. He knew Fallwyn was right, but his heart wanted to thrust him past his two companions and on to save Shahandra. As he turned around and walked slowly back down the corridor toward his next test, something of the boy in him died, and he felt the seeds of his manhood take root. Life seemed to be more sober for him at that moment and less romantic. Happy endings might be more a thing of bedtime stories told by old folks and less a thing of realities. The wishing that he could be there for her was in fact beyond the realm of his possibilities... his heart screamed a silent protest at the unfairness of life. His spirit was at the point of despair...

"Dalwan? Dalwan, stop right there... the upcoming room contains your next test."

Fallwyn did it again. The subtle magic in his voice immediately snapped Dalwan out of his somber emotional quicksand.

"Dalwan, you have great abilities and a long life ahead of you. Your power may be the key that unlocks the future for many more like Shahandra if you use it well and lend it to wise and noble pursuits."

Darric cut into Fallwyn's music, "What ma eloquent friend is trying ta communicate is that ya gotta go on from here... take yer next step toward a future ya can control and don't let yer emotions get trapped in a present or a past ya can do nothin' about."

Dalwan felt a flood of confidence flow over him, energizing every muscle as it sparked life into his mind. He wanted more than ever to get this test finished and get on with life, whatever its future held.

"O.K., Fallwyn," said Dalwan with fierce determination, "What's next?"

"Go into the chamber next to you. The stones you find there are the communion stones. They display your ability to touch the souls of the animals."

As he walked into the chamber, he noticed three small stones glowing faintly.

"What do you see, Dalwan?" asked the golden-toned voice.

"I see three little glowing stones."

"Excellent. Pick them up in one hand...and don't squeeze them very hard. Just hold them loosely."

Dalwan obeyed and stood for a moment holding them with no visible change occurring in the stone's appearance.

"Open your mind to me. Envision with me a cave lion stalking
you. Yes... that's it... No! Don't challenge! Make it feel content, easy... now
sleepy... yes, yes, that's it!"

As he did, a constant white light poured out from the cracks between his
fingers. At the same time, an arc of light formed between both hands with the
light traveling over his clothing like lightning, which shifted its path frequently,
and especially with every move he made. The vision faded, and the color of the
light went to a bluish white, similar to clear ice.

"Good Dalwan," came the soothing tones in Fallwyn's voice. One more
remains. "You can put the stones back now."

As he placed them carefully back on the little shelf, he was startled by
bright flashes of light as if the entire corridor had caught on fire with the most
intense flames imaginable. He rushed out the entrance of the little chamber to
discover Darric and Fallwyn walking toward him, shielding their eyes from the
massive swirls of light, intense color, and thunderless lightning that poured out
of the chambers as they passed.

"One more remains Dalwan...an' thar's a bit of a question surrounding
it..." said Darric in a very serious tone. "As ya know, the earth power is
consistent, varying only in intensity. However, it does its magic differently
through each race... elven magic differs from dwarven, and both differ from
man's. A true powermaster can use the combined power of all the races if it
was made by all three in concert... or at least that's the story we have about the
last test."

"What do you mean by 'story about the last test'?" said Dalwan
incredulously.

Darric looked at Fallwyn as they both broke out in laughter. "Well, ya
see lad... this test hasn't been tried for about two hundred years."

Dalwan opened his mouth to object, but was cut off abruptly by
Fallwyn, "In the realm of magic, art differs from art and all the arts differ from
species to species. So we have decided to use fire for the test because it is the
magic most closely related in all the races..."

"And also because it's the very same test used last time, so we da not
hav'ta reinvent the whole thing!"

"We have to go to the last chamber for this one," said Fallwyn,
motioning with his hand indicating the direction of the chamber.

Darric led the way with Dalwan following and Fallwyn bringing up the rear. As they passed another of the small chambers, like the others that Dalwan had gone into, Fallwyn instructed him to leave the sensing crystal in it, on its back wall shelf.

From that point on, the passage continued in a perfectly straight line with no more little chambers. The light from the stones left behind them quickly faded out as they got further away from the chambers. Each of the three companions used their fire art to provide light for traveling by. The passageway was closing in on them bit by bit as they moved down it.

Dalwan could see that they were quickly coming to the end of the corridor and was feeling anxious when they suddenly stopped.

"Here's the door, lad!" Darric exclaimed as his flame vanished. Fallwyn likewise extinguished his. Feeling oddly conspicuous, Dalwan followed suit and put his flame out.

"Dalwan?" came a voice of musical laughter, "Why don't you keep some light about for us?"

He quickly relit his flame, illuminating the area.

The dwarf and elf turned toward the wall on their left. Dalwan could see nothing unusual on the wall that would mark an entrance, no handle, no hinges, no seams or even cracks. But with a couple of mysterious hand motions, which the other two completed in unison, a door appeared and swung noiselessly open into the inside of a very dark room. Even for a gifted magician like Dalwan, the incident gave him chills.

Though the room was pitch black, something about the sound in it told Dalwan that it was immense. The air inside was cold and not stagnant. The others did not make a light with their art but allowed Dalwan to lead the way inside. His fire only gave light to the wall where they entered, but was totally lost in the cavernous darkness beyond. Dalwan increased his fire, and the definitions of the monstrous cave in which they stood took vague form. Fallwyn lit a set of torches that hung just inside the door. He left one hanging at the entrance and brought two others to stands near a table that sat by itself, only a dozen paces from the entrance.

Darric accompanied Fallwyn to the table, and together they began to unwrap something long and thin that was lying on it.

After a few curious moments, Fallwyn held up a sword. "This should do the trick. Dalwan, we can only attempt to duplicate this test. Because there hasn't been a reason for it in almost two hundred years, we don't have practice to confirm the writing."

Dalwan cut in, his voice cracked with anxiousness as he spoke, "If this hasn't been tried in centuries, how will you know if it succeeds?" His heart was now pounding as hard as it had been when he first entered the corridor of testing stone. He was both puzzled and irritated at the seemingly light-hearted way the elf and dwarf were treating this matter.

"We'll know lad, ya can count on that. Ya need ta listen now and try a bit of trust... maybe even as much as we have given ta you! Da ya really think that we've come this far ta simply guess at results?" Darric stood for an uncomfortable moment to let his words soak into Dalwan's consciousness. "Our problem's not what the outcome should look like, but how ta guide ya through the process." The dwarf was now speaking slowly in a fatherly tone... no trace of humor in his voice.

Continuing on after a brief chastising silence, he explained, "Dwarves and Elves have long shared their arts in fanciful ways. We've together created many a wonderful work. We've also fought side by side effectively when the times required it o'er the generations."

Darric took the sword from Fallwyn. "We've made a fire sword!" he said with great satisfaction while he turned to Fallwyn and exchanged a smile of accomplishment. As he spoke, he held the sword straight out from his shoulder, displaying its beauty to Dalwan. "Lord Fallwyn has given it elven fire, which is the finest an' most accurate. I've given the elven fire dwarven longevity. Elf fire, by itself, t'is of a nature ta be short in duration, comin' in flashes, extremely precise. Dwarven fire, while apt ta stray from its target at long distances, has a much longer duration, allowin' a good artisan to adjust his blast after it's let go. But together... what beauty!" At that very instant, he released a straight, thin, blue lance of flame streaking across the mammoth cavern, hitting the damp deposits of minerals on the far wall, which in turn sent back a delayed crack and sputtering. It held for a moment then vanished, leaving a faint lingering glow in the air, drifting silently sideways from where its path had been.

Fallwyn stepped forward and took the sword from Darric. "Your fire magic comes mostly in balls of flame, which vary in size, color, type, and intensity. Your accuracy tends to be good, but your fire spreads as it flies and can suddenly flare and lose its potency. Your fire has the greatest impact and highest potency. If it could be made to hold together in flight, over large distances, it would be altogether the most dangerous."

"So," said Dalwan, cutting in, "if my magic was mixed with both of yours, it could be an even more formidable weapon than it already is."

"Exactly!" continued Fallwyn. "Now, I'm going to use the sword. As I do, try and sense its power."

Fallwyn lit up the sword with a single line of piercing blue-white light. He swung the sword, and the light moved like a sabre through the air. The entire blade of the sword was bathed in the light. The intensity of the light varied as Fallwyn moved the sword. At times, it appeared to pulse almost as if attached to his heartbeat. Dalwan took and internalized the pattern of the sword's magic. As suddenly as it had come, it was gone. The fire's light had been so bright that it took a few moments for all of their eyes to readjust.

"Here. Your turn now." Fallwyn handed the sword to Dalwan handle-first.

Dalwan swung the sword around a few times to get accustomed to its weight and balance.

"O.K....here goes!" He paused for a moment, then a bright ball of red fire left his hand, traveled down the blade, and out about a dozen steps where it vanished in a brilliant flare.

Darric's eyebrows were raised in obvious disapproval of the effort, "The fire was too weak and ya didn't use the sword's power. The sword's not a pointer lad, 'tis a fire weapon!" He walked over and touched its blade. "It draws its power from you just like ya draw yers from the earth. Like those that receive power from the earth, it channels the power, changin' it into its own art. In this case, a long, powerful, accurate flame." Darric stepped back again to Fallwyn's side. "Try again, lad."

Without speaking again, he held up the sword and pointed toward the far wall. Nothing happened... he continued to hold it out, concentrating... still nothing happened... a seeming eternity of 'nothing' passed. Finally, the sword lowered a second time with the tip hitting the ground. Dalwan's shoulders drooped, and his chin dropped to his chest.

There was magic in Fallwyn's voice, "Dalwan, you cannot use only your magic. You must let go and blend yours with ours. Only then will you be able to produce the combined fire. Feel our magic in the sword. Go ahead, it's there."

Dalwan began to concentrate. This was the most personally stretching exercise in magic he felt he had ever performed.

Fallwyn sensed Dalwan's effort as he probed for the resident magic in the sword until he knew Dalwan had it, "Now!... That's it! Add your own magic without letting the others go."

Instantly, there was a gigantic flash of fire directly into the ground at the end of the sword, throwing flame in all directions along the ground.

"Pick it up, Dalwan! Quick!" Came shouts from both of his companions.

The flame faltered as he raised the end of the sword. Then there were several extremely intense, narrow streaks of fire that shot from the sword to the wall of the cave, sending small glowing bits of minerals shooting in all directions.

Fallwyn stepped to Dalwan's side, "control it... that's it... let it flow."

There were several rapidly repeated blasts of fire, then a more controlled, less powerful pulsating orange flame. The pulses increased in intensity, changing color to red and then blue. The blue flame created a sizzling and popping effect on the wet rock of the cave wall.

"Give it power, lad!" shouted Darric in something of a cheer.

Dalwan pointed it almost straight up, and the blue flame gave way to a startling white beam of light which hit a stalactite and shattered it instantly into a glowing shower of fragments.

Fallwyn and Darric dove laughing under the table as Dalwan dropped the sword and put up a monstrous green flame curtain that covered himself and the table. The rude shower was finished in one brief, hard downpour. The flame curtain turned away the worst of it...

In a flash, Fallwyn jumped up from under the table and was at Dalwan's side. He quickly picked up the sword and handed it to Darric, who had followed close behind. Fallwyn took Dalwan's hand in both of his and gave a powerful squeeze and a single shake. "You've done it, Dalwan...you have proven yourself to be a powermaster!" There was compassion and admiration in Fallwyn's eyes, but all Dalwan could see was a dark spot where his face should be. The brightness of the sword's flash left everything in front of him dark. Both Fallwyn and Darric had been watching the sword and were not blinded by the flash like Dalwan was. They led him to one of the very stately chair settings nearby against the wall and guided him into it so he could sit while he gave his eyes a brief rest.

Darric's enthusiasm was more animated than Fallwyn's. Once Dalwan was seated, he took his hand and shook it so hard and fast that Dalwan's whole body rocked, "Ya did it, lad...ya did it...I knew ya would!" A brief glance from Fallwyn brought a quick rephrase, "I mean, I thought ya would... I mean, I hoped ya could."

"We both had high hopes, and you didn't disappoint us. Congratulations!"

"It's true then... I'm a powermaster!" Dalwan's eyes were wide with amazement, and his mouth dropped open.

Darric and Fallwyn both broke out in full-blown belly laughs at the sight.

"Got yer eyes back yet?" asked Darric as he and Fallwyn moved to opposite sides of Dalwan and lifted him to his feet. "Come, lad. We've a long road ta cover bafore dinner ends."

Dalwan scarcely remembered the walk back to the wagon, and the ride back to the conference grounds was a blur. His mind raced like wildfire, driven by a strong wind, thinking of the ramifications of being a true powermaster... he would have a chance to wield the sword Fallonrod... possibly fight Danlion.

It was then that he realized Danlion had fought the sword once before and survived... and had now had over a hundred years to plan a strategy against it. While Dalwan knew that the sword would be a totally new experience for him!

They arrived back at the meeting grounds just after dark and before any of the delegates returned to the quarters from the dinner.

"Darric, will they have sensed our activity today?"

"No, lad. We were shielded by the rock of the cave walls."

"Let's keep this a secret, O.K."

"Indeed!" Darric's eyes darkened under his now tightly drawn eyebrows, "the fewer that know, the greater a chance ta surprise Danlion."

At the name Danlion, Dalwan felt his stomach tighten, his jaw lock, and his mouth fill with saliva.

"Lad!" said Darric in bewilderment, "why are ya so frightened? Have ya learned nothin' today? Do ya still expect to fight that beast alone?" Darric studied Dalwan's panic-stricken face before speaking again, "No doubt ya knew yerself that if ya proved out ta be a powermaster, a battle with Danlion would be a possibility... nay, even a likelihood. But that'll only be yer first test lad... only the beginning of yer trainin', yer adventures and experiences. And we've said from the start that we plan ta be there with ya. Pardon me fer sayin' so, but ta go alone would most assuredly be yer undoin'."

Dalwan could see the look of disapproval in Darric's eyes and could hear the chastisement in his voice. Tears of joy filled his eyes as he realized for the first time that they had not been testing for the use of the sword only, but for the potential of comradeship in the pursuit of Danlion... or was the pursuit of Danlion more of the testing? No matter...

"You mean you're going with me?"

"Not exactly lad," came the reply with a hint of scolding in it, "...we plan ta go together... tha'tis, ta accompany each other."

"I'm sorry... I don't mean to sound like that... I mean, I know I need lots of help... no, that's not what I mean..... I just thought I'd have to go alone or something... Shaylan always goes alone and Rhem too... and most of the time I practice alone... I guess I thought this was something I was somehow destined to have to do alone."

Darric sensed the relief that Dalwan felt in knowing that they were going together, "Y'are sure ya don't think yerself better suited ta work alone than with us, huh?" asked Darric with an exaggerated look of inquisitiveness which quickly faded into a broad-faced grin.

"You know I don't. Shaylan and Rhem have worn themselves out trying to figure out how to use the sword's power. I don't have a clue how to use it, even if I could come up with a real plan on how to get it!"

Fallwyn put his hand on Dalwan's shoulder, "Well, just possibly, between all of us, we might be able to come up with a plan that will do exactly that... get the sword and figure out how to use it."

"I reckon anythin' we devise'll be an improvement on what ya had dreamed up so far," said Darric, laughing at the same time, sporting a knowing glance toward Dalwan.

"All I had thought about was trying somehow to steal the sword and go find Shahandra... she's a good sensor... maybe..." Suddenly, he had a flashback of Shahandra in the fight. She was in a castle. Darric and Fallwyn both sensed his intense emotional change.

Fallwyn took him by both shoulders and looked, sensing, into his eyes, "Dalwan, what's..?"

"It's Shahandra... she's fighting... in a castle."

"Do you see it now, or is this from the testing?"

"The testing."

"See if you can use the same power you tapped in the testing."

Dalwan tried to see Shahandra again but failed.

"Try again, lad!"

He began again, and this time he sensed her, but could not get a grasp on where she was or what she was doing. "She's alive... but I can't get anything else... I can't see her."

"You best not use your magic anymore for now," said Fallwyn, letting go of Dalwan's shoulders. "We'll try again later when we have some distance between us and the others."

"Fer now though, we better be gettin' back inside ta wait the return of yer companions... don't want ta look too suspicious."

CHAPTER 17

Shahandra cleared the edge of the forest and slowed her pace only slightly as Lady started down the bank toward the river. She glanced back at the forest as they entered the water. It was gone! Nothing remained of the beautiful giant trees; even the outer perimeter of the smaller ones had vanished. In the dim light, she could make out a few small shade trees in what appeared to be a meadow of brush and grass. Lady sensed her distraction and stopped in the middle of the river. Shahandra sat confused. Had this been a dream of some sort? Had she somehow been enchanted into a dream stupor?

"It must have happened! It must have!!!" she thought, frantically, searching her memory for some trace of pure reality that she could grab hold of. "Am I riding off, crazed with fear, to find Eric who isn't actually in danger? I would never live it down... he would surely think me 'the fool'". She decided to go find Eric just in case, but the urgency had dimmed. Just then, she caught sight of her hand. It had irregular glowing patches of skin on it... "the berries!...ERIC!!!"

As she yelled, Lady bolted forward with a renewed sense of purpose. Shahandra rode with near desperation, trying to pick out the mountain top she had used as a landmark when leaving the enchanted forest. Only with difficulty did she avoid having her legs torn by the brush along the trail or being knocked from her horse's back by low-hanging limbs as she rode recklessly toward the place she had sensed Eric. After the second very close call with a tree limb, she realized that it would just be luck if she continued to avoid a disaster, then she would never reach Eric at all. She decided that her best chance was to find the road and ride hard. She pulled her wits together and quickly found a path that led her up the steep bank directly to the road. Lady landed on the road at a full run.

Meanwhile, Eric had sat up, startled to hear Shahandra scream some sort of warning... or was it a dream? He sat for a brief moment staring into the darkness, believing that he had seen Shahandra ride up. But as his vision focused in the darkness, he quickly picked out the silhouette of a man apparently frozen in his tracks. A scan of the horizon revealed two others similarly stationary, all of them coming from the general direction of the road. He chanced a fast look behind him to ensure that he was not flanked and rolled to his feet holding his sword, which he kept battle ready at his side when he slept outdoors.

Once the attackers realized they hadn't avoided detection, they all began
to run the twenty to thirty paces left between them and Eric. None of the
charging men spoke. One of them arrived about 10 paces ahead of the others.
Eric moved quickly to meet him and stumbled just as he got to the man. The
attacker took advantage of the mishap to raise his sword fully over his head for
a killing slice. There was a sudden, seemingly miraculous recovery by Eric, who
slid a dagger up through the man's stomach into his heart. He dropped almost
instantly... Eric's ploy had cost several men their lives in the past. He turned
just in time to deflect the sword blow of the next attacker. They were good
swordsmen. The only thing that kept him ahead of them in the fight was his
ability to sense their blows before they came... and the fact that he was clearly
more motivated than they were. The ferocity of his skilled fighting continued to
frustrate them. Every time they tried to get on opposite sides of him, he would
quickly reverse his position with one of them. But he had not been successful
in injuring either. They worked their way across the meadow to a place where
several scrub trees grew among the waist-high brush.

There was the roar of a cave lion from somewhere close by, seemingly
answered by the growl of a bear. They were only slightly distracted, realizing
that all the grunting and clanging of sword steel would draw the attention of
hungry territorial predators.

The men began to taunt Eric about getting tired and losing his
concentration. They told him that all they had wanted was his weapons, but
now they would have to kill him anyway because he hurt their friend. All the
while, the men continued to circle Eric. Suddenly as if by some signal that Eric
missed they were on him. He fought off an initial volley but was cut deeply on
his left arm in the second one. The pain was intense enough to make him
dizzy. He did manage to hit the hand of one of the men with the tip of his
sword, causing him to retreat a short distance with a howl and quickly wrap it,
while the other man continued to press Eric. The remaining man was the older
of the two and appeared to be tiring. But fatigue caused by the pain and the
loss of a lot of blood again balanced the fight.

The wounded man began to yell obscenities as he started back toward
Eric. Eric knew he could not hold out any longer against the two of
them. Suddenly, there was a flash of movement, and the wounded man went
down screaming amidst the muffled growling of a large cat. Eric took

advantage of the distraction to strike out at his immediate opponent. The strike was blocked.

Hearing the roar of the lion and the answer of a bear, Shahandra knew she must be close. She went toward the sound with her horse still full run. Shortly, she found the meadow she had seen in her vision... it was exactly as she had seen it, only darker. She used her sensing and quickly located Eric. He was fighting two men. One began to curse and run toward Eric as Shahandra entered the meadow from the road, still at a full gallop. Suddenly, the advancing man fell screaming. She saw Eric strike out at the other man, who blocked the blow and returned one to Eric.

Eric saw Shahandra coming, recognizing her manner of riding and distinct silhouette, he shouted, "Get out of here, Shahandra. Get away..." This time, the distraction was his, and the man took full advantage of it, striking Eric with a heavy blow that knocked him down. It was followed by several more blows, one of which cut deeply into the top of his thigh. Eric could scarcely hold his sword up any longer and lay back, reeling from the pain and blood loss, waiting for the final blow. To his dazed eyes, what he saw was a black cloud rise rapidly behind the man, obscuring the stars and crescent moon. The cloud simply swept the man away. Eric passed out.

Shahandra could not see Eric, but could see the man striking over and over toward a target at ground level, a target that must be Eric. She could still sense his magic, so she knew that he lived. The man stopped briefly and raised his sword over his head as a large bear rose undetected, head and shoulders above and behind him. One swipe of the powerful paw sent the man flying. The bear quickly had the man trapped in his powerful jaws and dragged him off without any further sound. Shahandra changed the magic she used on the lion and bear from protection of a cub to dinner.

She rode to the last place she saw the man strike. She felt that Eric was still alive even though she could no longer sense his magic.

Tears filled her eyes. She had been only a few seconds late... seconds she lost in the stream when she first exited the woods... seconds lost fighting the creek terrain instead of taking to the road early on... "No use whining about it... I have to take things where I find them now", she thought to herself as she dismounted near the place she last saw the man hacking at a fallen opponent. A gnawing feeling ate at her insides over what she might find as she advanced through the brush and grass in search of Eric.

As she pushed through a patch of moonlit brush, she could see a motionless body lying on the grass just beyond her, contrasted dark against the lighter grass. She ran the few steps that separated them.

It took only a brief moment to tell that he still clung to life. The light from the moon wasn't sufficient to illuminate his wounds well enough for her to heal them properly. He was unconscious and did not respond to any probing she made of his wounds.

"I can't see your wounds..." she mumbled as she awkwardly picked through his clothing, trying to find the source of the blood that soaked them. "I shouldn't have stopped... I should have just kept riding..." she had to stop and wipe tears from her eyes several times. As her frustration grew, her voice became louder, "...and if you hadn't left me to begin with, maybe none of this would have happened..." she finished, nearly shouting at him.

Exasperation overcame her, "I can't do this unless you help me, Eric... do you hear me?... wake up, Eric... WAKE UP!" She placed her hands on his forehead and used her magic to try to stimulate his mind.

Eric awoke very groggy, in pain, and sickened.

"Eric," said Shahandra softly, "Where are you wounded... what hurts?"

Eric took hold of her hand and moved it from wound to wound as she relieved the pain in them one by one. She ended with his head, which had a nauseating ache in it.

When he finished moving her hand to the most painful wounds, Shahandra moved around and placed his head in her lap. He lay deathly still for some time before opening his eyes.

"So... this is what it feels like to die... to need help... to want...to want someone to care..." he said in a barely audible whisper.

"Maybe I can help you, Eric... maybe it's not too late." Tears again filled her eyes... she wondered at her feelings. He angered her with his arrogance, but they were a team... a team that had a mission... and now that mission was over... they had failed in the worst possible way.

"You always help, don't you?" he whispered. He continued on with only the slightest sound leaving his lips, "...even when it's dangerous... even if it.. jeopardizes your mission?!" The admiration she sensed from him surprised her.

"Eric, many times helping is my mission within the mission," she answered as she stroked his forehead.

"Did you save the man yesterday?" She sensed an almost reverent interest in her prior activity, a deep searching that was all too obviously missing the day before.

She did not answer for a long time. Eric closed his eyes while he waited for her answer. "No, Eric. He just went to sleep and died."

She felt his spirit sadden. She sat for a long time without moving. Eric lay very still, his breathing became shallower and shallower until it was barely detectable. The eastern sky slowly lightened as she stroked his cold forehead and ran her fingers through his hair. Even though she hadn't slept, she felt strong and alert.

Earlier, she had retrieved her water skin from Lady and continued to give Eric some in very small amounts. She knew he was very weak from blood loss, but at the same time felt sure that his remarkably strong-willed determination might just be tough enough to pull him through... with her help.

She worked her magic again to awaken him, only this time she had to work longer and stronger to bring him around. Once aroused again, she made him drink some water before she spoke with him. "What do you think, Eric, should I just put you out of your misery?" Her question sounded so sincere that Eric did not immediately respond.

Shahandra rephrased her question, "Should I use my art to kill you or try and save you? I won't be able to make good time back to the castle if I care for you."

"Why do you... taunt me.... while I'm dying," he asked in childlike candor.

"Why did you leave me alone with the dying man?" came her reply without emotion.

"Because..." he closed his eyes to refocus his thoughts, "...because I had to... get the message...message to Oakbern... hundreds of lives... at stake... hundreds of lives..." even in his weakness and semiconsciousness, he could scarcely believe that she needed him to explain this to her.

"But you know he's going to find out the attack is coming before it actually happens," she chided.

"This talk... proves nothing... wait..... I know...you win, Shan... OK... you winnn...... I die...you live." His whispers were full of derision and self-pity.

After a prolonged silence he spoke again, this time in a raspy voice a little louder than his whisper had been, "You need... to go... go tell Oakbern... about Danlion..... give time to prepare..." he reached out and weakly took hold of Shahandra's arm for emphasis but his eyes did not open, "every... minute early... he knows... can prepare... call help... provisions from outside..."

"Don't you understand, Eric? I can't leave you now any more than I could leave the man yesterday. I feel your feelings, your pain, your weakness, and I can't ignore them... I don't know how to be like you... I don't even think I want to be." Tears again filled Shahandra's eyes, tears that she did not bother to wipe away.

"Then we fail..."

"Eric, our mission was to find the powermaster and persuade him to work with us. We did at least find someone who knows him... maybe even a friend of his. That's valuable... and Eric... he likes me a lot, I sensed that much."

Eric's eyes opened a slit, "..were not for... that witch...I would know... for sure."

"I think we all may have underestimated Dalwan. There is much more to him than meets the eye... or even the first sensing. Too many coincidences..." her voice drifted off with her thoughts. "He may even be the powermaster... I just can't believe it, but maybe..." she reflected.

"If you felt that way about him... why didn't you tell me?"

"I hadn't thought through it then... and you wouldn't have listened long enough to be sensible."

"You think you have.... have everything figured out.... don't you?" She detected arrogance and condescension in his question.

"Can't you see any good in my work at all. You would already be dead if not for me. Even now, I've saved your life, and my art keeps you conscious at this moment. I made friends with the only person who knows the powermaster's identity..." It sounded to Eric like she was yelling at him. To her, she was only making a point.

She continued speaking to him while he drifted off into hazy thought. He realized that she had fared well and accomplished a great deal, if only by luck. As he pulled his strength together and began to answer her, he felt a sharp pain in his chest that seemed to shoot through his whole body. All he got out was, "Shahandra..." before his breath was knocked out of him. His whole body tensed up and went limp.

Shahandra tried for a long time in vain to revive him. "It really did kill him to give me a compliment," she thought as she rose to her feet, leaving his body lying on the wet grass in the predawn twilight. She could scarcely believe he was dead. Only two men had fought him. That wouldn't have normally been a problem to such a man. Something somehow caught him by surprise, and the men he fought must have been very good. She decided to take him back to the castle for a proper burial. It was now only one hard day's ride back to the castle from her present location. She would need to find a way to get him up on and secured to his horse. She went back to Eric's camp and retrieved his saddle and the bag containing all of his personal things, special weapons, papers, and such. It was then that she discovered the third man's body, as yet untouched by any animal.

She used some rope that Eric carried as a tool of his trade and tied it around his feet. She ran the rope over the saddle of Eric's horse and tied the other end to the horn of Lady's saddle. She was then able to get his body up, lying across the saddle, where she tied him in place.

She found the swords that the men had dropped and wrapped them together along with Eric's, securing them to in his bedroll. She attached the entire bundle to Eric's saddle.

The first rays of sunlight were visible when she set out for Brandon Keep.

Shahandra rode until midday, stopping only briefly to refresh herself and water the horses. She was now riding through familiar countryside, having explored this far from Brandon Keep on numerous occasions. The road was more heavily traveled, and from time to time she recognized merchants and farmers, some of whom she could address by name. As she approached the hamlet "Greenspell", known for its large and tasteful vegetables, she was met by a unit of five soldiers from Brandon Keep. They had been dispatched early that morning to search for her. It seems that the night before, an enormous swell of power resembling all too closely her own power print was felt keenly by all the sensors in the castle. Two of the soldier-sensors and three fighting specialists were dispatched early to find her and, presumably, Eric. They led her back to Brandon Keep, listening with interest as she recounted her story of the recent events and the battle that claimed Eric's life.

Shahandra was only mildly surprised to discover that the castle gates were closed and that sensors were posted outside with the entry guards. She found out that perceptions by the castle sensors of a growing mercenary army led by a powerful and menacing madman had been further verified two days prior by scouting parties. It was confirmed that this was the same crimson-caped leader whose band had been raiding small villages, towns, and farms, killing, plundering, and kidnapping certain women. The sensors in Brandon Keep had been following the growth of power in this group and especially of its malicious and crazed leader. While they did not expect an outright attack on the castle with so few men, it was possible that the small army would try to slip in one at a time to spy out the defenses or create some mischief of sabotage, or terrorism.

It was late afternoon when they arrived. Once inside the castle, Shahandra was escorted directly to Lord Oakbern. She recounted the adventure from beginning to end, spending much more time on the last two days than on the prior events.

Lord Oakbern had hastily assembled a group of experts and advisors to hear Shahandra's report. Several more arrived during the course of her account. Of greatest interest to most of those attending was how Shahandra's power had increased so much in so short a time. Because of this, they questioned her in detail about the magic forest. They stretched her memory for every fine detail, including feelings, perceptions, texture of the plants, density of the light, and variations of its appearance, clarity and duration of the visions, sounds of voices in the vision, and on and on into the evening.

Finally, it occurred to Lord Oakbern that she had not slept for two days. Upon realizing this, he abruptly arose from his seat in kingly fashion and, without explanation, dismissed all but Shahandra and his own wife. With the look of bullied school children, those in attendance rose obediently and left with quiet, abbreviated farewells. Lord Oakbern apologized to Shahandra for his insensitivity and praised his loyal wife's perception, which, incidentally, played a very large role in helping his majesty surmise the poor girl's plight. Then he departed, leaving her in Lady Oakbern's care.

CHAPTER 18

While Darric and Fallwyn were away testing Dalwan, the Pretorian delegation in Thamerlain had made some headway in their quest for knowledge and help regarding the sword Falonrod. The dwarven council confirmed that a sword named Falonrod was known to have originated in Thamerlain itself. It was made in a joint effort between the Dwarves and Elves. Most remarkable of all, it was created for a man, a very special man.

The greatest number of details contained in the public library regarding the sword were uncovered by Fanx, the Dwarven delegation historian. He retrieved this information, after considerable searching, from the "Ancient" section of the archives. The writings were in the form of notes contained in a very old-looking leather satchel, wrapped in a thin leather sheath that was cracked and showed traces of mildew stains. It had obviously not been kept in a normal dwarven repository for books, or it would not have shown such wear and age. One of the most curious facts reported by Fanx to the conferees was that the contents of the satchel were not registered in the archive catalogue, and the satchel was not marked with classification numbers. He happened upon it quite by accident. The only marking on the outside of the satchel was a title, "CONFIDENCE".

Fanx read several sections aloud to the conferees, which detailed the turmoil of the times and the circumstances that precipitated the forging of such an extraordinary union: dwarf, elf, and man. The record made it clear that it had been deemed a reasonable and prudent risk by the military leaders as a possible solution to the ever increasing raids by men on outlying elven and dwarven territories. They hoped to avoid the necessity of going to war with men by giving one of them the power to stop the raiders who terrorized not only the dwarves and elves but also human settlements. The project was carried on in secret, with only a few members of the dwarven and elven races having knowledge of the undertaking.

They initiated a search for a man who had qualities and values as similar to those of the dwarven and elven races as possible. After several phases of searching, they discovered such a man, Maylore.

It happened that Malore and a band of warriors under his command had come to the aid of the elves when it was learned that a particularly malicious band of men had been raiding and pillaging small elven homesteads and outposts.

The elves had already begun a campaign to eradicate this nuisance outlaw group, so Malore and his men put themselves under the command of the elven authorities to assist as the elves saw fit. This so impressed the elves that they told the dwarves. When word reached the secret group looking for a sword bearer, they immediately went to investigate. After watching him and observing his values at work, they elected one of their members to become soulmates with him. In the end, he was everything they had hoped for.

As it turned out, this was very timely in the cause of preventing outright war with the men of bordering kingdoms. The Lord of Bearshire, a community of men east of the elven kingdom, had developed a power sword of some renown. A report came to the elves that their military leaders were proposing a strike against the elven capital for their gold and other precious treasures rumored to be stored there. With this bounty, they could finance a great war against the other kingdoms of men to the south of them.

While the elven army and its friends from the dwarves prepared for the battle, the small chosen band of talented magicians worked to make the sword. The sword was shaped, balanced, and finally charged with the magic that would allow Maylore and perhaps only Maylore to use its power.

The story stopped there, and Fanx closed the book.

Attleman jumped to his feet, "But what about the part implicating that only Maylore could use the sword? Is that true? I thought a powermaster could use any power sword?"

Fanx replied in a calm voice, "The understandin' o' the sword's power is ta be left in Darric's hands. He's the keeper of antiquities and 'ill know what power the sword holds an' who can or cannot wield it...if indeed such knowledge still exists."

"I suppose this means we'll need to await Darric's appearance before we can investigate this any further?" asked Attleman dryly.

Fanx turned and faced Lanamir, who was chairing the session for the Supreme. Lanamir answered, "Tha'tis correct Attleman... we're not able ta proceed with information on the sword's power because we simply don't have it ta divulge. Only Darric has whatever information we possess, and, as ya' have noted already, he isn't here."

Malan, who was sitting next to Attleman, stood and put his hand on Attleman's shoulder and intervened, "Can we safely assume, from the information you do possess, that no one less than a powermaster could control the sword Fallonrod?"

"Of that, ya may be certain, Malan... more than that we cannot say," answered Lanamir congenially.

Attleman turned to Malan as they were setting down and whispered loud enough for everyone to hear, "...but that's what I asked him..."

"Not exactly my friend...not exactly," said Malan with a chuckle. "You must ask precisely the question you wish answered. If you assume they read into what you say and interpret your question, you may indeed be correct. But they will always answer to their advantage and in the way least likely to create conjecture or outright misunderstanding."

Malan turned back and again addressed Lanamir, "Since we're not able to discuss further the sword's power, may we proceed with questions regarding possible candidates for use of the sword?"

"Ask."

"Judging from the process and requirements you used in choosing Malore to bear the sword, may we assume that you have a proposal regarding the potential sword bearer's character?"

"Yes," answered Lanamir with a pleased look on his face, "as a matter of course, an' requisite condition for our assistance in this undertaking, we do presume ta present a proposal. Thank you for yer sensitivity ta our feelings on this matter, Malan. We're willing ta assist ya, but for reasons of our own, which revolve more around the sword's magic bein' well-kept than any concern that Danlion may secure the sword to prevent its use for a time. Are ya prepared ta receive them now?"

Malan looked to the other Pretorian delegates for consensus. Each in turn gave a nod of assent. "We're prepared to receive your proposal."

"We'll send a delegation of dwarves an' elves of our choosin' ta accompany you. They'll check the sword ta ensure that i'tis indeed Fallonrod, they'll inspect it fer damage an' finally they'll evaluate the status of its magic. If they find it's in good shape, they'll further investigate the potential of its use, if indeed Darric has enough information ta make that determination. If, after all that, they're confident that it can be used, they'll remain and interview potential sword users. If some prospective user passes the interview, a soulmate 'ill be chosen from among our delegation an' the final test 'ill be conducted. If the prospective bearer passes that test, training and further knowledge regardin' the sword's power 'ill be arranged."

Shaylan stood and asked, "Is there anything else...anything regarding the role of the people of Pretoria in choosing the sword bearer? You haven't given us the specific character requirements, which we must presume you have already determined."

"The matter o' character is far deeper than mere written requirements can determine. That's why a soulmate must be chosen. It can suffice to say that personal nobility, honesty, concern for others, hatred of war and destruction, and most of all, some degree of sensitivity are necessary. The soulmate 'ill discover whether the candidate possesses the more subtle requirements."

Most of the Pretorian delegation were squirming in their chairs with exasperation, and resentment was building quickly. Shaylans tried to voice their concern without offending their hosts, "Is it not fair that the people who will be most affected be the judges of what character traits they desire for their leader to have?"

"Yer people are free ta add to or complement any part o' these requirements as long as ya don't alter their intent. But before ya let yer emotions run away with ya, consider this, how many powermasters do ya have waiting for this opportunity?... indeed, how many true powermasters even exist in the entire world at any given time?... One maybe two!? And lastly, what makes ya sure that any powermaster will be a competent leader?... Fools come with all shades o' magic do they not?"

Shaylan could sense the growing apprehension in his fellow delegates and knew that the dwarves were at least as sensitive to those feelings as he was. "We require time to discuss these matters in private... not too long, I should think... we'll doubtless return with some questions."

They were led to a closed room where they quickly began their discussion.

Draymoor was the first to speak, "Does this mean that we have no say in who wields the sword? I don't want to see them in the position of determining who may become a power wielder among our people and who may not... indeed, who may not even be allowed to try! Magic is not predictable... there could be a dozen candidates coming of age who might all be good wielders. I say we make it a requirement that any person we put forward be given equal opportunity to pass their test."

"Even then," said Attleman, pounding his fist on the table, "we'll be putting them in the position to eliminate our choices arbitrarily and without recourse on our part!"

"Gentlemen...you forget," said Shaylan in a fatherly tone, "We are here because we couldn't do this on our own. They owe us nothing that would demand this level of repayment...trivial favors, yes... but nothing of this magnitude. We, in reality, have no recourse now! At least they offer us hope... and we know that they will not choose someone fond of war or hungry for power."

Malan chimed in, "Are we just going to let them walk in and take control of the sword... just like that? I don't trust them!"

"I agree," said Attleman with vigorous determination, "they shouldn't be given access to the sword without our people there. We must make that a condition."

Malan's face fell, and he became somber as he flopped back into the soft armchair and sat slumped down. Speaking almost to himself, he said, "If we insult their integrity, they'll withdraw. I know them well enough to be sure of that."

It had not been until now that they realized just how compromising their situation was. Shaylan tried to salvage them from impending gloom, "Friends, why don't we give them a list of our requirements and see if we can work out a middle ground. We can't lose any more footing in this situation than we have already lost. I doubt they'll want to back out now since there is always that chance looming in the realm of possibility that we'll somehow find a sword bearer, and at that, one who may not be to their liking."

They all Agreed.

"Draxyl, ready your pen! Take down our requirements and mix them with theirs. We can present them as a combined document and see how they react."

They agreed on four requirements and documented them in short order:

FIRST: Only Pretorian-approved candidates will be permitted to attempt qualification for the sword.

SECOND: None of the visiting delegation would enter the Swordroom without an authorized Pretorian observer or direct permission from the Lord of Castle Crest.

THIRD: There would be no attempt on the part of the dwarves or elves to control the sword user before or after training unless he becomes a direct and imminent hostile threat to their land or their personal safety.

FOURTH: The Lord of Castle Crest has the right to terminate the contract and its requirements after consultation with the visiting delegation.

The document was accurately prepared by Draxyl's lightning hand and presented to the council. After a brief review in which they read it aloud and its intent was discussed, the dwarves required a recess to discuss it.

It took them only a short time to return.

Lanamir stood and responded, "Pretoria must recognize that the sword is a blighted treasure. We recognize that it was a selfish gift given by our ancestors to a human ta prevent the necessity of our entrance into yer wars. In our short contact with Darric on its power, he assured us that i'twas built with certain safeguards intrinsic in its creation ta protect it from misuse under certain circumstances. Most of yer enemies will be unable to use it... as probably will you. However, its reputation 'ill keep kingdoms seeking it because rumor 'ill always prevail over truth when concerning such instruments of power." Lanamir waited a moment before continuing to let his words sink in.

"With these things in mind, we've analyzed yer 'requests' an' have concluded that yer people's paranoia has precipitated the four stipulations you've brought forth. As for number four we accept that yer leaders have the right ta cancel the contract at their discretion...as do we. As fer trying ta control the sword user, that 'ill be totally unnecessary... we won't choose anyone who'll necessitate such a constraint... we therefore accept number three also. Regarding yer second stipulation, we find it ta yer discredit that you would ask us to assist ya in a crisis of kingdom proportion while at the same time embarrass us in that ya do not trust us alone with the object o' that crisis. We'll accept yer stipulation, hoping that the castle lord 'ill have more sensitivity and not disgrace us with unnecessary restrictions which 'ill damage our honor and force us ta terminate our assistance. The major stumbling block fer us 'ill be number one, the choice of the sword bearer. As before, we seek ta keep the wars o' men within the kingdoms of men. That's the reason we assist ya a'tall. It's not reasonable fer us ta explain the content o' the safeguards the sword possesses an' thereby subject those protections ta manipulation by those unqualified ta use it." Again, he waited for a moment while his words impacted the Pretorian delegation.

Draymoore stood up and in a stiff challenging tone addressed Lanamir interrupting his pause, "Does this mean that unless we let you pick our sword-bearer, you won't come? How would you handle such a requirement made of you by another race?"

"Draymoore, we don't go ta war with ourselves, so an identical parallel 'ill not be possible," answered Lanamir with a smile which aroused a brief chuckle from the other dwarf and elf delegates.

"In answer ta yer real question, which is 'will we still come if such a restriction is imposed?', I must seek further clarification. Do ya really want only the every few people ya bring forward ta be considered, or do ya simply wish ta ensure that only someone who is personally committed an' favorable ta Pretoria be chosen? We'll commit ta the later while opposin' the former."

"But that's the same as saying that you alone will be the final judges of who will bear the sword and who will not," answered Draymoore as he angrily pounded heavy-fisted on the table.

"That has always been our intention... and if I'm not mistaken, you have something less than chance as your ally in choosing a bearer if we are left out of this transaction."

A quick huddle formed around Shaylan.

"I hate having others determine our fate," grumbled Attleman whose remark was echoed by all the others.

"What will be made of us if we return having bargained away our sovereignty?" asked Draxyl, displaying considerable emotion. This was the only major contribution made by him during the entire negotiation and brought everyone face-to-face with their pride.

Shaylan broke the ensuing silence, "We simply can't get this close and let the opportunity to learn more about the sword's power and use be lost... we must use our reason here. It..."

Shaylan was cut short by Lanamir, "Men o' Pretoria... if ya don't trust us, don't waste our time an' efforts by bringin' us ta yer country. The sword was given to ya originally by our people for all o' our good. We've not interfered with its use up ta now and didn't come ta you requestin' audience regardin' it. If ya still wish our help, we offer it, with condition, in the same spirit that originally bestowed it ta yer land."

The men of the Pretorian delegation exchanged looks of chastised resignation, prompting Shaylan to stand, "We now recognize our reluctant pride and will put it in its proper place... out of the negotiations. We apologize."

"Accepted," shouted Lanamir over a round of unanticipated applause by the dwarf and elf delegates.

"Furthermore, we wish you to accompany us with the hope that you will consider us trustworthy enough to share your convictions about potential candidates and at least receive our input."

"Shaylan, we must first investigate the condition o' the sword. If i'tis fully operative, we intend ta chose a person who embodies as much o' the best characteristics ya each have ta offer... that is as much as can be found in one person from among yer people. And we must all recognize the possibility that no one may be found who even possesses the ability ta wield the sword." Lanamir sat back down and ordered a final draft of the agreement to be written for signing.

By early evening, the drafts were drawn and signed, and the delegations retired to the rooms to freshen up for the dinner which followed.

The dinner was delightfully prepared and presented. Most of the dishes were identical to the ones they had eaten the night before and pleased everyone just as much as they had the previous evening. The entertainment was not nearly as intense, consisting mostly of soothing music played by an elven group using instruments seldom heard by humans. During dessert, a dwarven quartet performed unaccompanied. Their harmonic melodies, with a combination of rich, deep and clear high tones, enchanted the dinner guests, bringing a sense of tranquility to the evening.

As soon as they finished singing, Frone stood up and thanked all the delegates on behalf of all three kingdoms. He then called out, each in turn, those responsible for the food preparation, the servers, and the musicians, all of whom received a rousing round of applause.

After that, he announced that there was to be a final summing up of the conference by the Supreme immediately following the dinner, and therefore all conference attendees were to remain. The Supreme would also identify the delegation that would accompany the men back to Castle Crest.

The Hall was packed with representatives from the three races. The Pretorian delegation was already seated at a prestigious table. They all felt very anxious and so exhausted that they sat solemnly still while waiting for the meeting to begin. The Dwarves and Elves were mixed together in several groups, some laughing and telling stories while others just listened with interest.

As he entered, the Supreme called the meeting to order. Everyone quickly found a seat, and silence filled the room.

He spoke in a kind but firm voice, "A few days ago, we received a delegation of men from Pretoria. As ya all are aware, the matter that brings them here and the coming o' their enemies ta our land, has cost us the lives o' twelve of our countrymen. Three died by the hand o' the shadowmaster employed by Danlion and nine soldiers in battle with the raiders, also in Danlion's employ. Dealin's with men in the trades of war-related magical power have always brought unnecessary death ta those we love, those who's friendship we cherished."

"Makes me feel real special about my heritage," said Dalwan aside to Darric.

"We are now faced", continued the Supreme, "with the rising Earth power and the inevitable wars that 'ill result from man's misuse of it. They will seek ta pit that power against one another in various attempts to assert dominance over the other...ta subjugate those weaker or more timid to the selfish wishes of the powerful." There was a murmur that went through the crowd of Dwarves and Elves, accompanied by a lot of head shaking and cool glances toward the obviously self-conscious men, who in turn shifted nervously in their chairs. The Supreme paused a short time for the noise to die down before he continued.

"We are now involved because we hold some o' the secrets o' the power sword 'Fallonrod' forged and empowered by our ancestors almost two hundred years ago. While we have precious little written information about the sword, what we do have has been helpful. The keepers of the sword sealed it in a stone room in one o' their castles, where it's remained untouched until recent events have caused it ta resurface as a viable weapon in the hands of a powermaster. Pretoria has sought our services ta either disclose its potential for use by their allies or determine the course of its destruction. We, the Dwarves and our distinguished friends the Elves, have decided ta return with the men o' Pretoria ta investigate the sword's power. Our goal is ta determine if any assistance is possible, whether by makin' it accessible ta their powermaster, should one be found who is worthy, or by discoverin' a means ta destroy it or at least render it useless." There was another brief time of murmuring, this time in more hushed tones.

Turning to speak directly to the Pretorian delegation, "Men o' Pretoria. We do not have a particularly good nor bad relationship with yer land. We've little ta gain from aidin' ya except that we may now have opportunity ta become influential in the selection o' the next sword bearer, should a qualified candidate be found. This we feel is an advantage in that the wrong bearer could bring disaster ta many lands an' peoples, includin' us.

We'll go with ya and share whatever knowledge we may possess or may discover, concerning the sword, with a suitable powermaster from among yer people. Much o' the knowledge 'ill not be shared with yer leaders nor with yer magicians. It'll be shared only with the one who'll be required ta use the swords power."

This brought an abrupt response from the Pretorian delegation.

"We knew that they'd be shrewd negotiators," said Attleman aside to Shaylan, but loud enough to be heard by most of the others. "I expected them to bend things to their advantage, but this is ridiculous!" This was quickly affirmed by the rest of the delegation.

There was a hushed debate that lasted only briefly, being stopped short by Shaylan, speaking in a harsh whisper, "Please! Men of Pretoria. Our actions now could jeopardize the entire venture. Let's at least hear them out. After all, what more would we know if they didn't come with us than we would if they came and didn't tell us anything? At least we have the possibility of an informed powermaster."

"We apologize for our rude interruption. Please continue," said Shaylan repentantly.

The Supreme resumed, "In this way we've been allowed ta present the sword to a worthy man and still have a say in his successor. Each time a new sword bearer is required, the Dwarves and the Elves 'ill have the option ta renew its use for men or deny it if need be." There was a strong resolve in the voice of the Supreme. The Pretorian delegation sat very still, having already realized there was precious little they could do or offer that would change the council's intentions. It was not defeat, but victory was clearly not in their control.

"We've already chosen the delegation that 'ill accompany ya back ta Castle Crest," continued the Supreme in a matter-of-fact tone. "They'll be given access ta the sword, open interviews with any person they choose an' final authority ta choose the eventual sword bearer, should one be found who is acceptable."

Attleman stood up in obvious irritation, "Honorable Supreme," he said, trying to control his emotions, "Why do you treat us as children? Are we not capable of discerning how to use the knowledge of the sword by ourselves? You've already taken our sovereignty of choice regarding the bearer away."

"Y'are quite able ta choose the person ya wish ta wield the sword. We've no doubt o' that. But there's a possibility that the person ya choose would not be one we would wish ta train in its use or give the secrets of its power to." The Supreme was very relaxed and confident without being overly arrogant. In fact, he sounded to Shaylan like a wise father speaking to a challenging young son.

Draymoor stood and spoke. "But the sword was a gift to us and belongs to us. Its knowledge and use should belong to us also!"

"Then use it!" said the Supreme with a gentle smile that made Draymoor sit back down in embarrassment. After time for the Pretorian delegation to reflect on the exchanges that had taken place, he spoke again, "We have not asked ya for the sword. You've asked us for its secrets. Yer desire is for the use o' the sword in its employ against yer enemies, those who would threaten yer land or possibly attempt ta use the sword against ya. We're willin' ta conditionally grant fulfillment of yer need, but on our terms only."

"I must also assume," asked Shaylan, "that Darric has nothing that he is willing to add to our earlier discussion regarding the power of the sword?"

"Tha'tis correct Shaylan. Thank you fer remindin' me so I could clear that up. However, after the investigation at Castle Crest, he may very well have much ta say to a powermaster, should one be chosen."

The Supreme turned to Elloewyn, the Elven dignitary who was to speak next, and gave a slight bow, after which he sat down, giving attention to him.

Elloewyn's voice was like deep music, "As we attend to the business of investigation and discovery of the sword's powers, we reserve the right to refuse communication of our knowledge to anyone. Should we choose to share it, we will do so with anyone we wish, before or after our mission to your castle. We will gladly interview any potential sword bearer or magician you wish to bring before us for the purpose of receiving information on the sword, but the right of refusal is with us and is final. Should we choose to reveal the sword's powers to one of your countrymen or women, we reserve the right not to reveal their identity to you before or after the endowment of knowledge if we deem it expedient."

"We object to the possibility of a woman wielding the sword," came the loud and emotional response from Attleman. "No woman should be made to bear such a burden!"

"I did not mention anything about giving a woman the task of wielding the sword, although a woman of your species may well be better suited to wield it than many of your men. I spoke of the impartation of knowledge regarding the sword," said Elloewyn calmly and without expression.

Cutting in, Draymoor asked, "Do you mean that you may give the secrets of the sword to one of our people and not reveal that person's identity to us?"

"That is precisely correct."

At this Shaylan stood up and intervened, "Most honorable Elloewyn, have you any more conditions to add before we retire to consider these most interesting provisions you have required?"

"Only that if our delegation deems it necessary, we may cancel our contract and leave the castle at any time we believe it would be to the best advantage of both parties. Furthermore, we must be guaranteed safe passage."

"We'll discuss these provisions briefly and return to you shortly with our final answer. Is there any gratuity or honor you wish from us in return for your service?"

Elloewyn exchanged glances with the Supreme and, looking back at the Pretorian delegation with a slight smile, said, "We require nothing."

"Then permit us to discuss this briefly, and we'll return promptly." Shaylan turned and walked toward a side room in the hall with Rhem close behind. Draymoor and Attleman were next, followed by Malan and Draxyl, who was still writing as he walked.

Shaylan was waiting in the room, poised to speak when the others arrived. He did not give any of them a chance to talk before opening his argument, "Gentlemen, we have nothing to offer them in return for their services. They are our best, and possibly our only hope of discovering the use of the sword. We can send one of our own ahead to present the conditions prior to our arrival. If they are unacceptable, we can cancel the arrangement prior to commencing the investigation. We have nothing to lose and we will not change their minds without something to bargain with...and indeed we are already greatly in their debt."

In light of this simple challenge, their arguments faded, and they all agreed to the provisions.

They returned and accepted the conditions.

As soon as it was officially recognized that the conditions had been received, the Supreme named Darric, Myletan, and Mornic as the Dwarven representatives in the delegation to Castle Crest. Elloewyn named Fallwyn, Angoleen, and Mayflyn as the Elven representatives.

As soon as he concluded, an elf woman with long silken auburn hair and who wore a shimmering royal green dress, stood and removed from a glistening cut crystal glass box an instrument that looked like a golden flute. A murmur of astonishment and excited anticipation filled the elves and dwarves, who each in their own way situated themselves for the recital. It's music filled the air in a way that at once seemed too clear and full for its size. Its music then reached inside the hearer and played to the soul as if bypassing the ears entirely. Its melody was haunting, telling of ancient days of peace and sharing the very music of love itself. Its music ended, leaving everyone who felt its power restored in spirit and full of peace. There was no applause... applause would have been irrelevant... just whispers of thanks and admiration.

Lanamir stood and quietly dismissed everyone. Sleep would be sweet this night to everyone who had heard the sweet music of the rare and wonderful "Magical Nightwind Pipe", one of the seven ancient treasures of the elven people.

The next day, the delegation spent their time sightseeing and picking up a few mementos while waiting for their counterparts to ready themselves. Dwarven guides were made available to every member of the delegation to show them the city with its art and wonders, both natural and of dwarven creation.

While the others went out, Shaylan stayed behind in the sleeping quarters to fill Dalwan in on the conference decisions, detail by detail. When he got to the place regarding the concession over choosing the potential sword bearer, Dalwan laughed out loud.

This so annoyed Shaylan that he stopped talking and stared deep into Dalwan's... sensing... probing into his soul. Dalwan was slow to catch Shaylan's invasion, and his attempts to block them were too late.

"Young man!" Shaylan's booming voice surged with intense warning tones, "This negotiation and its results are of the utmost importance. What happens may... no!, WILL affect the lives of a great many people. You may or may not become a part of the history to be made, but your emotions betray an arrogance, a self-important omniscient attitude that is more than dangerous for someone of your power... IT'S RECKLESS!" Shaylan's voice was so loud as he finished that it caused Dalwan to jerk back in his seat with eyes wide in astonishment.

Dalwan fought back the frustration he felt at Shaylan's misinterpretation. Before he could respond, Shaylan continued, only this time in very quiet, subdued tones, "...and worst of all, you blocked my sensing... you broke your commitment to me as your teacher... as your uncle... and as your friend." Shaylan finished just above a whisper with a sad, introspective look in his eyes. Shaylan was at an emotional standstill. He had feared that Dalwan would someday pass him by or reject his counsel. It had come sooner than he expected. Perhaps the dwarf, Darric, had somehow swayed him...

"Shaylan," blurted Dalwan as he jumped out of his chair, breaking the solemn gloom produced by Shaylan, "You're my teacher and friend...you just don't understand..."

At that instant, the door swung open and a very cheerful, loud Darric entered, "Come lad, we've much ta do today. Only one day ta prepare fer yer mission ya know!"

Shaylan faced the door in surprise. "What is going on here, Darric?"

"The lad has too much ta do today ta just sit and discuss things that can be talked over later... ya know... after we set out ta your castle." The dwarf had already walked over and grabbed Dawlan by the arm and was pulling him toward the door.

"What's so important, Darric?" asked Shaylan in tones resembling objection, "...and who is the 'WE' you are speaking of?" he continued as he followed them out the door.

"We must outfit the lad 'n give 'im a new sword," came the reply from the exuberant dwarf over his shoulder as he continued dragging Dalwan down the pathway.

"NEW SWORD? WHAT NEW SWORD?" yelled Shaylan. "You can't do that!" He had stopped flat-footed with arms crossed, as was his custom when making a judgment and pronouncement which he expected to be followed, only to realize that the others continued on at a steady clip. Shaylan had to trot down the path to catch up with them. "You can't just run off with the lad...er uhm... I mean, with Dalwan... You don't understand what he's all about... he's somewhat special."

Darric stopped suddenly, and his powerful grasp of Dalwan's arm made the boy look like a rag doll being swung around by an absent-minded child. Shaylan was now moving so fast that only with difficulty did he avoid running into them.

"Shaylan," said Darric in a hushed tone, "the lad's a powermaster!"

Shaylan's mouth dropped open, and for a brief moment, he was speechless, an extraordinary event in itself. Recovering only slightly, he blurted, "...Well uh... well you can't just... now wait a moment here, you can't know that for sure! This is not a matter for conjecture... you can't just presume..."

Darric cut him off as he firmly grabbed Shaylan's arm and half-dragged him along with Dalwan, "We've tested 'em an' found 'em ta be complete. We're gonna outfit 'im with another sword. 'Tis a magic sword, o'course! He'll have a need fer it in his work. Now, Shaylan, ya must hide these thoughts in the same way Dalwan hid 'em from you... an' ya need either ta trust us or come with us. But one way or the other ya must quit slowin' us up!"

"What kind of test?... and what's this about a 'new sword'? And what am I hiding, and from who? Darric, I need more information here!", shouted the now completely flabbergasted Shaylan, still trying to loosen his arm from Darric's painfully strong grip.

"Ya came here ta Tamberlain in desperation. Yer people needed our help. Ya should not have come if ya didn't trust us!"

"I never said we... I mean, I don't trust..."

Darric cut him short, "Now Shaylan," said Darric, his voice breaking with a taunting chuckle, "ya just questioned me 'bout givin' the lad a new sword, said that I didn't know what he was all about, and then inferred that I couldn't know fer sure that he was a powermaster... you'll have ta give pardon if that sounds like mistrust ta me." Darric looked upward out of the corner of his eyes, with brows raised in a chastising expression, meeting a red-faced Shaylan's embarrassed stare.

Darric's tone turned fatherly, "Just because ya don't understand what I'm doin' doesn't mean I'm a reckless fool. All yer questions 'ill be answered in due time. Meanwhile, yer best bet is ta trust us... this adventure was, after all, yer own instigation!"

At that, Darric let go of Shaylan's arm so suddenly that Shaylan spun around on his leading foot and almost tripped.

Quickly regaining his balance, he tried to catch back up with and match Darric's relentless pace, "Very well, Darric, you have my confidence", he said, never quite catching up with them. At that, he stopped on the path, his voice getting louder as they quickly widened the gap between them, "I'll just keep quiet about this... tell me only what you want me to know... and Darric...please take care of the boy, he's like a son to me!"

Darric suddenly stopped and swung Dalwan around again so both of them ended up facing Shaylan, "Did ya hear that lad... the man loves ya like a son... an' is trustin' ya ta my care. Shaylan, I'll treat him as my own life... ya have ma word!" Sensing Darric's intentions, Dalwan began to move around him

quickly, leading his movement to avoid having his arm jerked out of its socket
again, and they were off at a quick pace.

Dalwan glanced back to see Shaylan standing where they had left him,
staring in their direction. They moved quickly to the perimeter of the
conference grounds while Shaylan stood watching. Just before they moved out
of sight, Dalwan held up his arm over his head with his fist clenched, a signal to
Shaylan that he was OK. He saw Shaylan return it, but with much less vigor.

Shaylan had known the day would come when the world would take
possession of Dalwan. But that didn't make it easy for him to let go. He had
trained Dalwan, giving him the benefit of all the knowledge and wisdom he
possessed. Now it would be up to the powermaster to use his resources
well. Shaylan shrugged off his apprehension, turned, and walked somberly back
to the sleeping quarters.

Meanwhile, Darric and Dalwan were making good time working their
way to the bottom cavern meeting hall under Darric's mountain. There, they
met Fallwyn, who had another dwarf with him.

The dwarf was dark skinned with short curly black hair and eyebrows so bushy
that they almost hid his deep-set eyes in his broad face. His shoulders were
wider and his arms bigger than Darric's. His hands were rough with thick,
cracked calluses.

"Dalwan, this is Myletan," said Darric, pointing in the tough-looking
dwarf's direction, "He's the forger of the sword ya must bear. He put the magic
we gave 'im inta the sword fer just such a possibility as has come ta pass."

Myletan stood perfectly still until the introduction was finished and then
stepped forward and reached out his hand. Dalwan prepared himself to touch
the soul of the rugged dwarf as he had touched Fallwyn's.

Dalwan completed the now familiar grasp, and the rest came amazingly
easy. Their minds met with unexpected rapidity and clarity. Dalwan went
first. His images came in blue hues: first his battle; then several of his practice
sessions, including the one where Rhem and Shaylan persuaded him to learn the
sword; his meeting with the anderon; and finally his test for powermaster.

Myletan followed. His images were brilliant hues of red. It was as if
Myletan's soul was at one with the substance of the earth itself. Dalwan saw a
huge room with blocks of metal and powders. There were tools and fires,
forges and anvils - his soul filled with exhilaration at the sight, feel, and heat in
the room. There was immense power in it. The scene shifted to a setting where

a large number of dwarves were together. There was a large tree limb lying across two closely situated tree stumps. A powerful-looking dwarf stepped forward and swung a large broad axe, cutting the limb in two with a single blow, and landed directly on top of one of the stumps. Another even larger log was placed across the stumps. A dwarf in very fine clothes walked up to the log and looked around. He was obviously arrogant. A sense of great humor invaded Myleton. It made Dalwan laugh out loud. He handed the pompous dwarf a broad axe. The humor swelled but was being well controlled. Even more haughty than before, the dwarf stepped up to the log and swung the axe. It bounced off the log like a baton off a large drum, bringing a roar of laughter and delight from those watching. The scene shifted to a garden full of flowers where beautifully shaped and ornamented trees grew in a magnificently landscaped setting adorned with handcrafted stonework. Great peace and tranquility filled Dalwan. Another figure appeared, that of a dwarven woman. She had a stout frame and full figure, a broad smile, and big, bright, enchanting brown eyes. Her hair was pulled back into a thick braid that went to her waist. Myletan was deeply bound in spirit to this attractive dwarven woman. Dalwan was flooded with the emotions of respect and love. The woman and Myletan appeared together in the garden where the small trees were. She took his hand in one of hers, and with the other hand, she touched the trunk of a small tree. Suddenly, Dalwan was aware of the life in the tree. He sensed its vitality, its damp, cool roots, and its tiny leaves that fluttered in the gentle breeze. The magic was from the woman. The scene shifted again. This time, he saw Fallwyn and Darric in the forging chamber. He could feel the heat of the forge fire; it excited him. He was now pouring hot liquid metal into a long, thin casting tray. It was unmistakably a sword cast. He could see the metal puddle and crest in the center of the tray as if each drop had a specific mission. The smells of hot metal and the feel of the heavy smelting pot invigorated him.

As the metal began to cool, he saw Fallwyn approach the casting tray. He stretched out his hands together and held them directly over the tray, less than a handbreadth above it. A blue-green mist appeared between his hands. The air felt as if it were vibrating. He then felt a power in Myleton begin to grow and grow. It was a magic of mixing and bonding. He felt the magic keenly as Myletan projected something like a streak of red fire directly through the mist between Fallwyn's hands. The fire turned from red to violet as it traveled the remaining distance toward the cooling sword cast. There was a sensation of connection between Fallwyn, Myletan, and the sword. It was as if part of him actually was in the sword. He felt the sword's power.

The image changed again. There was the sensation of joy and accomplishment. Myletan was carrying the sword blank in forge tongs toward an anvil. He stopped near the anvil and set the new formed sword on a solid black table which was only two fingers on each end longer than the sword itself. The table was stone; he could feel Myletan's magic in it. Now Darric appeared, standing nearby. Myletan took hold of the end of the table with both hands, and the sword blade began to float upward until it was about two hands high off the table surface. It was unevenly balanced at first, with the hilt floating closer to the table than the tip. He could feel the sensation of deeper concentration from Myletan as the sword leveled out.

Darric approached the table, stretched out his arms, and blinding fire leapt from his hands to the sword. The sword began to spin on its axis and became bathed in the fire's glow. Dalwan could feel the power of the fire as Myletan's magic combined fire and sword.

Again, the scene shifted. This time, Myletan was holding the sword mid-blade. It had been carefully sharpened and was ready to be put together in its final form. He felt Myletan's now recognizable power surge into the sword as he held the handle piece to the blade hilt and began to join them. The handle glowed brilliantly, as did the hilt end of the sword where they joined to become one.

Very suddenly, the vision ended.

A callous hand released Dalwan's forearm, and blood began to flow toward his hand again.

"Did ya read the sword's magic, lad?" came Myletan's response to the encounter.

"Yes!" answered Dalwan with a questioning smile that Myletan understood immediately.

"The clown with the bouncing broad axe is Winsor, the son of the Supreme. He needed a little lesson in humility."

"Got one, he did!" chimed in Darric with wide eyes and a familiar chuckle. His eyes met Myletan's, and both of them erupted into full belly laughs.

Dalwan found it very hard to imagine having the courage to set up the Supreme's son for humiliation before such a large group of dwarves. He couldn't even envision what awful consequences might follow such a stunt if it were pulled on the son of a castle lord in his own land.

"Weren't you afraid of embarrassing the son of the Supreme?..."

"Hardly, lad," answered Myletan. "Every dwarf's born equal. The mastery of his arts and skills, his courage, integrity, an' personal commitment in the community 'ill determine his status an' reputation among his peers. Mere wealth an' property are only advantages to a wise dwarf who uses them well. What good are the magic arts ta one who doesn't practice an' master 'em? So i'tis among the dwarves with wealth, property an' family position."

Dalwan's thoughts drifted. He had always felt that life should be fairer... that everyone should have the same chances to excel. Nothing ever seemed equitable... the arts were random... you could be born into a position or power and maintain it even if you were a moron... and others, wise and noble people, were doomed to obscurity because they were born into the wrong family or in an uninfluential area. Worse yet, a fool could be greatly gifted in the arts while a person of virtuous character could be extremely limited in the arts. With all these inequities, men could not separate out the true value of a person from their wealth or position of personal influence. Those who suddenly became wealthy, even those who were previously humble, charitable folk, would become arrogant and even greedy, gravitating toward the powerful and removing themselves from those they once called friends. It made him feel angry, even sick. It was then that he realized, as a powermaster, if he lived through this little adventure, he would have power and wealth... or he "could" have power and wealth. Would he be able to escape these same snares? He felt a sort of panic set in. What would the dwarves do to protect themselves from this fate if they faced it personally?

"My people have even more pride and greed to trip them up than your people seem to," said Dalwan. "Even Winsor would be considered commonplace among us." Dalwan spoke so soberly that the others lost their smiles and gave concerted attention to his words. "My people often use each other by way of deception or even force to get what they want. How do you avoid becoming like that? How do you keep from becoming like the supreme's son? If I drift off... how do I get back to right thinking again?"

To Dalwan's amazement, they took him very seriously, much more so than he anticipated. He watched as they huddled for a few moments to confer on a response.

Darric spoke first. "Dalwan, all that ya seek ta understand in this, ya already know. Ya just don't see how ta make it work yet."

"You see," cut in Fallwyn, "right now you value the things of magic art and new relationships. You have worked very hard for your mastery of the magics and are well accomplished... very powerful for one so young..."

"Fer anyone o' any age!" added Myletan with a conviction that the others quickly affirmed.

"You feel strongly now about the ideals we're sharing," continued Fallwyn, "but the temptations that can snare you will come just as you've foreseen them. What will happen when you become tired of conflicts? And now adventure is great... when you're young and have a lot of life ahead of you... but what about when you wish to settle down?"

Darric picked up at that point, "Do ya provide fer yer family all the pleasures they desire? Where do ya draw the line and why? Ya know, Dalwan, the most beautiful women in yer land 'ill seek someone who'll provide them with all the frills they lust after. They d'not fancy personal sacrifice, adventure, and modest living... they want wealth, comfort, and prestige."

"I feel like giving up now... you guys really know how to cheer someone up," said Dalwan despondently. "I already realized all that stuff... that's why I asked you for help!"

"Now lad," answered Darric as he slapped Dalwan on the back with a good-humored but thunderous blow which all but knocked the breath out of him, "we simply wanted ta set things in perspective before givin' the answer we feel is best fer all our races. Y'are masterin' yer arts with great speed an' ability. Now ya must master yer heart with the same dedication ya use ta tame the arts. The inclinations of yer race 'ill lead ya ta the same evils predominant in most who 'ave gone before ya so far. But the seeds o' what we have in our culture are already in yers. All ya need is a change in perspective... a different way o' lookin' at things... a bit of a value shift."

Fallwyn chimed in, "Having more or bigger is of no value if you don't know how to use well what you already possess. With this in mind, we form a community. In your land, the communities are built around the rich and powerful, with each person hoping to receive some benefit from the relationship. Wealth and power are the keys to personal status among your people. Not so in our land. Our communities are formed around common needs and goods, but our personal goals focus on what we can contribute. We go where we are most likely needed, not where we can gain the most."

"With both our races sharing the same perspective," added Myletan, exuding enthusiasm, "we work together fer common goals an' share our gifts without limitation, bringing the beauty and wonder ta our land that ya've witnessed over the past days."

Darric picked up from there, "We d'not take more from the earth or land than we need. O'course we still seek beautiful things, placin' high value on items of necessity that have artful design and creative beauty. But the most important things ta us are relationships, not possessions... our people, not their wealth."

Dalwan felt overwhelmed with all the idealism they poured on him. "This all real nice for you and your races, but it's not real in my world... nothing like this exists except in some families... and even then I'm not sure it's so pure as what you do."

"Dalwan," answered Fallwyn, "if you wish to have this kind of life, you'll have to cultivate the seeds already present in your culture... there are those who will respond."

"An' plenty who won't," said Myletan, "...least wise not fast enough fer Dalwan ta see it before he dies o' old age. Why don't ya just give up on yer people an' come live with us?"

There was just enough taunt in Myletan's voice to bring Dalwan's feelings to the surface. "I don't even know if I can escape being exactly like the rest of my race... maybe it's something we're born with... like brown eyes or curly hair... it just happens and you can't avoid it... what then? What if that's just the way it is and we're all doomed to be like that in one way or another, especially if given even half a chance?!"

"Is that what you want?" asked Darric quite without emotion.

"NO! At least not now I don't... I hate it... but what if I change?"

"Master your change!" answered Fallwyn, "Let it be out of growth, not deterioration of spirit."

Darric studied Dalwan for a moment, sensing his mood as well as his thoughts. "Dalwan, why don't ya want ta be like the others?"

"Because there isn't much to admire in most of them. The way they act and treat each other... the things they work the hardest for... what they do to each other to get what they want. At best, they may perform a noble act of some kind now and then, but look hard enough and you'll probably find some ugly motive behind it... some desire for recognition or greed or hope of reward."

"Dalwan, we all need recognition o'some sort. Especially among our peoples, we have a need ta be recognized for our achievements or gifts, even our sacrifices. The difference is that we seek this honor for our comrades, not necessarily ourselves... and recognize it in every level of our society. Our rewards come in appreciation and personal honor, not necessarily in some monetary fashion."

Dalwan just sat without expression as Darric spoke. Darric waited a moment before continuing, "In yer observations ya sounded very much the philosopher and observer. What would things be like if i'twere up ta you ta mold the state of affairs?"

"It would be more like your lands... people would look for opportunities to outdo each other in different good ways... helping each other out. They wouldn't hoard stuff and would spend more time using their arts to support each other instead of using them to control each other..." at that, Dalwan went silent with a faraway look in his eyes.

"These're all great aspirations, lad." Darric stopped for a moment while he probed Dalwan's blank stare, "I take it that this's ta be yer way of livin'... or is this just yer dream fer everyone else?"

"I don't know... I just wish it could be that way."

"As a powermaster ya could make people do it! Ya could force them ta be nice ta each other and ta use their arts ta benefit yer community!" The look on Darric's face displayed the same taunting as Myletan's had earlier.

Dalwan knew instinctively from his past that this was their attempt to wake up some sleeping wisdom they believed to be dormantly awaiting expression. But all Dalwan could muster was a feeling of hopelessness. "Forcing people to be nice would only create hostility among them," he thought to himself, "even I can see that... and it would make great enemies out of the truly powerful and even worse out of the very arrogant."

"I don't understand what you want me to see," he retorted with a pouting anger.

"Simply this, Dalwan," said Fallwyn, "it all gets back to perspective... do you wish to live it yourself because you believe it?... or just to experience it because everyone else is doing it too? Do these values exist if only one person lives this way... maybe someone... like a powermaster?!"

"That's easy for you to say because your people already do it... it comes easy to them... and to you." Dalwan knew that somehow this conversation would come down to him having to be the leader and live all these principles as some sort of example to everyone else. Shaylan always did this to him, too. He was only sixteen now and resented being put in the position of being a leader just because he was born with lots of potential skill and power in the arts.

"It's no problem fer me ta live this way, lad. Ya're very correct," answered Darric as he turned to Fallwyn and Myletan, "Is this a problem fer either of you?"

"None for me!" said Fallwyn with a big smile and a wink.

"Nor fer one such as I," said Myletan with a firm nod of his head and a serious look that betrayed only the slightest hint of a smile.

"'Tis simple as a song ta spend hours doing work that no one 'ill ever notice... tha'tis if ya do it well enough," there was just a hint of a father's scolding tone in his voice as Darric spoke.

"As a matter of a fact," continued Fallwyn, "in my land, much of our service isn't ever noticed at all. We do it because we care about our country and our society. There are those among us who are available to orchestrate our duties, but they are generally the only ones who know for sure what each of us do in our voluntary public service."

Myletan continued, "There are lots of opportunities ta show off... and dwarves love ta do just that as much as the elves and even your race. Our competition is in fun an' there are rewards from time ta time... but the fun is in the sport, not the reward."

"If ya're gonna be a lover of such a life, ya can live it wherever ya want," Darric said as he stepped up and took hold of Dalwan by the shoulders to get his undivided attention. "We don't do it because our society does, we do it because we love our society. Our land and countrymen benefit from this. It's b'come the way o' life fer us as much as honorin' an' protectin' our resources is part of our life. It's b'come our heritage."

Dalwan felt totally overwhelmed, like a schoolboy surrounded and trapped by a handful of kind but adamant teachers. "You make it sound so simple...too simple!!..."

"But i'tis simple lad! Not easy... never easy... just simple. All ya need ta do is know what ya want ta be an' decided why. Then keep it before ya like a beautiful vision... let the results bring ya yer reward. The rest 'ill be just circumstances."

At this, Fallwyn cut in, "and share your vision... your motivation with others... a little at a time... if only when you perceive someone to be interested in some way or another."

Dalwan wasn't feeling much stronger, nor was his resolve growing.

"So many among all the races have neglected developing their arts," continued the voice with music in it, "but you have gone to great lengths to develop yours...Why? Wasn't it too much work? And you've gone to great lengths to remain undiscovered by your countrymen... was it worth it?"

Fallwyn's magic cut through Dalwan's despair; he felt himself shaking his head in agreement with Fallwyn's every word. His mind then cleared, and he blurted out, "Yeah, but hold on here! They made me practice... and the only way I could survive was to hide when I did practice," he said as if throwing in a tidbit of information they had overlooked.

"But the choice was still yours... you did what you felt was best and followed both counsel and instruction from those you trusted... right?" Again, the magic voice charmed away his objections and dulled his nervous edge.

"We here are among the most accomplished an' multigifted o' all the races," said Darric, looking for agreement from Myletan and Fallwyn, who affirmed with solid nods. "I'tis our faith in each other, an' common perspective o' life that makes it possible fer us ta do some o' the most amazin' things, things we've done tagether."

Myletan had moved to an exposed part of the stone wall and called out to Dalwan, "Even in our sportin' times we work together ta have the most fun we can... watch!"

He pulled out a short sword that began to glow and shimmer like a heat mirage in the desert. He thrust it into the stone wall and cut out a small conical chunk with one stroke. He tossed it into the air, and instantly, intense white flame streaked from Darric's hands and shattered it into liquid drops that fell toward Fallwyn, who had formed something like a pale green curtain of light that spread from his upheld, outstretched hands to the floor. The drops hit the curtain and flowed together into a molten puddle at his feet, which began to solidify into the consistency of putty. The curtain vanished, and Myletan touched the floor on both sides of the thickening blob. It began to pull together into a sphere. No sooner than it was a complete ball, it rose off the floor. As it began to float above the stone pavement, Myletan's hands formed a cup directly under it about a long handbreadth away. He raised it to the level of his own chest. When it stabilized, Darric put a mild flame to it and replenished its diminishing glow. As it warmed again, its liquified inside began to slowly move in a swirl of color. Fallwyn began to sing in tones that seemed as if there were many harmonic notes together simultaneously in one enchanting sound. As he did, he began to circle the floating orb with his palms, only a couple of fingers' distance away from its glowing surface. To Dalwan's amazement, neither Fallwyn nor Myletan was burned nor even seemed to experience any effect of the heat from the orb. It began to spin, slowly at first, then faster and faster. Fallwyn's hands began to shimmer like the curtain had, only this time they were clearly blue. The ball grew in size as it spun and cooled, until it was about twice its original size. Fallwyn moved to the side of the orb, opposite Dalwan. Fallwyn's hand continued to glow with the blue shimmering light.

"Look into the floating ball, Dalwan," requested Fallwyn, hoping that he could see the patterns created by the magic light he was putting inside of it.

As he did, he looked intently, not knowing exactly what he was looking for, he could see a scene of himself clearly pictured inside the spinning ball. He saw the testing chamber and the test of the sword. It was a perfect picture with crystal clear images, even the most intricate details clearly visible, down to the very sparkle in Darric's eyes and the etched runes in the blade of the sword. Dalwan wondered if the others could see the image.

A voice of crystalline tone and purity broke Dalwan's trance, "What do you think about that, Dalwan?"

The orb was no longer spinning. Myletan was holding it in his hands, extending it toward Dalwan. "Go ahead, grab hold of it and take a look. The outside was a combination of mostly clear glasslike material mixed with occasional milky looking swirls. Dalwan took it carefully. As he turned it, something like sparkles of fire jumped back and forth inside it.

"It's wonderful! What is it?"

Childlike glances of humor and inquisitiveness were exchanged between the three participants. They all moved a little closer to investigate.

Fallwyn looked at the other three again, then said, "We don't know." Fallwyn was joined in laughter by the others. "It's just a piece of rock we filled with magic," he said as he reached to touch its top.

Suddenly, the ball lit up and began to glow in very bright colors, like sunlight through stained glass. Then, just as suddenly, it went bright white. The others moved even closer to take a better look. There followed a wild confusion of images dancing inside it, so hectic in fact that it caused all of the observers to lose their equilibrium.

"Clear your mind, Fallwyn," shouted Dalwan with childlike excitement. "Let my mind control it."

"Go!" answered a calm, enchanted voice.

Dalwan sought out Shaylan's presence. Suddenly, Shaylan's image appeared in the light. It was fuzzy at first, but cleared within a short time. He was talking with a distinguished-looking dwarf.

"Look there!" whispered Myletan, "the Supreme!"

"Wish I could hear what they're sayin'," remarked Darric in an equally hushed voice.

Suddenly appeared an aura appeared around the orb that began to vibrate in concentric waves, racing around and then outward toward the watchers. Then came the sound. Their voices had the same overall tone that Fallwyn's did, but were unmistakably identifiable with those who were speaking. All four bent forward a little more to hear.

"Yes, that is correct, sir." Shaylan was talking. "He is with Darric as we speak."

The Supreme spoke next, apparently continuing the conversation, "When they return, we'll need ta assure that their plans are not hindered. Dalwan will be accompanied by a very select group. No one but you and those they chose ta tell 'ill know o' their mission or even that they are in any way especially connected to Dalwan."

"Very well, sir."

"And one more thing," the Supreme hesitated to ensure full undistracted attention.

Shaylan straightened up and made strong eye contact with the Supreme, "Go ahead, sir, you have my devotion."

"You'll not interfere with their mission save on view o' the surely imminent death of Dalwan." The Supreme stood staring at Shaylan, obviously waiting for some sort of reaction. After receiving a very nebulous nod from him, he continued. "Weigh these words carefully because many things may happen that may be designed ta distract or throw off a perceived adversary. Use yer sensin' power. Yours is indeed among the strongest I've witnessed."

"I take it, sir, that this is part of the covenants between the lands?"

"That is correct... and though unwritten, it is by far the most important ta the success o' this joint venture. You..."

The vision suddenly vanished.

All four of them stared in wonder at the orb as it continued to glow and display an ever-shifting variety of shadowy images.

Fallwyn removed his hands from the crystalline sphere, and the images ceased. He was more than pleased with the results of the exercise and amazed that their demonstration had worked so much more completely than they had anticipated. Dalwan had been able to see in the three of them what potential was possible when they worked together. But the next step had been accomplished quite by accident. He and Dalwan had mixed their arts together unwittingly and accomplished a most amazing result, completely unforeseen by any of those present. They had observed something in the orb that neither of them had seen in the past.

Fallwyn broke the retrospective silence, feeling an even deeper kinship with Dalwan than he had before. "We were able to do these things because we have each worked very hard, perfecting our arts. We believed practice to be important, so we continue even to this day. Your work has been alone, for the most part, until today. The three of us have done this before, but never with the results we got today. We worked together because we wanted to. In our society, we do the same thing for the same reasons. We believe in what we are doing and are not willing to compromise it or give it up even if some or even all of our countrymen do."

At this point, Darric continued, "The simplicity, lad, is in the fact that we've already decided how... that is, upon which principles, we intend to live. This IS us!... not what we do, but instead, what we are! Our countrymen 'ill not change this."

"Not much glory though," added Myletan, "mostly work... mostly unnoticed... the satisfaction comes from the quality an' value of yer own accomplishments."

Dalwan's senses were frayed. This seemed like far too much at one time. "Why are you doing all this to me... all at the same time... If I'm supposed to be some sort of apprentice of yours, you gotta give me some time to grow up. Don't get me wrong, I believe in all this... and you make me feel like I really can do it... but I'm no hero, ya know... I'm still just a kid with a lot of power."

Myletan walked forward and, facing Dalwan, took hold of both his shoulders with a hardy slap, "No ma friend...ya're not a kid any longer... ya'll never again be, nor have ya been far some time now, a kid!" Myletan's eyes etched a message in his mind... "'Tis time fer ya ta grow up!"

Dalwan wished that these dwarf and elf sorts would quit undressing his soul. He wanted to run and hide, but decided that this was a time for strength and resolve. The feeling vanished. He was going to make up his own mind, not let these folks, however complimentary they were, determine his thinking and future.

"You can't do this to me!" said Dalwan, defiantly pulling free of Myletan's grasp. "You can't make me into something I'm not." His tone was cool and confident now.

"What of all this don't you think is 'YOU'?" said Darric, meeting the coolness with a challenge.

Dalwan's cool defiance began to heat up around the edges, "This adult... this hero... this 'lead the people by example junk'... and I am too just a kid!"

"We've not told ya how ya must live... we've only answered yer questions. Admittedly, we've been forceful in our depictions, but yer life is the same now as when ya came ta us... it's yers ta live and yers ta decides how," answered Darric in a very matter-of-fact, detached tone.

"But one way or another," said Fallwyn, in his soothing, crystalline voice, "you'll never be a 'kid' again. You can laugh and play as we do. You can enjoy every moment, just like we do... but you are a powermaster... your magic has forced you into adulthood. We have simply shown you an alternative to living in the feudal and wasteful ways predominant with most of your leaders... an alternative we sensed would be acceptable and even desirable to you."

"But I'm no hero!"

"Don't worry 'bout bein' a hero then. Just live the way ya believe is best, in the little things ya do," added Myletan, trying to instill confidence in Dalwan.

"In whatever ya do be true ta yerself, lad...TA YERSELF!" finished Darric in truly fatherly fashion. "I've heard what ya believe. It's right thinkin' on yer part... it's best for you and fer yer kinsman. Hold on ta it, think about these things, dream about them... live 'em and experience 'em... even if no one else around ya does. After all, we're not suggestin' that ya live a life ya don't understand or love... just be true ta what ya already believe. It'll fill ya with peace and confidence because yer actions 'ill not violate who ya are."

Dalwan was amazed at what had taken place. They had taken him on an emotional wild rapids ride to get him to the place where he would at least be willing to try and live a life among his people that would, by nature, be an exemplary lifestyle. They had invested a great deal of energy into this effort. There was nothing casual about it. He knew that all this instruction and encouragement were because he was a powermaster. Everything told him that it was their specific intention to ensure that he ended up with the sword, Fallonrod. He knew instinctively that they would be very cautious about letting the sword fall into the wrong hands. "All of this," he thought to himself, "must be preparation for receiving the sword... maybe the sword's magic was somehow sensitive to motives...?"

"OK! I won't let you down," he said with resignation to this fate filling his voice, "I'll do the right thing."

Ignoring the downbeat tone in his voice, Darric slapped Dalwan on the back, "Good lad! GOOD!"

He then turned to Myletan with a victorious look in his eye and gleeful anticipation in his voice and said loudly, "The sword, most excellent Myletan! Bring on the sword!"

Myletan hurried to the back of the meeting hall and vanished right through the wall. He returned a brief moment later with a long leather pouch having a flap at one end secured against the sides with straps of leather. As he approached the others, the straps untied by themselves and the flap rolled up like a scroll.

Myletan reached in and pulled out a sword with a magnificent hilt, housed in a silver-trimmed hard leather scabbard. He turned the hilt end toward Dalwan and said, "Draw yer sword, Dalwan."

It slid effortlessly from its housing. Dalwan had not known what to expect as it was unsheathed, so he prepared his senses for bright light, a surge of power, intense heat, but not for what he found... a much heavier than he expected, very cold, ornate sword... no magic!

He held it up then swung it around a little, without attempting to apply any magic to it. The swinging of the sword caused his companions to move back a bit and give him respectfully cautious room. It was perfectly balanced.

"Does it have a name?"

"We just call it 'sword'," mused Myletan.

"How imaginative," said Dalwan with a smirk.

Dalwan began to move around with it, putting it through battle stances and routines. The room was well lit by an array of beautiful torches, but when he moved near the wall, his body cast his shadow on the blade, and he noticed a faint glow. He immediately stopped. The others watched in amusement as he sought out a place where the lamps were not so bright and he could get a better look.

"It glows! I haven't put any magic to it... how..." his puzzled look was met with laughter from the others.

Fallwyn moved quickly to Dalwan's side and took the sword with a serious look on his face but bold laughter in his eyes. Turning to the light and holding it up, he said, "There's no light in this." He turned back and handed it to Dalwan. The others were holding their breath to keep from laughing out loud.

Dalwan gave Fallwyn a wary glance while taking the sword and turning to shade the blade.

"OK, you jokers!"

They all broke out laughing.

"I know what I saw... the sword glows... I saw the glow in the shadow," he said while studying the smiling faces of his comically stumped companions. "What? Is this some kind of trick? Did you make this sword look like Fallonrod? I know that Fallonrod glows because of its great power. How does...uh... 'Sword' glow?"

Fallwyn, still sporting a broad grin, again took the sword from Dalwan and held it up. "The glow in this sword is the same glow that Fallonrod possesses. It is an art of the elves. It is a night glow. Its purpose is to allow its wielder to locate it at night. It can be turned on and off at will."

"Then all these years that Fallonrod has been glowing, with everyone assuming it was because of its great power, it was nothing more than a night light?"

"That's a sure thing, lad!" laughed Myletan.

"And it can be turned on and off at will?"

"Correct again," answered Fallwyn while putting 'Sword' back in its case, "Strap it on. We'll practice later. The light's off now. Better leave it that way until we need it."

Myletan picked up the orb and studied it as the others prepared to leave. Darric was already working the conical hole left in the stone by Myletan's short sword. He smoothed it over, leaving a hollow spot in the wall under a shallow skin of remolded stone.

Fallwyn joined Myletan in his inquisitive admiration of their strange creation. "Myletan, my friend, what do you make of this? It seems to heighten the sensing arts."

"That it does. Seems that there's much ta learn about it. I say we take it with us an' test it again on other subjects."

Myletan held up the globe, "Darric, any objections ta us takin' along our new toy?"

"Not as far as I'm concerned. What do yer senses tell ya, Fallwyn?"

After a brief pause for sensing, "Not safe, but useful!"

"Worth the chance?"

Another moment of pause, "Yes, worth the chance!"

"Then let's secure it an' be on our way. Myletan, bring Fallwyn some cloth and a skin if there's some close by."

Myletan trotted off again toward the back and through the magic door. He returned shortly with a roll of deep blue material and the complete skin of a medium sized animal. He handed them to Fallwyn, who went to work first with the fabric.

He wrapped the cloth around the crystal orb and, holding it while singing in low tones, it began to reweave in successive layers around the ball until it was six layers deep.

He then took the skin and began to fuse its edges around the cloth cocoon. When he was finished, the object looked for all intents and purposes like a large water skin, complete with saddle horn strap.

Myletan just stood staring as Fallwyn worked his magic. Dalwan was also impressed but noticed something very different between his reaction and that of Myletan. He, himself, felt a little envy, or maybe it was competition, mixed with his admiration. But not so with Myletan. It was pure admiration. No facade, no jealousy, just childlike, exhilarating admiration. This was strange to Dalwan. Myletan had caused the ball and the sword to float in mid-air. Dalwan had never seen that done. Myletan had forged the magic sword. Myletan had created a short sword that cut right through stone as if it were cheese. And now he stood in awe of Fallwyn, offering the gift of uncensored praise to his equal. "How different from the ways of man", he thought to himself, "how foreign to our nature."

Dalwan's thoughts were interrupted by a shout that came from Fallwyn just in time to alert him to the object flying in his direction. He barely had time to see it before he caught the now-disguised crystal, which had been tossed to him by Fallwyn.

"That should protect it from just about everything. Let's go finish our preparations for the quest." There was an unmistakable singing in Fallwyn's voice.

"What quest? Where are we going? Aren't we going back to Castle Crest?"

Myletan was close enough to Dalwan to grab him from the back and spin him around. Face to face, he took hold of Dalwan, pinning his arms against his sides and with a wide-eyed, broad-faced smile exclaimed, "Didn't ya hear the voices in the crystal orb, lad? We're goin' with ya. But, like the Supreme said, 'Not a soul's ta know!'" he finished in a whisper.

In Myletan's enthusiasm, he had partially lifted Dalwan off the ground, and when he let go, Dalwan had to dance a bit to maintain his balance.

As Dalwan was regaining his footing, it suddenly dawned on him that everyone was ready to go with him on a quest he wasn't fully apprised of. The Supreme already knew all the details... even those about him... apparently more about him than he now knows himself. Dalwan felt a little irritation that he had no idea what was going to happen, but this dwarf leader, whom he had never met, seemed to know the strategy of the plan and was somehow involved in choosing his companions and intimidating his friends.

About the time his irritation started to heat up toward anger, his thinking was stunned with the realization that it would be a great relief to have these new acquaintances with him on this adventure. He did feel safe with them, albeit somewhat in the dark. Shaylan seemed to be comfortable with this arrangement, or at least agreed to it. He decided that it must be a great honor to be considered a member of such a group as he had the fortune to fall in with... "Some luck!" he thought, "luck had very little to do with it... it was still a good fortune." He made up his mind to go along with them and consider it a privilege.

Suddenly, Dalwan realized that Darric was pulling him toward the door through which the other had already passed. "Let's be on our way, lad. Time enough ta daydream later."

Dalwan, Darric, Fallwyn, and Myletan arrived back at the conference grounds about dinner time. Dalwan carried the new sword in an old, black, unadorned scabbard. Fallwyn covered the hilt with a small black bag, which he custom fit around it so it wouldn't draw unnecessary attention. Dalwan laughed to himself as Fallwyn finished his work on the little bag, thinking how nervous Rhem would get if someone were to put this type of customary elven cover on his sword, in a politically sensitive situation that he was forced to allow. He doubted that Rhem's sword was ever in the scabbard long enough to ever need the protection from tarnishing or rain that the cover provided.

"The less attention to the sword, the better for us. You may uncover it after we leave for Castle Crest," said Fallwyn as he made the final adjustments to the bag.

"From this time on, we'll need ta treat each other as casual acquaintances... formal, not comfortable an' certainly not too friendly. No one among yer company must suspect our mutual alliance an' personal involvement with each other nor the quest we occupy ourselves with," said Darric as he watched and sensed Dalwan's response.

"No problem!" exclaimed Dalwan in strong, confident response.

"Excellent, Dalwan! Excellent!" Darric and Fallwyn were both clearly very pleased, but Dalwan didn't know exactly why.

Picking it up from there, Fallwyn continued, "We'll contact you when it's time to switch the swords. We may not be at liberty to discuss with you whatever plan we devise before we attempt it."

Darric cut in excitedly, "You'll need ta depend upon yer senses ta understand what's happenin', an' then trust us ta create an appropriate diversion."

"Our situation may be such that we'll only be able to casually suggest that you accompany us," continued Fallwyn. "It may be entirely up to you to act on your own in switching the swords when the appropriate time comes. You must use your senses and act swiftly without consideration for us."

Fallwyn and Darric stood looking expectantly at Dalwan, who stood listening expectantly for their next instruction. With eyes still fixed on Dalwan, they asked simultaneously, "Well?" Their voices were so perfectly timed that it sounded as if only one person had spoken. This in turn caused them to turn slowly toward each other with eyebrows raised and sheepish grins on their faces. With his eyes still turned in a humorous gesture toward Fallwyn, Darric said, "Dalwan, do ya understand and agree?"

Trying to understand how they could be so easily amused when he felt so terribly solemn, he answered reverently, "You have my word!"

It was difficult for Dalwan to understand how these very talented friends could be so easily distracted and amused by such small things as speaking the same word together at the same time. He was beginning to think that they were not as serious about this venture as he was. But then again, they were the ones who had managed to arrange everything, even to the point that the Supreme knew of the plans before he did. Even his traveling companions had been chosen and relationships established in detail before he was made aware that any plans even existed. It all seemed confusing. One moment, they are logistical geniuses, and the next minute, they are children at play. But to Dalwan, the stakes were too high to be taken lightly. Even switching the swords could be looked upon as treason of the highest order and death prescribed for the offender. But they treated it as little more than a fantastic adventure wrapped up in fun, secrecy, and strategically planned surprises. All he knew for sure was that he had bound himself to them in this adventure and, despite the unknowns, felt oddly comfortable and secure in their company.

"What should I tell Shaylan?" asked Dalwan as they prepared to separate.

"Just be patient, lad... everythin' in its proper order," said Darric with a wink and a reassuring smile.

They parted ways just before they entered the conference grounds, and each one went in a different direction. Myletan and Fallwyn went together, and Dalwan accompanied Darric.

CHAPTER 19

It did not take long for the news of Shahandra's adventure to reach the surrounding villages. With every new telling, her powers increased and her feats were enlarged. In the villages south of the castle, the story surfaced as a tale of a girl receiving power from an enchanted forest, and from that metamorphosed into a fabulous report of power so great that she was able to create an enchanted garden and forest from which she could speak with the dead and look easily into anyone's private life. Many people considered it fortunate that she was such a kind girl; otherwise, such power might be used maliciously.

****

Due to the raiding of outer villages, a large number of refugees and other strangers were passing through the villages near Brandon Keep in search of safe dwelling or in transit to some relative's home. Two such men happened into a make-shift village which had sprung up near the river at the entrance road to the castle. One of the men, Dorslin, was half a head taller than the next tallest man in the village. He looked, acted, and moved like a fighting man. The other, Moric, his companion, was a frumpy-looking man, head and shoulders shorter than Dorslin. He was balding and wore a short sword clumsily at his side. They found an open air pub and proceeded to inquire about the strange power they had sensed two days before. They explained that their village had been raided by a madman whose companions looted and destroyed their homes, killing all who stood up to them or who failed to escape. The two men announced that they were seeking to avenge themselves against this marauder by joining those in power who might be willing to stand against him. They hoped to find the one who wielded the great power they had sensed two days earlier.

The two men attracted an audience, as did anyone bearing a story about this malicious man and his ruinous friends. Most of the people who joined in the conversation had a story to tell about the mysterious power that had been experienced by many sensors. Each had a slightly different rendition, but the bottom line was that a very powerful girl had killed several dangerous men who had been responsible for a series of robberies and murders, allegedly in pursuit of their victim's weapons. She then created a magic forest at the south end of the valley from which she was able to look into any place in the land and find any person she might wish to locate.

"Was it possible", thought Dorslin, "that the men who were dispatched by Danlion to collect weapons for the campaign had all been killed? How could that be? They were among the most elite fighters in Danlion's dangerous little army. Would a girl of magic be wise enough in her use of power to defeat trained mercenaries?"

Moric found it difficult to believe that the powerful and focused sensation of intrusion that he had experienced with Danlion had been created by a girl... but the stories they heard seemed to be too coincidentally precise to be ignored. "Why was I the only one to sense the mysterious magical invasion?", he thought to himself, "unless.." he began to feel like such a fool, "unless the others were afraid and lied to protect themselves from potential danger!" He felt betrayed by his own simple-mindedness... "Of course, they knew it would bring them trouble. But being caught by Danlion in a lie would easily have brought a worse fate!" This made him feel a tiny bit better, realizing that he was such a bad liar that it didn't even take magic to detect it.

Moric was brought out of his daydream by Dorslin, who slapped him on the back as he stood to leave. It made Moric bite the end of his tongue, which characteristically stuck out of his open mouth when he daydreamed or slept in a sitting position. He immediately whelped like an injured pup. This brought laughter and jesting from bystanders. Moric called a curse on them all as he stood up from his chair and promptly stumbled and almost fell down. That put the entire pub into a roar of laughter as the two men left.

"There now, Moric", said Dorslin in his smooth baritone voice, "doesn't it make you feel good to give these poor hard-timers a nice laugh?"

"I'd feel better to see them burn," came the harsh nasal reply.

"All in due time", laughed Dorslin as he slapped Moric on the back so hard that he almost fell down again, "all in due time, my impatient little friend."

Moric hated being hit by this monster of a man, but could not figure out what to do about it. "Some day Dorslin", he thought with violence, "some day you'll be sorry you treated me this way." After all, he knew that they had to work together for now. They had strong but tolerant contempt for each other. Such was the case in most of the relationships between those who joined with Danlion...all in all, not a very amicable bunch.

****

Living at the North end of the valley and far into the rocky hills to the east and north were the various clans of Rocklin squatches.

They were generally a peaceful lot, only fighting to protect their immediate territory. They were, by and large, an ugly, smelly bunch with stooped posture, flat heads, fat noses, and too much unkept hair all over their body...not enough to be called fur but so much that their bodily features were obscured by it. They were hunters and scavengers, eating everything from bugs to animals, roots to leafy vegetation. They were very clannish and superstitious. They had the mental capacity of about a five-year-old human child. Off and on through the generations, men had tried to find ways to take advantage of their brutish strength. The problem was that the squatches were not selfish, aggressive nor greedy, so once they had their immediate needs met, they quit working. If captured or coerced into working, they became very depressed and, if unable to escape, soon died. It took so much effort to gain the desired results that exploiters gave up on them.

There had been several attempts to commit genocide against them in the past centuries, but the squatches proved to be very hard to kill and very dangerous to fight against as a group. The squatches did not use regular weapons; they used rocks. Their long, powerful arms could throw a large rock a tremendous distance with enormous momentum. The squatches always kept piles of appropriately sized throwing rocks throughout their camp for just such eventualities. They seldom ventured into the flat lands, preferring to remain in the rocky mountainous areas where they could more aptly protect themselves and where men seldom ventured.

There was also the issue of Dragons. It seems that there remained some strong tie between the squatches and certain dragons reaching far back into the past. Many casual observers felt certain that the squatches worshiped the dragons. The rumor has been widely spread that on a monthly basis, dragons would visit troll villages and, with each visit, the squatches would sacrifice one or more of their own to the beast in exchange for the dragon's pledge to protect the clan. Men considered this to be an advantage in that a few squatches would disappear, and the dragons didn't need to hunt as much food (cattle and other livestock would be safer)... they only really need one heavy meal a month and a few snacks to keep going strong.

The truth, of course, was much different. Many generations of squatches ago, when they were more migratory, a clan of squatches happened upon a small dragon lair late one afternoon. It was situated in a narrow rock-walled canyon with a small, fast-running stream flowing through it.

The squatches first noticed it when they spied a rather large, freshly dead dragon lying near the mouth of a cavern in the canyon wall. The dragon appeared to the squatches to be warming himself in the afternoon sun. Having a very healthy respect for such beasts, the clan crossed the creek and hid among the rocks and ledges on the far wall of the canyon to watch the dragon. They waited with animated expectation to see it move, and hopefully fly, something they enjoyed very much but seldom ever witnessed from a close vantage point. After a short time of watching nothing happen, a time that seemed like an eternity for the restless squatches, they decided that five of the largest of their number would venture to the other side and investigate. The small band circled wide upstream and worked their way back on a series of ledges to a place directly over the cave entrance. Though generally an intrepid group, they did pick up throwing stones in each hand as they approached the outcropping marking the top of the cavern opening. They were standing directly over the dead beast when a piercing roar came from within the cavern. All five squatches took giant jumps backwards, causing loose rocks and debris to fall over the side onto the motionless beast. The others on the far side of the canyon were on their feet, every muscle tensed, every hand containing a rock.

The sound was that of a large cave lion, a sound that, if ignored, could cost a troll his life. There was no sound or movement for a few brief moments. The tense silence was suddenly shattered by a different sound, a squeal of pain, followed by another roar. A heartbeat later, a baby dragon dashed out of the cavern mouth at a full run, stumbled on the rocks, and began rolling down the canyon wall yelping. In a flash, the lion bounded out in pursuit of his prey. In two giant leaps, he was upon the baby beast and came up holding its back leg in his powerful jaws. The dragon yelped and screamed, kicking and twisting helplessly and to no avail.

Almost as if driven by a single will, the five nearby watchers let fly their granite missiles, all of which pounded heavily into the unsuspecting cat, knocking it sideways down the canyon wall a little further. It did not let its fresh catch go but instead struggled to regain its foothold. It had no sooner steadied itself than it was hit with another volley of stones, one of which clearly broke the front left leg. The giant cat let go of the dragon as it fell screeching and writhing to the ground.

The now dazed little dragon limped away as a third round of rocks, this time from both sides of the canyon, battered and bloodied the cat. With fresh stones in their hands, they stood and watched as the lion convulsed and finally lay motionless.

The little dragon had stopped crawling and was lying very still with eyes wide open and very shallow, rapid breathing. The squatches approached the cat first and quickly removed its head with their crude stone knives. By the time this was completed, the other members of the clan had joined them. Together, they went to the dragon and surrounded it. It did not move or blink, but continued its shallow breathing. Seeing the wounded leg, two of the larger squatches picked it up and carried it to the creek with all the others jumping and yelling in excitement as they followed. Though just a baby, it was fully as heavy as a medium-sized male troll. They found a pool of water in a small side eddy and placed their little patient role in it. The two largest squatches washed its legs carefully. Several of the bravest young squatches joined in pouring water over the whole body and gently stroking it.

Then the clan mother was called (she was the oldest, wisest female troll, and functioned like a medicine woman). She carried a crude sack made of skins, which she used to hold the tools and medicines of her ancient trade. She packed the wound with some mud, which she mixed with herbs. She then wrapped the mud pack with several large leaves and bound them in place with thin, preshrunk leather strips.

It was only after she had completed her work that they spied a very large, very alive dragon watching them from the rim of the canyon. The alarm was sounded, and all but the two squatches who had carried the dragon fled back to the other side of the canyon and hid among the rocks directly across from the cavern.

The remaining two carried the baby back up the canyon wall to the cavern entrance, then fled to join the others.

Before they reached the other side, the ancient creature had spread its monstrous wings and was gliding effortlessly in a circular motion downward, finishing with a long glide up the canyon. It landed at the cavern entrance. Immediately, the baby began what sounded like whining as it dragged itself toward the much larger dragon. The larger dragon put its nose up to the bandaged leg for a moment, then raised its head and looked directly at the hiding squatches on the far side of the canyon. It then began a series of noises that sounded as if it were talking with the little one. To the squatches' utter amazement, the little one answered. After a few moments of continued conversation between the dragons, which included some apparent comforting and nuzzling, the dragon retrieved the lion carcass and, with two wing strokes, flew across the canyon, landing somewhat precariously about its own length away from the squatches. It laid the lion down and stepped back a few paces. There was ancient magic at work as they felt compelled to advance. Cautiously, they walked forward, stopping with each step only to continue the next with less fear. When they had crossed about half the distance between them and the lion carcass, the dragon gently stepped forward and nuzzled the carcass toward them, causing them to cheer and run the remaining distance to the lion.

Before any of the older squatches could stop them, three of the youngest ones ran the remaining distance to the dragon and began to stroke and pat its lowered giant head (which was easily as thick as the little ones were tall). The others instantly froze. The elders called out for the children to come back as the others waited, breath held and every muscle tensed. The three children did not respond to the call but just kept laughing and petting the dragon's head. Suddenly, the rest of the young squatches, at least those who were not physically restrained by terrified parents, ran to the dragon, laughing and frolicking. This in turn caused the dragon to laugh...a laugh like smoky thunder. The children shrieked with delight. The dragon had lain his head down flat on the ground to allow the children to climb on him, a gesture quickly responded to by the playful troll babies.

A very subtle voice began to speak in the minds of the adult squatches. It was not as much in words as feelings. It calmed their fears, it spoke peace and friendship, it called them to join their children. The great magical beast had called the children and was now calling them as well.

Over the next weeks, the squatches shared the cavern with the dragons. The children took the little dragon down to the stream every day to bathe its leg. The baby loved the attention, and the children loved the dragon. After they were finished, the clan mother would dress the wound. The larger dragon was still mourning the loss of his companion, whose body he had drug up the canyon and cremated. The clan mother had no medicine for such ailments of the heart except tenderness, which she was always very liberal with.

By the next full moon, the leg was healed. The larger dragon told the squatches that he and his baby had to leave and find another home with other dragons. The dragon provided the Elder with a smooth, round, clear stone about the size of two fists doubled up. He instructed the Elder to place it in a large open area on the morning before the full moon every month. He promised to return to them each month, wherever they traveled. The stone would guide him to them.

Thus began the monthly rendezvous between the dragons and the squatches. The squatches kept the tradition of their ancestors up to the very present. After quite a few seasons, the little dragon flew well enough to come with the larger one and finally replaced him altogether, continuing the tradition of his father, up to the present without fail. Without fail, that is, until this month! This month, he did not come. The clan waited and waited. They repositioned the ancient stone. They washed it and relocated it in the clearing...anxiously anticipating their friend, anderon! He had always come before the sun was halfway through its course. The children played at the edge of the lake, one eye always on the horizon, each hoping to be the first to spy his low-flying image. He never came.

Finally, it was dark. They decided to leave a fire going near the stone and stationed two of the young adults to stay with it and watch, just in case he came late.

The clan with the stone, the Holders, always invited at least two others, of the over 30 or so neighboring clans, to attend each month.

In the morning, the three clans that had gathered for the event took counsel together to decide what, if anything, they could do about this strange incident. They decided to send six adult males to find out what had happened and to perhaps help if he was ill or in need.

The next day, they set out to find the dragon. Their only help was a mental image the dragon had set in their minds of his home and the surrounding hills and forest. They were cheered and wished well as they left.

****

Meanwhile, Moric and Dorslin made their way back to Danlion's borrowed house. They told him all the news about Shahandra's adventure and her great powers. Danlion became enraged.

"She can't have had these powers long, or we would have sensed her work before", he murmured in a guttural hiss. "We must stop her before she discovers how to use her newfound powers!" He looked around, sensing the attitudes of his chosen companions.

"Are you frightened by this fledgling magician, by this GIRL?" said Danlion sarcastically, clearly mocking them all.

They shuffled nervously, but none answered.

"We need to take that castle and put out the fire of this girl's magic", came the words which Danlion mixed with such magical manipulation that everyone in the room was swayed in his direction as if drunken into an obedient stupor. Only Dorslin remained unaffected.

"We must take the castle," he said again with each word slowly spoken and clearly articulated in deep melodious tones, "we must take the castle...we must take the castle..." Each time he spoke the words, his mesmerized followers fell deeper into his spell. Over and over, he chanted it as he walked through the crowd, each one with glazed-eyed stares. As he spoke, several of those present lipped the chant with but a whisper, leaving their mouths.

The quiet rumble of Dorslin's voice cut through the air, "Lord Danlion. Your magic alone can't take the castle. You can turn these fools into slaves who'll die for you, but that won't gain you victory either. We need a larger army."

"A larger army or a smarter army with a good ploy, Master Dorslin," retorted Danlion with a hideous yellow-toothed grin.

"I'm pleased to know that you have a plan. I, for my part, will not be easily swayed to throw my life away on a lusty whim." Dorslin spoke dispassionately as he wiped off a small throwing knife he kept sheathed up the sleeve of his tunic.

"You are mistaken! I do not have a solid plan. But by this time tomorrow I will!" He spoke slowly as he walked toward Dorslin without breaking eye contact. "And, I will not tolerate any challenge to my authority!"

"Dorslin stood and faced Danlion as he approached. He showed no emotion. "I've given you my allegiance freely. I have fought for you, killed for you, and tolerated fools for companions in order to serve you. I do so for reward and for adventure. I do not commit my allegiance loosely, and I do not take my responsibilities lightly. But I will question foolish endeavors and purely emotional quests..." His eyes squinted as he continued speaking to the now stationary, glaring Danlion. "I do not serve arrogance!... Greed?... maybe if it includes my interests... intelligent power? Certainly!" Looking around at the pathetic cowardice displayed on the faces of his companions, "This group does not inspire me with any deep sense of personal loyalty or patriotism. I will serve you of my own will, for personal gain, or I won't serve you at all."

"Do you see me as a fool, Dorslin?" Squinted eyes, furrowed into the ancient wrinkles of Danlion's face, added to the impact of the question laced with malice.

Dorslin answered in a casual tone, seemingly without regard for the obvious threat imposed by Danlion, "I only suggest that you worry less about passionate revenge and focus your great power and abundant experience on becoming a strong but tolerable ruler. If all you wish to do is make a generation of people pay for what happened to you two hundred years ago at the hands of their relatives, whose names most of these people have forgotten, then you waste your life and ours."

Danlion paused a moment in reflection. A smile crept across his face, and the hint of a sparkle entered his eyes. "You shall be my public affairs officer should we succeed." The tone in his voice picked up a hint of humor. He was amazed at the ease with which Dorslin was able to defuse an intense situation and bring a face-saving remedy without violence. It amused Danlion. "Maybe," he thought, "I could really become a credible ruler if I could find the means of surrounding myself with men like Dorslin to buffer me from the contemptible masses." He had not actually considered a reign of power and reason. Cruelty and terror were much easier tools and required no rational negotiating talents or energies. He decided to consider it later. "For now," he said while turning away from Dorslin, "we must consider our next step in light of the significantly small forces we have at our disposal," he said, finishing with a conciliatory nod toward Dorslin.

There was a corporate sigh of relief from all those gathered. No blood... no burnt flesh... no familiar face turned to ash... no sickening clean up!

Dorslin and his minions left the house and went to the camp of his followers, which was located in a forested area surrounding a small natural pond in a rocky canyon. It was late afternoon when they arrived. They had not been in the camp very long when they heard a commotion at the top of the rocky ridge above the camp. There were yells and screams for help. The camp went to full alarm. Men were running with weapons in hand for the ridge path when suddenly a man flew off the edge of the canyon wall, backwards. Something huge moved into the forest from the exact place the man departed the cliff.

"Squatches!" shouted a man closer to the top. It was echoed by others back into the camp.

"Why squatches? Why here?" said Danlion almost under his breath. "Don't kill them!" he shouted. Then, realizing that his voice was too weak to be heard over the noise, he grabbed Dorslin, "Tell the fools not to kill them."

Dorslin's voice carried well, and the message began to work its way to the top of the cliffs.

Danlion was now moving toward the ridge trail as fast as his rickety legs would move. "Get someone up there with food...nuts, fruit, bread...they love bread..." almost frantic now, he yelled, "Hurry! And be friendly!"

It was Dorslin's turn to be amused. "Lord Danlion, are they friends of yours?"

"It could turn out that way, my skeptical friend. Did you see how far they threw that sentry? If we could persuade them to join us...let's see what brings them out of the mountains."

They made their way up the rocky canyon wall, stopping from time to time as Danlion sat and rested. Once at the top, they found about twenty men in a group, standing about a long stone's throw from six very large squatches. The squatches sat facing the men, next to a small pile of food, eating with one hand while holding a large rock in the other.

Once they were within clear sight of the squatches, Danlion went directly to the group of men. "Do you have any more food?" he demanded as he removed his cloak and laid it on the ground.

The men were amazed at how frail Danlion looked without his intimidating cape, but were not lulled by that appearance into any false sense of security. They complied grudgingly but with urgency, throwing the rest of the rations, which they had kept back from the squatches, onto Danlion's cape.

Turning to Dorslin, "I want you to accompany me in this little adventure."

Dorslin's face lit up with a very amused smile.

"Take off your weapon, Dorslin, and help me carry this food to them. If they understand our language, and some of them do, they may go along with what I tell them. They are simple and gullible, but in some ways, very cunning. Don't underestimate their intelligence.

Dorslin complied and was still wearing an infectious grin as he picked up one end of the cape, which Danlion had folded so that the food would be visible to the squatches as the two men approached them.

"Hold that smile!" said Danlion with almost childlike glee. "It will be very helpful."

As they left the group of men toward the squatches, one large troll dropped his food, jumped up, and stepped toward them, now holding stones in both hands.

"Keep smiling and hold up the food," Danlion said in a low tone. Then, much louder, "More food for our friends!" Danlion forced a friendly smile, which looked very unnatural on a face accustomed only to menacing grins.

The squatches all stopped eating and stared blankly at the approaching gift bearers. As the two men neared, a short exchange of words took place between the squatches, and then they all jumped up and began running toward Danlion and Dorslin.

Dorslin's attention shifted to Danlion to sense his response. Danlion called out loudly, "Yes... good! Come, my friends," he said, grinning more broadly than before.

With astounding speed, the squatches closed the distance between them.

"Quick," whispered Danlion, "lay the cape down."

They spread it out like a tablecloth. The squatches grabbed the food from the cape and returned to their original pile, leaving behind only the cape and the unmistakable smell of hot, dirty squatches.

"Come," he said, scooping up his cape, "we must join them." Danlion moved toward them as quickly as his ancient legs would carry him. This alone was humorous enough to cause Dorslin to chuckle under his breath as he accompanied Danlion.

The squatches returned to their original squatting positions, each facing the men and each still holding one rock.

"Leader?" asked Danlion in a strong but friendly voice.

There was a quick exchange of what sounded like grunts and whines. Then one troll pushed another, who laughed and pushed another troll. Then they all laughed with thunderous voices, then sat silent for another moment looking back and forth at each other, then spontaneously laughed again.

Finally, one stood and said in a deep guttural voice, "My turn, leader."

"I am Danlion and this is my friend Dorslin," he said, gesturing and half turning to Dorslin, who gave a slight bow of recognition. Almost instantly, all the squatches began to mimic the gesture, turning from one to the other and offering squat versions of the bow, each grunting with wide-eyed humor, mouths still full of food.

"Why have you come from the hills to the flatland?" asked Danlion, slowly articulating while using wide hand gestures for emphasis.

"Anderon not come," was the loud rumbling reply which sounded much like a pout.

There was a look of astonishment on the face of the ancient magician and a resultant moment of hesitation. Recovering gracefully, he tried to discover their errand. "Are you friends of anderon?" Sensing that Dorslin was about to speak before they answered, he put up his hand toward the giant man to silence him.

"For many lifetimes, we have been friends of anderon." All the squatches got up and moved very close to listen. They were deadly serious now and exuded an intensity that both men could feel.

"Why are you looking for him?"

"He did not come with round moon!"

"Does he always come with round moon?"

"Never miss since my father's days."

"So you are looking in the flatland for him?"

"Why you ask about anderon?" The squatches had now fanned out and half-way surrounded two men. Dorslin only now gained a full appreciation for the size of these beasts...he looked squarely at the ugly chin of the shortest one.

"We are his friends too." Turning to Dorslin, he looked for approval, "Isn't that right, Dorslin? The dragon, anderon, is our friend too, isn't he?"

Hiding his surprise and donning a very serious expression, Dorslin replied directly to the squatches, "Yes, a good friend...a very honored friend." His answer was so sincere that the squatches clapped and hooted in approval.

Danlion took immediate advantage of the troll's positive response to it.

"Do you know where anderon is?"

"Cha naw..." the troll speaking was cut off by the largest one, who mumbled something to the other squatches in troll language, which roughly translates, "speak to them in their language, they can't figure ours out. We don't want them to feel stupid."

The others obediently chimed in:

"We come to help anderon!"

"We find anderon and help him."

"Anderon need squatches to help."

They all spoke at roughly the same time, each with exaggerated seriousness and intensity.

Danlion waited for their response to die down. "Then you don't know why he didn't come?" he said, sounding very serious and earnest.

"NO!",they answered in unison. Each of them had a sad look on its face.

The largest one spoke again, "You find anderon?" All six of them bent forward toward Danlion with their hideous faces bunched together like flowers in a narrow-necked bottle, their eyes wide and their breath held.

Slowly, with a sad look, Danlion answered, "Yes, my friends. I do know where he is. He has been captured by magic workers and taken to a castle." Danlion sounded as mournful as the mother of a dead baby. "They are going to cut off his head and eat him."

The squatches spoke frantically among themselves in their language, then one asked in drawn-out words, "They going to eat anderon?" They all waited with horrified expressions on their faces.

"Yes...eat him!" came the answer mixed with a subtle magic that Dorslin caught right away, but which they seemed unaware of.

The squatches began to rant and make contorted facial gestures. "We help Anderon! We help!" they chanted quite out of sync with each other.

Very sincerely and with childlike animation, Danlion continued, "Maybe we can all help anderon!"

Their antics came to an abrupt halt. They again moved close to Danlion to listen, almost choking the air with their combined smell.

"If you could get more of your friends to help us, we could take Anderon back...we could get him out of the castle." His seemingly sincere, magic-laced words were very convincing. The squatches went into a huddle to talk.

It took only a few moments for the squatches to respond, "We get many friends. But what about the magic? squatches not have magic!" The troll speaking sounded very frightened, and the faces of his companions reflected that same fear.

"Dorslin and I have magic...lots of magic. But we need help...strong help." The squatches stood motionless as if waiting for something, fear and question still etched on the gruesome faces.

"Look!" said Danlion as he turned and walked toward the cliff. There was a tree growing near the edge of the cliff with numerous dead branches lying under it. "My friend Dorslin will throw one of these limbs off the cliff...watch."

Dorslin took a thick one with few branches on it and gave it a powerful toss up and out over the canyon. Danlion waited for it to finish its upward arc, and just as it started downward, he incinerated it in a flash of bright, colorful flame.

The squatches cheered and clapped. One ran to a much larger tree branch that lay under a giant tree nearby and bounded back with it. He did not even hesitate but threw it with enormous force out over the canyon. A bright white flash of fire split the flying limb in two. Almost instantly, two more flashes, one from each hand, blew the two pieces into flaming fragments which rained on the watchers standing on the canyon floor.

Again, the squatches clapped and hooted in approval. "We bring many friends to help." Their excitement could hardly be contained as they bounced back and forth from foot to foot, still clapping and yelling.

They didn't wait any longer than was necessary for them to pick up as much of the provided food as possible, which they stuffed into animal skin bags, and make a pledge to return. Then they were off. The possibility of saving anderon was the most powerful motivation these squatches had ever experienced. They departed at a run, glancing back with determined looks on their faces which only slightly changed to reflect a smile for their newfound friends.

Once they were completely out of sight, Dorslin turned to ask Danlion what he planned to tell the squatches when they failed to find the dragon in the castle.

Before he could speak a word, Danlion faced Dorslin, and looking over his shoulder with his menacing grin in full bloom, said, "What's that?" pointing behind Dorslin.

Dorslin turned to discover a full-grown dragon in heavy chains standing next to a carnival-style magician. The magician held up his hands, and there was a flash of light, and both disappeared. "You see, Dorslin, we will have to tell our hairy army of friends that the evil magician took the dragon back to his other castle, far away. You can then volunteer to show them that castle also."

As the two men started back down the trail toward the camp, Dorslin was trying to work out the logistics of this momentous alliance. "Lord Danlion, a large army, even a well-trained army, without a plan is an exercise in suicide." Danlion gave no response; he just kept up his slow pace down the trail. "There is quite a lot to do in a very short time if we are going to attempt both castles in one campaign."

Danlion stopped and sat down on a rock outcropping. "Yes, you are quite correct. We must prepare food and plans for the taking of each castle. We'll need all our stockpiled weapons and lots of stones for our rock-throwing friends," he said in a conciliatory manner. "I leave the logistics up to you, Dorslin. You are now second in command next to me. Your word is law."

Dorslin was quite taken aback. He didn't really want command of this group, but neither did he wish to attempt these feats without organization and advanced planning. "Very well, I accept your challenge," he answered with one eyebrow raised. "How many squatches should I expect and how soon?"

With a wickedly amused laugh, Danlion answered, "A thousand or more...and you may expect them in three to four days." His twisted grin was enhanced by the twinkle in his eyes. "We will obviously need to move quickly once they arrive. There isn't enough food in camp to feed them all even once. Round up as much as you can and be ready to attack the morning after they arrive."

Dorslin pondered all this in silence for a moment. "That many squatches on the prowl in the flat lands will bring alarm to everyone in the area. Might it cause the number of people seeking refuge in the castle to swell and make it more difficult to take?"

"I doubt they will open the gate again at all if they learn that hundreds of squatches are running loose. Even if there are more people to fight in the castle, our new friends will help clear the way for us." Danlion finished with a laugh that made Dorslin's blood run cold.

"One more thing, Lord Danlion."

"Speak, my testy friend," answered Danlion, who had now come to regard Dorslin's questions with a much greater tolerance and even a small degree of respect.

"About the dragon? Are you sure the image you present is close enough to that of the dragon which they seek, to fool them?"

Danlion was pleased to hear less arrogance and more caution in Dorslin's voice than he had earlier. "There is only one dragon that I know of left in this land. I have seen him several times and spoke with him once many years ago. The other dragons have gone further north, most of them over a hundred years ago. He either remains alone or returns periodically to check his cave. It's his image I have used. And the magician is the image I hoped to communicate through a little magic to the squatches. They are quite receptive to certain imagery. It is a gamble though...I admit there is at least a possibility of being discovered." They both were silent for a minute. "Is there anything else?"

"No, Lord Danlion. Not yet, at least."

"Good! If you require my services at any time, you need only to ask. I need to take my time getting back. I'm going to rest now. You go ahead and tend to business. I'll spread the word that you are in charge of our affairs. If you need any assistance in establishing your authority, I shall be glad to demonstrate my confidence."

"Thank you, Lord Danlion...you'll be a wise ruler for your people," Dorslin said as he turned and headed down the trail.

Dorslin got right to work making preparations for the coming hoard. Some time later, Danlion reached camp and word began to spread of Dorslin's new position. He was surprised to hear such a favorable response from the men.

"Maybe there is a future for this bunch of misfits!" he thought to himself as he set out for the house to plan for the arrival of their furry recruits. The camp spent the next two days feverishly preparing for their arrival.

****

Brandon Keep was shut up from the outside world. The gate would open briefly twice a day to allow traffic out and in. The guards outside the gates were experienced sensors and would carefully question any who desired to enter. They would not allow anyone access if they sensed even the slightest degree of deception.

There were always three guards keeping vigil outside the front gate day and night. If there was an emergency need to get into the castle, the guards on the wall would drop a rope ladder over the side and allow the person in question to climb up. If they couldn't climb up, they had to wait until the next opening of the gate. The rope ladder had only been used twice in the current castle closure. The polished dark stone surface of the exterior walls made it virtually unscalable. The even cut of the stones and small seams between them gave the castle the appearance of a monstrous piece of furniture created by skilled stone molders.

The inside of the castle was also a work of art. Over the generations, virtually everything originally handcrafted had been altered or embellished by some magician's trade. Many creations of magical origin were improved upon or changed to reflect some new trend or design enhancement.

Some of the original wooden floors on the upper levels of the castle had been replaced by layers of magically fused stone. Below several of these reworked floors, the wooden supports in the ceilings had been removed and replaced with a combination of molded stone and decorative metal arches. These would form a honeycomb lattice under the floor and provide very decorative, very strong support. The best work had been done in the King's Library, the Crystal Room, and the Inner Circle Strategy Room. Later magicians had used their arts to create highly reflective surfaces on the metal or stone in the ceiling structures. This became desirable as the quality of the lighting in the rooms improved, revealing more of the upper detail and intricacies.

The lighting fixtures had changed numerous times, reflecting advances in design from the earlier, very dirty burning torches to the more recent smokeless crystal lamps. The design of these crystal lamps was entirely from the imagination of the men at Brandon Keep. However, the very brightest burning of the smokeless oils was purchased from the Elves. The combination of these arts provided lighting that was the envy of every visitor to the castle.   The stonework in the floors and fireplaces was inspired and often breathtaking. The floor of the Entertainment Room had been molded by magicians to depict the heavens, with stones representing the sun, moon, and constellations of stars. The sun was a stone about as big around as a man is tall, made of a partially translucent bright yellow stone. The stars were various colors from orange to blue white, and each proportional in size to their appearance in the heavens. The moon was crescent, milky white with light grey swirls. All these were fused into what appeared to be single large smooth black stone slab. When the settling of the floor had caused cracks in the past, they were sealed so artfully that only the minor contour difference in the floor betrayed the areas where they had occurred.

The castle was not nearly as large as Castle Crest or the other two Pretorian castles, which were situated near large open spaces. But its eloquence made it the envy of all rulers and would-be overlords. Its drawback was the limited area of farmland near enough to provide sustainable commerce for a large population. It did support the merchants, castle attendants, and four hundred very talented soldiers who resided there. Many of them were competent in one or more aspects of magical art-assisted warfare. Some of them were skilled in Hauna, an art of sensing which they use to anticipate the enemy's moves. There were also several skilled in illusionary arts, an ability that made them very difficult to fight.

Of particular fascination to Danlion were the magical artifacts and special effects contained in the castle. The Crystal Room was a repository for many such items, including several source stones and crystal lights that would illuminate when held by a person who possessed the particular art responding to the stone. It was reported by those who had seen them that when someone with the corresponding art would pick them up, they would glow with varying intensity depending on the power and ability of the holder.

Danlion appreciated these things but had never pursued invention himself. He had instead sought to control, manipulate, and intimidate with his power, and when these failed his ends, destroy. During his long absence from the public eye, he had studied, practiced, and developed some very useful tricks with which to protect himself, but had still not pursued any usefully creative avenues for his arts.

He had managed not to betray his identity nor give rise to sustainable suspicions that he indeed still lived. Instead, he had waited until the earthpower had risen enough to assure him every protection he desired from potential ill-wishers...protection that his intentions would make mandatory if he was to succeed with his plans.

His goal was now to establish himself as a power to be reckoned with and to amuse himself along the way with the magical trinkets that so charmed him in his past life. Capturing Brandon Keep would provide both quite handily. Nowhere in any of the lands had so many magical artifacts been pulled together in one place as in Brandon Keep. It was this castle that Danlion had set his heart on possessing. The fact that the mystique of the castle would add to his image was an intoxicating attraction to him. And now, if his hairy friends could actually produce a formidable army, he could take the castle with only minimal losses to his own forces.

****

Jarmin made his way back to the last stronghold he had known Danlion to inhabit. The amulet had worked wonders on his damaged body as it continued to heal him and provide stamina for his journey. It had performed beyond his wildest hopes. In less than two days, he had traveled a distance that would have taken twice that time under normal circumstances, and still showed no fatigue.

He found the stronghold deserted. Knowing that Brandon Keep was Danlion's ultimate destination, he made his way there without resting. Jarmin was now forced to continually wear the amulet because it was the only thing that kept him alert. On the one occasion in his journey back, he took it off briefly to keep it from getting wet when he stopped at a stream to refresh himself, and he almost passed out from exhaustion. Even now, he could feel its magical warmth invigorating his body. He decided to wear it until he had met with Danlion.

Knowing that Danlion would send out spies to investigate the area near the castle, he decided to set himself up in the makeshift town nearby, hoping to recognize one of the band or be recognized himself. He arrived at the large outdoor pub in the early afternoon. He did not have to wait long. Two men walked in, one he recognized as belonging to Danlion's entourage. He was a thick-bodied, wild-haired man called Mic. The other man was not familiar to him. They had obviously been frequenting the place because they were greeted by name and exchanged boisterous, light-hearted talk with several men gathered there. After the last such exchange, Mic spotted Jarmin and, swinging his elbow out at the other man to gain his attention, moved to the small table where he was seated. After a quiet exchange of information, Mic and his companion led Jarmin back to the camp.

As they made their way past the outer perimeter of the camp, a runner was sent to announce Jarmin's arrival.

Jarmin entered the small "borrowed" house and found Danlion seated in a comfortable chair on the opposite side of a small table upon which sat a full stein and part of a loaf of thickly sliced bread. Dorslin was seated sideways to the entrance at the side of the table to Danlion's right. Three other men stood together near the entrance.

"Lord Danlion, I've brought news of the sword."

Danlion studied Jarmin for a moment without speaking, his eyes cold and searching, his face otherwise expressionless. "Jarmin, my friend," he said with a voice as cold as a mid-winter's icy north wind, "you've been absent a very long time. Have you been lost?"

Jarmin sensed the extreme danger in Danlion's voice. He was tempted to flee but knew that would prove fatal. He didn't know why Danlion was acting this way toward him, but felt that he could probably clear it up if given the time. "Lord Danlion, I was captured by the dwarves after I killed three of them. I escaped and have come here directly from my captivity."

Again, Danlion sat in concentration. Jarmin knew something was wrong, but couldn't put his finger on it...unless it was the amulet! "That's it!" he thought to himself, "he must be able to sense the elven magic." Jarmin wrestled with exposing it to Danlion but knew that to do so would most surely cost him possession of it. "It's mine," he thought with quick violence, "...it's part of me now...I couldn't give it up even if I wanted to."

Danlion stood and leaned forward, putting both hands on the table. "Come and sit then, Jarmin. You must be quite tired from your adventure."

Jarmin felt a secure warmth run through his body again, replacing the icy cold feeling brought on by Danlion's questioning. "Yes, my lord, I am very exhausted from my ordeal."

He had taken only two steps when a brilliant bolt of fire struck his head, incinerating it and setting fire to his upper clothing and the door frame behind him. "Lie to me, will you..elf?!" Danlion walked around the table toward Jarmin's body, sporting an evil grin and continuing to speak in a quiet taunting tone, "Didn't you think me capable of sensing your overwhelming elven magic? Some mistmaster you are...or were." He broke out in a deep, bone-chilling laugh. Everyone in the room was standing very still, all but Dorslin felt sickened by what they saw. The flames on the door flickered out.

"You must have been better than I thought," he said as he reached down and poked the lifeless body. You still have your magic even in death." Danlion stood over him for what seemed a very long time to those watchers who stood fearing to move. Still, he stood motionless as he just stared and sensed. The magic was growing, not diminishing. The headless body convulsed and began to thrash about. Danlion responded by setting it on fire. The smell of burning flesh and the choking smoke further sickened those in attendance, even affecting Dorslin. The other men finally fled the room, choking and gagging. Dorslin moved to a window and opened it so he could stand in the incoming breeze.

"What is this?" Danlion said in a surprised and curious tone. "Give me your sword, Dorslin." Danlion did not even look back at Dorslin but reached over his shoulder to receive the hilt. Once Dorslin placed it in his hand, he began to probe and poke at the damp, smoldering ash-covered lump on the floor. After a few moments of digging, he fished out the amulet. It hung dangling on the end of the sword, where Danlion studied it as he maneuvered the sword so he could inspect it from all angles. It was no longer glowing and was covered with ash and smudged with Jarmin's blood.

"Look at this, Dorslin," he said triumphantly as he finally took hold of the amulet. Danlion made a short, lame, distracted toss of Dorslin's sword back in his direction. Dorslin, however, moved quickly and easily caught it by the hilt.

Dorslin's first thought of wiping off the residue from his sword was abruptly disrupted by the brilliant green glow coming from the amulet held by Danlion.

"It's Elven magic..." the words rolled slowly, thoughtfully off Danlion's tongue, "...very old Elven magic." He looked down at what he now reassessed to be Jarmin's remains and quipped, "You should have told me about this...your little elven trinket. I might have spared your life!"

Danlion did not share with Dorslin the incredible energizing power he felt coming from the amulet, "some secrets are best kept to one's", he mused as he walked out of the house. He stopped briefly and spoke without turning, "Oh Dorslin, see to it that our weak constitutioned friends clean up this little accident, will you?"

"It will be cleaned," said Dorslin dryly, wishing at the same time that the entire house would have caught on fire and saved them all a lot of irritation.

Early the next morning, the squatches began to arrive. They came by clans ranging in number from a few dozen to almost two hundred. They did not come directly to the camp but went to the cliff where they first encountered Danlion. Dorslin had set up a camp there, hoping that the squatches would stay on the higher ground and not pollute the little canyon.

Dorslin had persuaded the men to move barrels of water and throw-sized rocks up to that area, hoping to make their guest feel more secure. He had his men collect additional fist-sized stones and load them on every cart, wagon, and pack animal he could round up or steal, to be moved to Brandon Keep. The canyon they were in proved to be one of nature's veritable repositories of such stones. At first, a few of the men had refused to perform the arduous task of digging up the rock-laden canyon floor. However, after their refusal had been met with a resultant short bout of hand-to-hand personal negotiations with Dorslin, they reconsidered, and the total effort went smoothly from that point on. Dorslin's power of persuasion was quite compelling.

On the very day that he first encountered the squatches, Danlion had sent out messengers to retrieve all the spies, scouts, missionaries, and mercenaries dispatched on earlier assignments. They had been arriving in small groups ever since.

Dorslin had been too busy with his duties to look up Danlion during the day the squatches began arriving. They came bearing some food and a few of their own hand-picked stones each. The main difficulty was communication, a task further complicated because the squatches were, by nature, very edgy around men. Finally, with the aid of several squatches more adept at understanding man's language, Dorslin got them situated. Their sheer numbers far exceeded that which Dorslin had anticipated, and by evening, there were so many settled in that they formed a perimeter completely around the camp of men. If Danlion's followers' location had been a secret prior to this time, and that is doubtful, it certainly was not now.

When Dorslin found a relatively free moment to contact Danlion, he discovered a remarkable change in his countenance. Danlion was noticeably more animated and energetic. He spoke a little faster with more volume in his voice. The "trinket" he recovered from Jarmin was hanging fully exposed around his neck, glowing bright green.

"Lord Danlion, the squatches have, for the most part, arrived. They have come by the hundreds just as you expected."

Dorslin waited briefly while Danlion acknowledged his news with a smile that seemed to say, "Was there some doubt in your mind?"

Dorslin continued, "I believe, sire, that we will need to strike early in the morning and be prepared to break camp and move on to Castle Crest by the following day if at all possible."

"Dorslin, my friend," came Danlion's reply in a tone as close to friendly as Dorslin had ever heard, "your optimism in my plan is flattering. But are you actually suggesting a half day to take Brandon Keep?"

"My lord," Dorslin was now smiling like a child with a secret that he was just dying to tell, "there are thousands of your giant friends waiting to rescue their dragon!"

Obvious delight crept across the ancient face as he whispered, "Thousands?!"

"Yes, Lord Danlion! Thousands!!" answered Dorslin, stretching the words and prolonging the "s" into a gentle hiss.

Both men laughed with evil delight.

"I take it then that there is precious little room or provisions for our hairy host of an army?" A broad grin covered his face, exposing his rising moon yellow teeth.

"Precisely why we must act quickly, my lord."

"Can we be ready by daybreak?" asked Danlion with a surprisingly strong voice.

Yes, Lord Danlion. We'll need you nearby as we breach the wall. Will you require transportation, or will you ride your horse?" Dorslin's tone of voice betrayed his observations in the renewed vitality displayed in Danlion.

"As you can obviously tell, my physical condition has improved. I shall ride my horse," he said as he rose to his feet and straightened up to a height much greater than Dorslin had suspected, almost as tall as Dorslin himself.

"If he weren't so stick thin, his mere height could be very imposing," thought Dorslin as they walked out to survey the camp.

****

News of the troll's arrival was greeted with outright terror from the entire community. In the evening of the day they began arriving, the merchants and farming families gathered at the gate of Brandon Keep seeking refuge. There were hundreds of families. Lord Oakbern opened the gate and screened the incoming refugees with teams of sensors. Few were left outside.

Oakbern had sent out four teams of two scouts each to assess the circumstances. Three teams returned, each with the same report, "hundreds of chanting , highly excited squatches moving in clans toward a small well-protected canyon in the foothills.

The last group observed a long column of men, wagons, carts, pack animals, and a virtual sea of squatches moving out of the canyon. They remained long enough to determine what direction the strange procession was taking and what their purpose might be. When it became evident that they were moving toward Brandon Keep, the scouts headed back to the castle. Although they moved quickly and in stealth, a group of squatches saw them and gave chase. They almost got caught. As soon as they arrived and announced their business at the wall, the ladder was thrown over and they climbed up, followed by the guards outside the gate. The last guard was one quarter of the way from the top when two squatches ran up and began climbing behind him. The two squatches were shadowed by about twenty rock-throwing companions who pelted the castle catwalk with the stones they brought. After the initial exchange of arrows and rocks, two archers bent over the side of the wall to try and stop the two squatches who pursued the last guard. The leading troll was within a body length of the guard when he cleared the wall. The sentry tending the ladder released the safety catches holding it to the wall, and both squatches fell back to the ground. It happened so fast that the archers didn't even get off a shot before they fell. The one who had been closest to the top got up and limped off to join his companions, several of whom had now been wounded with arrows. The other, who cushioned the landing of his partner, did not move. Another died from wounds inflicted in a volley of arrows that dogged their retreat.

Dorslin had observed the pursuit and followed out of curiosity. Once they were safely back away from the wall, Dorslin scolded them for their behavior. Though he was angry at their rashness, he was even more impressed with their courage and ability to work together. He was also struck with a small amount of personal fear over what might happen if these overzealous warrior recruits discovered the truth.

After seeing their speed and agility on the rope ladder, he thought it possible that these long-armed beasts just might be able to climb a rope. He guessed better than he had suspected. He had his men attach a length of metal cable to a grapple hook and then secure a rope to the cable. This would make it easier for them to throw up and hook onto the wall, but it would be difficult for the defense to detach. In a practice session near Brandon Keep, the squatches proved even better than he had hoped possible, given their large frame and massive bulk. They moved up the rope like fire up a wick string.

As soon as the last two scouts were rescued from the squatches, they reported to Oakbern that there was a large army of squatches, "thousands and thousands", accompanying a small, apparently renegade army of men, all of whom were arriving outside the castle as they spoke.

The castle was already coming to a state of full alert following the attack. Oakbern called a council consisting of the most experienced magicians at controlling animals and his chief military commanders.

"Is there anyone here who has had substantial contact with squatches?" Oakbern's words echoed back off the stone walls with violence. The answer from the twenty or so attendees was a deafening silence...no no one ventured even the tiniest morsel of information or even speculation.

"Is there anyone here who thinks they may possess valid information about their behavior?" This time, there was some nervous rustling, but still no answer.

"Can they be charmed?"

There was an initial silence which was finally broken by Shahandra, "My Lord, I'm sure that every living creature has some degree of susceptibility. These creatures are like children. They can surely be placed under the power of suggestion by one who knows their needs, emotions, or even desires."

"Thank you, Shahandra." Lord Oakbern looked around at the rest of the assembly. Few of them would meet his eyes. Looking back at Shahandra, he asked, "Could someone charm them all and hold them in control?"

"Not without all of us sensing it... and I have not the slightest sense of such a thing." There was such confidence in her voice that most of those present wrote her remarks off with their colloquialism, "speaking from your youth", which roughly translates, "confidently asserting a guess!" Few of them had any real knowledge regarding the charming of animals, except for those few experiences where other magicians had entertained them with wild animal acts supposedly directed through magic.

"How would control of such a mass of squatches be accomplished then, if not through magic?"

Siemon, the senior military advisor, spoke up, "Perhaps it was just a case of being able to deceive them into fighting..."

"Maybe with a reward of some kind," added Gesher, one of the other officers, cutting in over Siemon.

"It's not likely that the squatches would be mercenary," said Siemon, giving Gesher a rebuking look, "every kind of inducement has been tried in the past without any success...they simply aren't greedy or ambitious...more like Shahandra said...like children."

"Even children will cooperate for a reward, Siemon," said Oakbern, challenging his assertion.

"Not if the children already possess all they want, my Lord...and the squatches care for themselves very well...there simply isn't much that they desire which they don't easily provide for themselves."

Lord Oakbern sat for a long time without speaking. When everyone was feeling the weight of the silence, he spoke again, "Can we withstand an attack by the squatches? Will our walls hold them out?"

Before Siemon could answer, Gesher was on his feet speaking, "The guards on the wall said that the squatches were up the ladder four times faster than any man they ever saw climb it. They're sure that we would be quickly overrun if there are enough squatches with ropes and hooks."

"My Lord," broke in Siemon, who walked over to Gesher and put his hand on his shoulder in an obvious attempt to intimidate him, "the squatches are completely untrained in warfare and won't have the remotest idea how to hold and throw the hooks. Even then, someone would need to find enough surplus metal to make a sufficient number of them after the other implements they need have been made." Siemon pushed Gesher back into his chair in a seemingly casual manner while finishing, "My Lord, I've seen these beasts climb, unaided, straight up a virtually vertical cliff after bird eggs in a high nest. They are very resourceful and will likely figure out how to get over the wall by themselves if they perceive the need to be great enough."

"Can anyone think of a motivation powerful enough to get them out of the hills in this number and assembled together as an army?" There was great frustration on Oakbern's face.

Again, Shahandra spoke up, "Lord Oakbern, they must be united by a very powerful common thread. With the kind of determination they possess and a drive strong enough to bring them here together, apart from their families, they could prove unstoppable. Even now, I can sense a strength of immense force in them...they are driven with a deep sense of loyalty."

"Lord Oakbern," said Siemon, who was now seated again, "we have a great many excellent archers who will all be on the wall waiting for these beasts. As large as they are, they would make easy prey for our forces."

"But what if they all came at you from the same direction at the same time?"

"I don't know, my Lord...they move very quickly for their size and they are very strong...If they made a suicide run, my guess is that we couldn't stop them."

"There are too many unknowns in this situation. Prepare the escape tunnel. Get the women and children moving tonight, as soon as possible. Have them and our elderly already out by daybreak. We can retreat and secure the tunnel if need be, and they will be safe there no matter what happens." With that, Lord Oakbern dismissed all of them except Shahandra.

He waited until they were alone, "Shahandra, what could possibly drive these peaceful creatures so hard? What could this old magician Danlion have given them for a motivation?"

"There's strange magic in the air these days, my Lord. A few days ago, I sensed the presence of a strong magic watching me... when we were walking the perimeter with the military advisors... it seemed to be coming from a long way off, but at the same time, nearby. I don't know what powerful magic like that could do to the squatches."

"Shahandra, your magic was like that on the night you spent in that magical forest of yours," said Oakbern, looking very contemplative.

"All I know about squatches, sire, comes from only three sources: Old stories, the sense I had about them the only time I ever encountered one, and the strength of the sensation I sense coming from them now." Shahandra waited briefly for some sort of direction or response from Oakbern but witnessed only a faraway look in his eyes and a slow, rhythmic nodding of his head. "They're not very selfish creatures and wouldn't, in my estimation, become involved for any mercenary purpose. A response like we're witnessing here must be rooted in some very noble business... something they hold sacred... like protection of their families against some danger... or maybe a pact they have to help a friend. Beyond this type of thing, I don't think anything will motivate them to this kind of action... and I doubt they've ever bound themselves together like this in the past for any reason at all... it must be extraordinary whatever it is." Shahandra had now joined Oakbern in her own vacant-eyed stare.

Oakbern broke the trance, "Could Danlion have befriended these beasts over the past many years and now be asking this favor in return for something he provided them?" He stood up and began to pace in circles around the large table in the middle of the room. It all seemed to make sense to him now. Danlion would need lots of help when he tried again to regain his position...and what better place to hide all these years?!?

"Anything is possible, sir." Shahandra studied Oakbern, wondering if the tragedy in this had hit him or if he only thought of the military significance of the situation. "Isn't it sad that these dimly witted but very loyal creatures will suffer so much only because they were tricked?"

Oakbern continued to pace as she talked and seemed to be very preoccupied. At Shahandra's question, he suddenly stopped, his eyes focused on her's and he answered, "Yes... yes I suppose it will be quite a tragedy, especially if they ever really understand what happened to them." He stopped and stood quietly for a moment, staring into space, then abruptly excused himself and left without looking back.

Shahandra wondered if Oakbern would have used the squatches as Danlion seemed to be doing. She had often heard Oakbern use the illustration of a farmer deserving the meat of the deer who had for months feasted from his garden. She wondered if Oakbern would have used a similar rationale to exploit the squatches, and if this was true, did he admire Danlion's resourcefulness?

The night was filled with packing necessities, treasures, and supplies to take with them, knowing that most of their precious possession must be left behind. By daybreak, the men and women not essential to the battle, the children, and the elderly were safely inside the tunnel leading into the mountain. From there, they could move through a series of natural caverns joined by man-made corridors clear to the other side of the mountain range if deemed necessary.

Oakbern and the other warriors were standing guard on the castle walls, watching the growing hoard of squatches amass just outside the forest border, at the far side of the fields immediately surrounding the castle. There were piles of rocks mounded all over the fields, with many near the castle walls on the three most level sides. There were thousands of squatches. Even from the great distance where they were standing, their very large stature made it possible for individual forms to be clearly distinguished. They stood motionless in groups varying in size from a small handful to about a hundred. They were as quiet as they were still. They stood against the landscape like a giant, meaningless painting.

The quiet was something that Dorslin expected from his men but did not expect from the squatches. It spooked him a little and gave him a great sense of relief that they were on his side. Dorslin and Danlion rode up to the front line together. Danlion was strong and sat tall on his horse. They dismounted and brought their horses with them as they walked up to the largest group of squatches, which happened to be assembled closest to the castle. They had spent the evening spreading the command to the groups of squatches that they needed to get the gate opened as quickly as possible if they hoped to save the anderon. Until now, no squatches had argued or questioned the order.

The biggest troll in the group, standing easily over two heads above Dorslin, said, "We will get in and save anderon by ourselves."

"If you try," said Danlion in the friendliest voice his stone heart could muster, "you will be killed by the evil magician."

"No, we will be too fast for him," said the troll with childlike confidence.

"Try to reach me," said Danlion loudly as if playing a game.

A broad smile spread across the giant's face as he lunged at Danlion with catlike agility and speed.

Ancient hands responded with a powerful green flame curtain that picked up the troll and threw him backward a distance three times his height. He landed and tumbled awkwardly out in front of the line of squatches.

Danlion walked to the quite shaken troll and spoke loudly as he got up, "The evil magician inside the castle is very powerful too. Open the gate so I can fight with him and protect you.

"We will open the gate," said the now slightly stooped and still dazed troll. The other squatches ran to him and tried to comfort him, always keeping an untrusting eye on Danlion.

Danlion returned to Dorslin and asked if he had distributed the cable and hook devices prepared for the squatches. Assured that they had been distributed, Danlion finished, "Can any of them throw them well enough to set them on the wall?"

"I only had time to give them a couple of practice throws. All we need is one or two of the twenty to work for us. Then the squatches will see to it that they get over the wall.

Fully recovered from his battering by Danlion, the large troll walked up to them again, "Are you ready for a surprise?"

Danlion looked at Dorslin for some insight but got only a shrug of the shoulders and a puzzled look. Turning back to the troll, "Yes, my friend, show us your surprise."

The troll whistled, and all the groups of squatches began to yell. It was deafening. From the forest cover hundreds of squatches were running through the mass of standing comrades. Each set of four had a long, thin limb-stripped tree which they gracefully carried at a full run. As they reached the center of the mass of squatches, the entire group yelled even louder. Those with the trees did not stop but were joined by the entire line, all running toward the wall. There were over a hundred trees moving for the wall. With hands full of rocks, thousands of squatches joined them, yelling and leaping as they ran toward the castle.

Dorslin looked at Danlion with a wide-eyed, humorous resignation on his face, "Well, my lord," he shouted, compensating for the noise of the charging squatches all around them, "I guess the attack is on."

Both men were glad they had held on to their horses' reins; even battle-trained horses could panic in a storm of squatches. As they mounted, Dorslin was surprised at the speed and agility displayed by Danlion, who moved as smoothly as a young man.

Danlion's face showed obvious delight, even though the attack was out of their control, "Probably better to let them fight it their way," he yelled as he leaned toward Dorslin so he could ensure an attentive ear. As soon as the wave of tall brown hair had passed, Danlion shouted with up-held hand, "We'd better get going or we're going to miss the war and the opening of the gate."

As he yelled his command, Dorslin noticed the amulet shining through Danlion's tunic as if reflecting the sunlight. "Whatever the trinket is," thought Dorslin to himself as he watched Danlion's horse break into a full run with Danlion setting like a seasoned cavalryman in the saddle, "it has given him obvious strength and given his men a great advantage in seeing him looking so strong and responsive."

Dorslin's men had been assembled center mass of the waiting squatches and remained stationary as the squatches attacked. On Danlion's command, they broke into a charge, staying a safe distance behind the squatches.

To the warriors on the wall, what they saw coming at them resembled a giant moving matted rug with sticks in it.

Lord Oakbern assessed the charge with his commanders and decided to let the initial part of the hairy wave approach and see what their strength really was. It was amazing to those on the wall that even though there were hundreds of squatches hit by arrows, it did not stem the tide of their attack...if anything, it seemed to speed them up. The squatches threw their rocks so hard that, with the first wave of stones, two soldiers were knocked down from the sheer force of the blows to their shields. Some stones were thrown almost straight up and became a deadly rain. When their shields were up, their front was unprotected. The squatches were amazingly accurate and moved so fast that the archers were less effective than they had hoped.

As the rain of rocks continued from thousands of two-handed rock throwers, the trees began to arrive. Lord Oakbern's fears of a solid wave single-point attack were being played out in painful exactness and with devastating results.

Oakbern realized they were beaten soon enough to minimize further loss of life, "Retreat! Retreat!" The horns sounded, and the soldiers made quick work of escaping. He then stood on the wall with a handful of his most skilled archers and swordsmen until the rest of the wall was evacuated. The escape was well organized and carefully executed, but still, a few of his soldiers were killed on the wall, and some were killed by rocks thrown clear over the wall as they abandoned it. The wounded were laid on waiting carts and whisked away toward the escape tunnel.

Outside, powerful arms hoisted the trees to an upright position and made twelve nearly vertical ramps, each made of trunks which they laid together against the wall with their tips forming a point near the top of the wall. The squatches made quick work of climbing their impromptu ramps, traversing the distance with the same ease that a man would a bridge. Within a very short time, there were hundreds inside the castle, trying desperately to figure out how the gate worked. With precious time being consumed, Dorslin scaled one of the lean-to ramps and made his way through a wall of walking fur to get to the gate. There was no sign of resistance. He could see the back of what appeared to be a column of wagons very near the castle at the far end of a long, straight road leading into the city from the gate.

Dorslin's attention turned to the gate, which was being battered by a hundred frenzied squatches. The center of the gate had been sealed by a wood weaver and metal molder, so the two doors had literally become one piece. He directed the removal of the securing bolts from the top and bottom edges of the giant gate so that it would open freely when he finished his work on it.

Dorslin pulled his sword and held it up. It began to shimmer like water reflecting sunlight. Then it burst into a shaft of brilliant white light. He swung it hard at the gate hinge and cut through it like a hot knife cuts lard. The gate moaned. He called two squatches and had them lift him up so he could reach the other hinge. They ran to him and, with a little coaching, lifted him up, one holding each leg steady. Dorslin swung his sword so hard that the shifting of his weight caused the squatches to stagger; again, his blade cut through the hinge in one clean swipe. The gate immediately shifted and began to swing inward.

The squatches dropped Dorslin and helped open the gate, being aided by those outside who were pushing. It swung easily open, and Danlion entered, spurring his horse to a full run directly through the squatches, who had parted down the middle, forming a sort of parade route cheering atmosphere. He continued straight down the road leading into the city center. He was immediately followed by a fast-moving column of whooping, jumping, sprinting squatches. As he neared the halfway point of the road, he looked back to make sure the squatches would be able to see which little alley he turned down. The squatches had kept up with him, being only three or four lengths behind him. He spurred his horse on faster toward the last turn he could see, hoping to gain some distance on them, be far enough ahead to have the image intact, and give them only a glance before it disappeared. At the incredible speed they were running, there would scarcely be time for even that.

Danlion's mind was clear and his reflexes sharp as he reached the last possible turn, where he hoped there would be room for his illusion. To his right, there was a dead-end open courtyard surrounded by buildings. He swung in at a full run, causing his horse to almost lose its footing while slipping on the roadway. Instantly, the dragon was there, lying sideways across the far end of the courtyard, standing with the circus magician who was complete with a colorful, pointed hat, a red-lined black cape over his shoulders, and holding a golden chain attached around the great beast's neck. There were three stone buildings side by side along the road before it widened into an open square. The dragon was at the far end of the square in front of a very large building made of impressively cut stones. Danlion was down the street and about to enter the square when the squatches began to pour around the corner and toward the dragon. They cheered and yelled in a frenzied dash toward their friend. Suddenly, fire went from both Danlion and the magician, crashing together in a spectacular show of colorful flame about midway between them. The squatches came to a gasping halt, causing a rippling effect back through their masses as they crushed together. The illusionary magician held up his empty hand, and in a sparkling flash, both he and the dragon disappeared. The squatches began to howl and moan, covering their eyes and holding their heads in mournful, childlike grief.

As more and more squatches tried to enter the street, those inside were forced forward into the square. Seeing the potential for further disaster,

Danlion began to point back toward the corner from atop his horse and yell, "BACK! GO BACK!" Like a ripple in a pond, his order floated back up the street. Those who could were pointing back toward the corner in exaggerated motions, but most were still facing the square. By the time the order got back to the corner, every troll in between was now trying desperately to turn around and face the right direction. Some were so tight that they literally were forced backwards for a time until the moving river of squatches loosened up enough for them to turn around. The square and street began to clear remarkably fast for such a large number of squatches. It was as if they were somehow connected and could move in unison. They were all heading back toward the gate.

Danlion sat still while the street cleared of mourners. He was amazed how well they obeyed and how undamaged...indeed how untouched the surrounding buildings were, considering that the street had been visited by thousands of emotional squatches. "Amazing! He thought, An army that doesn't pillage and leaves its bounty intact!"

Danlion's horse cleared the corner, but he turned and headed at a gallop for the castle proper instead of back toward the gate. Like thousands of trained and obedient puppies, the squatches turned and followed, matching his speed and moving behind him like a giant brown train on an ornamental dress. As he reached the castle and before he could dismount, he was surrounded by an increasingly stagnant sea of squatches. He was not sure if it was because his sense of smell had been enhanced or because these hygienically foul beasts were now hot and sweaty, but the pungent smell was stifling.

a

At that, the squatches began to mourn out loud. Then they broke into a subdued chant, "anderon...anderon..."

Danlion raised his voice; it was charged with magic, "We can go to help anderon. We can go far away to help anderon. We want to help anderon..."

The squatches had become quiet as Danlion began to speak, but as he repeated his words over and over, they began to chant with him, "help anderon...help anderon..."

After a brief time, he stopped the chant, and so did the squatches. He raised his hand and pointed back toward the gate, "Dorslin will take you there...take you to anderon." There was a murmuring that went through the crowd in their own language. Some then began to shout and point back toward the city gate. The group began to move out again to find Dorslin. Soon, Danlion was almost alone. There were still some squatches who had split away and gone exploring, presumably looking for anderon. While the mass of them followed Danlion, there had been numerous groups of varying size that had spread throughout the city.

The escape tunnel was like a stairway into a mine shaft leading down into the earth. The entrance itself was made of two very large iron doors, which had been opened with the aid of horses and now lay flat on the ground. The last of those injured at the castle wall were being carried in as soldiers stood vigil, waiting for their enemy to come. Several sensors detected the use of powerful magic. It had stopped after only a brief time and was unfamiliar to any of them. A short time later, there was another use of magic which was even more powerful. It was definitely Danlion's, the magic experienced over and over when towns and villages were destroyed. This time, he was nearby. Shahandra had stayed near the gate during the evacuation to help with any wounded who might require her arts. She had attended the last to be moved and was still outside the tunnel when a group of eight squatches came running for the tunnel opening. Several guards stepped out with drawn swords to intercept them. Shahandra stepped out from behind them and, using her magic, touched their minds with a deep sense of friendship and peace. They slowed down in response and lowered the rocks and bricks they held as weapons. They came to a stop about twenty paces from the line of soldiers. Shahandra started toward the squatches.

"Your blood is on your own head, Shahandra," shouted one of the soldiers.

Shahandra did not give it enough thought to break her magic. She reached the squatches and spoke softly to them, "Do you understand my words?"

"You stole anderon!" said one of them, with the others shaking their heads in assent.

Shahandra's magic gave her the image they saw in their minds, "a? The dragon?"

"Dragon, yes! Dragon...anderon!" he repeated emotionally.

"We had no dragon here, not anderon or any dragon." The bad magician lied to you."

"No! We saw anderon...here!" The others again chanted agreement.

"What you saw was a magic trick...not real."

The squatches were very confused after their main speaker interpreted to several others what Shahandra had been saying.

"He tricked you so you would fight for him and take our home," she said, motioning around at the buildings.

Before Shahandra could say anything else, Oakbern broke through the line and shouted at Shahandra, "Your magic is giving you and us away. We've got to go now and seal the tunnel. Come on...NOW! Or we'll have to leave you."

"I have to go now, I'm sorry," she said as she turned and ran back through the line of soldiers who all backed into the mouth of the tunnel. The squatches stood silent and very perplexed.

A loud roar of crashing stone and falling dirt filled the air at the tunnel entrance. A high plume of dust rushed out and up through the doors like a geyser.

No sooner had the dust begun to settle than Danlion rounded the corner nearby at a gallop, drawn by the familiar magic. He was still alone.

"What did you see here?" he asked in an almost friendly tone as he dismounted his horse.

"Men going into the hole," said the one who had been doing most of the talking.

"Did they talk to you?" he asked, looking around to see if there were any other squatches visible. He saw none.

"They said you lied about anderon."

Without a moment of hesitation, Danlion let go of a huge green flame curtain which hit six of the eight squatches, knocking them down. White fire hit the other two in their heads before they could even react. While they were still falling, he burned the other six likewise with a brilliant flash of fire.

"I'm grieved to hear that you think I misled you," he said as he remounted his horse and turned back for the gate. As he passed the tunnel entrance, he paused for a moment of appraisal, then moved on without getting off his horse.

At the gate, he met with Dorslin and had him send some squatches to fill the remaining part of the tunnel entrance with rocks. While that was taking place, the soldiers made a quick search of the town to assess if all inhabitants were gone. No one stayed behind.

By early afternoon, plans were being drawn for the attack on Castle Crest. All day long up to that point, more squatches had continued to arrive from the hills, following the trail of their relatives and friends to Brandon Keep. With now over ten thousand squatches, there were far too many for Brandon Keep and too many to keep feeding for any length of time. The castle had enough food left in it to feed the entire troop, maybe once. Because of this and for sanitary reasons, the march for Castle Crest began that night. Danlion had addressed the troll army in part and convinced them that the dragon could be saved if they hurried. He promised that he would join them as soon as they arrived at the castle. They were ready to move by early evening.

Danlion kept a majority of the almost eleven hundred recruits in his army with him at Brandon Keep, sending only about two hundred with Dorslin. He felt sure that he could hold the castle with the men he had if he could be sure all secret entrances were secure.

Dorslin was now in charge of the most unusual army ever assembled. The men who went with him were not excited about fighting with an army that smelled worse than it looked and looked like a huge mass of knotted brown hemp. They were willing, though, because of the riches and power of being on the winning side.

Before they departed, Danlion gave Dorslin a long, thin box and a special pair of gloves. "See that you retrieve the detestable sword and return it to me in this box. Pick it up with these gloves and apply no magic to it. It will not harm you if you do as I say." With that, they were dispatched to Castle Crest.

CHAPTER 20

Morning seemed to come quickly for the departing party. They had received provisions for the trip before they had gone to sleep the previous night. A hot breakfast of sweetbreads, portage, and fruit was awaiting them when they arose. They quickly ate and were on their way before the sun had risen. It was a beautifully crisp morning with a clear, bright sky. The monstrous trees that decorated the center of the city stood like gentle spectators, pondering the mission of the odd-fellow band of travelers. There were numerous Dwarves who came to bid their countrymen good fortune in their journey, not knowing for sure what it was, but certain of its importance. At the edge of town proper stood a small group of Elves, including Elloewyn, who came to send their friends off with an Elven blessing in song. They sang in tones and words that were altogether foreign to the men who listened. Lanimar pronounced the dwarven traveling blessing, and the little group was off.

At the outskirts of town, they were joined by an army of Dwarven warriors approximately the same size as that which had escorted them into the capital. They were informed that a band of men matching the description of those destroyed at the crossroads had been seen in the area. The army would accompany the delegation the entire distance to Castle Crest. It was most certain that the men in question were those dispatched by Danlion to stop the delegation from reaching their destination. While it was embarrassing that the men were not thought capable of protecting those who had come with them to help Pretoria, it was at the same time very comforting to have the proven dwarf army along.

The trip to Castle Crest went without incident. Malan went ahead of the entourage to acquaint Lord Falock with the conditions of the arrangement arrived at with the Dwarves and Elves.

Lord Falock had received and read the document prepared by Draxyl and signed by the Supreme and Elloewyn. "I knew they would be difficult to deal with." He spoke with near rage in his voice. "Why can't I have competent people in my employ! Why can't I have people who can discover the answers to these secrets without having to bring these scheming outer-race foreigners into my castle... only to be manipulated by them to their gain?"

"Perhaps, sir," answered Malan cautiously, "because the scheming outer-race foreigners created this most powerful of swords!"

Lord Falock stood silently staring at Malan for a brief moment, contemplating the situation, then said, "Yes, I suppose you're right," he said as he turned and walked a few paces away from Malan as stood facing a blank wall. "Let alone the fact that we haven't been able to make a power sword to match Fallonrod, we can't even control the one we have..." Falock seemed to drift into his own world and spoke quietly as if to no one in particular, "The Earth Power seems to have chosen favorites among the races... it distributes its power without equity or recourse." He paused a moment, working through a maze of emotions. "Malan, you know the Dwarves best of any of the delegates. Do you trust their intentions?"

"My Lord Falock, they are not totally safe as a race. They know how to manipulate situations and circumstances to their advantage, which undoubtedly they are doing now. But they are a very good race, and the Elves are their equal in this characteristic also. Whatever their plan, its eventual outcome will be intended for the greatest benefit of our people, from their perspective."

"Do you sense that they already have a plan?"

"Undoubtedly, their conditions contain something of their plan. Expect them to have very carefully organized their conditions to reflect their intentions. Also, realize that anything left out of their conditions may have been done so very intentionally. Even if they do not have a specific plan worked out, they have concocted a framework that will allow them to operate to their own ends." Malan finished in a very dry and matter-of-fact tone.

"I don't know of any alternative available to us."

"Nor could we discern any at the conference, except to trust to luck and hope we could discover the sword's secrets before it fell into the hands of some enemy. Besides, they may be able to provide the bearer with secrets about the sword's power that may never have been discovered by a powermaster even if he was forced to learned to use its power on his own." Malan was trying to be as objective and unemotional as possible, and still managed to clearly portray to Lord Falock his trust in the character of the Dwarves and Elves.

"Your words don't make me comfortable with these conditions, but there's a confidence in your voice that tells me of your trust in their abilities and intentions," Lord Falock said with a probing grin on his face.

"My Lord, I do not wish the burden of this decision based upon my feelings. Make the decision based upon your own sense of the matter."

"Don't be a coward, Malan. You were chosen out of all the land as one who knows the Dwarves better than any other. Your feelings and experience aren't simply requested, they're essential! You are a chosen advisor. Whether you like it or not my decision must be based at least partially on your sense of things, a sense which you have clearly portrayed to me today. Your confidence in them, coupled with their historical dealings with other people, compels me to trust them now. We have little alternative other than perhaps to try and protect the sword from ever being used at all." Lord Falock resolved himself to accept the conditions. He felt helpless in the matter and especially irritated with the prescribed condition, making it possible that he might never know for sure if someone actually had been chosen and given the knowledge of the sword's power. However, he knew that it would be impossible for someone to take possession of the sword without him knowing it. So whoever possessed it could be courted into service. With this in mind, he gave his seal of approval, accepting the plan.

He dispatched a detachment of soldiers from the castle to relieve the Dwarves from the necessity of escorting the delegation the entire distance. He also sent Malan back with the soldiers to accompany the delegation to Castle Crest.

The delegation reached Castle Crest in the early afternoon. Upon arrival at the castle, the Dwarves and Elves were immediately introduced formally to the castle leadership and the other visiting delegations of Pretoria, then shown to comfortable rooms in which they could refresh themselves in preparation for a midday buffet of cold cut meats, breads, and fruit.

Lord Falock knew that the Dwarves and Elves were both very aesthetically oriented races, so he had been busy for days trying to prepare for their arrival. He had gone to special pains to ensure that the castle grounds and the castle proper were in the cleanest and most orderly condition possible. He had instructed Alsdorf, the head of the castle staff, to ensure that the rooms being prepared for the visit were properly decorated. Alsdorf had visited the archives and retrieved some items of historical interest with which to provide both beauty and intrigue for the visitors. Among these items were several trunks of relics previously owned by the bearer of the sword Fallonrod, several ancient oil lamps of Elven origin, two tapestries containing scenes from legends of the last battle of the Great War depicting Fallonrod's victory, and several pieces of Dwarven-made furniture.

The sleeping quarters were set up in two quads. Each quad had a single large entry into a comfortable setting room complete with unique decor, a small library (books taken from the castle library, chosen especially for the guests using the quad, and placed in the room for their recreation), comfortable stuffed leather chairs, a dining table, and a large fireplace. On both sides of the setting room were two sleeping rooms with a bed, a small wardrobe, a bed-table and basin, a cistern, and a water jug. The Dwarves were placed in one quad, the Elves in the second. The remaining members of the other Pretorian delegation each joined the members of their own visiting entourage, partaking of their assigned accommodations.

At the buffet, the Elves announced that they had appointed Angoleen as their spokesman. The Dwarves chose Mornic. These two would be the official representatives to any meetings and would communicate any necessary information or requests to the Pretorian leadership or castle representatives according to need. This would free up the others to continue their investigation uninterrupted.

This was puzzling to the Pretorian delegation in that both of these appointees were outranked by delegation members of their own races. However, this was accepted upon the advice of Shaylan and Malan.

Angoleen was a typically strong, lean elf with piercing green eyes that always seemed to be laughing. He moved with a smooth grace that made him appear to float as he walked. Even the quickest maneuver was accomplished with such agility that he had sometimes been suspected of using magic and illusion that would enhance the appearance of his moves, though no one ever sensed it. He spoke with a deeper voice than most of his race, but retained the characteristic musical quality. Angoleen was a very talented sensor and mistmaster (the Elven counterpart of the human shadowmaster). His primary duty to the delegation was to keep vigil on the human responses to the delegation's progress and methods of operation. He would be able to warn the others against any who might become anxious or too suspicious.

Mayflyn was an artist. He was an elven metal molder. His arts were most effective as applied to putting magic into metal and, therefore, being able to discern the magic in an object of metal. His job would be one of the most dangerous, the probing of the sword. Because Darric had recovered some records regarding the forging and empowering of the sword, they had a good basic knowledge of the sword's original power. There was, however, no way of knowing if that power had been altered either by the war, the last owner, or the long amount of time it had lain essentially dormant. Mayflyn was the best hope of discerning any changes. He would then become invaluable in determining the possible uses and extent of power. Myletan would assist him as best he could, but would be at some disadvantage in that the scanty records had revealed that an elven magician had put the power into the sword, not a dwarven magician.

Mornic was a very powerful-looking dwarf. He was a dark dwarf with very hairy arms and large, powerful hands. He had a thick, bushy black eyebrow that went all the way across his face, shadowing his dark eyes. He was a student of man's warfare, a weapons master, and a brilliant strategist. As a matter of record, Mornic was the principal architect of much of the plan already in motion to recover the sword.

As soon as the midday buffet was completed, the delegation insisted on a viewing of the sword. They were led to the sword chamber, where they entered one by one. They were accompanied to the entrance by Lord Falock and a select few Pretorian dignitaries. The only ones who actually entered the room were the elves and dwarves.

They circled the sword, allowing the faint glow from its blade to be the only light in the room. For a few silent moments, each member stood staring in the darkness at the creation of their ancestors. They wondered at its exquisite craftsmanship. They sensed its power. As they stood watching it, the center of the grip suddenly began to glow, eventually exceeding the brightness of the blade. As they looked closer, they realized that the grip was stone, a fire crystal which was reacting to the presence of someone who possessed that powerful art. While they stared in wonder, a faint arc of light formed in a pulsating rainbow of color between the sword and Fallwyn. Everyone stepped back a step except Fallwyn, who remained somewhat mesmerized by the experience. The waves of pulsating light moved toward Fallwyn, changing color as they increased in speed until finally they became a blur. Changing direction, the waves again began to lose speed, still changing colors. Then, just a suddenly as it had started, it vanished. The entire incident may not have been noticed at all in a well-lit room. Finally, the light in the fire crystals went out altogether.

"You're correct in your estimation of the sword's power, Darric," came the musical voice of Fallwyn. "There appears to be more than one separate source of magic in the sword."

"That could make it very difficult to use..." said Myletan, who was cut off by Mayflyn, who continued...

"Not to mention dangerous and unpredictable!"

"Let's have a better look," said Myletan, who was already moving toward the opening in the wall. "We need some light in here," he called through the hole in the rock wall.

A moment later, a man stepped through the hole with two torches, which he handed to Myletan, then immediately returned back through the hole.

With the area surrounding the sword well-lit, the details of the sword became more vivid. The group again gathered close around the sword for a closer look. They visually studied it for a long time, then began to probe it with their magic arts. The use of magic rapidly became so pronounced that they found themselves interfering with each other's ability to perceive correctly. This brought a spontaneous burst of laughter from everyone present, which continued on briefly as they each recounted briefly their distorted perceptions. They decided to probe it one at a time, with the others standing close enough to perceive impressions from the sword with each successive inquiry. After each had taken their turn, the group made their way back out of the room to the waiting delegation.

"We'll return to our rooms for a time to rest and meditate on what we have learned in our brief encounter," announced Angoleen. "We'll need a brief preparation time before the evening meal. If you'll be so kind as to send an announcement of the meal sufficiently early to permit this. It's very likely that you'll find all of us in the graciously provided sitting room of the Dwarves' quarters."

Lord Falock agreed, and the group was guided back to their quarters.

There was a polite irritability among the Pretorian dignitaries. Men were usually impatient. They wanted analysis almost instantly, and answers to follow quickly. They were annoyed that there was not even the courtesy of a hint from any of the findings nor assessments from the spokesman. They knew that it was unlikely that they would be able to discover much in such a short time, but they wanted something... anything... just a word or an emotional response. But the elven spokesman, true to his race, was characteristically cautious, reserved, and seemingly secretive while remaining polite. The men bore their frustration in silence, but wore it blatantly on their faces.

Each member of the examining party went to their own room and spent the next hour sorting through the images and sensations they had received from the sword. Some made notes on parchment while others relied on their memories and left their interpretation open to new revelation. Everyone in their number was a master in one or more magical arts. Each had been amazed at the response they had received from their probing of the sword.

After sufficient time had been allotted for perusing the impressions, Angoleen called them all together in the dwarf's sitting room. They discussed their impressions of the sword and came to the conclusion that they were dealing with a very powerful magical tool that somehow responded to every magic they had tested it for. Due to the fact that so many of them had been able to access the magic of the sword at the same time, they entertained the possibility that there was indeed more than one source of magic at work in the sword. If it were true that the sources were actually independent sources of magic, then Mayflyn's earlier assessment of the potential unpredictability of the sword was possibly its greatest danger. If, however, there was a bridge in the magics that bound them together in one source, then that danger would be diminished. If there were more than one source and no bridge to bind the magics together, then the user could inadvertently cause the sword to act against itself. Worse yet, a sophisticated and knowledgeable magician could cause the sword to act against the bearer. They determined to devise a test that would discover the truth. This would be impossible without putting someone in jeopardy. One of them would have to hold the sword for the test to be conducted!

After a brief discussion of the merits of an experiment that would carry such a dangerous potential, it was decided that the knowledge which might be gained could easily outweigh the obvious perils of such a test. If it results gave the potential sword bearer the necessary understanding he would require to control it and use it respectably it would be worth the risk. It was already common knowledge that Fallwyn lacked only the art of water control, which was the rarest art in any of the lands, to complete him as a powermaster. Only Mornic, among all those present, possessed this rare art. Indeed, there were presently no known powermasters in either the dwarven or elven races. They decided to meet the next morning and devise a plan to test the source of magic in the sword. Fallwyn would hold the sword and be the conduit for the magic. They all sat quietly meditating upon the possible combinations of arts which might test the sources with the least possible backlash or danger to the sword or Fallwyn.

All of the members mourned privately that their friend would face such grave danger in this test, a test which was made necessary by mankind's proclivity towards violent conflict. But each one knew that their ancestors had created the sword to be used by a man. They also knew that the correct sword bearer could easily prevent their races from ever having to fight in human wars, indeed could possibly even prevent war among men!

The evening meal was announced in time for the group to pull their thoughts together for a brief synopsis of their discoveries. Then they all adjourned for dinner.

Dinner was served in the main dining hall. It was decorated in festive colors with wall hangings and colored lamps. Each of the fourteen tables had a unique cloth covering. Some were multicolored weaves, some dyed cloth, and two had embroidered scenes on them.

There was a great deal of sensing taking place in the room, enough to prove distracting for a truly sensitive person. Most of it was subtle, not overtly challenging. But not all of it was directed at the dwarves and elves. Darric and Angoleen both detected men who were subtly searching for signs of deception from Falock's personal staff. Angoleen found it sadly amusing and very human for them not to trust one another's intentions. After discussing the matter briefly, Darric set out to ascertain who the sensors were and which delegation they belonged to.

"If they'll probe their allies," thought Darric, "what trouble might they be to us?"

It took very little time to discover that all of those active in this clandestine operation were from Lord Linx's delegation. Their castle was physically closest to the potential danger from Danlion and would gain the most from having the defense provided by the sword. They did not want to be deceived or cut out of whatever support the sword might provide should it become accessible. After all, they had sent men and supplies to Castle Crest to protect the sword, and that entitled them to its use. Darric approached one of the men, a tall, thin man named Vestor.

"I'm Darric," he said, slightly bowing in a gesture of acknowledgement.

"Honored!" came the baritone reply mixed with instant mistrust. "I am Vestor, court counselor to Lord Linx." He returned the bow without losing eye contact, a sign of mistrust among the dwarves and elves. "How may I be of assistance?"   Darric sensed in his offer of service a definite intention of deception. "Glad ya asked!" answered Darric, thinking to himself that this man took himself far too seriously and that the most pleasure he probably ever gets is at the completion of a mission... missing everything in between the conclusions of life's pursuits, only finding joy in the successful culmination of a quest... what a pity. Then he continued to Vestor, "What's yer function here at this time?"

"As I already mentioned, I am a counselor in court affairs to Lord Linx." His speech was cautious and coolly polite.

"That's the case at your castle, sir. But how 'ill ya provide this counsel here at Castle Crest?" After giving only enough time for Vestor to gather his thoughts for a response, Darric continued, "Do ya go around gathering information, confirming suspicions, interrogating bystanders, and peaking behind closed doors? Or do ya conduct interviews with Castle Crest officers whose duties are ta ensure that visiting allies receive timely information?"

Darric sensed Vestor's inward rage but did not see it on his face or hear it in his carefully worded reply, "I assure you that my intentions are most noble. I hope that I have not in some way offended your sensitivities. At times, the nature of my business causes me to unintentionally probe where I have no actual need to do so. I catch myself doing this from time to time. I am as aware as you have demonstrated yourself to be that allies of such longstanding relations have no need to suspect evil motives or duplicity regarding each other's actions or plans. Again, my apologies if I have caused you concern." With that, Vestor excused himself. His rage had subsided, and he had worked very hard to mask his impulse for revenge, but Darric had clearly picked it up.

As Vestor walked away, he knew that Darric had seen right through him. He prided himself on virtual invisibility to the powers of other sensors. He had felt violated, and his pride was deeply wounded. "After all," he thought to himself, "it's my duty to keep Lord Linx as well informed as possible. If it meant 'confirming loyalty' of allies, then my job would be pleasant and reassuring to Lord Linx. If it means exposing some dire plot, then I will have served well. The dwarf's job was to make the sword accessible, not to police the activities of other delegation members!" The more he thought about the dwarf's actions, the more irritated he became. He did not like being caught at his own game.

Darric knew that even men of common alliances would not completely trust each other. He also suspected that even if there was no instruction from their leadership directing delegates to spy, some of the overzealous types would nevertheless do just that. It made him glad that he was a dwarf with friends like the elves. This would never be necessary between their races.

The dwarves and elves spent the evening telling stories and listening to the men recount all the myths and rumors surrounding the sword. There were a great many theories about the power of the sword and exactly what its uses might be. Stories from the last war were recorded on tapestries and written in numerous books. But they only chronicled stories about the results of the sword's use, not how it worked. Most curious of all, but not unexpected by them, was the assessment that the leadership of the kingdom in the last great power war did not care much for the last bearer of the sword. He was not the typical hero and not a natural leader. It even had angered some that the sword had come to him instead of some "more worthy" bearer.

Before going to sleep, they had agreed that when they awoke, they would devise a plan for discovering the sources of the sword's power and carefully calculate its risks. They had also made arrangements with Falock to discuss with him their immediate assessment of the potential problems they may encounter with the sword and the hopeful results of any plan of action that they may come up with. Knowing that the power of the sword, as it was being tested, would most likely attract the attention of every sensor in the kingdom who was awake, they decided to inform him of the timing of their intended experiment, minus the details about having someone hold the sword

Before breakfast, they met to discuss their ideas and forge a plan designed to prove out the sword's power source or sources. After some very creative possibilities had been brought forward, they decided to have Fallwyn hold the sword with Mornic's hands wrapped around Fallwyn's hands. This would combine all the understood magics that might bring the balance of power to the bearer, in this case, Fallwyn. Fallwyn would use the sword to fight off an attack of fire, which was to be thrown by Darric. At the same time, Angoleen was going to bring his considerable power as mistmaster to bear on the sword in an attempt to forge the appearance that the sword did not operate correctly. The thought was that if there was only one power source at work, it would fend off the fire attack and expose the attempt to veil its magic in illusion. In theory, the sword was supposed to protect the bearer against multiple magical attacks. If an illusionist attempted to make the sword appear ineffective, the sword would defeat the illusion. In order to tell the difference between the effect of an illusion thrown against the sword and the attempt to create an illusion through the power of the sword, Angoleen would first attempt to make the sword look powerless through an illusion of his own. Then he would try to infuse his own power into the sword and use it against the bearer. There was no way of knowing how the sword might react.

After they finished mental preparation for this adventure, they departed for the dining room for breakfast. They found human food somewhat different from their own delicately seasoned and carefully prepared meals, but adequate for satisfying hunger. They were joined by most of the dignitaries from the different delegations, all of which were very serious and overanxious to get on with the work. The dwarves and elves, on the other hand, were animated, conversational, and in no apparent hurry to get to their tasks. They were too busy enjoying the breakfast company. This, in turn, irritated the men who would have preferred to skip the meal together and get down to business... whatever that was to be. The contrast was not missed by the jovial visitors. They deliberately prolonged the meal by asking a multitude of cultural questions regarding subject matter in which the men had absolutely no interest. They continued on for some time because it was so much fun soliciting "polite responses" from their extremely agitated and increasingly more impatient hosts.

Finally, Angoleen intervened to bring the games to an end and shift their attention to the initial experiment. He stood and announced that he and Mornic would be joining Lord Falock to explain their current plans while the others prepared for their encounter. As soon as he finished speaking, the other dwarves and elves rose from the table and excused themselves, to the utter relief of the men with whom they had been conversing.

Once Angoleen and Mornic had joined the Pretorians in a library-type sitting room, they explained that they intended to activate the sword's power using two separate sources of power at the same time. They further explained that their attempt for activating the sword must be accomplished to insure that the sword would be safe from harm by any potential trespasser. Mornic explained that the art of illusion was very powerful if used correctly at just the right time. "If, for instance, a very powerful mistmaster were to make the sword appear not to be working through employing the power of the sword itself to create the illusion, the bearer might abandon its use prematurely to his own demise."

Angoleen continued, "It's precisely this magic that we are going to attempt today. If the sword can be activated to counteract fire and, at the same time, activated to resist illusion from a separate source, the sword itself has more than one source of power in itself. This would make it a difficult and dangerous tool to handle. A truly worthy opponent would attempt to manipulate the sword in just such a way."

Cutting in as if this presentation was a carefully rehearsed review, Mornic continued, "You see, your Lordship, it is a much easier task to put several sources of magic into a power sword of this type than it is to make the sword totally responsive to all the magics from a single source. Either way, the magics are bound together and require a powermaster to operate without causing destruction to the would-be user."

This short session shed more light on the power of the sword than Lord Falock had received since the entire crisis began. He graciously thanked the odd duo and allowed them to return to their work. They determined to meet at the sword chamber a little later in the day with anyone whom Lord Falock chose to invite.

By the time the others arrived at the chamber, Myletan had enlarged the hole in the wall through his powerful use of molders' magic. He not only enlarged it and smoothed it out but also decorated it with minor alterations to the stone surface resembling wood trim around the outside top and sides. The speed with which he had molded the stone alarmed the Pretorians, who knew that it had taken very talented magicians a long time to accomplish very little smoothing out of the magically molded stone after the initial breach by the invaders. Respect mixed with a healthy degree of fear replaced the complacent disregard that some of the men had displayed for this unassuming dwarf.

Stepping through the newly molded opening to the room, each member of the delegation of "outer-race foreigners" proceeded without speaking, directly to the glowing sword. They all carried unmistakable respect for the power of the sword and admiration for their ancestors who had created it. The men remained outside by choice, having seen what had become of the invaders who had attempted to use the sword, never knowing that had they desired to enter, they would have been denied.

Seriousness now sets in hard on each member of the group. Every heart was pounding, and every mind was keenly focused. Mayflyn moved close to the sword to assess if there were any discernible changes in it since their initial encounter with it yesterday. He could, since nothing was different or unbalanced. While he was probing the sword, Fallwyn and Darric shoved a freestanding book cabinet against the hole in the wall, thereby preventing those outside in the hall from entering or seeing in. They said it was to protect the Pretorians in case something went wrong in the room.

When it was determined to be safe, Fallwyn reached down and pulled the sword out of its stone sheath. It was warm to the touch and slid out effortlessly. He held it up in the air without applying any magic at all to it. Its glow was the only light in the room. Mornic moved over to stand next to Fallwyn while Darric and Myletan moved to a point on the opposite the hole in the wall and as far away as they could get from Fallwyn. Mayflyn stood next to the cabinet covering the hole in the wall to discourage any who might wish to peek or enter. He lit an oil lamp and trimmed it for low light, then set it on top of the cabinet. It was far enough away that it did not mask the sword's glow. Angoleen took a position next to the fireplace to the right of Fallwyn and Mornic, who were both facing across the room toward Darric and Myletan. Mornic stood to Fallwyn's left and reached up, taking firm hold of Fallwyn's hands, which already gripped the sword.

"Go ahead, Angoleen, my friend," came the strong, calm voice of Fallwyn.

Angoleen raised his left hand in an open-handed gesture toward the sword, and the glow went out. Everyone froze for an instant. Nothing happened.

"Is that illusion or is the light actually out?" questioned Mornic as he stared somewhat expectantly at the sword.

"The magic was directed at the aura surrounding the sword, not the sword itself." Angoleen was clearly pleased that the illusion was working. "I will now remove the illusion." Without even a move on his part, the illusion vanished and the glow returned.

Darric shifted anxiously from foot to foot and said, "So far so good! Let's go ta the next step."

There was a brief moment when everyone's heart jumped in preparation for the energizing of the sword.

"Good fortune to us," whispered Fallwyn as his concentration turned to focus on the sword. "Here goes!"

There was a brief moment when nothing happened at all. Suddenly, the glow went out. Every eye was wide in anticipation. Nothing else happened.

"It's yers, Fallwyn?" breathed Mornic, almost fearing to interrupt Fallwyn's concentration.

"Yes...got it…"

Muted nervous laughter of approval and relief filled the room for an instant, then died to dead silence.

"Ready?" Darric was raising his hands.

"Go!" answered Fallwyn, at which time the entire sword turned to a cobalt colored flame.

Fire jumped from Darric's upheld hands toward the flaming sword. It was instantly absorbed. Again, the fire flew, this time blue flame in an intense attack against the sword. It was as if the sword was hungry for fire and ate with a ravenous appetite. Not the tiniest portion of a flame passed the sword.

Angoleen raised his hand again and gestured toward the upheld sword. The flame appeared to flicker briefly but did not go out. He held his hand fixed in the direction of the sword. But nothing happened. "No result!"

"Next phase," shouted Darric, moving a little closer to the sword. "I'll try ta hold a flame on the sword as long as I can."

A steady stream of flame shot toward the sword again and was devoured. Angoleen moved closer to the sword and tried to use the power of the sword itself to create the illusion of the sword disappearing. At the same time, Fallwyn threw a small green flame curtain toward Darric. Darric's flame cut through the curtain as it flew toward him. The sword continued to absorb the flame thrown by Darric. The instant the green concussion flame hit Darric and Myletan, Angoleen disappeared. It happened so quickly that no one knew exactly what had transpired.

Mayflyn was the first to perceive what had happened and yelled, "Stop the magic. Angoleen's gone!"

Both Myletan and Darric were spun around by the concussion of the green flame and were just regaining their bearings when the flame went out on the sword. Neither Mornic nor Fallwyn let go.

Angoleen did not reappear.

"Angoleen!" shouted Fallwyn. "This is no time for a game. Speak up or show up."

They neither saw nor heard anything.

Fallwyn ignited the glow in the sword, and Mornic let go. Fallwyn slid the blade back into the slit in the floor. "Where are you? I can feel you... what's happened?" Fallwyn began to walk toward the last place Angoleen had stood. He bumped into something that felt like a heavy curtain, but he couldn't see it. He began to push at it and feel its contour.

It was then that I heard a faint voice, "Help!" He could feel the curtain moving slightly against his arm. Again, "Help! I can't breathe very well in here."

Everyone ran to the place where Angoleen was apparently trapped. Each gathered around the invisible curtain and began to probe it. They could hear the faint voice but could not push through the curtain. The curtain was about a large stride through and about the height of a tall man. It felt cylindrical in shape. It totally enclosed Angoleen.

"Stoop down, Angoleen," yelled Darric as he shot a white hot flame toward the top of the invisible prison. The flame passed right through without phasing it.

Angoleen yelled, "Stop! Stop! You're cooking me!"

Myletan took out his sword and swung it at the top of the magical container, only to have it bounce off.

Fallwyn walked over to the sword, pulled it out of the floor, and returned quickly to Angoleen. "Mornic, take the sword with me. Let's see if we can get rid of the curtain."

He took it, and they aimed the sword at the place where Angoleen was trapped. Fallwyn tried to undo the illusionary magic that Angoleen had used against the sword. Nothing happened. "Let's try to cut through it." The sword passed through without resistance but left no hole.

"Come on, Mornic. We're going in." With both of them holding on tightly, they entered through the curtain. Once inside, they could see Angoleen, but no one outside could see them. Angoleen fell to the floor, almost unconscious. It was then that they noticed how very thin the air was. Mornic let go of the sword and bent down to pick up Angoleen as Fallwyn neutralized the sword's power. "Walk carefully and slowly so I don't lose contact with your arm," said Fallwyn in a very serious tone. "Let's get out of here. I'm getting dizzy." As they walked, the curtain moved with them. They could not get out. No matter which way they moved, so did the curtain. They had moved passed those outside the mobile airtight cage and were now standing behind Darric and Myletan. Darric sensed that the presence of the magic had moved and was trying to locate it again. It was difficult because the magic was so powerful that it filled the room. Only the balance of power showed movement.

"Hold still, Mornic," gasped Fallwyn. "Put him down and grab my hands." He quickly complied. Fallwyn held up the sword, and the blue flame lit. Almost instantly, there was an explosion of rushing air. They were free.

Both Fallwyn and Mornic fell to the ground while the others outside almost jumped out of their skin. A cheer went up as they realized what had happened and that everyone was free. Laying the sword down, Fallwyn went to Angoleen's side, being joined simultaneously by several others. Mayflyn reached down and touched Angoleen's forehead and stood for a moment. Soon Angoleen opened his eyes and began to stretch and yawn, and rub his eyes. Applause and cheers erupted from the entire group.

As soon as they were refreshed, Fallwyn explained that the invisible curtain was the sword's response to Angoleen's attempt to make the sword appear to vanish. The illusion was thrown back at him, intensified to such an extent that it trapped him and sealed him inside of it.

"If that is true, why didn't the sword react more drastically to Darric's attack?" asked Myletan, who was only now realizing how dangerous it had been for Darric and him.

"I don't know for sure," Fallwyn said as he went into a deep meditation, "unless..." his eyes brightened, "unless it was because I was in control of the fire and therefore in control of the response!"

Mayflyn had the best vantage point to observe and assess what he saw, "At least we know that the magic could not be accessed directly by Angoleen, and it did not work against the sword. The magic must be of a single source. It must be tied into the user's ability in its response. Even though Fallwyn was not directly using the mistmaster art, the sword responded using his type of power."

Darric had been working hard to remember exactly what he had sensed just prior to being hit by the green flame. Only after Mayflyn shared his observations did his recollection clear. "Yes, that's it," there was considerable excitement in his voice. "I clearly remember sensin' Fallwyn's magic in the sword's response ta the illusion by Angoleen...'twas not a return of Angoleen's magic but clearly Fallwyn's!"

Fallwyn retrieved the sword and walked back to the group. "Mornic, what is your weakest art?"

After thinking for a moment, Mornic answered with a little embarrassment, "stone molding." He had always loved metal, and even though he could have been a stone molder of considerable power, he had never mastered it due to his preoccupation with metal, a preoccupation that had won him a place in this delegation.   "Excellent," said Fallwyn in a voice that could only be interpreted as both relieved and very pleased. "You must try to use the sword's power to work the stone. Come on and take hold with me. Try to make the stone flow out of the wall to form a shelf."

As Mornic took hold of the sword with Fallwyn, Fallwyn continued, "The rest of you see if you can distinguish the power source molding the stone."

The group found the place where the original door had been and opened it, revealing the magically molded stone that surrounded the room. Mornic concentrated on the molded stone wall with the sword tip in contact at the place he wished to mold. There was no change in the appearance of the sword, but the stone began to flow like thick portage out of a bowl, leaving an awkward-looking indentation in the wall and a blob of stone forming a lip at the bottom of it. Suddenly, as if made of the wettest clay, the blob began to transform into an ornate shelf with clearly detailed indentations in the wall above it. Stone flowed like hot wax as the point of the sword moved across the wall, forming this beautiful creation.

There was a spontaneous applause, "It was clear when you joined in Fallwyn. I could feel your magic coming to life", exploded Darric with his characteristic enthusiasm.

Myletan's brow was furrowed, and a curious look took his face. "Mornic, can you mold at all?"

"Not this much on 'untreated' stone", came the answer in an amused voice. "That was much faster, and on molded stone at that!"

"So, the sword increases the magic's effect but not the ability of the user", came Myletan's conclusion. "Lots of power that is not well under control may lead to a giant catastrophe!"

"But Myletan, my friend," cut in Mayflyn, "That's what a power sword is all about!"

Darric caught Myletan's point immediately, "No! If I understand what I have heard, it means that an almost totally undeveloped art was just used to mold magically treated stone, a feat not easily performed by any casual molder. That would have been very difficult for an inexperienced molder. Mornic did it with ease, and doesn't even qualify as a novice."

Angoleen joined in, "This means that, since we now know that the sword can accomplish more than one art at a time, the user must be very careful how he wields his magic."

"He could work a developed art without hardly being aware of having done so!" added Mayflyn, sounding somewhat foreboding.

"Gentle friends!" came the deep voice full of magical music. "We've seen some remarkable things here today. But we all know that this power sword was created by our ancestors. It was made as a formidable tool to be used by a human. We must expect it to be an exceptional creation. As a true power sword, we must expect it to operate through the spectrum of magical power. But because it originated with our people, we must look for the unexpected. Maybe a condition placed upon the user, or some special responses it may bring to attacks upon it. It may even have built-in limitations." Angoleen wandered over to a chair and sat down. "It was able to turn illusion into reality, something that we must combine our efforts together to accomplish, and then only with the greatest care. I wonder if it does the same thing with other arts or applications of illusion."

Darric's face lit up, "I wonder if a mistmaster could actually move through solid objects as he can appear to? Or possibly become as untouchable as he is unseen?"

Fallwyn went over to the sword and retrieved it again. "Mornic, come to the wall with me." Mornic took hold of the sword while everyone moved around them to watch. Taking the sword in their hands, Fallwyn made it disappear. Then he moved the sword to the wall. He had to struggle with his concentration to keep from activating the molders' magic as the sword came near the wall. Still, the sword passed through it. It moved as though it was being swung flatwise through water. Though there was some resistance, the wall remained unchanged to the eye. He immediately shut down the magic in the sword. The group rushed to the place where the invisible sword had entered the wall and investigated. Darric brought a magical flame up in the palm of his hand to shed light on the details of the affected stones. Nothing!

They stood speechless for a moment, running their hands over the wall and looking at the sword.

Fallwyn was the first to speak, "I heard of such a thing as a child, but only as a story. I never actually suspected that there could be any truth in it."

"It may actually be true what the legend said about Maylore, Fallonrod's first master, that he could walk through walls and vanish without a trace, only to reappear in the most unexpected places," said Mayflyn in a manner that betrayed his obvious amusement with the possibilities of such an art.

Suddenly, Mornic became very serious. "How can we stand here an' seriously consider givin' this sword to a human. We have the ability ta remove it without bein' discovered. They'll never know it's gone."

Darric waited for a moment for someone to reply or rebut the idea, but no one spoke. It had occurred to all of them that this was a possibility. They all mistrusted humans. But they also knew that the wars would be inevitable. "Friends, I know your thoughts. I have them too. But they're wrong. This sword was built for a human ta use. If it was made by our ancestors for men and given ta them, it's not our right ta take it back. Our way o' life is on trial here. Our integrity is bein' tested. We must be true ta ourselves

and our beliefs. Besides, it's our choice who 'ill wield it. We've found one that
has all the signs o' bein' able ta uphold proper ideals an' use the sword
courageously, that is, selflessly!"

"Sometimes, Darric, it's hard to weigh out such things," said Angoleen
without moving or making eye contact with the dwarf. "But the wars will come,
and this sword, in the hands of the correct person, will bring a greater
possibility of peace, or at least, shorter wars and less killing."

At that, the others renewed their commitment to bring the sword into the
hands of the chosen human.

"I pity the boy. The responsibility he'll bear for the rest of his life will be
oppressive," Fallwyn said as he walked away from the group to return the sword
to its stone cradle.

Trying to pick up the spirits of the group, Darric, half shouting in a jolly
tone, said, "He may surprise us all!"

"I hope it's a good surprise, Darric. A real fine investment of his power,"
said Myletan, heading toward the bookshelf and dragging Mayflyn with
him. "Let's air out our minds for a while."

As soon as they pushed the cabinet aside, the group climbed out in single
file without saying a word to the anxiously waiting group.

Angoleen was the last one out of the room and announced that they
would retire to one of the sitting rooms and discuss their findings, and then
bring a report to Lord Falock and the other Pretorian delegates.

Those waiting outside were very annoyed at being put off, and it almost
caused a confrontation. Only the intervention of Lord Falock prevented it. He
physically grabbed Lord Linx by the arm to restrain him from following the
retreated group with demands for information. The men grumbled quietly
among each other as they walked away in a clot, leaving Lord Falock and Lord
Linx in a somewhat heated debate.

"How can you let them just walk away, saying nothing. The sword is in
your castle and is useless to you. We all know that they activated the sword...
everyone in the kingdom who can sense at all knows that the sword has been
brought back to life." Lord Linx was yelling like a brother would yell at a
sibling, no threats, just frustration.

"Calm down, my friend. You're going to make yourself sick. They're probably just testing us to see if we are 'worthy in their eyes' to have the information they now possess."

"Are you really that confident that they're going to give you what you want?"

"I'm not really sure what I want. But they are very honorable races. They'll honor their commitment. They actually owe us nothing! But they've given us their word that they'll help us.... and we can expect that they'll do just as they've promised."

Lord Linx became agitated again, "But we don't know HOW they'll fulfill their promise, or in what form it will come!"

"There is the very real possibility that we won't recognize the actual fulfillment of their commitment when it comes. But at the same time, we've gotta recognize that they gave us the sword to begin with, and it proved to be the key to our winning the wars and preserving our land. And besides all that... we really don't have any good alternatives," said Lord Falock as he led Lord Linx back down the hallway. "Some ale should soften all this irritation. They'll come through for us if we give 'em their way now. If we push 'em, they just might pack up and run out on us in a fit of indignation."

"I still don't like them dictating our future. I don't like the prospect of THEM having the final decision over who 'ill be given a chance to wield the sword and who won't even be allowed to try!" pouted Lord Linx as they walked away.

Back in the elven sitting room, the group gathered to decide their next step. They were very concerned about the impatience they sensed in the group of men who had been waiting outside the sword room after the encounter with the sword. They now knew more about the power of the sword, but nothing of its possible hidden traits. It was obviously the work of very powerful magicians who had carefully invested it with magical abilities. Knowing the care and planning that must have been put forth in the creation of the sword, it was easy to surmise that the makers could have also put personality into it. Specific traits could have been infused that were designed to prohibit its use by certain types of people. Perhaps certain attitudes would trigger it to shut down, or even destroy the user. It may be that those killed by the sword were not destroyed because they were not powermasters, but because they possessed that characteristic against which the sword was designed to rebel. But how to test such a theory?

The results of the intrusion into the sword's power by the invaders had proven disastrous for them. Wisdom would then dictate that this time, greater care should be taken in thinking through any plan they devised to test the sword's response.

They talked over many approaches, but in the end decided to put off any further testing until they had given their minds time to ponder the problem.

When Mornic and Angoleen went to fill in Lord Falock regarding their encounter with the sword, Falock decided not to disturb Lord Linx, who had gone to his room after having consumed a few too much ale. He was unable to locate Lord Welton. Apparently, he had left the castle to venture through the streets and walk off his irritation toward the elves and dwarves, whom he called "the mystics and their jolly little playmates". They met together in the library, which was immediately adjacent to the banquet hall. Mornic and Angoleen informed Lord Falock that they had successfully activated the sword and discovered that it was indeed a power sword with a single power source. They explained how it had almost taken the lives of several members in the process of testing. This information made Lord Falock very nervous. He was further agitated that they would not give him a detailed account of the test.

Falock was about to express his irritation when the sound of muffled yelling erupted out of a small reading room, which was situated through a set of closed double doors. Before they could move or otherwise react to the noise, the doors broke open and Darric tumbled into the room, holding Vestor around the waist.

"What's the meaning of this?" yelled Falock in a deafening roar. Both combatants collected their wits and climbed to their feet, Vestor mumbling curses at the dwarf and Darric attempting to look dignified while smiling broadly.

"I will only ask one more time. What is the meaning of this?"

"I'll defer ta Vestor," said Darric with a bow and a not-too-subtle grin.

Vestor stood for a moment, staring loathsomely at Darric. He then turned his face toward Lord Falock and explained, "Sir, I had been doing a little exploring of the castle again, being that it had been quite some time since last I had the honor of visiting, when I heard voices coming from the next room. Being curious as to who I might find in this room, I put my ear to the door to determine if I could identify the voices or not. It was at that very moment that this dwarf with the overactive imagination ran at me from the rear, startling me so much that I yelled, then grabbed me so that we both fell against the door and landed here in your presence." At this point, he turned and threw a purely vile glance at Darric. "There's really nothing left to tell. I do beg your pardon, Sir."

"And you, Darric, how do you defend your actions?" asked Falock with one eyebrow cocked.

"Lord Falock, I can lay no claim ta ignorance o' this meetin' nor of the location at which i'twas takin' place. I had become aware of a vague sensin' bein' used, an' set out ta investigate it. Ya see, I have twice before detected it an' wished ta secure better knowledge o' the wielder of such a refined an' subtle art. It led me ta this room and ta Vestor. Knowin' that this meetin' would be attended by any ya wished ta call, an' not attended by others, I took offence at this man's efforts ta listen in uninvited. I must admit that in my haste ta apprehend him, I did not visually identify him before I jumped upon him." Darric ended abruptly and simply stood, a hint of a grin still present, and faced Lord Falock.

"You finish as though there were more Darric," said Falock in a tone that solicited a reply.

"If so, then yer Lordship 'ill need ta supply it from yer own observations," explained Darric in a matter-of-fact tone.

Lord Falock looked back and forth for a moment at each of them, then excused both of them, "Vestor, you need to be more discreet in your adventures. And your Darric, you honor yourself in your intentions. I only hope I correctly judged them. Let's put this incident behind us, shall we?" Both of them nodded agreement to Lord Falock, then to each other, turned, and left the room.

As they were walking away, Vestor, who was a few steps ahead, spoke quietly over his shoulder, "You had better exercise more than discretion if you ever give thought to such an adventure as that again." He had barely finished the statement when he turned down a hallway heading away from the dwarf.

Darric returned to the sleeping quarters and set about getting their group together. He had already filled in the others regarding the incident in the library when Angoleen and Mornic returned from their meeting with Lord Falock.

"I sensed strong malice in Vestor," said Darric as he went to the main entrance door and shut it, and turned the key to lock it from the inside. "Vestor's up to some evil invention, I assure ya of that! For some reason, or lack o' reason, he doesn't trust us." He returned to the center of the room, where he stood and looked around the circle of attendants. "Now I don't trust him. He'll no doubt attempt ta violate our relationship with the Pretorians in the name of 'Security'. This could put our plans in jeopardy."

Myletan leaned forward in his slightly overstuffed brown leather chair and voiced what was already on everyone's mind, "We cannot afford ta have our plans discovered or lives might be endangered..."

"Would most certainly be lost!" exclaimed Mornic, cutting off Myletan mid-sentence.

There was a tension in the air that charged their powers of concentration and knit them together in a tighter bond than most humans will ever experience.

Fallwyn stood up from his corner spot at the center table and strolled thoughtfully toward Darric, who still stood in the center of the room. Without so much as a word passing between them, Darric shouted, "Wonderful idea Fallwyn..." and with a wink and a nod headed straight into his sleeping quarters.

"I hate it when they do that," said Angoleen, bringing laughter from everyone. "Care to share the secret with us?" he said with a chastising smile on his face.

A little embarrassed, Fallwyn cleared his throat politely, "I seriously doubt that he even knows what happened..." they all laughed again. "He's gone after our little rock orb."

Fallwyn realized that Angoleen, Mayflyn, and Mornic knew nothing of the strange creation so he began to tell them the essential facts as Darric returned with the stone ball. After the briefest of explanations, with a promise to tell the entire story later, they set it on the table and all gathered around it.

"Dalwan was the host last time," said Myletan with a little uncertainty in his voice. "I wonder how it will work this time?"

Darric put his hands on the ball for a moment, and everyone else just watched. It came to life. The inside began to swirl in a brilliant display of color and light. Fallwyn put his hands on the now brightly shining orb, one at a time, as Darric removed his. There was a brilliant explosion of colored light that threw shadows on the wall of the already well-lit room. Images began to form in the swirling colors. At first, they were phantoms, lasting for only an instant. Then firm images began to take shape, becoming more and more distinct until they were crystal clear. The first was that of an elven woman... beautiful... colorful... sitting quietly, making something in cloth with her hands. The vision vanished. Darric appeared in the stone ball, an amused look on his face. There was a vibrating light around the crystal clear image. Darric moved closer to get a good look.

"Will you look at that!" he said as the vibrations around the orb changed into distinctive patterns, obviously reflecting his voice. The voice coming out of the orb was an elven version of his own. Everyone was now gathered close to gaze at this wonder. Darric glanced away in the direction from which the stone seemed to be looking at him. He could neither see nor sense anything unusual. "The magic here seems mute."

"Hard to tell though," added Mornic. "There's so much magic coming from this ball that any subtle magic could be masked."

"True enough." Darric stepped back a pace, trying to sense the room. The image changed again. Lord Falock came into view.

"Where is it coming from?" he was asking.

"From the visitors' room, sire," came the answer from a man none of them remembered meeting.

"Very well. Stay close and inform me if it changes or if you sense any danger. They are our guests, and they are some of the most powerful artisans of their races. They'll not deliberately harm us. See if you can identify what they are doing. We may learn something from them." With that, Falock dismissed the speaker.

The images faded as Darric stepped up again to Fallwyn's side, "Can you find Vestor?" The images swirled while Fallwyn tried to focus on Vestor.

"I don't have a good enough feel for him." Brilliant light flooded out of the swirling maze of colors in the orb as Fallwyn looked at Darric, obviously waiting for some help. After a moment of intense concentration, a glint of light sparked in Fallwyn's eye, "Darric, come and put your hand on this thing with me. See if we can control it together."

"But we don't know what it 'ill do," he answered with concern in his voice.

"And we never will unless we try it," said Fallwyn with childlike challenge in his voice.

With that, Darric reached toward the fiery ball. A brighter ray of red light jumped across the distance to his hand as it neared. Instantly, the light changed and the images began to form, confused at first then clearing. Vestor's image formed crystal clear. There was no sound at first, but he was clearly speaking with two other men. He was obviously passionate about what he was saying. One of the men was shaking his head in some form of disagreement or disbelief. Suddenly, Angoleen stepped forward and peered intensely into the orb.

"He is using magical manipulation on them. I can sense it coming through the orb." Angoleen closed his eyes, trying to sense more keenly.

"I've got him now," whispered Fallwyn. Instantly, the light began to vibrate around the ball, and voices followed in clear tones.

"...why you must go along with this!" said Vestor in impassioned tones. The one man was still shaking his head in what was now seen clearly to be disagreement.

The second man spoke, "How do we know that you aren't just overreacting to them?"

The first man joined in, "This could explode in our faces and bring disgrace and embarrassment to us and our Lord's."

"You can no doubt sense the power they are using at this very moment," said Vestor in an enchanted voice. "What do you think they're doing? What sort of manipulation or twisting of events to their own selfish advantage do you suppose they are up to? Did they send their best here just to honor an ancient covenant?"

"Maybe they did. Maybe that's exactly what they're doing," said the first man.

Cutting in quickly, the second man spoke angrily, "...and we could undo every bit of help they might offer if we spy on them and get caught."

"I'm not even sure that we can spy on them without them knowing it. They're even better than we are at these things." The first man was now shaking his head again, having a glazed, contemplative look on his face.

"Then we'll use a distraction to keep them focused on what we want them to sense," said Vestor, who was becoming desperate. "We must find out what they're up to. I guarantee you it's no good. If we sit by and do nothing when we could have acted wisely, we'll be forever disgraced. If we do something, even if it is wrong, it 'ill be out of a sense of honor and love for our land that we do it. If we get caught, we confess our error in judgment and suffer only embarrassment. Better that than a witless fool!" His words were full of magic.

"How can they miss what he's doing?" said Fallwyn with an amused grin on his face. "He'll make fools of them in spite of their intentions."

The first man continued, "How do you actually plan to pull this inquisition off?"

"I'm pleased that you asked," said Vestor, regaining his calm, cool composure. "There is a chamber directly below their fireplace where we can listen to their conversations. First, we'll place one of us there throughout the day to discover their every intention. Then we'll follow them and wreck whatever subversion or false plans they intend. After all, if their intentions are noble, they have nothing to fear from us."

The second man stirred as if from a daze and slowly stood to his feet. "Alright, I can't argue with your logic. But we must all be in agreement if we decide to act on anything they say or do."

"Agreed!" said Vestor with a triumphant grin.

Reluctantly, the first man also stood as both of the others stared expectantly at him, "Count me in, but only on Brillman's conditions."

"Then we're all in agreement. I'll take the first watch. Come on, and I'll show you how to get in. The main entrance to the inner wall corridors is guarded at all the hallway doors. There are two entrances from the rooms." Vestor's thin frame was already moving quickly toward the door even as he spoke.

Fallwyn laid the ball down, and the figures were swallowed by the orb's swirling lights. The light then died down to a flicker and went out altogether. "We have a good plan, and I see no need to alter it at this point," said Fallwyn, looking directly into Darric's eyes. "We'd better act now. The room isn't well guarded at this point. Let's take advantage of it."

"The rest o' ya stay here an' play with yer magic. That 'ill keep our friendly spies busy." Darric said, dressing his words with a broad grin. "Fallwyn, find our friend."

Fallwyn picked up the stone ball, and with a brilliant flash of light, it focused quickly on the image of Dalwan. Everyone moved closer to check out the area where he was seated and see if they could identify it.

Suddenly, Dalwan turned and faced into the crystal's perspective. Without disturbing those around him, who were busy carrying on some sort of conversation, he began to probe the sensation he had of being watched. It was familiar... very familiar. Finally, it came to him that it was the magic he had sensed when the orb had been created. He looked around to see if anyone else could sense it, but none appeared to. He then looked back directly into the perspective of the orb again, winked, and gave a small wave. At that, Fallwyn put the stone back down, and they all exchanged astonished glances.

"Remind me to play with this thing some more later. This could prove to be great fun!" They all laughed as Darric and Fallwyn headed for the main library, where they had seen Dalwan.

They walked directly to the library and made a grand entrance, laughing and talking loudly. Once inside, they stopped short and apologized for intruding so disruptively. Then they discovered several of Lord Falock's personal attendants and advisors sitting and talking with Shaylan and Rhem. The interruption was well received, and they were asked to join the discussion. They said that there was something they had left in the swordroom that they needed to retrieve. They promised to return and talk for a while. They stopped to talk for a moment with Dalwan, exchanging pleasantries in a casual manner quite which reminded those listening of men talking with a child. They were walking away, having gone only a few steps when, after a brief exchange between themselves, they stopped, turned, and called back to Dalwan, "You may join us if you like; we should be coming back this way shortly."

Dalwan looked back at Shaylan, whose protection and invitation he was bound to. Shaylan gave a symbolic gesture of permission, and Dalwan bounded out of his chair and joined them as they walked out of the room. They were pleased to see that Dalwan had remembered their request to keep his sword handy; he had it on.

As they walked toward the swordroom, the three made small talk while making subtle gestures warning Dalwan that sensors were active. They approached the swordroom with enough commotion that the guard had plenty of time to prepare himself for their arrival. They reached the room and requested entry to retrieve a needed article. The guard said that he would permit them to enter, but not Dalwan. Darric tried in vain to embarrass the man into letting him enter. Without even the slightest warning, a huge beast pushed through what appeared to be an invisible door right into the hallway, only 10 paces or so from the door. It was head and shoulders taller than the guard, who himself could look over the top of Fallwyn's head. It was covered with hair and wore a thick leather belt containing a mace, sword, and coiled bolo. There was a glow around the beast, and his eyes shone with light against the dark, torchlit hallway. Fallwyn and Darric closed their shoulders in front of Dalwan, blocking him from entering the conflict. The guard pulled a sword and challenged the beast while yelling for reinforcements at the top of his voice. The beast bared fierce, pointed teeth and stepped forward. To Dalwan's surprise, both Fallwyn and Darric were frozen in their tracks. The beast sported a small, round shield on his left arm, which amply blocked the first intense blow that the guard threw. There was a quick flurry of blows, and the beast was beaten back a few paces. The guard was now in full control of the fight and had stopped yelling except for battle shouts as he swung his sword.

Suddenly, Dalwan remembered the sword. He could take it now, or was he supposed to? He hesitated. Still, neither of his companions moved. Dalwan turned and dashed through the door toward the glowing spot in the room. Without so much as a hint of magic, he pulled the sword from its stone sheath and switched it with his own. To his utter amazement, his sword slid effortlessly into the hole left by the power sword. As quickly as he had entered, he left. It was too easy. Something had to go wrong. He entered the hall to find that the group had moved a few paces further away. The beast was still losing to the skilled guard. There was a giant blinding flash of light, and the beast disappeared. There was a breeze of air that brushed past the group and toward the direction from which they had approached the room.

"Shadowmaster!" yelled Darric, and they all pursued except the guard. As they turned the corner, there were three men running toward them with swords drawn. One of them was knocked down by an invisible force moving past him. He fell directly into the other two men, causing all three to stumble, each trying to avoid stabbing each other or themselves.

"We'll pursue the shadowmaster, you seal off the castle," shouted Darric as they ran past the recovering men.

"They made three corners and were out of sight of the guards when Darric and Fallwyn ducked into a room and dragged Dalwan with them. They began to laugh and lean against the wall, holding their mouths to keep from being too loud and being discovered. Dalwan stood looking at them with total bewilderment on his face. This caused the other two to almost choke with muted laughter.

Finally, Fallwyn caught his breath enough to squeeze out a few words. With his hands on Dalwan's shoulders, he gasped out, "It's all a figment." As he finished, he buried his head in Dalwan's shoulder and laughed until he cried. There was enough amusement watching the two of them carry on that it finally brought a smile to his face.

"What is so funny, you two?" said Dalwan, trying desperately to understand the humor in the incident.

"Lad," groaned Darric, holding his stomach, "It wasn't the incident as a whole, it was the beast." Again, both of them broke into laughter that caused tears to flow down their faces.

A voice filled with music filled the air, "Dalwan, we couldn't control the movement and the looks of the beast at the same time since we had never gone this far with the fantom. Its head kept changing. One moment it was a beast with fierce teeth, then a silly hairy critter with a stupid grin."

"Then it would just go dim, leaving glowing eyes with no features," said Darric, cutting in.

"The guard started overpowering it with the strong blow of his sword..." Darric said as he lost the battle to control his laughter.

Fallwyn finished, his voice full of laughter, "...and every time we concentrated on making the beast's shield stand up to the sword strike, the beast changed colors a little."

Darric went humorously serious for a moment and spoke with wide eyes staring right into Dalwan's, "At one point, the poor guard almost turned and ran when the beast opened his mouth, roaring wide, bearing sharp white teeth.."

Fallwyn finished in hushed tones, as if telling a horror story, "...and at the back of his gaping mouth, clearly visible, was...the wall behind him!" Both broke into laughter again.

"Ya should have seen it lad... just as clear as could be... the wall!!!"

"The poor guard glanced back at us and almost ran. But we appeared to be standing our ground, so he swung hard again, this time striking the beast's sword..." said Fallwyn, looking to Darric to complete the sentence.

"...and it stopped the blow from his sword with no sound." Darric was holding his sides, which began to ache from the laughter, and gasping for breath. It was hard for him to laugh quietly, which made the pain just that much worse.

They could hear men in the hallway making their way from room to room toward them. They quickly collected their wits and entered the corridor.

"The magic vanished and left no trace of the bearer," said Fallwyn.

Only seconds later, Vestor came walking quickly around the corner at the end of the hall toward the group gathered around Fallwyn, Darric, and Dalwan.

"The magic stopped in this very area. Who was here when it happened?" questioned Vestor in an authoritative tone.

"I'll do the questioning if there's any to be done, Vestor. This is not your domain!" said a rather tall, rotund man in a stately dress. "They have already testified to the facts you spout so boldly. I'm sure we can do as apt a job as any at getting to the bottom of this." Turning to a group of five guards standing with them, he instructed them to keep at least two alert guards in this area of the corridor for the next two shifts. He wanted them to watch for any return of the "thing, whatever it was."

The man introduced himself as Damian. He was the captain in charge of the castle security, replacing the recently retired captain. At Lord Falock's request, he sent relief to the guard at the swordroom breach and had him join them all in the State Room, where Lord Falock was to convene an inquiry.

When the inquiry began, it was attended by royal members of each delegation as well as security from each delegation. Fallwyn and Darric explained exactly what they observed. Dalwan was only questioned after the final testimony of the guard. It was determined by the entire group that what was experienced was a phantom, not a reality. It was still baffling that it had substance enough to fight with a guard. Its source left a question after Darric and Fallwyn both deferred to Lord Falock's people, citing that men would have better credibility in judging such matters in their own land.

Dalwan was sent back to Shaylan's room, and Darric and Fallwyn returned toward their room. As they walked back, they decided that ending their visit soon was a vital necessity. They set a plan in motion to secure an honorable exit.

Several hours later, they had secretly made the others aware of the plan and prepared to set it in motion later that night. Knowing that their conversations would be monitored, they began to talk about "retrieving the book." They mentioned that they had searched the libraries and had narrowed it down to one library where it must be kept. Darric then said that he had been en route to check that library when he stumbled upon Vestor earlier. They then talked as though they had decided on a late-night raid to retrieve it.

Mornic was later dispatched to retrieve Lord Linx to the rendezvous point. Once there, they described their entire conversation to Lord Linx and what they expected to happen when they arrived at the library.

Under the cloak of magic provided for everyone by two of their party, Lord Linx and one of his security officers, accompanied Darric, Fallwyn, Angoleen, and Mornic to the library, unseen but clearly sensed. They entered the very same door that Darric had crashed through with Vestor earlier. Once inside, they uncloaked except for Lord Linx, the security officer, and Fallwyn. They strategically placed three small lamps and moved to the bookshelves in three separate areas of the room. Suddenly, the doors burst open and Vestor entered, followed by his two cohorts and two security officers, one from Lord Linx's delegation and one from Castle Crest security.

"What sort of games are we playing tonight, 'guests of Pretoria'," said Vestor in a brash, accusatory tone, putting an additional derogatory emphasis on the last part. "I sincerely hope you can satisfactorily explain your actions to the Lord of this castle." There was pompous glee in his voice.

At that instant, he sensed the presence of Fallwyn's magic as a mistmaster's illusion. "And you, come out from behind your magical disguise. You're as clear as if we could see you." Vestor was looking directly toward the source of Fallwyn's magic.

A compliant voice full of music answered, "As you wish, sir."

With that, the magic faded slowly, disclosing the unmistakable presence of three forms. Vestor went pale as the image of his Lord crystallized in front of him.

"And I for my part hope you have a good explanation for me regarding your actions here tonight, Vestor," said Lord Linx without the same glee of discovery Vestor had displayed.

Turning toward Fallwyn, Lord Linx spoke quietly, "My most profound apology for this very unfortunate series of circumstances. I don't even know how to explain it except to say it was loyalty to a fault that has brought this about."

Angoleen stepped forward, accompanied by Mornic. "Since we're not treated as guests nor respected as allies, we find no other alternative except to leave at daybreak. We'll leave our departure up to you to arrange and explain," said Angoleen with something approaching sympathy in his voice.

"As you wish." Turning to Vestor, he said, "Lock yourself up somewhere and lose the key." Vestor slinked out of the room alone. Turning back toward Angoleen, "If you should decide to reconsider, please let me know before daybreak."

"It may be, sir," said Fallwyn in a compassionate tone, "that history will write this incident as fortunate."

Lord Linx stood facing them for a brief moment as if to say something, then just turned and left.

The most confused of all were the guards who were left to their own observations to determine what had occurred. Though they did not know the circumstances that led up to this, they knew that what transpired was not very pleasant for Lord Linx and would be even less pleasant for Vestor.

The dwarves and elves were packed and ready for departure with the rising of the sun. Very unceremoniously, they filed into the State Room where they made their last appearance before Lord Falock.

Angoleen spoke on behalf of the group that stood shoulder to shoulder in a single line directly in front of Lord Falock's throne, "Lord Falock, your hospitality has been very gracious and your patience exemplary. We know that you do not understand our response to the incident, which has now led up to our departure, but we strongly believe that time will show us to have acted wisely. The additional secrets of the sword which we have learned upon our visit will be made available to you at a future date, which we shall choose at our discretion. It is the general lack of trust shown by your race for others, both of your own kind and ours, that has given us the most discomfort in undertaking this adventure. It is in response to this mistrust that we decided upon our course of action and now take leave of any further commitment here at your castle. We wish you no disrespect."

With that, he turned and joined the others who were still facing Lord Falock. They all gave a roughly simultaneous half-bow and filed out single file without even waiting for a reply. The way was clear, and the doors opened up all along the path leading out of the city. They did not stop or look about until they cleared the front gate. They went about half a day's journey to await Dalwan at a prearranged rendezvous point.

CHAPTER 21

Dalwan joined Shaylan soon after the exit of the Dwarves and Elves in apparent indignation. He was so anxious to get out of the castle that Shaylan had to physically restrain him by grabbing his shoulders and shaking him into submission. "Get hold of yourself, boy. We'll do everything in its proper order and according to etiquette," chided Shaylan as he loosed his grip and began pushing Dalwan by the back of his elbow down the long hallway toward the dining room. "This has indeed been an unfortunate adventure. We are now without the help of the Elves and Dwarves... help which we need badly. I'm not sure if Lord Falock will look kindly upon any of us after this. All of our efforts are lost, and our work must begin all over again. I don't understand these other races. They willingly gave us aid and now have abandoned us without finishing. Most of all, they have left you in a lurch..." At that, Dalwan suddenly stopped in his tracks. Shaylan was too distracted with his speech and hanging on to his elbow so securely that before he realized it, he had swung around and ended up face to face with him.

"Shaylan, hold on...give me a chance here!" Dalwan was so agitated at Shaylan's monologue and not having a chance to explain what had transpired that his face was red.

Shaylan threw up his hands in total frustration and said loudly, "What is it, boy! What! What!!!"

"I have the sword," he said in a whisper with a tone that sounded much like lecturing.

Shaylan's mouth dropped open. Coming to himself and looking around to see if anyone was listening, "You mustn't tell anyone!" he said with a panicked look on his face. "You haven't told anyone, have you?" he said as the panic look took on an anxious edge.

Shaylan quickly looked around like a man positioning himself for battle and then again took hold of Dalwan's elbow, heading the opposite direction this time. "We must get away from this place as soon as possible." Shaylan was walking faster than Dalwan had ever seen him walk, with the look of a man who had just seen a ghost.

Trying to keep from laughing at Shaylan's response, Dalwan pulled his elbow away from Shaylan's rigidly painful grip, then said in a quiet voice,

"Shaylan, no one's ever gonna know that the sword's missing. There is a look-alike in its place..."

Shaylan came to an abrupt halt and spun Dalwan around, taking him by both shoulders and shoved his face eye to eye about a handbreadth from Dalwan's with a shocked look on his face, "What possessed you to do such a thing. The imposter will be discovered. The sword is a national treasure. How will we ever explain this? If you are caught, they'll..."

Dalwan cut in, pushing Shaylan back away from his face by the shoulders, "It's already done! No one suspects it. And now it's time to leave." With that, he turned and began to walk toward his sleeping quarters, leaving Shaylan stunned and completely befuddled.

Shaylan was so nervous that he went directly to his quarters and packed his bag. As soon as he finished, he set out to retrieve Dalwan, who had wandered off to say farewell to several new acquaintances. After a very brief and officially polite exchange with those in Dalwan's presence, he drug him out to search for Rhem. In short order, they found him in the library reading one account of the sword's use during the battles of the last great war. Shaylan was unable to recount everything there because there were two other people working with him, but he did manage to communicate that he was leaving the castle immediately, with intentions to revisit the Dwarves. Rhem vowed to catch up with him as soon as he finished his current business.

When they had traveled to Castle Crest from the council with the Dwarves and Elves, they had spent the night in a mountain pass. While staying there, Darric had taken Dalwan to visit a small wayhouse (small in every sense of the word, being made expressly for Dwarves) used by Dwarves when they traveled through that area. That became the designated meeting place should they become separated. Dalwan and Shaylan made their way to that place and met the rest of the group, who were patiently waiting. Shaylan then returned to the road to await Rhem's arrival and lead him there also.

As soon as Shaylan had returned to the road, the group quickly got up and broke camp. They quickly set out following a deer trail, which went up the side of the mountain and eventually over it to the other side. It then went back down where it crossed the road, which had followed the base of the mountain.

Rhem showed up much later, just before dark. When Shaylan took him back up to the camp, they found it abandoned. It was so late by that time that they spent the night at the wayhouse. That evening, Shaylan told Rhem everything Dalwan had shared about the events surrounding the taking of the sword and their leaving, although Dalwan's information was sketchy on everything except the switching of the sword. Both men felt great apprehension about Dalwan being coaxed into fighting Danlion with the sword when so little is known about its power or the method of its use. They realized that since the dwarves and elves had taken him away secretly that it would be very difficult to locate them again until they wanted to be found. With that in mind, they decided to return to Castle Crest. The difficult part would be deciding whether or not to tell Lord Falock about the switch.

Darric led the small but distinguished group along the single file trail as it wound its way through the rocks and high brush. No one spoke, but all of them felt a strong sense of destiny and personal exhilaration. The trail was heading in the same direction now as the road, up toward a pass.

Just before they reached the road again, they stopped near a ravine and uncovered a well camouflaged large bag wrapped in water-resistant, treated hide. It contained traveling clothes which were obviously made for moving through the wilderness without being noticed. To Dalwan's surprise, there was also a set for him, complete with a cloak. They changed clothes and put their discarded ones back in the bag. They then uncovered another bag, similarly water-resistant. This one contained food, personal weapons, and camping utensils, all organized into individually fitted backpacks. This time, it was not so surprising for Dalwan to find that there was one for him also.

Once they were properly outfitted, they set out again. They walked the road through the pass and then partway down the descent, veered off onto another deer trail.

It didn't take Dalwan too long to figure out that they were all prepared to keep going and to assist in the destruction of Danlion and his plans as soon as possible. He knew that the threat from Danlion was growing, but didn't see why they had to be in such a hurry to get to him right then.

When the group stopped for a short time to rest and take a drink, Fallwyn explained that Danlion's power was only part of the problem. It was Danlion's ever growing band of misfits and deceived followers who now worried everyone. They had become a danger to everyone, men, elves, and dwarves. It would not become easier to stop him, only harder. More lives would be lost with every passing day that his influence and deception went on unchecked. This would be the best time to stop him, now, before he suspected that the sword had left the castle.

One benefit that they had derived from trying out the sword at the castle was the discovery that the sword did not have a magic print of its own but only reflected the magic of the user, as it had Fallwyn's when the sword acted on its own, trapping Angoleen in the power bubble.

"It remains to be seen if your use of the sword will tip off Danlion that it's back in service," finished Fallwyn as they rose again to continue the journey.

The small group skirted every town and every group of houses in order to avoid detection. They kept hidden for two days, passing Thamerlain and heading into the hills Northeast of the dwarvian countryside. On the second day, they sensed a short burst of intense magic, lasting only long enough for them to locate the direction it had come from and to identify Danlion as the source. After some discussion and rough "in-the-dust" map drawing, they came to a consensus that the location from which the magic had come must have been Brandon Keep. Dalwan knew that Danlion would try for the castle sooner or later, but no one had considered that it could happen this soon. He felt anxious at the possibility of Shahandra being caught or killed in the battle. Several days before, he had felt her magic keenly, powerfully. It was so clear that at first he had imagined her being close. Then, as it continued and he focused on it, he realized that she was far away. How had she become so extremely powerful? He wondered if she had discovered some power-enhancing tool or become heir to one at Brandon Keep. Dalwan wondered what would have happened if he had allowed her to know his true abilities. Would she forgive him for deceiving her? He wondered if two people with such great power could ever become truly close. He felt a lump in his stomach that seemed to work its way up to his throat as he thought of her... her smile, her energy, her dreams, her beauty. He drifted on in his thoughts, walking in a daze, scarcely aware of his surroundings. Suddenly, his thoughts returned to the powerful burst of magic they had perceived from Danlion and the probability that it signaled war at Brandon Keep. For now, all his daydreams were doomed to be lost in the fog of uncertainty that hung over the fate of Brandon Keep. He felt a powerful urge to go there, "NOW!", and save her from the ancient evil called Danlion. He was gripped with a fierce new determination.

About the time he got this new burst of energy and determination, he realized that his traveling companions were stopping again, this time for the evening. He hadn't realized that the time had gone by so quickly. They were now in a remote mountain area with rugged rocky crags. Their camp was situated in the wide ascending valley floor that went through the middle of the Greystone mountains. The valley floor had a rapidly running stream in it and was populated with trees that had trunks so large you could put a small house inside of them. They we close enough together that very little sunlight got through. Where sunlight did manage an appearance on the forest floor, bushes and ferns flourished. It was an ancient place where all who entered were struck with an inspired sense of awe.

As they were setting up camp, they made a decision to have Dalwan try out the sword. It was Darric's job to supervise the effort.

"Now lad," Darric said in a fatherly tone, "first of all ya must think o' the sword as an extension of yerself. As we've been telling ya, it 'ill act with and for ya. As ya're using it, it may do thin's ta protect ya that ya don't expect."

Dalwan took off the hood that covered the hilt and unwrapped the strap securing it to the sheath. The sword slid out as easily as if pushed by an unseen hand over an oily rag. It felt good in his hand. It was perfectly balanced and glided through the air effortlessly.

Angoleen and Mornic, who had been spending a lot of time together sharing stories and magic, had laid a bed of logs in a fire pit, custom-made by Mornic of stone from the river.

Darric simply pointed at the wood and said, "Start our fire."

Dalwan pointed the sword, and the logs burst into flame as if being lit from the inside. The sword did not change. No fire leapt out... no flash of light... the logs simply caught on fire.

There was a hush over the group as they tried to fathom what had taken place. Fallwyn's job was to sense the magic of the sword.

"The only power I sensed was Dalwan's!" said Fallwyn as he walked over to the fire and studied the logs, now fully involved in flames. "Dalwan, what did you do here? I sensed your fire but saw nothing. I sensed no illusion. Did you cover the sword's fire?"

Dalwan stood holding the sword hilt with both hands, the sword tip resting on the ground. He was equally amazed.

"All I did was aim the sword and prepare myself for throwing fire. I had the firepit logs firmly in mind... I envisioned them bursting into flames, AND THEY DID! The magic happened, but I don't know why," he said with a quiet, glazed-over look on his face.

"I don't know what I did. I don't know why it worked." Dalwan quickly searched the eyes of each in attendance for answers, but found none. He was both inspired and a little frightened. His potential power frightened him. He wondered if he held enough mastery of his abilities to control that much power. With this much power, he would automatically become the best friend or worst and most feared enemy of every would-be ruler or conqueror. He would become like the anderon, sought out and hunted down. He would not be able to move about freely without fear of being challenged or just killed outright. On the other hand, when others discovered that he was a powermaster he would be sought out anyway... why not have the sword for protection?! "What could stand in my way?" Almost instantly, he caught himself midthought... "This is what I don't want to happen," he thought with something like violent pouting. "I don't want to be this kind of person." It was one thing to dream about glorious conquests and being the hero of the land... or its tyrant! It was quite another thing to have the potential to make those dreams a reality and therefore to have to deal with the consequences. He looked to Darric for help, wearing his apprehension clearly on his face.

"Lad," Darric said, addressing him in a compassionate fatherly tone, "ya are a powermaster. Yer magic gives ya away. Yer spirit and yer abilities give ya the right ta bear the sword. With or without it yer a power ta be reckoned with. Remember what ya've been taught. Ya needn't worry 'bout bein' a tyrant if ya keep yerself accountable to yer friends an' hold on ta yer ideals. It can be done. If anyone can, you will!"

"But I don't feel wise enough or careful enough to wield it."

"You'll learn as ya go. Remember, lad, the sword's only an extension of yer own power. It's got no mind of its own. Control yer thinkin' when ya use it, and you'll control the sword. Yer magic doesn't act on its own an' neither will the sword's. It must be in concert with yer power and'll never act contrary ta yer own magic."

Dalwan stood staring at Darric with sad, frightened resignation in his heart.

It was Mornic who broke the gloom. "Dalwan," it took Dalwan a moment to turn and focus on Mornic. As soon as they made eye contact, he prodded him light heartedly, "We need some more wood for the fire. Use yer sword an' cut this tree limb up for us." Mornic was busy dragging a heavy branch, about the thickness of a man's thigh, to a fallen log on which he laid it as he spoke.

Dalwan walked over to the log, fully cognizant of Mornic's attempt to pull him out of his emotional quagmire. He raised the sword over his head and swung with all his might at the white barked limb. The sword stuck solid about half the thickness of the blade into the wood.

"Powerful swing, lad!" Darric said as he moved closer to look at the damage while Dalwan worked the sword in a seesaw motion until it came loose.

"Can ya cover up this gash in the log with your art?" Darric asked as he squatted down, running his finger across the slice Dalwan had inflicted.

"Sure I can," answered Dalwan, bending over to touch the wooden scar. With a smooth stroke of his hand, the wood pulled together, and except for a very thin white line where the blade had stuck, the limb appeared undamaged.

"Good lad! Excellent!" All the others joined Darric, gathering around to look at the handiwork. "Now, lad," continued Darric, "lay the blade at another spot on the log."

Dalwan complied, putting a sharp edge down on the log.

"Good. Now focus your power through the sword to cut the limb in half."

Dalwan stood for a moment, and nothing happened. Suddenly, the sword slipped through the branch and into the stump below as if passing through water. The log separated noiselessly and fell to the ground, cleanly cut in half.

This demonstration of power further unnerved Dalwan. He couldn't believe the way that the sword accentuated his own ability. It was at once both extremely stimulating and shocking.

Sensing his turmoil, Mayflin spoke up, "Think of the wonderful things you can do. Think of the excellent service you can lend in times of trouble or emergency... how fast you could cut a fire break. This kind of power is the fabric of legends... Dalwan, you're the very embodiment of magic, and therefore, you belong to all races. It's so fortunate that the power falls on one who is so sensitive... so in touch with life and those around him. Don't ever fear it... simply use it well... choose your companions well, folks who share your views and similar goals... who understand and applaud your perspective in life... folks like us!" he said as he ended with a sweeping gesture pointing at his comrades.

Fallwyn walked over to Mayflin and slapped him on the back in approval, "My friend, you're not often given to speeches... especially with such eloquence... what brings this on?"

"It feels a bit like jealousy!" he answered with a grin. This brought laughter from his companions, knowing that the other races are not much given to jealousy... competition, yes, but not jealousy. "OK, OK, I'll be serious," he said, trying to keep a straight face, "we found him, can we keep him?" This brought a roar of laughter from them all, even managing to break a smile loose from Dalwan's stoic face.

After everyone finished wiping the tears from the laugh lines in their faces, Darric added a final word, "As ya doubtless know, our friend Mayflin doesn't speak much unless he becomes quite moved. When he does speak, it's always worth givin' a listen to. Yer gifts are indeed inviable an' yer powers 'ill likely generate a song 'r two if ya use 'em well. But while ya have the power ta change many a life, ya should seek those activities that speak of yer values... do thin's that help those around ya... those ya claim to act in support of... do things that those who become most affected by yer power, will approve of. An' lad... don't take yerself too seriously. As yer friend Mayflin inferred, seek counsel, lots o' counsel, especially when there's time enough ta do so... depend on the counsel of yer friends fer the tough decisions."

It was dark when the evening meal was finished and the camp clean-up completed. Fallwyn, Mornic, and Dalwan cleared out an area near the camp and started another fire for light. They spent more time trying out the sword's defensive capabilities.

"Dalwan," said Mornic, who was one of the best sword fighters in the group, "let's see if the sword'll help ya fend me off."

Dalwan went into a defensive stance facing Mornic, who held an impressive-looking mid-length sword. Dalwan felt exhilarated as he began to intercept Mornic's blows, each of which he all but announced in advance.

"Everythin' seems ta be in order," shouted Mornic, who was bursting with enthusiasm, "let's move up the pace!"

"I'm game!" said Dalwan with overwhelming confidence.

Mornic began to increase the speed and impact of the blows as Dalwan, in turn, began to depend more and more on the sword's magic in combination with his own to defend himself. In spite of the sword's weight, it glided as if weightless and felt as if it moved on its own to intercept the oncoming blows. Mornic was working hard to conceal his upcoming blows and began to use more of his own weirding magic to fight. Fallonrod never faltered.

"Ready ta up the anti," shouted Mornic while continuing his now relentless attack.

"It depends on what you have in mind," answered Dalwan, who was not even feeling the effects of Mornic's vigorous onslaught.

"Fallwyn, why don't ya join us?!" he said, watching for Dalwan's response.

Fallwyn moved close to Mornic so as to come at Dalwan from the same direction.

"OK," said Dalwan with some reluctance, "but remember, I'm on your side!"

Fallwyn began to mix his blows synchronously with Mornic's. Dalwan easily defended against every attempt. His arms did not tire as they guided Fallonrod with lightening fast reflexes to match with ease each opponent's attack. Even when they moved apart, as much as they could with Dalwan using his very good fighting skills to keep them closer together, they could not get close to him with Fallonrod protecting against every swing and thrust.

Fallwyn lowered his sword and moved back a few steps. "Let's try fire."

The others stopped and looked with some reflection at each other while assessing the request.

"What if the sword reacts and does something destructive?" said Dalwan, feeling apprehensive about experimenting against friends.

"Dalwan," answered Fallwyn, "Only defend... only use your magic to protect yourself... you can't go on the offensive."

"I hope this works... I don't like experimenting with something this dangerous... didn't you already get in trouble with this thing in the sword chamber?"

Dalwan's words brought back frightening memories for Fallwyn. "I don't trust the sword Dalwan, but I trust your skill... let's try... we'll start with red fire."

"I'm ready... go ahead, but don't use too much power."

A short streak of red fire shot from Fallwyn's sword directly at Fallonrod. It simply devoured the fire. Nothing else happened. Again, Fallwyn threw red fire at Fallonrod, but this time in a longer, slightly hotter blast. It did not even phase Fallonrod. Dalwan chanced a touch of the blade... it was cool to the touch!

"Try blue."

Blue fire was followed by white fire, both of which the sword soaked up like water into a waiting sponge. Finally, Fallwyn dropped his sword and, using both hands, threw a powerful green flame curtain. The sword sliced it in two and propelled it away from him at a faster speed than it had been thrown.

"What a marvelous protector i'tis," said Mornic, reaching out to touch Fallonrod's unscathed blade.

"Well, we certainly made a spectacle of ourselves tonight... most every sensor within two kingdoms must be setting on pins and needles over what they felt," said Fallwyn, reflecting on the arts they had used. "This must have felt like a full-blown war!"

"An' ya can be sure that Danlion has taken notice too!" added Mornic. "Ya can be sure o' company over this little party here tonight."

By this time, Dalwan had become at ease with the sword. It was the first time he came to believe that the sword was nothing more than an extension of his own power, not some possessive magic that would warp him into something hideous.

They returned to the main camp confident that the sword was everything
and even more than they had hoped. And best of all, Dalwan felt comfortable
with it for the first time.

Sleep that night was at best unsettled for them, all knowing that
tomorrow they would arrive at Brandon Keep. Each dreamed of different
battles against terrifying odds, of dark dangers without form, of suffering and
the loss of companions. But all contained a common thread, the specter of a
tall, thin shadow with red eyes, a dark cape, and a yellow grin... the ultimate
enemy!

They arose not very refreshed but completely resolute to face the
unknowns that they were bound to encounter. They quickly broke camp after a
rather hasty breakfast of cured meat, bread, and jam.

They headed straight up the middle of the valley between the crags. Its
beauty was breathtaking as the rising sun's glow touched the tops of the trees in
an ever-increasing array of splendor. The slope of the valley increased, and the
water in the creek ran faster and shallower as they neared the top of the
pass. At the top of the pass, the ground was much more rocky and the trees
shorter, most of which showed signs of periodic harsh weather. There was
snow visible on the highest rocks surrounding them. Wispy waterfalls broke
their way to the canyon floor down sheer rock faces.

They worked their way through a flat gorge, passing between high rock
canyon walls. There was a path that picked its way past rock slides and massive
chunks of the canyon wall, which had detached and fallen to the floor, partially
blocking passage.

They approached an area where the pass opened up and began to slope
ever so slightly downward. The center was relatively flat but was bordered on
one side by significantly large rock slabs, some of which leaned high against the
canyon wall. As they entered its leading edge, both Fallwyn and Angoleen
stopped the group simultaneously.

"Feel it?" said Angoleen, sensing in the direction of the largest rocks,
only the distance of a long stones throw from their position.

"Yes!" Fallwyn said, pulling his sword. Everyone froze.

Dalwan was back at the tail end of the little procession, talking with
Myletan. He began to sense the surroundings, searching for that minute magic
that had warned the others. No sooner had he begun to sense than an arrow

flew past his head from up in the rocks and struck Myletan in the top of His shoulder near his neck. Myletan dropped to his knees with a slight whimper.

Dalwan's sword was out in a flash. In fact, it was out so fast he had no idea how it had happened. The sword was ablaze, as if he held a pillar of flame. Arrows flew at him from two directions. He saw them both for an instant, then his vision was blurred by a forked flash of fire from the sword resembling a stream of burning fluid which reached out and incinerated the incoming arrows midair. The attackers had only been partially visible and, at that, for only a short time, quickly retreated back into the cover of the rocks.

The rest of the group quickly dropped their packs and scattered, leaving only Myletan and Dalwan in the open. They went into the rocks on the side of the valley from which the attack had come. Magic was thick in the air. Dalwan could sense so many arts at work among the rocks that it became almost impossible to distinguish them.

His attention was drawn back to Myletan, whose breathing was labored and mixed with a very distinguishable gurgling sound. Dalwan kept his sword up as he bent down on one knee and touched the wounded dwarf. He could sense that his life was slipping away.

Suddenly, from behind him, came the clear sense of a shadowmaster... no two! He sprang to his feet, turning with sword still raised. The sword flew from side to side, jerking him so violently that he almost lost his footing. He shifted his concentration to the sword fighting arts, and instantly his opponents became invisible as brightly shining silhouettes. His confidence swelled, and he became the aggressor. One attacker stepped back and went around to Dalwan's side, obviously not aware that Dalwan could see him. The other man stepped back as if thinking it would confuse Dalwan's senses. It was just the break he needed. He turned and set his fire magic in action, burning a fist-sized hole with white fire, mid chest in the man who had skirted him. This so surprised the other man that he became visible for an instant, his very last instant. Fire engulfed him from the inside out.

Dalwan had not seen what took place behind him while he fought the shadow masters. No sooner had he turned to receive his invisible guests than the two original archers reappeared to try their luck again, only this time against a distracted target. They had scarcely gained full footing when the one on the left threw his hands straight out and up with arched back and a chilling scream. The other turned with an arrow strung toward his companion, now face down, only a few steps from him. An instant later, he saw the flash of a long, thin knife blade as it appeared out of nowhere, spinning end over end, and buried itself in his forehead. He fell limp to the ground, like a bag of rags, sending the arrow ricocheting harmlessly off the rock. Before the arrow fell to the ground, Fallwyn was again on the move, invisibly passing through the rocks toward the others who were searching further ahead among the boulders.

Dalwan turned his attention back to Myletan. As he reached him, Myletan appeared to focus for a brief moment, then his eyes rolled up and closed. His breathing was shallow and very labored. It sounded to Dalwan like he was drowning. "If only Shahandra were here," he thought in panic. "She's so good at this sort of thing." Tears fogged his vision. He started to get angry with himself for crying again, but suddenly it didn't matter that tears were in his eyes... this was his friend... his comrade... a dwarf who had called him friend... tears are probably the only appropriate response!" He realized that he was wasting precious time in hesitation. He quickly wiped the tears away. Fighting back the indecision, he dropped his sword, grabbed the arrow with both hands, and pulled it out with a powerful tug that scooted the dwarf about a handbreadth closer to Dalwan. He touched the wound and it immediately closed up, leaving only the slightest scar and discoloration. The dwarf didn't show even the slightest reaction to this maneuver. His breathing was all but stopped, and his skin was a pale milky color. Dalwan tried to sense the wound and somehow to feel what he needed to do next. Nothing he could sense helped him; again, panic flooded over him, causing him to jump to his feet and look around as if there was someone he could call that would help him save Myletan. There was no one in sight. He dropped to his knees and gently placed his hand on Myletan's shoulder, "I'm sorry, my friend..." he whispered, "I'm sorry I couldn't help you... I just never had anyone who knew enough about healing to help me learn. I wish.... I wish......" Dalwan's head dropped to his chest, and he just let the tears run quietly free.

Meanwhile, Angoleen and Mornic located the two remaining attackers who were now hiding under a large flat rock that was lodged against the canyon wall, forming a small cave-like hole. The entrance was so small that the men had found it necessary to back into it, scooting on their bellies.

Angoleen was the one who actually discovered them, so he called them out, "I know you're in there, so you might as well come out so I don't have to cook you out."

As the first man emerged from the darkness under the rock, a medium-sized man covered with smudges of dirt and carrying a quiver of arrows, the bow was nowhere in sight. Angoleen disarmed him as he cleared the hole. Mornic made him lie down and guarded him while Angoleen coaxed the remaining man out, a taller, stouter man with a bushy beard and just as dirty as the first. Angoleen likewise disarmed him.

Angoleen took a leather cord out of his tunic and secured it to the wrist of the last man out, using some small magic to ensure its security. He then motioned to Mornic to escort the other man close enough to be bound to his companion. Mornic pushed him toward Angoleen. The man took only one step before sending a powerful kick straight back, hitting Mornic mid chest in an attempt to knock him down so he could escape. Instead, he hit something that felt like a tree stump with his arms. Mornic inflicted a painful injury to the side of his shin with the steel butt of his sword and simultaneously grabbed the leg with his free hand. In an instant, with a powerful twist, the man found himself sprawled out flat on his face. He lay still for a moment, then quickly rolled over and pulled a concealed knife out of his sleeve. Before he could do anything with it, Mornic threw his own sword and caught him solidly mid chest. He collapsed instantly and died. The other man looked dispassionately at Angoleen and said, "Obviously, he never fought a dwarf before."

Angoleen used the remainder of the cord to further secure the last man.

"Why did you ambush us?" asked Angoleen as he finished synching up the cord and again using magic to fuse it together.

"Danlion sent six of us out to find the one he suspects as a powermaster... he told us not to come back without him," answered the man very dryly.

Angoleen led the way out of the rocks while Mornic got behind the man and prodded him to follow. As they reached the edge of the rocks, Angoleen stopped to sense the area for any other possible danger. Immediately, Mayflin appeared at the far side of the clearing, coming out of the rocks. He held up his fist and made a giant circle two times, which was a sign that all was clear where he was.

Angoleen's attention turned to the center of the clearing, where Dalwan was holding Myletan.

Dalwan was feverishly trying everything he could to keep life in Myletan. Two times Dalwan felt his heart stop, and both times he had been able to somehow get it going again. He pulled Myletan up into a sitting position and had his arms wrapped around the dwarf so he could more accurately sense everything about his physical condition. Myletan never regained consciousness. His heart stopped again. This time, he felt the rest of Myletan's magic vanish. He tried to bring him back, but couldn't. He sat holding him for a brief moment as rage began to build.

Suddenly, he stood up and held up both hands over his head, fists clenched, and yelled his grief and anger to the canyon walls. 'NOOO! NOOO!" The echo was eerie. It lingered in the canyon without losing its potency, hanging in the air much longer than nature would allow.

He began to look around as if in a panic until he located his sword and quickly retrieved it. He then turned and shouted, "If you want me, come and face me, you cowards!!! Come out and fight me face to face... you want me? Here I am!"

At that moment, he spotted Angoleen standing at the edge of the rocks with the prisoner. He began to run straight for them. Angoleen recognized Dalwan's state of mind and positioned himself between Dalwan and the prisoner.

Dalwan stopped a few steps away, breathing heavily. "You killed my friend!" he shouted in one rapidly exhaled breath. "Now you'll pay!" He raised his sword and moved to see around Angoleen, who jockeyed his position to keep between them.

This went on through several moves in which Dalwan appeared not to even notice Angoleen, but tried to skirt him as one would an inanimate object. Suddenly, Dalwan stopped and focused on Angoleen with a new air of irritation evident on his face.

Angoleen drew his sword and squared up against him. "He's my prisoner, Dalwan. I have bound him, and it's now my duty to protect him if need be."

"Then cut him loose and give him a sword!" shouted Dalwan to a visibly calm Angoleen.

"I won't make sport of death," Angoleen said, stepping toward Dalwan to close the small distance between them, "his or yours."

"He killed Myletan... don't you understand! He's dead... they didn't even give him a chance to fight!" he said as he looked around Angoleen into the cold, unemotional eyes of the captive and added, "Coward!"

"My friend, I don't think any of us could have saved his life." Angoleen's words were fast and went right to Dalwan's heart.

The tip of Dalwan's sword dropped to the ground, and he himself plopped to a cross-legged setting position like a rag doll, "I tried..." he said in a whisper, looking into Angoleen's eyes for answers that he knew wouldn't be there. "Oh, how I tried..."

Mornic pushed the prisoner up to Angoleen's side and walked over to Dalwan and put a strong hand on his shoulder. "We're all gonna miss him somethin' terrible... we're all gonna feel this for a long time."

"Thanks for savin' my life from this pathetic boy," said the prisoner aside to Angoleen in a derogatory tone that Angoleen recognized immediately as a manipulative attempt to drive a wedge between him and Dalwan.

"It's not your life I sought to save, mercenary. It's the boy's. His pain wouldn't have been eased with your death..." answered Angoleen. Then he stepped around to get eye-to-eye contact with the man, "Even though I also have a duty to uphold the ways and honor of my people in protecting a prisoner in my charge... Dalwan would have dishonored himself by killing you... and don't think for a moment that I could have stopped him if he really wanted you!"

Mornic turned and looked back at the man, "None of us hold much love for those whose loyalties and ideals can change as quickly as money passes between hands!"

"What are your high ideals won for you, dwarf!? Huh? You're friend's dead, and before this is all over, you'll die too, Danlion 'ill see to that!" answered the prisoner snidely. "All for nothin'! At least my pockets 'ill be full."

"My friend died in honor, surrounded by those who'd have gladly given their lives for his sake. He'll be remembered with honor. 'Tis more than I can say for those who died here today among yer companions."

Angoleen pushed the prisoner out from between the rocks and toward some trees on the downhill side of the pass in the Brandon Keep direction. Mornic stayed with Dalwan. Fallwyn, Darric, and Mayflin were approaching them as Angoleen departed. Darric and Mayflin continued on toward Mornic and Dalwan while Fallwyn jogged to catch up with Angoleen.

"Mind if I shadow you?" said Fallwyn in a most amused tone of voice. The prisoner had not even the slightest hint of Fallwyn's approach. When Fallwyn spoke from the side opposite Angoleen, the man jerked his head around so hard that he strained his neck. The man winced in pain, drawing up his shoulder and closing his eyes.

Angoleen recognized what had taken place and said, "Fallwyn, you're such a nuisance... always bothering someone! I bet this mercenary thinks you're a pain in the neck, too."

Fallwyn rolled his eyes at the bad humor, then obtained permission with a glance to tend the man's injury. With a strong hand, he reached out and took hold of the man's shoulder at the base of his neck. He recoiled slightly in a mixture of pain and surprise. The muscle healed in Fallwyn's skillful hand with a warming feeling that left his entire shoulder and neck relaxed.

As Fallwyn completed the healing, they reached the line of trees that bordered the trail leading down from the pass.

"Has Danlion begun his siege of Brandon Keep?" asked Fallwyn as he removed his hand from the man's healed injury.

"It took him less than one day to take it... as a matter of fact, it took less than half a day!" the man laughed. "You think that you're gonna walk in there with your little band of out-landers and take it back?! You won't survive long enough to meet him, let alone get the opportunity to try your skills against him... he's no one's fool!"

"How did he take the castle so quickly? He can't have that many men or resources," asked Angoleen.

"The Rocklin squatches are close personal friends of his... they brought all their hairy host to assist in ridding Brandon Keep of its squatters," he answered with some humor in his voice.

"What about the inhabitants of Castle Crest? How many survived?" asked Fallwyn.

"Most of them are dead... killed by the squatches," he said with a malicious laugh that betrayed his lie far better than his words had.

"And the city... how many men are guarding it?"

"Not too many now that the squatches are gone... we only had about 300 to start with," he said, again exposing his lie to the keen sensing of both elves.

"How about patrols outside the fortress... how many patrols are out at one time?" asked Angoleen.

"Not enough men inside to let any go out... everyone, 'ill be needed to defend the wall if any remnant of their army returns."

"How about the squatches... why did they help Danlion?"

"I told you, they're long-time friends, Danlion and the squatches... they help him whenever he calls."

"Where are the squatches now?" asked Fallwyn.

"Gone I guess... he didn't need 'em anymore 'n couldn't feed them, so he let 'em go."

Every one of his answers contained at least some remote element of truth mixed in with lies, and gave enough information to the elves to be very useful.

They continued to walk into the forest as they talked. Fallwyn chanced one last question, "What is Danlion going to do next... what's his next quest?"

"I'm just a soldier... he feeds me and lets us keep the spoils of our battles... he tells me what to do and I do it. He told me and the others you met here to come out and kill the power wielder and not to come back until we did. Other than that, Danlion doesn't confide in me much," the man said quite sarcastically.

By this time, they had traveled about a long bow shot distance into the woods on the downhill side of the pass perpendicular to the trail. Angoleen stopped next to a tree that was large enough for a big man to reach around and just barely touch his fingertips together on the other side of.

"This'll do just fine," he said with a glint in his eye. "Fallwyn, my friend, will you burn a straight hole through the tree about knee high on the left side, facing downhill?"

Fallwyn complied without a word and with only the hint of a smile on his face. He pulled his sword and pointed at the appropriate spot in the prescribed direction, and let go with a stream of fire. It began to burn and hiss its way through the tree. Before he was halfway through, Darric appeared and peeked around a nearby tree, having been drawn by the use of fire magic.

Fallwyn greeted him with a smile and a wink, having sensed his presence long before he actually saw him.

"Ah!" Darric said, highly amused, "The ole Elven stocks!"

"Just the prescription for a problem such as ours," answered the low musical voice of Angoleen as he glanced with a raised eyebrow smirk at the prisoner.

Soon, Fallwyn had finished a hole straight through and began to scrape the interior walls of it with his sword blade to remove any still-smoldering embers.

"It's all clear and ready for occupancy," said Fallwyn as he moved around behind the prisoner, who was now seated about ten paces from the tree near Angoleen and Darric.

Angoleen helped the man up and walked him over to the tree, then cut the cord that bound him. "Make this easy on all of us and just put your left arm in the hole, mercenary."

The man looked from face to face of his captors, then silently complied.

"That's it... all the way through now... OK!" said Angoleen as he took hold of the back of the man's hand. He began to mold the wood of the tree around the man's forearm and wrist, making the fit very snug around the wrist and forearm. He then let go and moved around behind him and slightly enlarged the hole from the elbow outward toward the man.

By the time Angoleen finished, the man's arm was through the tree from wrist to mid biceps.

"I hope you answered our questions truthfully, mercenary. Your life most likely depends on it," said Angoleen as he stood up and stepped around in front of him. "This 'ill be fairly uncomfortable, but if we fare well by your shared knowledge, we'll be back in a day or so to remove you."

Fallwyn stepped into the man's view, next to Angoleen, and continued, "However, if you gave us bad information and we all die, you'll most likely die also... out here alone."

The man had a water bladder over his shoulder, which he had been allowed to keep. Angoleen stuck the man's sheath knife in the ground near enough to so he could retrieve it with a little effort.   "You'll likely need your knife at night for protection," Angoleen said as he stepped back a few paces as he prepared to leave. "Is there anything you wish to tell us before we leave?"

"Only that you're fools and Danlion, 'ill see you all dead," he answered bitterly.

"Ya're so fatalistic!" said Darric with a scolding chuckle as they all turned to leave, "Don't worry, we'll be back fer ya."

"If any of you come back alive, I'll become a model citizen," yelled the man to the backs of the quickly retreating trio.

When they reached the location of the ambush, they found Dalwan and Mornic standing on top of a large flat rock about the size of a homestead cabin.

Mornic looked pale and sad. Dalwan's eyes were red.

"We're gonna put him in stone," Dalwan said in a stuffy-nose voice.

"There's nothin' he would 'a' loved more," said Darric solemnly. "I'm gonna miss 'im somethin' awful." His eyes welled up, but his voice stayed strong and steady.

Fallwyn took up from there, "He loved the earth... the stone and metal... the heat of the forge..."

Mornic cut in, "The caves were where his heart soared."

Dalwan pointed Fallonrod at the surface of the rock they stood on, and the stone began to flow from the center outward, forming a rounded crater with a mounded edge that resembled a wave radiating outward. He began to back up with the sword point held close to the surface of the rock until he had fashioned a curved bottom sepulcher about waist deep in the center, one stride wide and a little more than two strides in length. The flowed stone stood in a large heap around the lip of the hole, except at the end, where Dalwan finished, which stood open like a doorway. After a brief pause, he again lowered the sword tip and touched the stone at the edge where he stood. The bowl shaped side began to flow at the top to form the first small step. One after the other, he formed small steps going into the hole until they reached the bottom.

"It's fit fer a king, Dalwan. 'Tis a work o' reverence!" said Darric, obviously pleased with Dalwan's offering.

Myletan was carried into the sepulcher by Darric and Mornic who laid him there and stood in customary fashion for a brief time meditating on the character of his life. Then, without a word, they climbed back out.

Dalwan molded the stone back over Myletan in a dome shape about a wide handbreadth thick. Darric went to work on the legend, which he placed on the molded stone surface that Dalwan created. It read:

MYLETAN OF THE DWARVES

A TRUE FRIEND OF MANY

HIGH MASTER OF METAL AND STONE

FORFEITED HIS LIFE IN SERVICE

FOR THOSE HE LOVED

They took the other three bodies out of the rocks and piled them together with the burned remains of the two men Dalwan fought. Darric raised his hands over his head. As the others backed away, he poured intense fire onto them. They turned to ash with remarkable speed.

It was now well past midday. They went to the small creek, which had its origin at the top of the canyon wall, and washed up, then sat down in a circle to eat. They were all emotionally exhausted. They ate only because they knew they must... none of them felt hungry.

They decided to try to reach Brandon Keep by nightfall and see if they could locate any survivors from the fall of the Castle. They knew that Danlion would have sensed the battle and that most likely would now know more of their powers and abilities. They decided that the men who attacked them may have been thought expendable by Danlion and possibly sent only to discover, through their demise, the art of those coming against him.

One way or another, Danlion would now know more about them and would suspect that they were coming to visit him soon. As a result, they decided to continue to travel off the trail wherever possible.

They took up their packs and headed out with Fallwyn leading the way. Once they reached the valley, they avoided the roads altogether. They used only the slightest magic and then only when absolutely necessary, mostly for sensing. Several times, while the others hid, Dalwan went into small villages to seek out information about survivors, only to find the streets mostly deserted. Those few remaining occupants were generally not very cooperative.

At dusk, they sensed the use of magic which resembled a scaled down version of their earlier battle.

They began to move quickly in the direction of the commotion, staying in the woods close enough to the road to observe any traffic. It didn't take long for them to close in on the scene. In the darkness and from a long stone's throw away, they could make out three men tying up someone who appeared to be a woman or a small long-haired man. After closer observation, they could see that one of the men held a kneeling man by the hair with a knife or sword at his throat.

"She's all tied up now. She can't hurt no one else," said the man behind the woman.

The man holding the knife to the kneeling man's throat said, "Now isn't that convenient?" and slit the man's throat and threw him forward, thrashing on the ground.

"You promised!!" screamed the woman as she began to kick at the man with the sword.

He slapped her across the face so hard that it knocked her down. "I don't keep promises to people who kill my friends, lady."

"Get 'er up an' throw a cloak around her so no one'll see she's tied. I don't want any more trouble," said the same man who had slapped the woman.

Dalwan thought that the woman resembled Shahandra, but then again, every girl reminded him of Shahandra. He hadn't been able to sense any of her magic, and the scream was too shrill to identify. "No matter," he thought to himself, "they're coming right toward us... I'll know soon enough." While he watched, the other men raised the woman to her feet, and they all began to move down the middle of the road toward Dalwan and the others.

"Let me go out and meet them," asked Dalwan in a whisper directed toward Darric and Fallwyn, who were crouching next to him. "I think I can find out what's goin' on."

They agreed, and Dalwan stepped out into the road. It was straight for about a long bow shot, and the men were still a stone's throw away. He started toward them. There was one man walking about three paces in front of the other two, each of which flanked the woman. The man in front had a noticeable limp that Dalwan sensed was from a fresh wound.

They didn't notice Dalwan until they had covered about half the distance.

"Hello!" Dalwan shouted as soon as he was sure they had seen him. "That leg looks sore," he said as he continued at a regular pace.

The largest of the two men in the back drew a short sword and moved quickly around the front man without a word, and jogged a few steps before slowing to a fast walk. The other two stopped. None of them spoke.

Dalwan stopped and pulled his sword without putting any magic into it, "Don't let me alarm you... Ya see, I'm hungry and just need some food... thought I'd offer to heal your leg for a bite to eat."

The man with the sword stopped about five paces away and squared up against Dalwan. "Oh, I understand!" he said as if just figuring out a puzzle, "You're just protecting the woman... I assure you I have no intention of harming anyone," he said, looking around the man toward the deeply shadowed faces of those behind him. "Ma'am, I mean you no harm... just some food if you please."

Still, none of them spoke a word.

Dalwan was trying to see the facial features of those behind the man, "I see you're not much for talkin'... I suppose it does seem strange meeting out here at night with all those mad men at Brandon Keep... never know what sort of folks you're talkin' to."

Still without speaking so much as a single word, the man began to advance slowly toward him with sword in fighting position.

"If you intend to kill me, you'd better get on with it," Dalwan said in a tone that sounded very cocky and much more confident than his appearance and stature would suggest.

Before another heartbeat was complete, they were fighting. Dalwan didn't have to use magic to fend him off; his knowledge of sword fighting was totally sufficient. As they exchanged blows, out of the corner of his eye, Dalwan saw his opponent's companions drop without a sound, and a shadow carry the woman off. He circled the man so he too would notice what had taken place. Dalwan watched for the recognition in the man's face. When it came, he took advantage of the distraction and ran him through. He fell with a groan but never did say a word.

Almost immediately, he was joined by Fallwyn, Mayflin, and the woman. She walked with Fallwyn, holding his hand. She dropped his hand and walked up to Dalwan, pulling the cloak back off her head as she did... It WAS Shahandra.

She gave him a powerful hug, then backed up arm's length, still holding him by the waist, "Dalwan! You! Here! Now!" Her sensing powers were probing him deeply. "And this time again, the powermaster is close by." She looked back at Fallwyn, "Wyn, is it you?"

"No, my lady. You hold him in your arms!"

Her mouth dropped open, provoking a round of laughter from the shadows along the road. The others stepped out onto the road from both sides.

Dalwan was surprised by their appearance. He had not heard nor seen them. A wave of fear went through him as he realized again just how dangerous his traveling companions were. Power or no power, he did not feel the equal of any of them.

"I'm sure glad we're all on the same side," he said, still collecting his wits.

He still had his hands on Shahandra's shoulders and quickly came back to his senses. "It's been a lifetime since I saw you. I hope we'll be able to spend some time after this is done," he said, pulling her close for another brief hug. He turned her around, keeping one arm wrapped around her shoulder, and called to the others to come closer.

"Shahandra, I guess you already know Fallwyn... This is Darric, Mayflin, Angoleen, and Mornic. They've taught me so much... Shahandra, they're the best there is in any land."

"You honor us, lad," Darric said with a laugh. Then aside to Shahandra, "Actually, I think he likes us because we amuse him and make him laugh."

"Others coming!" said Angoleen as he turned with Mayflin to run back and pull the two bodies from the road while Mornic and Darric drug Dalwan's opponent off into the trees. In an instant, the road was clear without so much as a hint of magic. Shahandra went with Darric and Dalwan.

A ragged group of eight men passed by heading in the direction of Brandon Keep. They talked loudly with boisterous laughter and showed very little concern for their safety.

After they passed, Shahandra asked, "Why are you here? Are you alone or just some sort of scouting party?"

"We've come to fight Danlion," answered Dalwan with enthusiasm.

"I hoped that was why you came," she said. "I want to help... whatever you need, just let me know."

Darric cut in, "Ya can do us a favor if yer of a mind ta help. Arrange a meetin' between Lord Oakbern an' us."

"I'm sure he'll meet with you any time you want."

While they were talking, Angoleen joined them, "Fallwyn and Mayflin have gone to watch the entry procedure for Brandon Keep. They said they'll meet us back here as soon as they can."

"Very well," said Darric, "let's get this lovely lady back ta her people. If all goes well, we should be back about the same time."

They escorted Shahandra back to a place near a secret entrance to the caves where most of Lord Oakbern's fighting and support staff were staying.

Shahandra went in alone and explained to Lord Oakbern what had happened to her and her now dead companions. She further explained about the group that rescued her, and that they wanted a meeting with him.

"Do you mean to tell me that two dwarves named Darric and Mornic and three elves, including Fallwyn and Angoleen, are here?" asked Oakbern, scarcely able to believe that a group of this renown would have come together to fight for Brandon Keep. "Shahandra, do you have any idea who they are?"

"I know Fallwyn because I met him before, but the only other one of the group I know, is the boy I told you about, Dalwan."

"Is the boy with them, too?"

"Yes, but I'll let them explain."

Oakbern sent for two of his chief military officers and two personal aids as well as three of his personal bodyguards, to accompany him to the rendezvous. It took only a few moments for them to arrive.

"Now, Shahandra, tell us precisely where to find them. I don't want to keep them waiting," said Lord Oakbern as he strapped on his sword.

"I'll be glad to show you, sir," answered Shahandra.

"That won't be necessary, Shahandra. We'll handle it from here," he said in a tone that had dramatically shifted from friendly to kingly authoritarian.

"Sir, I need to return also... I have unfinished business with them," Shahandra said with equally strong resolve.

"Were you this much trouble for Eric?"

"He treated me like a child, sire."

Lord Oakbern paused for a reflective moment, cooling his rage at being challenged and yet quite intrigued. "Very well, if this is that important to you, you've certainly earned the right to go with us. But your blood is again on your own shoulders."

"Agreed!" shouted Shahandra with childlike glee, clapping her hands together. Then controlling her enthusiasm in a more dignified manner, "Thank you, my lord."

"I've never met someone who has had such luck as you, to be in so deep and yet be saved by the most unlikely folk... I couldn't even begin to calculate the chances that have favored you."

Fallwyn stepped into the road directly in front of a group of eight heavily armed men led by a woman he sensed to be Shahandra. It was so dark that only the vaguest silhouettes portrayed the travelers.

"Shahandra?" Fallwyn's musical voice cut the darkness.

She instantly recognized his voice, "Wyn! They've all come. Have you found a good place for us?"

"Yes, my lady. Please follow me." With that, he turned and slipped into the woods.

Oakbern was already nervous, and this made him even more sensitive. "I could hardly see you on the road... eh..." then aside to Shahandra, who was with him, "what's his name?"

"Fallwyn, sire."

"Eh... Fallwyn!" he said, almost yelling. "Make some noise or something... we can't see you..." he continued with some low tone mumbling, "cursed elves and their perfect night vision."

There was a brief musical chuckle which was followed by the most beautiful whistling, like the purest high woodland pipes. The melody was at once mesmerizing and soothing. It arrested their fear and pinpointed the path in the darkness.

Soon, they were in a clearing that had a small fire burning in it. There were five equal-length logs positioned around the fire.

Darric met the group as it entered the clearing and escorted them into the circle. "I'm Darric, welcome. I must apologize that we have no refreshments ta offer ya, only the comfort o' this small fire and a log ta rest on." He extended his hand toward Lord Oakbern, who took hold in a two-handed shake, an ancient sign of trust and admiration.

He introduced Mornic and Angoleen, who had been seated in the circle. "Fallwyn ya've already met. Mayflin an' Dalwan are out checkin' the area fer yer safety. They'll return shortly."

Lord Oakbern introduced his men, and all but two of the men sat down. The two went out to the perimeter of the clearing and positioned themselves on opposite sides as security. As soon as they were all settled in, Mayflin entered the clearing midway between the two sentries and whistled. Angoleen responded with a hand signal. Mayflin went back into the woods briefly and returned with Dalwan.

Anger flared on Oakbern's face, "This was to protect the boy from us, not to protect us!" he protested accusingly but without raising his voice.

"Ya're very perceptive, sir," retorted Darric. "But the mission they went on was designed fer yer protection as well as ours. It jus' so happened that it also kept Dalwan away until we could better assess the situation here with you. He is our youngest member and possesses arts which 'ill be crucial to our efforts here."

"Do you trust us now?" Oakbern asked with a hint of challenge in his voice.

"Why do ya challenge our intentions? We brought the boy in, didn't we?"

"Is the boy the powermaster everyone's been looking for?"

"The boy's powerful, an' many have sought lad. But how does one ever know fer certain that he's a powermaster?"

Dalwan arrived at the circle just then and positioned himself standing behind Fallwyn.

Oakbern continued, "Enough of these games, what do you want of us?"

"First of all, don't judge us too harshly because we protected our own... you doubtless would'ave done the same. We've come ta stop Danlion. We'll attempt this with 'r without ya. Yer knowledge o' the castle and yer ability ta distract its new inhabitants would be a great asset... but if driven ta last resort yer service is luxury we're prepared ta do without." He finished talking and stared stoically at Lord Oakbern.

"If you're good enough to accomplish this without our help or counsel, why did you even call for this meeting?"

Darric had little patience for games of diplomacy with belligerent players and cut right to the point, "I'm sorry fer ya that ya don't understand my previous explanation... I'll say it another way... we're goin' in after Danlion! Will ya assist us?"

"I know most of you by reputation only, and none of that involving the taking of a castle. Do you expect me to place my men under the command of a handful of dwarves, elves, and a boy?"

"Well, Lord Oakbern... we can hardly do worse than ya've done yerself!" chuckled Darric, who was joined in the laugh by his companions.

Lord Oakbern stood with a fierce look on his face and was quickly followed by his attendants. "Don't you think we would have already retaken it if it were that easy? We would have moved in as soon as the squatches left if it were so simple a task? These things take careful planning. Danlion by himself is a formidable foe for any small army if he knew they were coming. Throwing away the lives of my people is not some sport for me as it may be for other castle lords."

"Very well!" Darric said quite unemotionally. "We'll do the job ourselves... but we make no commitment ta ya regarding our activities or approach... we go ta remove Danlion and 'ill do what e'er it takes."

"Danlion has perhaps a thousand men and is an ancient master of many arts. You'll not have as easy a time as you suspect," said Oakbern callously while motioning for his men to prepare to depart.

"Boy, to stay with these dwarves and elves in their attempt is to throw your life away. If you come with us, your own people, I'll show you how best to use your power and be a part of a strategy that will work!" Lord Oakbern stood motionless and waited for Dalwan's answer.

Dalwan's companions never looked at him but continued to watch Lord Oakbern's men.

"I prefer ta stay with my friends and, if need be, die with them."

"Spoken like a true BOY," said Oakbern as he turned in disgust and headed back toward the little trail. His men stood for a moment, then quickly filed out of the fire circle and followed him into the darkness.

Shahandra hesitated, looking with tear-filled eyes at Dalwan. One of Lord Oakbern's bodyguards grabbed her around the waist and walked away with her tucked, squirming under his powerful arm. Her yells and struggles looked insignificant to him as they disappeared into the trees. The noise continued as they moved further and further away.

Dalwan started to move in her direction but felt such immense ambivalence that he faltered. Fallwyn stepped out and restrained him by the shoulder. "Let her go. She'll be safer with them." That swung Dalwan's feelings decisively away from rescue.

Soon, all was quiet, with only the distant call of a night hawk touching their ears.

By the time they turned back toward the fire, the others were already gathering up their things. Darric extinguished the fire, and they prepared to leave.

Suddenly, Fallwyn stopped them and was instantly joined by Mayflin... "Listen... someone coming," said Fallwyn in a whisper.

"Quick, sure-footed steps..." added Mayflin.

Then the faintest sensing power...

"Shahandra!" shouted Dalwan as he dropped his pack and ran to the place where he knew the trail to empty into the meadow. Again, he called, "Shahandra!"

"Here, Dalwan!" she said with some laughter in her voice.

Dalwan strained against the darkness to separate her image from among the trees. She had stopped moving but still sent out the slightest magic of sensing.

"No Dalwan... over here!"

Her voice finally pinpointed her, and he made his way through the perimeter trees to her location just a few steps in. "What are you doing? Why'd you come back... HOW'd you come back?"

"I ran Dalwan! How else do you think I got here?" she laughed.

"I know you ran... I heard you run... but... you're lucky you didn't break your neck?" he scolded.

"No Dalwan!" came a reply from Fallwyn, who was now right next to him.

Dalwan almost jumped out of his skin, "Don't you people ever make noise when you move?"

"No!" said Fallwyn matter-of-factly.

"And we see very well in the dark," added Shahandra. She laughed at the silly look of disbelief on Dalwan's face, being able to see him much better than he could see her. "Close your mouth, Dalwan... it doesn't become you."

"You're an elf?

"At least half elf," she answered with a great deal of pride and a grin that was barely visible to him. "Your turn to be surprised!"

Dalwan's mind raced back through her extraordinary gifts and the hint of elven features in her face that he loved so much. His feelings began to give him away completely, so he quickly changed his thoughts. Just then, Fallwyn rescued him, "We'd better get back to the others so we can find a place to sleep before the sun comes up."

The group walked for a little while until they found another area where they could comfortably bed down. They slept in a circle with Shahandra in the center, and took turns keeping watch.

They woke with first light and ate a hearty meal. After the meal, they hid all their belongings and supplies except their weapons.

Shahandra explained the general layout of the castle compound and where it sat in relation to the rest of the walled city.

Fallwyn handed her a piece of parchment and asked her to draw a diagram of the actual castle floors with the major rooms.

"I can do better than that," she answered, "I'll take you there."

"Now, little lady," said Darric in a fatherly tone, "we don't want ta be responsible for puttin' ya in a dangerous situation... it would bear heavy on our conscience."

"Quite the contrary," she retorted, "It's me that's going to put you in the dangerous situation."

Fallwyn took Shahandra by the hand and looked deeply into her eyes, "We're all prepared to die in this excursion. You won't be safe."

"Wyn, I'll bet I'm safer in there with you than out here alone."

Darric walked over to her and put his hand on her shoulder, "I can see that yer not ta be dissuaded. We all recognize the danger an' as such, each that goes on from here does so at their own risk."

"I wouldn't have it any other way," she answered.

"Very well, but ya need ta know that after we're inside, no more arguin' or fightin'... we work as a team."

"I'm sorry," Shahandra said with eyes lowered and a slight blush.

Shahandra led them to an outcropping of rock behind which they were concealed from view on the wall. She left the others and climbed partway up the rock, where she stopped and began to poke around and brush off lose debris. After a few moments of searching, she found it, a short sword-length shard of rock matching the surrounding surface and fit flush with just a fingerhole at the top disclosing its presence. She took out her knife and ran it along the seams, then blew out the finger hole. She then put her finger in and pulled the lever out and downward with some considerable effort. She then slid a few paces to her left, to a place where the surface of the rock was split and cracked, and pushed hard. A doorway swung open inward.

"It leads through the wall to a tunnel inside, which then goes to a closet in the castle proper," she said, talking so fast that they had difficulty keeping up with her. "We can only go single file."

They all, in turn, crawled up the rock to the doorway and entered.

CHAPTER 22

They entered into pitch blackness. The air was very heavy and stale. A stagnant chill touched them all. Even though the earth ordinarily shielded wielders of magic from detection, these were extraordinary times, so, being careful not to expose themselves with the use of magic, they started a torch on fire with a small tool Mayflin carried. They were inside a small entryway that led through a cut stone hallway barely wide enough for one person to walk through. A very large or fat person would have been extremely uncomfortable. They found another torch and handed it to Angoleen, who was to bring up the rear. Shahandra led the way. They walked at a downward slant for a time, then back up. The walls were very well formed, varying only slightly in dimension and proportion. There was an occasional place where the side of the tunnel broke away into a small open area, and one place where there was a room-sized cavern complete with stalactites and stalagmites.

Finally, they reached a stone stairway. About halfway up the staircase, the walls turned into cut stone masonry. The size of the tunnel corridor still did not vary from the one cut out of the mountain. They continued to climb until they were inside a hallway which had several alcoves, none of which contained a visible door. They came to the end of the corridor they were walking in, having made two turns off the one they started in, and found themselves dead-ended in a small alcove barely large enough to hold three of them.

Shahandra reached over to the left side of the alcove and, while pushing down with her foot on a stone lip at the bottom of the wall, she pushed in on a stone in the wall. It slid easily into the wall about twice the thickness of her hand, then stopped. She then turned to the open wall of the alcove and pushed gently. A door swung open. It was no larger than the corridor had been. There were several unseen items that they could hear slide along the floor inside the dark closet as the door moved, so she pushed even easier so as not to make undue noise.

There was barely enough room for all of them to stand in the closet once the door was closed and the items, which turned out to be cleaning buckets, were returned to their original places. As they stood in the darkness, they could sense several types of magic at work from time to time. They used only the briefest and faintest sensing magic for fear of being discovered. They stood and listened for a few moments. Finally, they decided to venture out into the castle and begin their search for Danlion. Their best hope was to find him alone and together destroy him. It had been determined that Angoleen and Mayflin would be the first to split off as a distraction if that became necessary, then Mornic and Darric, and last of all, and only as a last resort, Fallwyn would leave Dalwan to fight alone if no other alternative presented itself. Shahandra was on her own, charged to do what she thought best to take care of herself. She pledged to guide Dalwan and his companions as far as luck would allow her to go.

They were on the ground floor in a closet that opened up near a hallway into a giant room with a beautiful floor depicting the heavens. It was empty except for some debris consisting of glass, pottery, pieces of wood, two piles of ash which appeared to contain human bones, and several pieces of broken furniture. They entered without a noise. They could hear voices in rooms nearby but saw no one. They tried to sense Danlion's presence but could not.

"This is the ballroom," whispered Shahandra. "This way!" she said, motioning for the others to follow her. She turned and headed down the nearby hallway. They worked their way toward the Council Room, thinking that Danlion may be there.

"The Crystal Room is right down this hall and around the corner to the left. We can go upstairs to the Council Room through the Crystal Room stairs, without being seen," said Shahandra, talking so quickly in a whisper that to Dalwan she sounded like steam escaping from a tightly closed kettle.

When they reached the kitchen, three armed men stepped into the hall laughing and talking loudly. It took the men too long to comprehend what or who they were facing. Before they could react, the first man caught Mornic's dagger in the throat. Angoleen and Mayflin were on the other two with drawn swords. Their yells for help were too late to save their lives. Angoleen met the next man out of the kitchen with the point of his sword. The man fell back into the kitchen.

Shahandra grabbed Dalwan and pulled him into the room across the hall from the kitchen. It was the staff lodging quarters. It was a mess, having been ransacked by the invaders. All but Angoleen and Mayflin followed them into the room. Darric closed the door behind him.

Back in the hallway, Angoleen used his magic full force to create an illusion of half a dozen angry armed squatches standing in the hall at the kitchen entrance. The kitchen staff and other soldiers fled from the illusion through another door. Angoleen and Mayflin retreated back toward the ballroom.

Shahandra and the others waited for the noise in the hallway to die down. They continued to sense Angoleen's use of magic to distract the pursuers.

Fallwyn was sensing, and Darric was listening with his highly sensitive ear against the door. Darric stood silently with his eyes closed for what seemed to the others to be an eternity. Suddenly his eyes popped open and, grabbing the door handle as he spoke, announced, "Time ta go! Not a moment ta waste!"

As he pulled the door open, Mornic led the way out with a quick visual check.

"Still clear!" he shouted in a whisper.

Shahandra was next out, pointing again in the direction of the Crystal Room. She quickly moved around Mornic and led the way.

As they reached the final turn in the hall, Fallwyn felt a strange sensation that caused him to motion with his hand for everyone to stop.

"It's Elven magic," he announced in a whispered caution.

"Yes! I feel it too," said Shahandra, trying to sense the direction of its source.

"It's above us," Fallwyn said confidently after sensing for a moment to assure himself that he had accurately pinpointed the direction.

"That's it then. He is in the Council Room. Let's go!", Shahandra said with great resolve as she again began moving toward the Crystal Room door. Darric was the last to make the final turn. He had no sooner cleared the corner than a large group of men entered the far end of the hallway he had just left. They were making lots of noise and checking the rooms along the way as they went.

Mornic and Darric stayed behind at the door to the Crystal Room as Shahandra, Dalwan, and Fallwyn entered cautiously. The room was dark and appeared empty and untouched.

"All clear!" said Fallwyn back to the dwarves. Shahandra led the way to the right corner of the back wall while Mornic and Darric took up positions near the door to intercept any who might enter.

Going to the next-to-last panel on the wall, Shahandra took hold of a wooden molding trim on the side of the panel and, while pushing down on the heavy bottom trim with the toe of her boot, pushed it back, breaking lose the panel. It swung open on hinges. They entered and resecured the panel in place. It was pitch black inside.

"This staircase leads to a similar panel in the Council Room and another in the hallway. That way, someone could go upstairs and enter the Council Room through either door," Shahandra said, sounding much like a child playing hide and seek. "There are no lights in the rack," she said, feeling about in the darkness, "we'll need to go in the dark."

As they mounted the stairs, Dalwan noticed that the only footsteps he could hear were his own. He whispered twice to locate the others. Once they reached the top of the stairs, there was a landing on which they could stand together, still in pitch darkness.

Shahandra took hold of a sleeve on the arm of each of the other two and pulled them closer to her. "Which way do you want to enter from?" she asked. She motioned, pointing with their arms, which she still held, to indicate the direction of each panel door.   "I think we should go through both doors", whispered Fallwyn. "If we can enter from opposite directions, we stand a greater chance of defeating him quickly. I'll use magic in the hallway, which will make him think we're entering from that direction. Wait until you sense his defenses and my power, then make your move."

"But what if there's a lot of soldiers in the hallway?" shot back Dalwan in an embarrassing motherly tone.

"Dalwan, I'm counting on the company. It'll make the show in the hall more believable to Danlion."

It sounded all too heroic for Dalwan, but he knew that this was why they had come and that he needed to listen to the council now more than ever before. Here he was, in the exact position that he never wanted to be in. He began to feel sorry for himself. After all, he was only a boy and probably about to die... The realization of the possibility of death captured his imagination for a moment. Suddenly, he became embarrassed when he realized that he was actually the most likely one to live through this ordeal. All the others were much more vulnerable than he was. Even now, two of the most wonderful beings he had ever met were risking their lives just to be with him in this moment.

"We'll see you inside, my friend", whispered Dalwan with a confidence that left them all ready to go. Shahandra was still holding their arms, so she moved them together until their arms met. They locked on to each other's wrists in a brief shake, then parted.

Shahandra pulled Fallwyn to the hallway entrance. "It'll open into a small alcove where there's a door into the next room. It'll keep you from becoming visible to those guarding the door," she said as she pushed the panel open cautiously after several unseen maneuvers to unsecure it. There was no one in sight from the alcove opening as Fallwyn slipped out. Shahandra closed the panel noiselessly behind him. He found himself in a doorway that faced a hallway. He peeked around the corner and saw that there were two men standing guard with drawn swords at the door to the Council Room. They were about four or five long strides from him. There was no one else visible.

Fallwyn drew his sword and stepped into the hallway. He did not wait for the men to perceive him before he struck them both with white fire. They fell dead without even making a noise. However, his magic drew attention from inside the room. He heard an old voice, strong and loud, yell, "Out in the hall! They're here, get them!"

In an instant, the door swung open and four men poured out into the hall, almost tripping over each other. Fallwyn had retreated into the adjacent hallway, the one facing the alcove he had entered through. He sensed that at least one of them could use fire, but could not tell how developed his art was. He chose to wait just around the corner, about four or five paces in, and throw a green flame curtain at them when they rounded it into his hallway.

Having sensed the battle in the hall, Shahandra loosened the panel and pushed it open. Dalwan had drawn Fallonrod without putting any magic into it. He entered first. The room was about twice as long as it was wide. It had a cut stone floor with a large wooden table set in the center. There were six large chairs on each side of the table and one at each end. The most ornate chair was at the end of the table in the direction Dalwan was entering from. There were several large tapestries hanging from various ceiling beams and on the walls around the room.

As he came through the door, he could sense the powerful magic of a shadowmaster, magic with Danlion's print. There were three identical-looking men standing facing the front door. Because the panel was at the back corner of the room, they did not see him enter. Shahandra followed noiselessly.

Dalwan stood motionlessly, watching carefully to determine if the images there were actually three men with two magically disguised or if there was only one with two illusions. There was a loud noise in the hallway that caused the three men to react by moving... they all moved exactly the same, keeping their attention on the door. Dalwan held up his pointing finger to indicate that only one of the images was real. Shahandra nodded in agreement.

They could both sense the presence of elven magic but could not isolate the one from which it came. The job was complicated by Fallwyn, whose magic was close enough to interfere with perception.

Dalwan knew that if Fallwyn broke through the door, he would be in serious trouble. He had to act now to distract or perhaps destroy Danlion.

Dalwan felt certain that a well-placed surprise attack could destroy Danlion before he knew what was taking place.

He raised Fallonrod, charged it for fire, and let loose with a white fire blast that virtually blinded both him and Shahandra. He swung the sword across all three images, watching as best he could to see which was real. The fire passed through all three. They were all illusions!! "Brilliant!" he thought to himself as he reassessed the situation. Danlion had to be close; he could sense the elven magic coming from the direction of the table.

The images did not move nor did Dalwan. Flame flickered from two tapestries and several wooden support beams in the rock wall. Shahandra had been standing behind Dalwan and decided to move around him for a better look.

At that same instant, an enormous green flame curtain flew toward them from the area of the largest chair. Dalwan held up Fallonrod as he shoved Shahandra back behind him. The curtain was split by the sword and pounded into the panel wall behind him in two pieces.

Almost instantly, he returned white fire again, this time to the chair. The top of it exploded in a shower of tiny flames that turned from blue to red as they dissipated. The other three images of Danlion vanished. The sense of Elven magic filled the room.

The remainder of the large chair slid back, revealing a large black hat lying on the table in front of it. A green flame curtain flew from the front side of the chair toward the burning tapestries and smoldering timbers. The concussion put out the flames and scattered burning embers on the stone floor. Smoke already covered the high ceiling, concealing the uppermost open beams. A thin hand reached out, took hold of the hat, and placed it on the head of the rising figure as he turned around.

****

Deep in a remote Pretorian forest, in a cave situated in a small canyon forested with towering trees, an ancient beast stirred. Its healing sleep, now almost complete, had been interrupted by the sense of a familiar magic. The magic was a magic mixed with strong emotions of fear and uncertainty. It was battle magic, and it was the only human magic he had ever cared for. The great anderon stirred to full consciousness. There it was again...white fire... Dalwan was at war with someone.

Giant wings unfolded and long dormant wounded legs stretched, both with some pain. The anderon's sense of loyalty and bond of friendship drove him to the cave entrance. It was midmorning or a little later. The anderon began to stretch his mighty wings, knowing well that he could not fly for some time, not until fresh blood had strengthened them. The damaged wing had healed much faster than his age should have permitted... "It was," thought the beast in fond recollection, "no doubt the boy's magic!"

The wisdom of his age cautioned him to only try flight when he was fully ready or he would not reach his friend at all. He would fly as soon as he was sure he could. "Time seems always the enemy in these things," he mused as he waited.

****

Danlion turned toward the two intruders with an ear-to-ear, yellow-toothed grin.

"You have remarkable power for one so young," he said, strolling a few steps toward Dalwan. "It's a shame it will all be wasted... Yes, wasted," he said,

423

drawing out the sound of each word for maximum impact, "...as its potential is extinguished here in this room."

Danlion's words were slow, drawn out, and distinct. There was a melodious rhythm to them, almost hypnotic. "I can teach you things and help you develop into a great leader and powerful master of the arts. I will rule from seclusion, and you will be the one seen by the world as its leader."

"Dalwan," shouted Shahandra, "he's enchanting you. His words are laced with magic. Fight him."

Dalwan stood motionless with Fallonrod still held high. Another blast of white fire flew toward Danlion. Again, it was deflected and exploded into a shower of sparks.

With an evil grin on his face, Danlion said, "I take it from your actions that you refuse my offer. Very well," he said in a casual manner, "perish!"

At that instant, he sent a shower of flame at Dalwan that looked as though it totally engulfed him. The flame continued in a stream as Danlion walked closer and closer to Dalwan, laughing wickedly as he neared.

Suddenly, a brilliant green curtain became visible around Dalwan and Shahandra. Slowly, as if against a heavy current of water, the curtain began to open up and spread out until it reached twice the size of Dalwan's height. It began to move toward Danlion. His laughter stopped and was replaced with shouts of rage and cursing. Dalwan kept Fallonrod pointed directly at the curtain, feeding its strength as it overpowered Danlion's flame.

Danlion's fire stopped abruptly, and the curtain rushed towards him with enormous force. About arm's length from him, it burst apart into pieces that flew in different directions, sounding like an avalanche of boulders hitting the walls and floor. Danlion was knocked to the floor and lay dazed. The amulet blazed brightly through his loose-knit tunic.

Dalwan sent out a blast of what he now called lightning rope, which wrapped around Danlion where he lay, encasing him in a blazing cocoon. Danlion was motionless for a moment. Dalwan and Shahandra stood transfixed as his new bindings began to break apart and move across the floor like a storm of static sparks through cloth, with the floor absorbing them. Its departure gave way to a stationary green curtain, like a flame curtain, only it didn't move. He sat up and slowly rose to his feet. Dalwan stared in disbelief.

"Don't let him make the first move, Dalwan! DO SOMETHING!!" shouted Shahandra.

Dalwan threw flame at the ties that held the tapestry secure to the beam over Danlion's head. It fell perfectly and covered the ancient wizard. Instantly, it blew apart. It was hard to tell if it had been Dalwan's follow-up with fire on the tapestry or simply Danlion's own defense.

"Foolish boy! This is no game we play! Now you die!!" screamed Danlion in a hideous voice that seemed to shriek at him from all corners of the room. A rainbow of fiery streams flew toward Dalwan from Danlion's raised hands and were absorbed by Fallonrod like water to a sponge. Danlion stared in disbelief at the sword that protected the boy and his friend without allowing so much as a singed hair. He began to back toward the front door. "Your power will soon fail you, boy. Your luck can not hold," said Danlion, resuming his ugly yellow grin. In a flash, Danlion had thrown a dagger concealed in a flame at Dalwan. The sword jerked Dalwan's hand with lightning reflex to knock the knife away and absorb the flame. Danlion's eyes narrowed as he tried desperately to sense the sword, as if looking for that hint which would identify something hauntingly familiar about the boy's magic. Nothing came.

Dalwan began to advance on Danlion with Fallonrod held high. He tried to work his way toward Danlion's right so that he might circle around and get between him and the door. Danlion pulled a sword from under his cloak as Dalwan approached.

Danlion spoke clearly and quietly as Dalwan, shadowed by Shahandra, moved close to the wall as they skirted him, "Your sword is powerful, but mine has strange magic, magic from another age, magic of fear, the very magic of madness. It will steal your mind." He followed with a hideous laugh. "He raised his sword and pointed it at Dalwan, who was now only a handful of paces away. For an instant, Dalwan saw spiders crawling quickly down his sword toward his hand, then they disappeared, and Danlion yelled as his arms and hands were covered with the hairy visions. Something like a light made of sparks flowed down from Danlion's head across his cloak, and the visions disappeared. By this time, they had taken the few additional steps around Danlion and were now both on the door side of the table, with Dalwan near the wall and a little closer to the door than Danlion.

While Danlion and Dalwan battled, the dwarves guarded the downstairs door to the Crystal Room. They had situated themselves in the dark room so they could intercept anyone who might enter searching for them. Mornic hid behind the door, and Darric crouched behind a crystal display case. They had heard the sound of men shouting in the hallway. It got louder then subsided. About the time they started to relax, a man entered the doorway with a torch. He pushed the door completely open without entering. It struck Mornic, who was standing as close to the wall as his stubby body would permit. The man looked through the crack between the hinges and fled. They knew that it was only a matter of time before he returned with reinforcements. They fused the door closed using their arts and waited for those outside to return and try to break in. Meanwhile, they were being entertained by a marvelous display of lights from the crystals in the Crystal room. They discovered that there were several source stones that lit up in magnificent colors, throwing light all over the room. The stones were obviously being fueled by the dynamic battle taking place above them between Dalwan and Danlion. It became difficult for the dwarven duo to concentrate on their job with such a display to distract them.

As the dwarves watched a brilliant light show during Danlion's use of white fire, a group of men gathered outside the door had begun to use a large, solid object of some sort to batter the door. Using his sensing powers, Darric realized that those outside the door far outnumbered the two of them. Darric moved back to the hidden panel door in the wall and, after a couple of failed attempts, got it open. The main door was beginning to splinter when Mornic closed the secret panel behind them. They headed upstairs, hoping to discover enough signs of the other's passage to join them. Magic was so rampant in the castle by this time that sensing with any surety became difficult. This, however, gave them the freedom to use some small magic to light their way up the stairs without fear of being discovered. There was enough dust on the floor for them to follow the footprints through the passageway and thereby discover the upstairs secret entrance. Mornic began to try to release the panel using the now familiar pattern for such tasks.

Meanwhile, Dalwan struck out at Danlion and found Danlion's sword quick and responsive to his every move. Danlion did not have the strength that Dalwan did, but the magic in his sword seemed to make up for it. Dalwan tried to use his metal molders' magic on Danlion's sword, hoping to cut it up or melt it down. It would deform, then regain its shape.

While this was taking place, Shahandra got separated from Dalwan. She had moved to the rear of the room when she sensed magic from the direction of the back corner. She concentrated on it to isolate it from the many other magics at work, trying to identify the user. She became convinced that it must be dwarven magic. Hoping that it was, and that it belonged to Darric and Mornic in the hidden stairway, she moved to the panel to let them in. She activated the release just as Mornic felt sure he had figured it out. "I got it!" he whispered triumphantly. The panel swung open and revealed Shahandra's back as she continued to monitor the battle between the very cautious warriors

The three worked their way stealthfully behind Danlion's back about halfway between the table and the back wall, as the battling magicians fought on the opposite side of the table, almost directly in front of the door.

"Can't you help him?" whispered Shahandra into Darric's attentive ear.

"No! The sword 'ill work against us if we try anythin' of magic!"

Dalwan was clearly the aggressor as he threw blow after blow in a relentless attack on Danlion. Danlion's sword responded smoothly and systematically to each swing of Fallowrod. As Dalwan stepped back to reassess his attack, Danlion glanced back at the three who had flanked him. He quickly raised his sword straight up, and it errupted in an erie blue glow which flowed out from it like a cloud. Ghostlike fingers, like radiant blue fog, touched Shshandra and the dwarves. They each fell to their knees, gasping and holding their chests in terror. At the same time, another denser finger of cloud completely engulfed Dalwan. Instantly, it swirled like a cyclone and returned violently onto Danlion.

Danlion gasped, staggered a few steps, and doubled over. The blue cloud dissipated into the floor like iron filings drawn by a lodestone. There was an immense flash of green light from the stone around Danlion's neck. He regained his composure, rising again to full height, his vigor revived.

"You see, boy, you'll never win...you and your friends will all die!" he said with sadistic glee, looking around as the others got back up off the floor.

Dalwan advanced on him with a flurry of blows that clearly surprised Danlion in their power and intensity. Fallonrod began to glow brighter and brighter with every strike. Danlion's sword answered in brightness and color while it absorbed every blow. Dalwan backed Danlion up almost to the table.

Fire began to dance between the swords, flashing back and forth in blazing arcs. It appeared as if they were fighting with pillars of fire.

Sensing that Dalwan was beginning to fatigue, Danlion started his attack. "You tire boy!" he said with vicious delight. "I knew that I waited you out, you would falter." Danlion abandoned his defensive posture and began to throw a few well-calculated blows as he spoke.

You're an unseasoned warrior boy...and you've failed in a big way...you're too worn out to fight anymore, aren't you, boy."

Dalwan felt as if all his strength was being stripped away.

"Yes...YES!" laughed Danlion. "You feel the failure, don't you, boy...the disillusion is setting in, isn't it?"

Dalwan felt his strength start to give way, then very suddenly there was a strange ripple in the air between he and Danlion, and the dispare vanished just as Danlion's sword tip fell to the floor, as if he needed it for support.

At the same instant, Shahandra yelled,"Don't listen to him, Dalwan! It's his magic...he's..."

As she began to speak, the amulet around Danlion's neck flashed even brighter than it had the last time. Danlion recovered with amazing speed, and while Shahandra was still speaking sent a stream of fire in her direction. Darric responded by putting green fire between them and Danlion. The burning stream simply vanished without effect into the green flame.

A loud bang drew everyone's attention to the door as it swung open, revealing a tattered but quite alive Fallwyn. Instantly, Danlion shifted his attention to Fallwyn and prepared to throw fire. Dalwan countered with an enormous green flame curtain to protect him. Instead, Danlion threw an enormous ball of flame at Dalwan. Fallonrod answered with explosive force, collecting Danlion's fire and sending it back against him, greatly multiplied in force. The blast sent Danlion flying, though unsinged, across the table and directly into Shahandra.

Dalwan ran to the table directly between Fallwyn and Danlion. Immediately, Fallwyn stepped around the protective flame curtain and, with a wave of his hand, attempted to turn off the amulet that Danlion was wearing. Nothing happened!.

Danlion and Shahandra fell to the floor and landed tangled up together. The tell tale glow of the amulet continued on unimpeded. Again, Falwyn tried to extinguish it...NOTHING!

Danlion stirred to consciousness.

Fallwyn shouted, "Dalwan, MOVE! Fallonrod's stopping my magic!"

Danlion's face mirrored fear, then rage, "Fallonrod? HERE?! In a BOY'S HANDS?!"

Before Danlion could pull himself together to react, Dalwan moved aside, and Fallwyn quinched the amulet.

Danlion's eyes bugged in terror as he constricted into paralysis. He gasped and then writhed. Shahandra sat up to find Danlion's quivering head in her lap. She placed her hand on his forehead while everyone in the room watched, frozen in their places, each holding their breath.

Shahandra stroked his head and sensed his inner being. She felt his anger and rage, his bitterness and sense of betrayal, his immense emptiness, his sadness, his cruelty. She stroked it again and soothed his fear and calmed his agitation. She sensed his lostness and his exhaustion. There was a wave of rage, and she sensed desire for revenge. She calmed his feelings with her warm magic. He was confused and could feel his own life slipping away.

"I know you..." he whispered. "I know from somewhere..." his dry, raspy voice wheezed out. For a moment, he focused on her face. "It was you in the room..." his eyes closed. He convulsed briefly and went limp. A short flash of fire went out from the fingers of both hands as they lay motionless out to his side. The fire streaked across the floor in wispy trails like tine bolts of lightning, each snaking along in its own direction and dissolving into the stone. Nothing was harmed or caught fire. He again became fitful. She could tell that his magic had become very dangerous and that it was no longer thoughtfully controlled. She put her hands on the top of his bony head and employed the same art she used to calm frightened animals. His breathing returned to a slow, even rhythm. Still using her art, she cleared his mind of thoughts, leaving only a feeling of warmth. Danlion was asleep. It was the most peaceful sleep he had experienced in many years. No fear, no anger, no vengeance, only peace. Shahandra placed her hands on his head as the others watched in awe and gave him his final release. He breathed his last in peace.

"Ya took quite a chance, dearie," said Darric with clear admiration in his voice. He and Mornic went to either side of Shahandra while Fallwyn turned his attention back into the hallway. Ya're quite the woman, and I for my part am very proud o' ya." The others joined in complimenting her.

During the entire fight, each of them had sensed the nearby sporadic use of elven magic.

Mornic and Darric picked Danlion up and moved his body so Shahandra could get up. Darric removed the elven amulet from Danlion and tossed it to Fallwyn.

"There are men coming down the hallway, I can hear them," said Fallwyn, chancing a look back through the open door.
"No sight of them yet."

"Let's get back down to the crystal room," said Mornic, moving back to the hidden entrance. "At least we're in a better position to escape." Everyone agreed so they all made their way back except Fallwyn, who watched the door and hallway until the last moment. The men in the hallway were still around the corner and out of sight, but he could sense them and even hear them. They apparently were either afraid or waiting for someone to join them before trying an entrance. After seeing six of their companions lying dead on the floor, they were obviously exercising some additional caution, just enough caution to give Fallwyn time to get to the back panel entrance unseen.

It took them only a few seconds to get to the bottom floor secret entrance of the Crystal Room. They sensed the room and could detect no one in it. Shahandra opened the panel with great caution. The room was still dark. The front double doors were broken out of the frame at the right hinges and hung slightly open. The men had apparently left the room after finding no one inside when they broke the door down.

Again, Fallwyn went quickly to the front door to check the hallway. It was vacant. He pushed the door back into the frame where it hung awkwardly, being somewhat splintered.

"We have to find out what has become of Angoleen and Mayflin," said Darric with discernible concern in his voice. "I have sensed some changes in his magic in the few times I have perceived it."

"I think someone is hurt," Shahandra said slowly, thinking back on her perceptions of the magic the two elves had used the last time. "Which one uses the healing art, Fallwyn?" she asked in a louder voice so Fallwyn would be sure to realize she was talking in his direction.

"Mayflin used the art that you sensed," he answered, only partially turning his head in response. "I couldn't tell if it was on himself or someone else."

"Let's just hope he was being his normal helpful self and assisting some innocent bystander, if such a person exists in this mess," Darric said as he walked over to join Fallwyn at the door. "Fallwyn, someone must go out and bring our two adventuresome friends back to us."

"I've been hoping that I could sense some advance on their part, but I can't even discern their activity now at all," said Fallwyn in a voice that's music was sad.

"I'll go," said Dalwan without hesitation.

"I'll go with him," volunteered Shahandra so quickly and enthusiastically that it made Dalwan's heart jump.

Fallwyn's attention turned to Shahandra. "You've been an invaluable friend and an inspiration to us all. I think you must now stay with our dwarven friends to guide them out should Dalwan and I fail." His words were filled with emotion and obvious love for Darric and Mornic.

"But I know the cast..."

Dalwan cut in before she could finish, "Shahandra, we're both sensors. We may not quite have your gift or knowledge of the castle, but we'll find them and get back. We'll all need you safe when we return so we can get out of the castle in one piece."

Shahandra sensed something in Dalwan's speech that no one else detected. He cared so much more for her than she had known. This shocked her enough that she had to rethink what he had said just to understand it. It did make sense. "Alright. But don't get lost," admonished Shahandra, sounding so much like a mother warning her children that Fallwyn shook his finger at Dalwan in a pretend warning, bringing quiet chuckles from the others.

Like quicksilver in gravel, Dalwan and Fallwyn were out in the hall. They decided to move back to the place where Angoleen and Mayflin first split off from the group and attempt to retrace their steps. They encountered no one in the first hallway, but could hear loud shouting coming from an area some distance away. Without hesitation, they both started moving quickly toward the commotion, knowing that their group was the only one intruding and would therefore be the only one likely to be causing a disturbance of the magnitude that they now could hear.

They knew that they were on the right track by the body count along the hallway. It made Dalwan a little sick to see such a waste of life. Fallwyn must have picked up on Dalwan's feelings or been thinking the same thing himself, "Sometimes the powers we possess make us the most responsible for the very things we detest.

They encountered no one through the next two hallways. They came to a corner where they could hear nearby voices that seemed excited. "Here comes the ram!" they heard someone yell. "Now we'll see who lives and who dies!" yelled a distinctly different voice. The ram must have been coming from the other end of the hall in which the men waited, because it had not come past Dalwan and Fallwyn.

The corridor that the men were in was one that split off the hall that Fallwyn and Dalwan were in. "I'm going to very obviously sneak across the hall to attract attention. I'll keep going and draw them away. After they pass, follow us invisibly down the hallway until I turn around. Then we will finish them off," Fallwyn instructed Dalwan. Fallwyn did not even wait for a response but set out immediately. He moved very slowly across the opening, looking all the while at the men. When he was almost at the far side of the opening, he dropped his knife because they still hadn't noticed him. Five of the ten men at the door began a very loud and disorganized pursuit of Fallwyn. Dalwan vanished from sight, hoping that there were no more sensors close by, or at least that if there were, they would be distracted.

It worked so well that he didn't even have to wait for stragglers. They ran in a pack. Never suspecting that there was someone behind them, they pursued Fallwyn down past two rooms to the end of the hall, where he turned and held up his sword. The men pulled up short to regroup and assess their enemy about four paces from him. Three men stood in front of the last two, all facing Fallwyn. Dalwan did not bother to become visible but simply cut down the last two men as Fallwyn squared up against the group. As they were falling to the ground, the men in front had begun to advance against Fallwyn. They were distracted by their dying companions just long enough for Fallwyn to move in on them. Dalwan leapt over the bodies and killed the middleman who had stopped a step behind the other two. Fallwyn made quick work of the man on the right, and the one on the left turned and ran back past Dalwan, who struck him down on a back swing. He became visible again.

"It seems too easy. It just isn't a fair way to fight," said Dalwan, wiping his sword off on the last dead man's shirt.

"Don't ever forget those words and don't ever let this become sport for you." Fallwyn's voice was icy cold as he spoke. "Under other circumstances, these men might have become allies. Killing in this manner is at best an unfortunate necessity caused by evil or gravely misguided people." The two made their way back down the hallway as they talked. They reached the corner in time to hear one man say to another, "Go see if you can see them and if they need help."

"Let's become invisible again and just stand here for a moment," Fallwyn said, fading into a shadowy image, then out of sight altogether. Dalwan followed suit immediately. The man rounded the corner and shouted back at his companions that it looked like they were dead at the end of the hall. Two of the men had begun to use the battering ram on the door. When they heard that report, they dropped it and ran with the other two men to check out the situation. Suddenly, fear filled the men. Such terror overcame them that they all turned and ran down the hallway back past the door they had been trying to break down and out of sight at the end of the corridor.

"That was an excellent idea," remarked Fallwyn with the first sign of admiration he had ever heard directed at himself by the elf. "I had no idea that you had perfected your enchanting so well."

"And no one else had to die," Dalwan said, satisfied that at least these five men had lived.

"Let's not be too naive, Dalwan. We're dealing with human pride here. Remember what they were saying when we first heard them at the door? ...'we'll see who lives...?" said Fallwyn as they both began cautiously walking down the hallway toward the door the men had been trying to force entry on. "Most likely, the men will return with everyone they can find."

Fallwyn's words cut Dalwan to the quick. "Then why didn't we just kill them?" he said bitterly.

"That's the dilemma of power such as yours. You and I are powerful, past that which most rulers of this world could even hope for personally. We, and the little group we travel with, represent power that comes to but one in a hundred thousand. It'll bend you if you aren't very careful. You must notice that I said 'WILL', not 'CAN'. Remember Danlion? He was just a young man once, probably a lot like you." They both stopped talking as they reached the door.

"Angoleen! Mayflin! Are you in there?" shouted Fallwyn.

"Yes," answered Mayflin. "Are you alone?"

"Dalwan's with me."

"I'm going to move so you can open the door. You'll have to use a lot of force; it's sealed." Mayflin said in an exhausted voice.

They gave Mayflin a moment to move, then Fallwyn pulled his sword and simply cut a new door out of the larger existing ones using a thin white flame. He pushed the new door in, and it fell to the floor with a resounding crack.

Inside, Mayflin was sitting on a rug next to Angoleen, who had a bloody wound on his head. Mayflin's clothes were torn in numerous places, several of which had evidence of blood.

"He's alive but unconscious," said Mayflin with tears in his eyes. I haven't been able to do much for him.

"Dalwan, I'm going to carry him," said Fallwyn. "You'll have to protect our back as we make our way to the Crystal Room. We're in your hands," he said, talking quickly as he picked up Angoleen and headed for the door.

Dalwan was moving much faster and stepped into the hall with reckless abandon of caution.

"We need you alive, Dalwan, be careful. An arrow you don't see can fell you just as fast as anyone else." Fallwyn's words scolded Dalwan back into a sense of reality.

They were out in the hall and fully committed to their retreat when the far end of the hall filled with the sound of angry men. Dalwan couldn't even count them.

"Run!" yelled Dalwan to the others as he turned to face the coming mob.

Archers stepped out in front of the mob and shot as they moved toward him. He did not move except to hold Fallonrod up to intercept the coming arrows. The men did not move any faster than the archers, letting them have the front. Soon, they realized that the archers were not being effective. When they had moved to within twenty strides of Dalwan, they stopped, and another man stepped in front. He had a sling.

Dalwan yelled out a warning, "We haven't come for you. We've done what we came to do, and we'll leave without harming anyone else if you allow us to."

Someone in the crowd answered with fierce anger, "...and I suppose you're going to bring all our friends back to life on your way out?" This sobered Dalwan up even more. The losses some of them felt were no less severe than those Dalwan and his friends had experienced.

"We don't want to kill anyone else. I'm a powermaster, and I'll use every weapon and magic I possess on you to save my friends. It's too late for your dead comrades, but not for those living. The choice is yours," said Dalwan in words that just kept coming to him as if written in some script prepared just for this occasion.

It seemed to be working for a moment until the man with the sling decided to take matters into his own hands and strike. Dalwan realized that anything in a sling would take immense fire to destroy at that close range, so he simply hit the front of the group with intense white fire just before the slinger let go. There were screams of rage and pain. Men were scattering down the hall, and several arrows returned in Dalwan's direction only to incinerate midair. He turned and ran with all the speed his shaky legs would give him. His head was spinning. This was everything he thought it would be... a living nightmare. He came to the main hallway and rounded the corner just in time to see Fallwyn round the corner at the far end. They were still O.K.

He had only taken a few steps when an arrow went clear through his tunic on top of his shoulder. He felt the sharp pain of a razor cut. He turned in time to incinerate the next arrow. There were only two men in the hall, and only one of them had a bow. He lifted his sword and pointed it. The men ducked into a room. He became invisible and began to run again toward Fallwyn and the others.

As he rounded the corner into the hallway, which led past the ballroom, he noticed that Fallwyn, still holding Angoleen, was standing with his back against the hallway wall, looking into the ballroom. Dalwan realized that there was an entrance from outside at the rear of the ballroom, which could have been accessed by others since they had passed by. Still invisible, he made his way to the opening that Fallwyn was staring into. There were at least ten archers with arrows nocked and maybe 30 other men behind them, standing ready. Mayflin was standing in the entrance with his hands raised. His sword was on the floor next to Angoleen.

One of the men was yelling at Mayflin, "How many of you are there?" he asked as he paced back nervously behind the row of archers. Mayflin didn't answer.

"Come now, I know you understand me. How about me killing your injured friend? If you don't talk, I will!"

Dalwan moved into the room next to Mayflin and whispered, "Mayflin, it's Dalwan. I'm right next to you. I'm going to make a dragon appear so they'll empty their bows. As soon as they shoot, RUN." Dalwan felt quite proud that the dragon should come to his mind as a decoy... "Now to make it seem real..." he thought for only a few seconds... "that's it!!!"

Dalwan moved quickly and silently toward the back wall that bordered the outside courtyard as Mayflin began to speak slowly to the man. This gave him enough time to get behind the men. He placed Fallonrod against the stone wall and, with the most powerful blast of magic he had ever used against stone, undid the center section of the wall. It crashed spectacularly to the floor. He filled the gap with a perfect vision of an anderon, complete with roar and, to add that much-needed touch of terror, real fire. It worked like a charm. Those hit by flying debris from the wall scattered across the floor, some on their feet, others tangled up with the rubble. The others turned in terror to gaze at a nightmare the likes of which most of them had never seen. Arrows flew and passed through the image. The archers learned their folly too late to restring. Dalwan use Fallonrod to throw several flame curtains in their direction. The effects left him the only person standing in the room. Angoleen and Mayflin were out of sight. He wasted no time getting to the door. Before the men could regain their feet and begin the pursuit, Dalwan was on the heels of his companions, trying to prod them on while covering their backs. Dalwan covered them all with a cloak of invisibility.

They were nearing the final turn in the hallway leading to the crystal room when a group of men rounded the corner far behind them. Two of them had bows. One, who appeared to be in charge, shouted, "They're probably invisible, just shoot!" The two men opened up with a shot each. Both arrows

clearly missed. They restrung and shot. This time, Dalwan had to counter with
fire to stop the arrows.

Dalwan shouted for his friends to keep going and stopped to face the
attackers. He became visible to face them. He wondered if Fallonrod could
throw other magic the way fire was thrown. He knew from a comment made
by Shahandra that several of these hallways had corridors directly below them.
The two men had restrung and moved a little closer. Dalwan pointed Fallonrod
at the floor in front of them, using the same magic he had used to undo the wall
moments before. The men continued to move forward and shot again. Dalwan
diverted his attention briefly to incinerate the arrows, then back to the floor.
The archers remained in the front with a growing group of others hanging
behind them. Dalwan's disappointment swelled as nothing happened to the
floor.

By this time, his companions had rounded the final corner, so he turned
and ran to join them. He became invisible to give himself an edge in escaping.
He heard the men behind him shout and begin to run in pursuit. This was
followed almost immediately by an enormous crashing and brief screams of
terror. Dalwan glanced back as he rounded the corner to see the floor from
wall to wall completely missing just in front of the place he had been
concentrating on. All the men were missing with the floor.

Fallwyn had just disappeared into the Crystal Room as Dalwan cleared
the corner. There were no more sounds of pursuit. By the time he reached the
room, Shahandra was tending Angoleen and Fallwyn was lying on the floor
exhausted. Dalwan could feel his own heart pounding throughout his body and
could hear it in his ears, pumping faster than his feet had run to escape.
Adventures were so fun to hear about, but not nearly so much fun to be
involved in. "This would indeed be a story to tell if they lived through it,"
Dalwan thought to himself as he bent down to see if there was anything he
might do to help Fallwyn. Darric was already with him.

Every muscle in Fallwyn's body seemed to be cramping. Dalwan placed
his hands on Fallwyn's right leg, which seemed to be suffering the most, and
began to apply very familiar magic to it... This was one of the few healing arts
he knew well. Muscle by muscle, Dalwan tended Fallwyn. This took his mind
off the fact that every muscle in his own body was now tingling with near
numbness and exhaustion.

During this time, Darric, Mayflin, and Mornic secured the door back in place using a variety of mixed magics. It was now quite literally part of the wall.

Meanwhile, giant wings had already begun to thrust the ancient beast toward Brandon Keep. He flew invisibly at great speed, spurred on by a most curious combination of magical arts coming from Dalwan.

The room was now lit with several small candles and, from time to time, by a little magic. The heavy smell of smoke filled the room, making all of their eyes sting. They began to discuss the possibilities for escape.

"Won't they just leave if they discover that Danlion is dead?" asked Dalwan.

"No lad," said Darric with the hint of a laugh in his voice. "They realize that they have somewhat offended the people whose castle they stole. Ta simply say, 'Well this little plan o' ours didn't work out, so ya can have yer castle back now!', might not sit well with the displaced group."

"What'll they do, live here forever?" asked Dalwan, totally exasperated.

"They'll either make an escape plan or run for their lives if something extraordinary comes up. But either way, it's not likely to be very soon," Darric said as he walked over to Fallwyn, who was now setting up against the wall near the place where Dalwan had treated him. "We'd better make a plan ourselves before our hosts grow any more impatient with us." Fallwyn nodded in agreement.

Dalwan stood up and shook his head as if he had been hit and needed to regain composure.

"Stand up too fast?" laughed Mayflin. "Careful now, especially after a battle."

"No... I don't know what it was..." As Dalwan was speaking, certain of the stones in the room showed dim lights and then went out.

"Did ya see that?" said Mornic, walkin' over to Dalwan. "Better settle down, lad, an' rest."

As Mornic took hold of Dalwan's arm to help him set down, the lights came again, only brighter this time.

"If only we could get the anderon to fly us out." Dalwan was clearly in a dazed state. The lights faded, and his mind cleared again. "What's happening to me? Something's wrong." He took hold of his head as if in great pain.

" 'Could have had a head injury in the fighting," said Fallwyn, struggling to his feet and bounding over to tend Dalwan.

Before he could get to Dalwan, the stones lit, and Dalwan went to his knees in a swoon. This time, they were much brighter, and there were wisps of connecting light beams between some of them.

"The anderon could help us out... he could fly us out!" Dalwan's eyes were closed, but he sounded much more lucid.

"He must be injured," Fallwyn said as he reached Dalwan and knelt beside him. The lights in the crystals dimmed but did not go out completely. "Look at the combination of magics that are coming from him. It's as if he were unlocking them all at once." Fallwyn and Mornic each held an arm to steady Dalwan. "What do you make of this, Darric?"

The lights intensified, forming clearly visible multi-colored light bridges between themselves in several places.

"Anderon...anderon, is that you?" Dalwan sounded as though he was caught in a dream. "Where are you? What 're you doing up? It's too soon..." The lights were starting to bridge to Dalwan, the floor, the walls, and to each other in greater numbers and variety.

"Darric, I've never seen anything like this. Is he OK?" shouted Mornic. "You're the great magician, DO SOMETHING!"

"I'm open for suggestions if ya got any," Darric answered a little more excitedly than any of the others had remembered hearing him before.

The lights formed a glowing ball in the middle of the room over Dalwan, and a form began to take shape in the center of it. Slowly, the movement clarified until it clearly resembled the silhouette of a flying anderon. The room was completely quiet as they watched. Soon the image cleared more as the details of the great beast filled in: wing talons, scales, and finally his eyes.

"Are you near us, anderon?" shouted Dalwan so suddenly that it made everyone's stomach jump.

"Is that what they really look like... is this a real image or just a dream?" Shahandra asked, moving as close as she could to get a clear look.

"Not many of us can say that we've actually seen one close enough to say for sure. But it sure looks like the real thing," Angoleen said as he sat up in his makeshift bed of cloaks to take a better look.

Fallwyn looked into the image and smiled, "Yes, friends, that's exactly what they look like... I think I know him!"

The light in the ball began to quiver, and a voice spoke out of it, "I'm almost with you. Hold on to my thoughts for a few more moments."

"Do ya actually suppose that he's comin' ta Dalwan?" Mornic said as his heart swelled. All his life, he had wanted to see one of the grand beasts but had been denied the opportunity.

The monstrous wings folded back, and the image made a sudden downward plunge. There was a burst of fire, and the beast turned up with a powerful wing stroke. He repeated the maneuver. Both times, there was the brief sound of men shouting in panic. The third time, he went all the way down, slowed, and landed, revealing the grounds outside the castle mansion.

The light in the ball began to quiver again, and a voice said, "All of you standing there looking at the light, close your mouths and move to the inside wall."

They stood looking in disbelief for only a brief moment. Then there was a louder command from the voice, this time shouting in a deep growl, "MOVE!! NOW!!"

They all moved quickly. Fallwyn and Darric hoisted Dalwan up and half-dragged him with them. The lights moved with him as if they were cords tied about his body.

Immediately, the lights formed a giant, blinding column connecting to a single spot on the outside wall of the room. The spot started about the size of a large melon and grew until it was about as big around as a large man is tall. Suddenly, the wall disintegrated into a shower of fragments, forming a hole through which came a monstrous head.

"Dalwan. It's so good to see you alive. You've been quite busy, haven't you?" There was so much expression and intelligence in the immense face that it made all the others laugh and cheer. "I assume that these are your friends?"

"Yes, my friend. And yours too if you choose," answered Dalwan, completely recovered. He quickly gained his feet and ran to the familiar head and gave him a hug. This not only surprised the others but shocked them so much that they simply stood silently and stared, wide-eyed and open mouthed.

The anderon studied the small group and answered, "I have already made that determination with the one called Fallwyn, I shall decide on the others later. Suddenly, the anderons' eyes got large, then narrowed in irritation. His head withdrew from the room, and a deafening roar exploded in their ears. When the reverberations of it ended, all that they could hear was the muffled yells of men in retreat.

The giant head reappeared with what was clearly a smile. He knocked a much larger hole in the wall as his head reentered. "It seems that for some reason they felt quite confident that I was but an illusion!" said the deep rumbling voice as his stare fixed solidly on Dalwan. "Can you imagine what possessed them to think such a thing?" he continued with unblinking concentration on Dalwan.

"I apologize," said Dalwan, barely audible to the others.

"I'm sorry... I didn't hear you!" growled the very animated and inquisitive anderon.

Speaking up a little, at the insistence of the anderon, he recounted the story of their escape from the ballroom using the anderon image. "I used your image without your permission. I'm sorry I violated your trust."

"Humility! And at that, from a man! I love a humble soul!" he said so loudly that the sound could be felt in the stone. "You're forgiven the trespass."

Darric stepped up to the anderon's head and spoke Dwarf-to-face with the beast, "We're here as a result of a common mission to destroy a tyrant..."

Before he could finish, the anderon cut in, "Yes, yes, I know of your adventure from my friend Dalwan." The words "my friend" burned into the ears of everyone present. Such a thing spoken by an anderon of any type at any time in the past toward a man was unheard of. "I suppose that I can be of some assistance in helping you out of this little predicament since you are all friends of Dalwan." There was the unmistakable air of humor in the giant voice. "I'll take a quick look around and determine what the foe is up to," he said as his head withdrew again from the hole in the wall.

Shahandra was completely astonished, "How many more surprises are in store for us, Dalwan?" she said, looking at him much differently than ever before. "Next, I suppose we'll find out that you're really some old magician in disguise."

Before Dalwan could respond, the anderon was back with an unmistakable grin on his face. "It seems that everyone has decided to leave. I wonder... could it be my breath...?" His massive face reflected shock at the thought. This made them all roar with side splitting laughter to the great delight of the anderon. The expressions on his face and his timing were perfect.

They all climbed out of the hole in the wall to find a deserted castle yard. There was no sound save that of the gentle breeze blowing through nearby garden trees. To everyone's surprise, there were no bodies near the anderon or anywhere in the area they could observe.

"I do not intend to remain here any longer," said the anderon, looking around at the castle grounds, "far too artificial for my taste!"

Dalwan stepped up in front of his giant friend's face to explain his intentions, "I need to return to Castle Crest because Danlion..." he was abruptly cut off by the anderon at the mention of Danlion.

"Danlion!? I have heard quite a few nasty tales surrounding this ageless and twisted little man. Is that who you fought here?" There was a hint of smoke trailing from the hinge part of his mouth as he spoke, giving him a very menacing look.

"Yes," said Dalwan, continuing, "Danlion has sent an army of squatches to..."

.   "Squatches?" the anderon said loudly and in great surprise, "SQUATCHES? FIGHTING?" Smoke blew in a stream from his mouth as he roared the words. "They're not given to fighting," he said, continuing under a little more control, allowing only a hint of smoke to escape, "Why are they fighting?" His eyes were squinted in obvious anger.

"It seems," said Shahandra, "that Danlion has tricked them into believing that men captured some anderon that was their friend with the intent of harming him. For that reason, they're now en route to Castle Crest to free their friend from his captors."

"Castle Crest is the place where the sword Fallonrod was entombed," added Darric. Danlion apparently wanted control o' the sword's resting place so that it couldn't be used against him."

"So he obtained a disposable army!" snorted the anderon in disgust. "I'm going to stop them from this outrage. They're simple, gentle beasts with the sense and trust of children. Today they are MY children." The menacing tone in his voice made shivers run through them all.

"I'll help you if you'll take me with you," shouted Dalwan as the anderon turned away from the group and began to stretch his wings in preparation to fly. The wings curled back in, and the giant head swung around with a mysterious grin on his face.

"That would be different... yes!" hissed the anderon in delight. He sensed for a moment toward the rest of the group and turned his attention toward Shahandra... "Yes, you may come too. Dalwan, you must find a rope and use your magic to bind you and Shahandra to my back just in front of my wings, or you'll be blown off by the force of the wind."

Before any of them could even think about where they were going to look for a suitable rope, Darric was pulling one from a satchel that hung by his side. "I carry a little of everything for just such occasions."

Dalwan climbed up with Shahandra holding on tight behind him and secured the ropes tightly around them and then around the anderon's muscular neck.

"We're ready when you are!"

"No, you're not", laughed the anderon in a smoke spewing full-belly laugh that shook them violently. "But here we go anyway!!"

In an instant, they were airborne. The mighty wings pulled with incredible force. For one instant, Dalwan and Shahandra were forced powerfully against the toughly scaled neck, and the next instant, they were straining at the rope to keep from flying off. This reoccurred with every flap of his wings as they gained speed and altitude. Suddenly, as they cleared the castle wall and began to soar toward the tallest tree tops, the anderon disappeared. Shahandra screamed, and Dalwan felt his stomach in his throat. Before another instant passed, Dalwan realized that he and Shahandra were still firmly attached, tethered to his friend. He collected his wits and made both he and Shahandra disappear. The anderon continued to climb at a steep angle. The ride finally settled down after they were high in the air, where they leveled out and the monstrous wings picked up a smoother sweep.

After they were far up in the air, the great beast and his friend met in the secrecy of their minds to form a strategy. It was more grand than any experience Dalwan had ever had, sharing the thoughts and ancient wisdom of the most admirable creature he had ever met.

Dalwan and Shahandra began to chill to the bone as the wind whipped against them. Dalwan found a way, through the same fire magic that started the logs with visible flame, to warm them both from time to time. He was amazed that his magic worked at all that far up in the air.

After what seemed like a frozen eternity, the anderon announced that the castle would soon be in sight. Both Dalwan and Shahandra had closed their eyes for most of the ride because the cold wind dried them out and blurred their vision, especially when they were flying over the mountains. The anderon had begun to slow down and was now only gliding. They opened their eyes to chance a look. They were flying along the mountain range at the base of which the castle sat. They could see the castle in the distance. Under them, they could see the farms and villages cut out of the landscape in the most remarkable patterns.

The anderon and Dalwan joined minds to assess the situation as they overtook the castle. The invisible trio approached the castle from the air, where they could clearly see a brownish wave pouring across the fields heading for the castle. There were thousands upon thousands of squatches running full speed for the easily approachable east wall. They were still a considerable distance from the wall but closing rapidly. Thousands of tiny figures stood motionless, crowded together on the walls. Safely behind the squatches and about in the middle of the charging wave rode a small group of men on horseback, keeping up with the attacker's pace.

As the anderon and company glided overhead, they could see the long, thin poles, which the squatches had made from small trees, bouncing along, being propelled like miniature battering rams by small groups of squatches. As their plan quickly crystallized, laughter broke out spontaneously from the anderon and Dalwan, causing Shahandra to feel a little left out. Dalwan quickly explained as much as he could while they made a giant loop, swooping down to a flying height about equal to the top of the castle wall. They were now flying in a straight line between the wall and the charging squatches. When they reached the center of the wave of attackers, they abruptly became visible and landed. This caused no small disturbance, both among the squatches and on the castle wall. Shahandra and Dalwan quickly dismounted. The charging army gained momentum veering in their direction. The anderon took to the air again and headed straight at the squatches.

There was a deafening roar from the surprised and obviously delighted squatches. The anderon glided over the massive hairy army and headed directly over the small group of men riding in the rear of the line. As he flew, the anderon called to the squatches, a gesture that was hardly necessary at this point. He accelerated his flight and quickly put a considerable distance between the troll line and himself before coming to a rest in a large open field directly on the opposite side of the men from the main mass of squatches. He then let loose with a roar and billow of fire and smoke that could be seen and heard from the castle wall, now a sizable distance away. The extremely agile squatches made the adjustment in direction and were converging on their friend at amazing speed. The horsemen had a greater difficulty adjusting to the change in direction. They were now flanked by a very hostile-looking dragon behind them. Before they could fully decide on evasive action, they were mid-stream in a tidal wave of ecstatic squatches. They and their horses went down before they knew what happened and were trampled by thousands of heavy quick quick-moving feet. As the squatches reached the anderon, he began to move away from the castle, coaxing them to follow. When they had all reached him, he led his jubilant host off toward home without stopping.

As the reunion between squatches and anderon was taking place, Shahandra and Dalwan were making their way toward the area where the men had gone down. They both used some healing magic to stimulate their cold, stiff muscles as they tried to work up to a run after the long, sedentary ride. The squatches had made the distance look small as they had pursued the anderon. It proved much harder for them to close the distance.

As they ran toward the downed men, the castle gate opened, and an army of horsemen came pouring out, racing toward the men. Rhem and Shaylan had judged correctly that Dalwan was with the dragon and had received permission to lead the charge from the castle. An even dozen men appeared to have survived the crush of squatches and were up and moving, some better than others. Among the trampled bodies, several horses were being brought to their feet. As Dalwan closed in to within longbow range, he could see that several of the men were fighting over horses. Two men rode off toward the hills together. Another man struggled to his feet as if he had been unconscious.

Several of the men were still trying to rouse horses and comrades, while the others progressed to sword battles over the standing horses.

Dorslin had been knocked unconscious when he hit the ground. His horse went down on the troll side of the stampede, giving some protection to Dorslin. When he awoke, he saw most of his men dead, some of those left were fighting among themselves, his horse was dead, and there was an army of horsemen coming in his direction. He got to his feet a yelled for his men. Their fear of him was so great that they quit fighting and quickly gathered around him.

"If we stay here, we'll be killed," he said, pointing to the oncoming army of horsemen. "There are ten of us left and five horses." He pointed at the three smallest men, "You three take the largest horse and ride that way... go! NOW!" he shouted. He did the same thing with the others, sending them all in different directions. He and another man mounted the remaining horse and headed toward the hills in the same direction as the two earlier men had gone before Dorslin regained consciousness. Dalwan was about a stone's throw away when Dorslin rode off. He drew Fallonrod and threw a thin, powerful flame. Dorslin had his sword out also. The flame flew like lightning toward the retreating men. Dorslin's sword deflected the flame from him. It sliced into the other man, sending him flying from the horse. Dorslin kept riding, holding the sword between him and Dalwan. Dalwan withheld further attack.

As he lowered his sword, he could hear the shouts of the oncoming castle horsemen. He turned to see Rhem at the lead and Shaylan about halfway back in the group. The horsemen split up in smaller bands and pursued the fleeing men. Rhem saluted as he passed Dalwan and Shahandra in pursuit of Dorslin. Shaylan was closing in behind him with another six riders. Several men stopped to look over the remaining attackers to ensure that any survivors were captured and secured. None were found.

Shahandra wasted no time in tending to the injured and dying horses. During the time that she searched among the animals, she was able to heal a few broken legs, bringing three horses back to their feet. Because some of the horses had run away when their riders had been thrown into the crazed pack of squatches, there were fewer dead horses than men.

Meanwhile, Dorslin made his way back to the base camp, where they had left seven men tending all their supplies. The two men who rode off first had returned there also. The area was heavily forested. It was set on a gentle slope with a small creek running through it. A partially overgrown and obviously seldom-used road led through the camp. Dorslin dismounted and ordered the others to join him in fighting the pursuers. Three of the men had bows. They spread out in a crescent at the leading edge of the camp, taking advantage of the trees for cover.

Rhem was ahead of the rest of the group, entering the forest about a long bow shot behind Dorslin. He knew that the single rider wouldn't stop until he reached a place of relative safety or else the most advantageous place from which to make a stand. He decided to slow his pace and ride in with the rest of the soldiers and the Shaylan.

They caught up with Rhem rather quickly. After regrouping, they decided to move with a little more caution. Rhem was an excellent tracker and would easily pick up and follow the trail of a running horse through the woods. The fleeing horse would not be able to maintain its speed for very long, so it would be only a matter of time before Rhem and his companions would overtake it.

Rhem took the lead, and the others followed in pairs with Shaylan in the rear. It wasn't long before Rhem put up his hand in warning. The old road they had followed took a turn and entered a gentle sloping area. He could see a wagon sitting unattended through the trees. Shaylan began to sense the area for the use of magic and detected the presence of several magics at work, one was fire. Rhem backtracked, taking the others with him.

"I'm almost certain that there are several men waiting for us in there," he whispered. "Let's go in from different directions."

Everyone agreed, so Shaylan and three others went around an outcropping of rocks that bordered the camp while Rhem waited until they were in position before entering by way of the road.

The Shaylan and his companions made good time getting around behind the camp. The running of the water in the creek and the breeze in the trees masked their approach from the rear. When they were in position, they clearly saw two of the archers waiting in ambush, so they broke into a run, yelling and making as much noise as they could. This quickly brought Rhem and those with him charging in from the road.

The soldiers with Rhem and Shaylan had small shields with them and held them up as they attacked. Arrows flew to no avail, and the archers quickly abandoned their bows for swords.

Shaylan dismounted and approached a stout-looking soldier who mocked Shaylan's age, "This must be your day to die, you feeble old man." Rhem was close enough to hear the challenge and almost abandoned the two men he faced to join Shaylan. At the instant of his temptation, he instead turned and engaged the men who were moving to opposite sides of him. He often practiced this situation.

As the Shaylan approached the man, he ordered him to drop his weapon and surrender, something that his conscience made him do. The man began to laugh so hard that the Shaylan became embarrassed. He pointed his sword at the man and let go with a blazing stream of white fire. As the man dropped face-first into the dirt, he saw Rhem in a single move pull his sword out of one man and parry the thrust from the other man behind him with a long knife.

Shaylan's attention was drawn to a very tall, thick-bodied man whom he could sense also possessed fire. He virtually incinerated one of the men who had ridden in with Shaylan. As the man was falling, Dorslin was en route to assist another comrade with another soldier. Shaylan saw what was going to happen and called to Dorslin, not knowing his name, "Why don't you stand against me, coward!"

Dorslin turned and looked with interest at the old image moving toward him. He was about a stone's throw away from Shaylan and half that distance in a different direction from the fighting men. He hesitated for an instant, then continued on toward the two men. The soldier had almost disarmed Dorslin's man when Dorslin arrived and took over the fight for his man. His first blow cut the man's sword in half, and his second cut off the rest of the blade at the hilt. Before the man could move, he was run through. Dorslin turned and said something to his man and then moved in Shaylan's direction.

Shaylan raised his sword and stood his ground as Dorslin approached. Dorslin did not speak as he approached. When he was about ten paces away, Shaylan hurled a giant ball of blue flame at him. It was easily deflected by Dorslin's sword.

Dorslin countered with a spinning green flame curtain. Shaylan met it with an equally large green flame curtain, which pounded into Dorslin's. The impact sent fragments spinning into the ground, brush, and trees nearby. Dust flew into the air, and leaves fell like rain from every place the flames hit.

Meanwhile, Rhem had made short work of another opponent and was heading toward the last of Dorslin's remaining companions he could see. The man had just defeated one of the horsemen who rode in with Shaylan. It was at this instant that he heard the concussion of the green flame curtains. He turned to look and almost went to Shaylan's aid. He turned back to assess the remaining opponent heading for a wounded horseman who was leaning against a tree about halfway between them. He turned away from Shaylan and ran toward the advancing swordsman.

The man wore all black. He had thick, wavy black hair and a single black eyebrow crossing both of his deep-set dark eyes. A sickening grin crept across his pockmarked face as he began to swing his sword about in an artful routine, obviously performed to frighten Rhem. The bloodied sword swung loosely in quick maneuvers as the man passed it from hand to hand until finally bringing it to a halt, pointed directly at Rhem. While this was amusing to Rhem, it did not intimidate him nor did it even slow his advance. This very obviously disturbed the man. Neither of them spoke as they squared off against each other.

Shaylan was only beginning to size up his opponent again through the dust when he sensed movement behind him. Instinctively, he stepped to the side while ducking and turning with his sword up. A powerful blow, meant for his head, was deflected by the tip of his sword. Dorslin was now moving toward him from the back. Shaylan disappeared.

"Swing at him, you fool!" shouted Dorslin at the other man, "Strike again! He's gotta be right there," he yelled even louder at the astonished swordsman who flailed haplessly at the air with his sword.

It gave Shaylan just enough time to regain his composure and side-step the oncoming Dorslin, who also thrashed the air wildly with his sword. Shaylan had timed his moves perfectly to pass directly by Dorslin and get behind him. Dorslin was so angry that he pounded the man in the chest with a punishing blow that sent him sprawling onto his backside.

Suddenly, Dorslin was being tangled and tied in fire rope by Shaylan. He wove it like a panic-stricken spider. Dorslin began to cut his way out with his power sword, sending fragments scattering like miniature lightning bolts.

Before he had cut his arms free, Shaylan hit him with several balls of white fire, which he aimed at the areas that Dorslin had freed with his sword. Dorslin screamed and fell writhing onto the ground. The man, still lying breathless behind him, scooted away, sliding backward on his seat in a crab-like retreat from the grotesque sight.

Rhem began the fight with a few carefully placed blows, which his opponent easily blocked. They exchanged blow for blow and block for block. He did not see the blazing end of Shaylan's fight but did perceive the flash from the white fire.

Both of the swordsmen were tired from the fighting they had already done, but continued on without perceptible loss of power. He could sense that the man had use of some magic, but could not discern what type it was. He assumed he was a sensor who could use his art to perceive Rhem's intentions and preempt his moves. Every move Rhem made was artfully blocked and vice versa.

Finally, Rhem just stood completely still with his sword in position to defend himself. His opponent hesitated for a short time, then moved on him. Rhem blocked blow after blow but returned none. After quite a few blows by his opponent, Rhem suddenly swung. As the man blocked it, he kicked the man in the stomach with such violence that he dropped his sword. Before he could regain composure, Rhem swept his feet from under him. The man fell backwards away from his sword. Rhem pulled his sheath knife and challenged the man to surrender.

As this was taking place, Shaylan was walking his captive toward Rhem at sword point. Seeing this, Rhem's opponent surrendered.

Having sensed the battle, Dalwan and Shahandra had mounted horses that she had healed and had ridden to the battlefield. They arrived just as Rhem's opponent was surrendering. Dalwan scouted the area and found that everyone else except two horsemen were dead, and one of them was at the point of death from blood loss. Shahandra went to his aid and stopped the bleeding.

Rhem tied up the captives and quickly hitched a wagon up to the horses they had. They put the wounded men in the wagon and set out for the castle, pulling the captives along behind the wagon.

Dalwan decided to try the same healing magic he had used to give the anderon strength on the most seriously injured man. To his amazement, it worked.

"Will you teach me to do that, Dalwan?" asked Shahandra in a tone of voice that totally disarmed him. His heart began to beat rapidly, and he must have blushed because everyone within ear and eye shot laughed. He knew that Shahandra must have sensed his feelings for her because she blushed. Throughout the remainder of the ride, they kept exchanging smiles, then grins, and finally laughter... but words just came out jumbled. This just made them laugh even more.

"We did very well today, old man," said Rhem with a grin.

"I venture a guess that this'll not be the last battle we'll see together, my friend," answered Shaylan in his characteristically serious voice. "But let's wait for a while until my old bones get rid of these bruises."

"I know just the place for us to rest up," said Rhem in high spirits with a way too animated grin. "...you know...one of those 'EARTHY' places that you promised to go to with me."

"OH, the trouble I bring on myself!" said Shaylan while sporting a look that pleaded for mercy.

As they approached the gates, Shahandra leaned over and whispered to Dalwan, "I found this wonderful place where there's a magic forest. We could go there for a while and rest. What do you say?"

"I'm gonna need a rest after this... let's do it!"

Another voice also answered... somewhere inside their heads... a familiar voice, "Not without a chaperon you won't... must keep everything proper for ones such as yourselves. I will find you when my friends are safely home... I'll see you there... an enchanted forest you say...hummm??? There's a legend of such a place among my kind... I'm going to enjoy this."

Shahandra smiled at the thought of an anderon playing in enchanted grass.

www.ingramcontent.com/pod-product-compliance
Lightning Source LLC
Chambersburg PA
CBHW030328120726
47901CB00007B/1722